Ga

LOVE CHILD

The satyr opened the door of the hut--an untanned hide hung from crude wooden pegs--and motioned for Arvin to enter. Arvin stepped inside and felt excitement course through him as he spotted the object of his search.

Glisena lay on a sheepskin near a fire pit. She stared up at the ceiling, hands on her enormous belly, her long hair damp with sweat. Even over the smell of wood smoke, Arvin caught the odor of sickness; a fly circled lazily in the air above her head. Glisena still wore the dress she'd had on when she used Naneth's ring to teleport away from the palace; her winter cloak and boots lay in a heap against the far wall. Through the fabric of the dress, Arvin saw Glisena's stomach bulge momentarily: the baby kicking. Glisena gave a faint groan.

At least mother and baby were both alive.

Arvin should have felt elation. Instead he felt sadness and a grim sense of foreboding.

The satyr gave Arvin a shove from behind. "Heal her."

Serve the House of Serpents

House of Serpents
Lisa Smedman

Book I
Venom's Taste

Book II
Viper's Kiss

Book III
Vanity's Brood
March 2006

Also by Lisa Smedman

R.A. Salvatore's War of the Spider Queen, Book IV
Extinction

Sembia
Heirs of Prophecy

VIPER'S KISS

HOUSE OF SERPENTS

BOOK II

LISA SMEDMAN

VIPER'S KISS
House of Serpents, Book II
©2005 Wizards of the Coast, Inc.

Distributed in the United States by Holtzbrinck Publishing.
Distributed in Canada by Fenn Ltd.

Distributed to the hobby, toy, and comic trade in the United States and Canada by regional distributors.

Distributed worldwide by Wizards of the Coast, Inc. and regional distributors.

Cover art by Raymond Swanland
Map by Dennis Kauth
First Printing: March 2005
Library of Congress Catalog Card Number: 2004113604

9 8 7 6 5 4 3 2 1

US ISBN: 0-7869-3616-9
ISBN-13: 978-0-7869-3616-8
620-17678-001-EN

U.S., CANADA,
ASIA, PACIFIC, & LATIN AMERICA
Wizards of the Coast, Inc.
P.O. Box 707
Renton, WA 98057-0707
+1-800-324-6496

EUROPEAN HEADQUARTERS
Wizards of the Coast, Belgium
T Hofveld 6d
1702 Groot-Bijgaarden
Belgium
+322 467 3360

Visit our web site at www.wizards.com

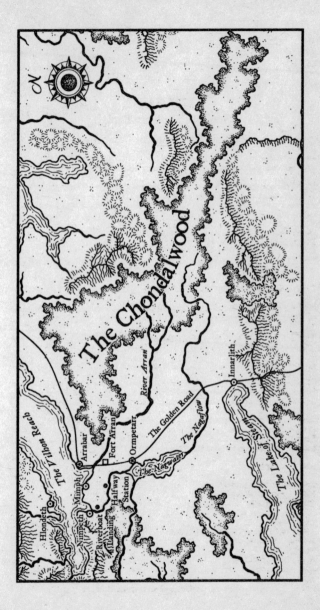

The man on the ship's fo'c'sle would have gone unnoticed in other circumstances. Of average build and height, and with dark, shoulder-length hair drawn into a knot at the back of his neck like a sailor's tarred bun, he would have blended into any crowd. His ornaments were few: a slim chunk of clear crystal hanging on a leather thong at his neck; a bracelet of braided leather around his right wrist; and a thumbnail-sized dark blue stone, flecked with gold, that he wore on his forehead in the spot where the Learned painted their marks.

Two things, however, made him remarkable. The first was his pose. He lay facedown, his rigid arms holding his upper torso away from the wet fo'c'sle deck, his head bent back so that he appeared to be looking straight up at the spot where six sailors toiled above him, reefing the foresail. The second was the fact that he was unclothed, save for his tight-fitting breeches and a black leather glove on his left hand.

Unclothed—on a gusty, open deck in a winter far colder than was usual for the Vilhon Reach—the man seemed oblivious to the brisk wind that blew a spray so chilling that the sailors above worked with clumsy, cold-stiff fingers as they hauled up the canvas sail. He'd been there since dawn first paled the sky, unmoving, unblinking. And not shivering, even though the sun was only now just starting to shine on the gray waters of the Reach.

As the sun crested the horizon, limning the ship in a faint winter light, the man at last moved. He did not so much rise from the deck as flow up into a crouch, then into a standing position. A series of poses followed, joined one to the next like the steps of a flowing dance. The man moved as sinuously as a snake, even though he was human, without a hint of yuan-ti about him. The pupils of his dark brown eyes were round and his skin was smooth and not patterned. When he assumed the final pose, standing on one foot and staring up at the sky through hands that were slowly coming together, as if crushing something between them, the teeth that showed as he grimaced were square and white. Slowly, he lowered his foot to the deck and his arms returned to his sides. Then, his exercises complete, he reached for his shirt.

A wave caused the ship to roll. The man steadied himself by grabbing one of the rope ladders that led up to the mast. Suddenly his smile disappeared. His gaze became unfocused, as if he were staring out at something on the distant horizon. A moment later, he blinked. "The hemp in one of the ratlines is rotten," he called up to the sailors. "If you don't replace it, one of you will die."

He spoke with such certainty that the sailors above shivered. One of them began to whisper a prayer.

The man below dressed himself, pulling on his trousers, shirt, and boots, and belting on a knife so that its sheath was snug against the small of his back. Then, rubbing himself briskly and at last shivering, he strode along the rolling deck and disappeared down the hatch that led to the passengers' cabins.

CHAPTER 1

Arvin leaned on the ship's rail, staring across the waters of the broad bay the ship had just entered. Ahead lay the city of Mimph. Like Hlondeth, it was a port, its harbor crowded so thickly with ships that their masts resembled the bare trees of a winter forest. But there the resemblance ended. Hlondeth had been built by serpents—it was a city of round towers, gracefully arcing viaducts, and ramps that led to rounded doorways reminiscent of the entrance to a snake's burrow. The buildings of Mimph, in contrast, were squat, blocky, and square. The city was a series of sharp angles and edges, from its square windows and doors to the jagged-looking flights of stairs that led up from the piers that lined the waterfront. Where Hlondeth's buildings were of green stone that glowed by night with the residual energies of the magic used to shape them, Mimph's structures were of plain gray granite that had been hewn by hand.

By human hands.

As the ship sailed slowly into the harbor, making its way between the dozens of ships already at anchor, the only other passenger aboard her joined Arvin at the rail. He tasted the air with a flickering, forked tongue then gave a slight sniff. "Humans," he hissed under his breath.

Arvin glanced sideways at the other passenger—a yuan-ti half-breed with a distinctive diamond pattern on the scales of his face. The yuan-ti's head was bald and more snakelike than human, and his lower torso ended in a serpent's tail. He wore an expensive looking winter cloak, trimmed with white ermine fur, that draped all but the tip of his tightly coiled tail. He hugged a stove-warmed stone to his belly; his breath, unlike Arvin's, didn't fog in the winter air. His unblinking, slit-pupil eyes stared with open distaste at the city as he sluggishly turned his head to stare at it.

"How they stink," he hissed, completing his thought.

Arvin's eyes narrowed. He smelled nothing but clean sea air, wet canvas and hemp, and the tang of freshly cut pine drifting over the water from the dockyards, where dozens of naval vessels were being constructed to counter the threat from neighboring Chondath. Arvin said nothing, even though the yuan-ti's remark was designed to goad him. He was the only human aboard this ship who was not a slave; the sailors who toiled above, calling to one another as they furled the sails, all had an S brand on their left cheek. The yuan-ti obviously couldn't resist an opportunity to remind the one free human about his place in the world.

Arvin smiled. Enjoy it while you can, he thought. Here in the Barony of Sespech, it's the humans who run things.

Foremost among those humans was Baron Thuragar Foesmasher, the man who had wrested control of Sespech away from its former baron—a Chondathan lackey—nine years ago. The barony was now fully independent, a rising star among the states that lined the Vilhon Reach. It was a place where a man with the right skills and talent could go far.

Arvin, with his psionic talents, was just such a man. And this trip was going to give him the opportunity to prove himself to no less a person than the baron himself.

Six days ago, the baron's daughter Glisena, a headstrong young woman of eighteen years, had gone missing from the palace at Ormpetarr. The baron's spellcasters had been unable to find her; their clerical magic had failed to reveal even a hint of where she might have gone. With each passing day the baron's fears had increased. There had been no ransom demand, no boastful threats from his political enemies. Glisena had just . . . vanished.

Desperate, Baron Foesmasher had turned to his yuan-ti allies. Lady Dediana's militia, he knew, included a tracker said to be the best in all of the Vilhon Reach, a man with an extremely rare form of magic. Perhaps this "mind magic" could succeed where the other spellcasters had failed.

That tracker was Tanju, the psion who was Arvin's mentor.

Lady Dediana, however, was loath to loan Tanju to Baron Foesmasher. There was pressing business within Hlondeth for him to attend to, and he couldn't be spared. Yet a failure to respond to Baron Foesmasher's plea might fray the alliance that had recently been woven between the two states.

Tanju had proposed the solution. In recent months, he told Lady Dediana, he'd taken on an "apprentice," one with a quick mind and immense natural talent. This apprentice, he assured her, could do the job. Delighted at being presented with a solution that would swallow two birds in a single gulp, as the old expression went, Lady Dediana had readily agreed. And so, early yesterday morning, Arvin had set sail for Sespech.

If all went well, he'd never have to return to Hlondeth. Tanju had agreed that, when the job was done—assuming the baron approved—Arvin could remain in Sespech. From time to time, Tanju might contact him and ask for information on the barony, but otherwise, Arvin would be his own master.

Staying on in Sespech suited Arvin just fine. After months of constantly looking over his shoulder, wondering if Zelia was going to suddenly appear, he could at last relax. He felt more at ease already than he had since last summer, when the yuan-ti psion had tried to take over his body with a mind seed. Arvin had narrowly defeated her by planting a false memory of his own death in her mind. In order to maintain that deception, he'd had to remain in hiding since that time. It hadn't been easy.

A light snow began to fall. The yuan-ti beside him hissed once more, tasted a snowflake with a flicker of his tongue, and slithered back to the passengers' quarters. Arvin watched him go, wondering what urgent business had stirred the yuan-ti out of his winter torpor and sent him south across the Reach. This winter was colder than any Arvin could remember, and yet the yuan-ti were more energetic than ever. They seemed ... restless.

As the ship drew closer to the spot where it was to unload its cargo of wine, sailors scrambled down to the deck where Arvin waited and stood ready with heaving lines. The gap between the ship and the pier narrowed and the sailors whirled the lines—each weighted at the end by a large "monkey fist" knot—above their heads. At the captain's order they let fly, and the lines, looking like white streamers, arced toward the pier. They were caught by dock workers, who hauled them in rapidly hand over hand, drawing toward them the thicker ropes to which the heaving lines were tied, then looping these over bollards on the pier. The sailors, meanwhile, scrambled to the ship's two capstans and grasped the wooden arms. The ship jerked abruptly to a halt as the mooring lines pulled tight then gradually, as the capstans were turned with rumbling squeals, was drawn closer to the pier.

The hull snugged up against the large, ball-shaped fenders of woven rope that hung against the pier to protect the ship from scraping. One of the fenders tore apart with a wet ripping sound, and Arvin snorted disdainfully. Whoever had made it must have used substandard materials. Not only that, but the weave was sloppy and uneven.

He waited patiently while the ship was secured. Unlike the yuan-ti—who was lethargically directing the sailors hauling his numerous heavy trunks up onto the deck—Arvin was traveling light. A single backpack held his clothing, travel gear, and the handful of magical items he'd been able to make for himself without the Guild finding out about them. Collecting these from their various caches throughout the city had been tricky. If anyone in the Guild had realized that Arvin was thinking about leaving Hlondeth for good, the Guild would have seen to it that he was stopped. He owed them an enormous debt; it had been the Guild that had helped him hide from Zelia these past six months. And Arvin was a valuable resource—a source of magical ropes and nets at mere coppers on the gold piece. Too valuable to ever be let go. If they found out he was planning on running, they'd make sure he'd never do it again. They'd probably lop off a foot, this time.

He sighed and adjusted his pack into a more comfortable position on his shoulders. Inside it, carefully wrapped in cloth against breakage, was a magical item Tanju had given him—a crystalline wand called a dorje. Made from a length of clear quartz as narrow as Arvin's forefinger and twice as long, it pulsed with a soft purple light: the psionic energies Tanju had charged it with. Using it, Arvin would be able to view Glisena—and her current surroundings—as if he were standing next to her. All he need do was touch the dorje to something that had once been close to her. A dress she had worn or, better yet, a hairbrush with a strand of her hair in its bristles.

Once Glisena was located and returned home again, Arvin would, no doubt, be rewarded by a grateful baron. Coin would be involved. Much coin, since Baron Foesmasher was known to be a generous man. Arvin would use the coin to set up shop in Sespech—an independent shop, not one controlled by the Guild. He would at long last reap the full profits of his magical rope making and net weaving, without the Guild dipping a hand in the purse. He'd make a new home for himself far away from the demands of the Guild, the reminders of his years in the orphanage—and the constant slithering hiss of the City of Serpents.

When the ship was secure, one of the ship's officers—a muscular fellow whose braided beard hid most of the slave brand on his cheek—shouted directions. The other sailors unfastened the hatches and swung a crane into place, preparing to unload the barrels that filled the hold. Another officer—this one a yuan-ti with patches of yellow scales on his cheeks and forehead, slithered over to the rail and coiled himself there. He watched the crew with unblinking eyes, one hand gripping a wand whose tip was set with a hollow snake fang. The slaves glanced nervously at him over their shoulders as they worked. The yuan-ti officer did not speak, but his message was clear. Any human seeking his freedom ashore would meet a swift end.

Arvin ignored the yuan-ti officer, taking in the people on the pier instead. The dock workers all appeared to be free men—many were bearded, an affectation that was forbidden to all but the most trusted slaves. Four teenage boys stood on the pier next to them, jostling each other and waving up at the ship, trying to catch the eyes of its passengers. Their voices overlapped as they shouted up to those on deck.

"Come to the Bluefish Inn! Good food, good ale."

"Clean rooms, just five silver pieces a night at the Travelers' Rest!"

"Hey, Mister! Let me show you the way to the Tangled Net Tavern. It's close by."

"Cheap rooms! Cheap rooms at the Silver Sail."

A handful of women were also present. One walked behind a boy who trundled a wheelbarrow laden with a steaming pot of dark red liquid, a ladle in her hand. "Hot mulled wine!" she called. "Sweet and hot, six coppers a cup." The half dozen other women were all doxies in low-cut dresses that were too thin for the winter air, strolling back and forth across the pier in an effort to keep warm.

Arvin's eyes were immediately drawn to one of the doxies, a woman with high cheekbones and dark hair that fell in a long braid down her back. She was pretty, but what had caught his eye was the gesture she just used. She'd raised a hand to her face, pretending to rub her eyes with fingers that were spread in a **V**. As Arvin watched, she lowered her hand, rubbing her fingers against her thumb, then pointed at the ship on which Arvin stood, directing someone's attention toward its passengers.

Arvin nodded. So Mimph had a rogues' guild as well, did it? He supposed that was only to be expected. He glanced around the pier and easily spotted the weedy-looking boy lounging a short distance down the pier. The boy—who looked about fourteen, the age Arvin had been when he found himself on the streets and was forced to steal to survive—acknowledged the doxy with a quick nod of his right fist, then began making his way toward the ship.

Arvin was glad it wasn't the doxy who would be attempting the grab. That was how things had started, the last time around. He looked around, trying to spot the other rogues he suspected would be somewhere nearby. There would probably be three or four in total, all working together in a carefully choreographed routine that would see whatever was stolen passed from one hand to the next. But the others—assuming there were more than just the woman and boy—didn't tip their hands.

Arvin slipped his pack off his shoulders, checked to make sure its flaps were securely fastened, then put it back on. He made a show of nervously patting a trouser pocket, drawing the boy's eyes to it. The only thing in that pocket was the remainder of Arvin's breakfast—some nuts and a dried cheese, wrapped in waxed cloth. His coin pouch with its supply of the local currency—small silver and gold coins called "fists" and "plumes," respectively, after the symbols stamped onto them—was tucked safely inside his boot.

As the ship was made fast, Arvin's eye ranged over the waterfront. The businesses lining it were typical of any port city: warehouses, boat builders, sail and rope makers, taverns, and fish-salting houses. There were also a number of stables, judging by the whinnying coming from some larger buildings farther down the waterfront, buildings that were fronted by fences that led to ramps on the pier. From these, the swift-footed horses of Sespech's famed Golden Plains were loaded aboard ships.

Instead of fountains, which could be found everywhere in Hlondeth, the people of Mimph seemed to prefer religious sculpture. At the top of a short flight of steps leading up from the pier where Arvin's ship had tied up was a low stone dais that supported an enormous gauntlet as tall as a man—the symbol of the god Helm. The statue was brightly polished and appeared to be made of silver. The fingers were stiff and erect, as if the gauntlet were saying, "Halt!" It faced the harbor; on its palm was the symbol of an eye, outlined in blue. The pupil of the eye was an enormous gemstone. Judging by its rich blue color, it might have been a sapphire.

Arvin whistled softly under his breath. Even if the gauntlet were only coated with a thin layer of hammered silver, it would have been worth a fortune. It should have been locked away behind temple doors. Yet there it sat in plain view, unguarded. It might be too heavy to carry away, but surely thieves like the pair below would have found a way around whatever magical wards the statue bore to pluck out the gemstone at the center of that eye.

A horn sounded from somewhere near the center of the city. Once, twice, three times it blared. At the final note, all activity on the pier below stopped. Dock workers, vendors, doxies, the boys from the inns and taverns—even the two thieves—turned toward the sound and raised their left hands in a gesture that mimicked the gauntlet's, their lips moving in silent prayer.

Straining to see past the warehouses that lined the docks, Arvin caught a glimpse of a larger building topped with a square watch tower. Its crenellated battlements had led him to assume it was a keep or well-fortified noble home. He realized it must be a church—one devoted to Helm, the Vigilant One. Unlike the Chapel of Emerald Scales in Hlondeth, which was topped by a spouting serpent, this church was devoid of any representation of its deity. Instead, its tower was capped by a curved object, also of brightly polished silver, that Arvin guessed must be the horn that had just sounded.

The midday genuflection was brief; moments later the dock workers were back at their tasks. Aboard the ship, two sailors brought out a gangplank, ran it over the side, and lashed it to the rail. Arvin moved toward it, then remembered the other passenger. He stepped back, eyes lowered, as the yuan-ti slowly made his way to the gangplank. The yuan-ti gave a smug hiss as he passed Arvin and slithered down the gangplank to the pier.

Arvin watched, amused, as the weedy-looking boy—pretending to be one of the cluster of touts for the inns and taverns—crowded around the bottom of the gangplank with the other boys. The gangplank suddenly tipped—one of the dock workers must have bumped it—and the yuan-ti stumbled. The boy jumped forward to steady him. As he caught the yuan-ti, his left hand darted into a pocket inside the yuan-ti's cloak. The yuan-ti bared his fangs in an irritated hiss, and the boy backed away, bowing and making a sweeping gesture with his right hand in order to draw onlookers' eyes away from the object he'd palmed with his left.

The yuan-ti wasn't fooled. His slit eyes narrowed, and he touched his pocket with slender fingers. "Thief!" he hissed.

Arvin, descending the gangplank, was surprised by the speed of the yuan-ti's reaction, given the fellow's earlier sluggishness. The yuan-ti lunged forward, grabbing for the boy's wrist.

The boy was faster. The yuan-ti's hand caught his shirt cuff, but he wrenched his arm free and danced back out of the way. His hands—now empty—were spread wide. "He's crazy!" he protested. "All I did was help when he stumbled."

The doxy moved into position at the base of the flight of steps. Arvin knew what would happen next. The rogue would turn and flee—only to run headlong into her. During this "accidental collision" whatever he'd just stolen would be exchanged. Eventually he would be caught, and searched, but by this time the doxy would be well on her way down the pier and out of sight, passing the object off to the next rogue.

The yuan-ti, however, wasn't playing along. Instead of calling out for the militia—or whoever patrolled this city—he used magic. No words were spoken, no gestures used, but suddenly the young rogue's face blanched and his hands started to tremble. Arvin knew just how he felt, having been the target of a yuan-ti's magical fear himself.

"You've . . . made a mistake, sir," he gasped.

The yuan-ti raised a hand and flicked his fingers. Acidic sweat sprayed from his fingertips, striking the boy in the face. The young rogue howled and clawed at his eyes.

"Give it back," the yuan-ti demanded.

The boy turned and ran—blindly, crashing into the dock workers and shoving them out of the way. As he neared the base of the steps, the doxy opened her mouth as if to call out to him then thought better of it and turned away. The rogue waved his arms around, feeling blindly for her then staggered up the steps.

The yuan-ti turned to the officer on board the ship. "Use your wand," he hissed. "Stop him."

The officer shook his head . . . slowly.

Nearly spitting with anger, the first yuan-ti slithered after the blinded rogue. The stairs slowed him down somewhat—he slithered back and forth along them, humping his serpent's body up them one by one—but the boy's progress was even slower. He ran headlong into a pair of dock workers who were carrying a heavy sack between them and careened backward down the stairs. As he scrambled to his feet again, the yuan-ti lashed out, trying to bite him, and just missed. The yuan-ti's fangs caught the boy's collar, tearing it, and the boy shrieked. "He's trying to kill me! Stop him, somebody!"

Arvin strode down the gangplank and onto the pier.

He caught the doxy's eye, made his left hand into a fist, placed it on his open right palm, and jerked his hands upward. *Help him.*

The doxy's eyes widened as she saw Arvin using silent speech. For a heartbeat, she hesitated. Then, as the young rogue on the steps screamed a second time, she shook her head and hurried away.

Arvin was furious. The doxy could easily have saved the boy by "accidentally" colliding with the yuan-ti. She still had eyes to see with, and could have run away, but she'd abandoned him instead. Muttering to himself—and wondering what in the Abyss he was thinking, getting involved in the local guild's business—Arvin ascended the steps. He slipped his gloved hand inside the back of his shirt and grasped the dagger that was sheathed there. With a whisper, he vanished the weapon into his glove; it would make a persuasive backup if his psionics failed. He readied himself to manifest a charm and felt the familiar prickle of energy coiling at the base of his scalp, waiting to be unleashed. But as he reached the top of the steps, he paused. Maybe—just maybe—this dispute would resolve itself.

The young rogue had backed up against the dais that held the statue of the gauntlet. He threw down whatever it was he'd stolen; Arvin heard a metallic clatter as the object hit the cobblestones. "Take it!" the boy screamed. "Take it, and let me be! You've blinded me—what more do you want?"

The yuan-ti slithered over to the object—a small silver jewelry case—and picked it up. He slipped the case back inside his pocket and smiled at the boy, baring his fangs. His long forked tongue flicked in and out of his mouth, tasting the young rogue's fear. "Your death," the yuan-ti answered belatedly. Then he slithered forward.

None of the people in the small plaza that surrounded the statue came to the aid of the blinded boy—thieves must have been as despised in this city as they were in Hlondeth. And yuan-ti must have been just as greatly feared. The humans had parted to let the angry yuan-ti pass, though Arvin noted they weren't lowering their gazes. Instead they stared at the yuan-ti, faint smiles quirking their lips, as if expecting something to happen.

They didn't have long to wait. The young rogue, hearing the rustle of the yuan-ti's tunic and cloak against the ground, spun in place then leaped. His jump carried him up onto the ankle-high dais, where he crashed into the gauntlet. He clung to it like a drowning man clutching a log as the yuan-ti reared above him, savoring his terror. A drop of venom fell from his fangs onto the boy's hair. Amazingly, though the young rogue flinched, he did not move.

Arvin manifested his charm.

The yuan-ti cocked his head, as if listening to a distant sound, then shook it.

"Master yuan-ti!" Arvin called in as obsequious a tone as he could manage, sorry that he hadn't bothered to ask the yuan-ti his name during their day-and-a-half-long voyage across the Reach. "You're needed back at the ship. The crew aren't certain which trunks are yours. Don't waste your time on this boy. You got your jewelry case back. All's well now, friend."

The yuan-ti stared at Arvin for several heartbeats while flakes of snow drifted down between them. His lips twitched in a sneer. "Friend?" he asked.

"Damn," Arvin muttered. Quickly, he spoke the command word that made the dagger reappear in his gloved fist. He started to raise it—but a man beside him caught his arm. The fellow—a large man in a food-stained apron, his lack of a cloak indicating he'd stepped out of a building to watch the fight—shook his head. "No need, stranger," he whispered. "The gauntlet will provide sanctuary."

While Arvin was still trying to get his arm free—the man beside him might have been stout, but he had a grip tight as a coiled serpent—the yuan-ti lashed out at the rogue, fangs bared.

Halfway through his lunge the yuan-ti jerked to a halt. He strained for several moments against an unseen force, his body quivering, then slowly drew back. He studied the rogue for a moment, swaying back and forth, and glanced at the gauntlet. Then he reached down to grab the young rogue's ankles.

It was clear to Arvin what the yuan-ti intended—to drag the boy away from the gauntlet, which obviously was providing some sort of magical protection. But once again, the yuan-ti jerked to a halt, his grasping fingers just shy of the rogue's ankle. The yuan-ti shook for a moment in silent rage, and his face flushed red where it was not covered by scales.

A woman in the crowd chuckled.

The yuan-ti spun and lashed out at her instead.

Screaming, she jerked away, clutching her shoulder. She tried to get to the gauntlet, but the yuan-ti slithered into her path, cutting her off. The crowd, suddenly fearful, broke apart. Several people shouted, and some ran.

The young rogue, still gripping the gauntlet, turned his head from side to side, trying to hear what was happening through all the commotion.

Arvin felt the hand fall away from his arm. He still held his dagger but was jostled by the panicked crowd and could not get a clear throw. Too many people were between him and the yuan-ti—but the crowd was quickly thinning.

The woman who had been bitten, her face pale, backed up until she was against a building then stared with wide eyes at the yuan-ti. "No!" she moaned, her hands clasped in front of her. "Please, no." The yuan-ti's first bite must have failed to penetrate her thick cloak, but his second one wouldn't. The yuan-ti's head wove back and forth, his eyes fixed on her bare hands. If Arvin didn't act swiftly, an innocent woman would die.

Just as the crowd thinned and Arvin raised his dagger, a deep male voice shouted from somewhere to the right. "Hold!" it cried.

Arvin caused the dagger to vanish back into his enchanted glove and turned, but the command wasn't for him. The two armored men who had appeared in the plaza from out of nowhere had their eyes firmly locked on the yuan-ti. Both wore breastplates of brightly polished steel, each emblazoned with the blue eye that marked them as clerics of Helm. Their helmets were without visors, leaving their faces bare. Crimson cloaks hung from their shoulders. Their gauntleted fists were empty; amazingly, neither seemed to be armed.

"You," one of the clerics ordered, pointing at the yuan-ti. "Step away from that woman."

The yuan-ti turned slowly. His lips twitched into a false smile, the effect of which was spoiled by the forked tongue that flickered in and out of his mouth. "I was robbed," he said. He pointed at the young rogue. "By that human."

The second cleric strode over to where the young rogue knelt and took hold of the boy's cloak, dragging him to his feet. "Did you steal from this...." The cleric hesitated, then glanced at the yuan-ti as if uncertain what to call him. "From this gentleman?" he concluded.

The rogue shook his head, but the cleric raised his left hand, turning the eye on the palm of his gauntlet toward the boy. The boy nodded. "Yes," he said in a broken voice. "I stole from him. But I gave back what I took. And he *blinded* me."

The crowd, recovered from its earlier panic, drifted back into the plaza. The yuan-ti drew himself up, imperiously wrapping his cloak around himself. "Take the human away," he ordered, pointing at the rogue. "Throw him in the pit." He began to slither back to the ship.

"Not so fast," the first cleric said, stepping between the yuan-ti and the stairs. He turned to the woman the yuan-ti had been menacing. "Did he harm you, miss?"

Before the young woman could speak, the yuan-ti gave an irritated hiss. "Step aside," he told the cleric. "Step aside, human, or it will go badly for you. I am an important person. I will not be trifled with. Step ... aside."

Arvin felt the hairs on his arms raise, as if he'd just shivered. Once again, the yuan-ti was using his innate magic—this time, in an attempt to bend the cleric to his will. In another moment the cleric would either step obediently aside—or would feel the sharp sting of the yuan-ti's bite.

Ignoring the yuan-ti's order, the cleric raised his gauntlet and turned its eye toward the woman. He stood, waiting for her answer.

"He bit me," she replied. "By Helm's grace, my cloak stopped his fangs. If it hadn't, I'd be. . . ." She shuddered, unable to say the word.

The spectators crowded forward, calling out to the two clerics.

"I saw the whole thing. . . ."

"The boy did give the jewelry case back. . . ."

"The yuan-ti spat in his eyes. . . ."

"It was a silver case. It's in the serpent man's pocket. . . ."

The yuan-ti's eyes darted right then left. Slowly he raised his hand. Acid trickled down his palm; he was about to use the same trick he'd used to blind the rogue. Arvin opened his mouth to call out a warning—

No need. The cleric neatly sidestepped the flick of acid. A weapon appeared in his fist—a translucent mace that glowed with an intense white light. He used it to knock the yuan-ti's hand aside. The blow was no more than a light tap, but as soon as the mace touched the yuan-ti, his body became rigid. He stood, paralyzed, his eyes wide, the tips of his forked tongue protruding from his mouth, so still and silent that Arvin wondered if he was still breathing.

The cleric's glowing mace disappeared.

"That'll teach him," the man beside Arvin said—the fellow who had grabbed his arm earlier.

"What will they do with him?" Arvin asked him.

"Throw him in prison."

Arvin's eyebrows rose. "But he's a yuan-ti."

The other man shrugged. "So?"

"But...." At last it sank in. In Sespech, the yuan-ti were afforded no special status. Arvin had heard this—but witnessing it firsthand made his mind reel. It was as if sky and earth had switched places, leaving him dizzy. With the realization came a rush of satisfaction that bent his lips into a smile.

"Intention to kill," the stout man continued. "That's what they'll charge the yuan-ti with. If he pleads guilty and shows repentance, the Eyes of Helm may allow him to make atonement. If not, he'll be branded with a mark of justice. If he tries to bite or blind anyone again, he'll suffer a curse—as foul a curse as Helm can bestow."

Arvin whistled softly, glad the clerics hadn't seen his raised dagger. He watched as the second cleric placed a gauntleted hand on the rogue's head and chanted a prayer.

"And the boy?" Arvin asked.

The cleric's prayer ended. The rogue blinked, looked around with eyes that had been fully restored, and fell to his knees, weeping. His right hand raised above his head, he broke into fervent prayer.

Once again, the man beside him shrugged. "He'll probably be released, since he seems to have genuinely repented."

Arvin shook his head, incredulous. "But he's—" Then

he thought better of what he'd been about to say. The young rogue could no more cast off his guild—and its obligations—than he could shed his own skin. But if Arvin said this aloud, the fellow next to him might think back to Arvin's earlier actions and draw some conclusions that could bode ill for Arvin. It was bad enough that Arvin had drawn his dagger. He should have been more careful and stuck to his psionics. "—a thief," he concluded.

"Yes," the man said. As he spoke, he scratched his left elbow with the first two fingers of his right hand—probably the local sign for guild.

Arvin pretended not to see the gesture. The last thing he needed was to get enmeshed in the web of the local rogues' guild. He clenched his left hand, and the ache of his abbreviated little finger—the one the Hlondeth Guild had cut the tip from—enforced his resolve. This time, he'd stay clean. The whole point in coming to Sespech was to make a fresh start.

"And the gauntlet?" Arvin asked. "Can anyone use it?"

"Anyone. Even thieves. It shields the petitionary from blows, weapons—even spells that cause harm. But not," the man added with a twinkle in his eye, "against justice. Use it carefully, if you've committed a crime."

"Sound advice," Arvin replied. "But I don't intend to commit any."

He watched as one of the clerics laid a hand on the paralyzed yuan-ti and spoke a prayer. An instant later they both vanished; snowflakes swirled in agitation in the spot their bodies had just occupied. The second cleric touched the young rogue gently on the shoulder then waved him away, dismissing him. Then he, too, teleported away.

The snow continued to fall, dusting the ground with a thin layer of white. The crowd began to disperse.

The man beside Arvin shivered. "Need a place to stay,

friend?" he asked. "That's my inn over there: Lurgin's Lodgings."

Arvin shook his head. "Thanks, but no. I'm just passing through Mimph. I hope to catch a boat for Ormpetarr this afternoon."

The man placed a cupped hand over his heart. "As you wish."

Arvin turned and walked away, still awed by the treatment the yuan-ti had received.

He was going to like it in Sespech.

CHAPTER 2

Arvin squinted, trying to peer through the falling snow. He'd never seen it fall so thickly; usually the lands surrounding the Vilhon Reach received no more than a sporadic, wet slush that quickly melted. This winter, however, had seen more than one snowfall like this one; the thick, fluffy snowflakes had piled up ankle-deep.

Despite the snow, the wagon in which Arvin rode was making good time as it crossed the frozen fields east of Mimph—though Arvin wondered how the driver could see where he was going. Arvin could see no more than a few paces in any direction; beyond that was only the occasional dark blur—thin and tall if it was a tree, short and squat if it was a cottage.

The driver, a dwarf with a thick red beard,

stared resolutely ahead over the backs of the two horses that drew the wagon. He gave the reins an occasional flick or clucked to the animals, encouraging them to keep up their pace. The only other sounds were the crunch of wheels on snow and the tinkling of the tiny bells that hung from the horses' braided manes. Steam rose from their backs, mingling with the swirling snow.

Arvin tucked the heavy wool blanket tightly around his chest and legs and shivered. He was able to block out discomfort while performing his *asanas*, but not for a whole afternoon at a stretch. The cold bit at his ears and nose and caused a throbbing ache in his abbreviated little finger, and the snowflakes settling on his shoulders and drifting down into his collar chilled him further. He glanced across at the wagon's only other passenger, wondering how she could be so comfortable. Her own blanket was loosely draped about her knees, and she wasn't hugging herself, as Arvin was. Her winter cloak was open at the neck, and she hadn't bothered to brush away the snowflakes that dusted her long black hair. She stared over Arvin's shoulder at the snow-blurred landscape that fell away behind them. Judging by her dusky skin, she came from the warm lands to the south and shouldn't be used to cold. Her breath, like his, fogged the air. Yet she looked as comfortable as if she were sitting beside a crackling fire. Arvin decided she must have magic that helped her to endure the cold. Maybe that bulge under the glove on her right hand was a magical ring.

Envious though he was, Arvin couldn't help but glance at her. She was exquisite, with eyes so dark it was difficult to see where pupil ended and iris began, and long lashes that fluttered each time she blinked. Her cheekbones were high and wide, and the hair that framed her face was lustrous and thick, with a slight wave. Arvin imagined brushing it back from her face and letting his fingers linger on the soft skin of her cheek. The riverboat wouldn't be leaving until tomorrow morning; perhaps she could be persuaded to....

She shifted on the wagon's hard wooden bench, at last shaking the snowflakes from her hair. Arvin caught a glimpse of an earring in her left ear—a finger-thick plug of jade, its rounded end carved in the shape of a stylized face with drooping, heavy lips. Then her hair covered it again.

Her eyes met Arvin's. Realizing he was still staring at her, he blushed. "Your earring," he stammered. "It's pretty."

She stared at him for several unnerving moments. Then her gaze shifted to his forehead. "That stone. Is it your clan?" She spoke in the clipped accent of the southern lands, each word slightly abbreviated.

"This?" Arvin touched the lapis lazuli on his forehead. The fingernail-sized chip of stone was a spot of warmth against his chilled skin, joined by magic with his flesh—and joined with his thoughts, when its command word was spoken. He'd put it on as soon once the ship was safely away from Hlondeth and had left it in place since. There didn't seem to be any reason to hide it anymore. Zelia—the stone's original owner—was far behind him now, gods be praised.

"It's just a decoration," he answered at last.

"I see." She glanced away, seemingly losing interest.

"You're from the south?" Arvin asked, hoping to continue the conversation.

She nodded.

"I'm from Hlondeth, myself."

That got her attention. She studied him a moment. "You are not a yuan-ti."

"No. My name's Vin," he said, using an abbreviation that was as common as cobblestones in Hlondeth. "And yours is...?"

She paused, as if deciding whether to answer. "Karrell."

"You're going to Ormpetarr?" It was an unnecessary question, since the only reason anyone would be taking this wagon would be to reach the riverboats that plied the Lower Nagaflow.

She nodded.

"Me too," Arvin continued. He plunged into the carefully rehearsed story that would explain his presence in Sespech. "I'm an agent for Mariners' Mercantile. I hope to encourage Baron Foesmasher to buy from our rope factories. Those new ships he's building are going to require good strong hemp for their rigging." He patted the backpack on the seat beside him. "I've brought samples of our finest lines to show him."

Karrell raised an eyebrow. "You are meeting with the baron?" She glanced at his cloak—woven from coarse brown wool—and the worn boots that protruded from the blanket draped over his legs.

Behind her, the driver chuckled into his beard and flicked his reins.

"These are my traveling clothes," Arvin explained. She obviously thought he was a braggart, trying to impress her. He drew himself up straighter. "I'll change into something more suitable once I arrive in Ormpetarr, before going to the palace. Ambassador Extaminos has graciously agreed to introduce me to—"

"Dmetrio Extaminos?"

Arvin blinked. "You know him?"

"I know his work. He has a great love of architecture. He restored the Serpent Arch, the first Hall of Extaminos, and the Coiled Tower." She paused to stare at Arvin, as if expecting a reaction.

He shrugged. "Old buildings don't interest me."

It was the wrong thing to say. Karrell tossed her head. "They interest me," she said. "That is why I came north: to study architecture. The yuan-ti have a particularly graceful style, with their arches, spirals, and towers."

Arvin realized there might be more to the woman than just a pretty face. "Are you an architect?" He glanced at the bag at her feet. Like him, she was traveling light.

"Architecture interests me," she said. "I make sketches of buildings." She tilted her head. "Old buildings."

Arvin scrambled to salvage the conversation. He dredged up what little he knew about the subject, casting his mind back to the "lessons" the priests had given at the orphanage—lessons that were delivered to the backs of the children's heads while they worked. The lessons helped the priests convince themselves they were educating and instructing the children, not just profiting from their labors.

"The Coiled Tower was built in...." Damn, the date had eluded him. Was it 641 or 614? He could never remember. "In the year of the city's independence," he continued, reciting what he remembered of his lessons. "The Extaminos Family erected it to honor the snakes that saved Hlondeth from the kobolds. The ones Lord Shevron summoned with his prayers. The snakes, that is—not the kobolds."

Karrell's lips twitched. A smile?

"The year was 614," she said. "Eighty-five years after your people and mine first made contact."

"Your people?" Arvin prompted.

"My father's tribe." Karrell made a dismissive gesture. "You will not know their name."

"I might," Arvin said. "Where did you say you were from?"

"The south."

She was right. He knew little of the people to the south and probably wouldn't have recognized the name of her tribe. But he wasn't completely ignorant of geography. "By your accent, I'd say you were from the Chultan Peninsula," he commented. "That's where the flying snakes come from, isn't it?"

She gave him a sharp look.

She obviously didn't like snakes—they had that much in common, at least. Arvin quickly changed the subject. "You must have been traveling a long time," he continued. "What places have you visited?"

"I was most recently in Hlondeth, sketching the buildings that Dmetrio Extaminos was restoring. I had hoped to meet him and talk to him about his project but learned he had returned to Sespech to take up the ambassador's post."

"Is that why you came to Sespech?" Arvin asked.

Karrell shook her head. "No. I came to sketch the palace at Ormpetarr. But I am glad to have met you." She leaned forward and rested a hand on Arvin's knee. "Will you introduce me to Dmetrio Extaminos?"

Arvin hesitated. Karrell's answers to his questions had been short and evasive. What if she was a spy, or even an assassin? Even if she was exactly what she claimed to be, he could think of a dozen reasons to say no. Dmetrio didn't know about Arvin's mission—to him, Arvin would be nothing more than a "rope merchant's agent" that he was to introduce to Baron Foesmasher. This would give Arvin an excuse to chat informally with Dmetrio, to find out—with a little prompting, in the form of a psionic manifestation—if Dmetrio knew anything about Glisena's disappearance. Dmetrio had been courting Glisena for several months; there was a chance that her disappearance was part of an illicit elopement. If it was, the alliance between Sespech and Hlondeth would unravel as quickly as a frayed rope.

Arvin didn't need a stranger hanging about while he asked Dmetrio delicate questions. Nor did he want her tagging along behind him in Ormpetarr. The next thing he knew, she'd be asking for an introduction to Baron Foesmasher and a tour of the palace.

On the other hand, Karrell was the most beautiful woman Arvin had ever met. And the touch of her hand on his knee—even through the thick wool blanket—was sending a welcome flush of warmth through him.

Karrell raised her free hand to her chest, making a brief, imploring gesture that reminded Arvin of the silent speech. She leaned closer still, whispering a plea in her own language, and Arvin caught a whiff of the scented oil she must have combed into her hair to make it shine so. She smelled of the exotic flowers of the south, of orchids underlaid with a hint of musk. A snowflake landed at the corner of her upper lip, and Arvin was filled with an urge to kiss it away.

"Please," she breathed. "It would mean so much to me to meet Ambassador Extaminos, to share my sketches with someone who appreciates the subject as much as I do."

Arvin swallowed. "I'd like to see your sketches, too."

Karrell's dark eyes shone. "So you'll introduce me?"

Arvin tugged at the neck of his cloak, loosening it. The snow was still falling thick and fast, and the air had chilled as the sun went down, but he was suddenly very warm. "I...."

The wagon jerked to a halt. "We're here," the dwarf grunted—the first words he'd spoken since their journey began. "Riverboat Landing. The Eelgrass Inn." Bells tinkled as the horses shook their heads, taking advantage of the slack reins.

Arvin glanced around. The wagon had pulled up beside the largest of the half dozen inns that lined the bank of the Lower Nagaflow. Several piers splayed out into the river like fingers. Tied up to them were the riverboats—wide-hulled sailboats with tall masts, canvas sails furled tight against their yards. Snow had blown into drifts on the decks of most, but one had been swept clean. Aboard it, two men were fitting a repeating crossbow to the port rail amidships. A second repeating crossbow was already mounted on the starboard rail.

Arvin caught the eye of the dwarf, who had climbed down to tie the reins of the horses to a hitching post. "Why the crossbows?" he asked. "Are they expecting trouble?"

The dwarf's feet crunched in the snow as he walked back to open the door of the wagon. "Slavers," he said as Arvin climbed down from the wagon. "From Nimpeth." He pointed across the river at the far shore. "They have their own boats. Sleek and fast."

Arvin caught Karrell's eye as she rose and gathered up her bag. "Don't worry," he assured her. "If the slavers do attack, there will be more than just crossbows to stop them. I'm armed with a magical weapon—and I'm very capable in a fight."

Karrell gave him a bemused glance. She swept back her cloak, revealing an ironwood club, with a knobbed, fist-sized ball at one end, that hung from her belt. "So am I."

Arvin's eyebrows rose. "But you're—"

She stared down at him, eyes narrowed. "A woman?"

"No," Arvin said quickly. "I mean yes. You're *clearly* a woman." He realized he was staring not at her weapon, but at the curves the drawn-back cloak had revealed—at weapons of a different sort. "And there are lots of women in the Guil—" He caught himself just in time and took a deep breath. "I meant that you're ... an artist," he finished lamely.

"And you, so you say, are a rope merchant's agent," she said, giving the final word a slight emphasis, as if to imply she thought he was an agent of a different sort.

Arvin swore to himself. What had he been thinking,

bragging to this woman? To a complete stranger. She might have been anyone—even a spy from Chondath. She seemed to have guessed that he was more than he was pretending to be, but then, so was she. Arvin glanced at her bag. It didn't look big enough to hold an artist's ink pots, quills, and scroll tubes. Even so, he had a feeling he could trust her.

A gust of wind caught his cloak, and he shivered. The inn the wagon had stopped in front of was two stories tall, with walls made of roughly squared logs and a roof whose eaves were crusted with icicles. A signboard hanging above the front door was painted with a picture of a snakelike creature winding its way through submerged river grass. The door opened briefly as a man—one of the sailors from the riverboats, carrying a hand crossbow—exited the inn and headed for the piers. The smell of stew flavored with winter sage and onions drifted out in his wake.

The dwarf grunted and marched back to the hitching post, his feet crunching in the snow. "I need to rub down my animals," he grunted. "When you're done chatting." He untied the reins and stared pointedly at the stable that adjoined the inn.

Karrell nodded. "Of course." She stepped down from the wagon, glanced up at the inn's signboard, and picked her way gracefully toward the door.

Arvin trailed after her. "You're taking a room here?"

Karrell nodded.

"Maybe we could share it," he suggested. "To save some coin."

She paused, one hand on the door latch, and tilted her head. "We have only just met. Perhaps once you have introduced me to Ambassador Extaminos...."

Arvin nodded eagerly. Then he realized something. Once he got to Ormpetarr, he was going to be busy with his mission. And he didn't think he could wait until then. Karrell was an amazing woman, as quick-witted as she was beautiful. If he didn't win her over now, someone else surely would.

Karrell opened the door, releasing a gust of warm, savory-scented air that was thick with conversation. At least two dozen people were inside. Several glanced up from their meals as the door opened. More than one man raised his eyebrows appreciatively or whistled under his breath at the sight of Karrell.

"Listen," Arvin said, desperate now. He dropped his voice to a low, confiding whisper. "I won't have time to spend with you once we reach Ormpetarr. I'll be too busy. You were right—I'm not really here to sell rope. I actually came to Sespech to find someone. She—"

The words froze in his throat as he saw who was seated at one of the tables. A woman with long red hair, slit eyes, and skin freckled with green scales. She lifted from her plate what looked like a raw egg that was still in its shell, swallowed it whole, and licked her lips with a forked blue tongue.

For the space of several heartbeats, Arvin stood rooted to the spot, unable to breathe. The chill that filled him was colder than the thickest ice.

Zelia—here?

She glanced up.

Arvin jerked back, putting the half-opened door between himself and Zelia. He stared at Karrell, who was hesitating in the doorway. Suddenly, Arvin saw her in a new light. The flame of desire that had almost driven him to confide his mission to her had been snuffed out the instant he'd spotted Zelia. He recognized it now for what it was—a magical compulsion.

He'd been charmed by Karrell. And she'd led him straight to Zelia.

Or . . . had she? Karrell glanced once at Arvin, then back through the open door, her eyes ranging over those within. She obviously realized that Arvin had spotted someone inside the inn who terrified him—but she'd made no move to force him inside. Instead she had a thoughtful expression on her face.

She *wasn't* in league with Zelia. But if Arvin didn't act quickly, she'd give him away.

"Go on," Arvin said, flicking his hands at Karrell, frantically motioning her inside. Sharing a room with her was the last thing on his mind now. "This place looks too expensive. I'll find a room somewhere else."

Karrell frowned. "Will I see you in the morning?"

"Perhaps," Arvin said. "If not, safe journey." He turned and walked swiftly away. Thank the gods that it was dark. The night's gloom hid his face—and, most important, the lapis lazuli on his forehead. He spoke the word that would loosen it and peeled it from his skin. Then he vanished it inside his magical glove. He ducked around the corner of the building, his heart still pounding at his narrow escape. Why hadn't the sixth sense that had been plaguing him, ever since he'd begun a serious study of psionics under Tanju, given him any warning that the person he most feared was lurking within the inn? All his premonitions could do, it seemed, was give him unsettling glimpses of the dangers that *other* people faced. The vision he'd had on the ship—of a sailor falling from the ratlines and snapping his neck on the deck below—was a prime example.

Keeping low to avoid being spotted through the inn's windows, he made his way to the rear of the building.

What now?

Every instinct screamed at him to flee, to put as much distance between himself and Zelia as possible. Should he steal a wagon and return to Mimph? Or maybe try for Fort Arran? He stared at the falling snow and realized he would only get lost in the darkness.

No, there were only two ways out: as a passenger on one of the wagons back to Mimph or on tomorrow morning's riverboat. Either way, he'd have to be careful not to be spotted. If by wagon, he could hide overnight in the stables then board at the last moment after making certain Zelia wasn't also catching a wagon back to Mimph. Bundled in a heavy blanket, he'd be indistinguishable from any other passenger. There was always the risk that some stable hand or driver would find him in the stables, but he could give the simple excuse of not having enough coin for an inn, and charm the fellow into agreeing to let him sleep in a stall.

If by riverboat, he'd also have to find a way to board without Zelia seeing him.

Two men were approaching—the sailors who had been mounting the repeating crossbows on the boat earlier. Fortunately, the snow was still falling. Screened by its mottled white curtain, Arvin stepped into the shadows at the rear of the Eelgrass Inn and watched the men enter another of the inns. He glanced at the boat they'd just come from. Of the dozen tied up to the piers, it was the only one with a guard—Arvin could see him moving on the boat's raised stern, beside a dull red glow that must be a brazier. The guard obviously wasn't going anywhere, which meant the riverboat had cargo loaded on board. It was the one that would sail in the morning. It would be an easy matter for Arvin to use his psionics to distract the guard then slip into the hold and hide. That would ensure that Zelia wouldn't see him. Then, with Tymora's blessing, Arvin would be on his way to Ormpetarr. Zelia would never even know that he'd nearly blundered into the inn where she was staying.

Unless she, too, was planning on leaving by riverboat.

Arvin couldn't very well hide in the hold for the whole of the two-day journey to Ormpetarr. He had to know whether Zelia was planning on being aboard the riverboat tomorrow morning. More important, he needed to learn what she was doing here. Had she heard that Arvin was alive and on his way to Ormpetarr, then positioned herself at the one place he was sure to pass through on his way there?

In order to find the answers to his questions, Arvin had to take a risk.

A very big risk.

Taking a deep breath, he placed a hand on the rough wooden wall next to him. He withdrew into himself, drawing his consciousness first into the "third eye" at the center of his forehead and deeper, into the spot at the base of his throat. Tightly coiled swirls of energy were unleashed in each location; a heartbeat later he heard the low droning noise that accompanied his manifestations of this power. Silver motes of light sparkled in his vision then flared out around him, sputtering into invisibility as they moved away from him.

They penetrated the walls of the inn. Following them with his consciousness, Arvin quested about mentally, looking for the distinctive disturbances that accompanied the use of psionics. He found none. At the moment, Zelia was not manifesting any of her powers.

Thus reassured, Arvin shifted his consciousness away from his throat and into a spot at the base of his scalp. Energy awakened there with a prickling that raised the hairs on the back of his neck as he manifested a second psionic power. Once again, the silver sparkles erupted around him. He sent his consciousness into the inn a second time, searching, this time, for thoughts. He skipped lightly from one patron of the inn to the next. Strangely, he could not locate Karrell—had she left the inn without Arvin spotting her? But Zelia's mind, powerful as it was, rose above the others. Catching his breath, he listened.

She wasn't thinking about him. Instead her thoughts were focused, impatiently, on someone she was waiting for: a male—someone who couldn't come inside the inn, for some reason. This someone probably wouldn't arrive for another day or so, given the unusually snowy weather. She was stuck here until he arrived, and she wasn't happy about it. But all she could do was wait. He would send her a message as soon as he was in the vicinity of—

Arvin felt Zelia's thoughts jerk to a sudden halt. There was a faint tinkling noise at the edges of her awareness—the secondary display of the power Arvin was manifesting. Zelia focused on it. Someone was trying to contact her. Was it—?

Instantly, Arvin disengaged. He scrambled away from the Eelgrass Inn, putting as much distance between himself and Zelia as possible. The power that allowed a psion to detect manifestations in his or her vicinity had a limited range, typically no more than twenty paces. Likewise the power that allowed a psion to detect thoughts—a power Zelia also had.

Only after he'd slipped and staggered through the snow and put a hundred paces between himself and the inn did Arvin slow to a walk. Panting, he looked nervously around. That had been close. "Nine lives," he whispered, touching the crystal that hung at his throat. The power stone, a gift from his mother, was long since used up. He wore it on a thong about his throat for sentimental reasons only. But old habits died hard.

Listening in on Zelia's thoughts had nearly alerted her to his presence. It had been worth it, though. It seemed that Zelia's presence here was a coincidence. She wasn't looking for him. Not yet, anyway.

Unfortunately, Arvin had gleaned neither a name nor a description of the fellow Zelia was waiting for. Now he had to watch out not only for Zelia, but for her ally, as well. But at least it sounded as if the fellow wouldn't be here tonight. Arvin could take a room at an inn, wait until just before dawn, then slip aboard a riverboat and be out of here, leaving Zelia behind.

Of course, that didn't mean that she wouldn't drop whatever she was doing and come slithering after Arvin, once she learned that he wasn't dead, after all. Which she would quickly realize, if Karrell mentioned the name "Vin" and "rope" within earshot of Zelia.

If only Arvin knew which room Karrell was staying in, he might be able to prevent her from giving him away. One charm—let's see how *she* liked being on the receiving end—would see to that. Trouble was she didn't seem to be in the Eelgrass Inn. And he couldn't very well go around using his psionics to search for her. That would be certain to attract Zelia's attention. It would be like dangling a live mouse in front of a snake. No, it would be better to save his psionic energies in case he needed to mount a defense against Zelia—futile though that defense would be.

If Zelia did discover him, Arvin was a dead man. He knew Zelia nearly as well as she knew herself. The mind seed that had been lodged in his head for six days had seen to that. If there was one thing Zelia savored, it was vengeance. Exacting it upon a human who had thwarted her would be especially sweet. She'd stop at nothing to obtain it. Not to mention the fact that he knew more about her—and her secret dealings—than anyone else in Hlondeth, save perhaps, for Lady Dediana. Arvin knew a number of details that Zelia would kill to keep secret: the identities of several of the mind seeds that served as her spies, for example.

He toyed, for a brief moment, with the thought of sneaking into Zelia's room. He could lay in wait for her, attack her when and where she least expected it. But he quickly rejected that idea. The last time he'd tried to get the drop on Zelia, he'd failed miserably, even after springing several magical surprises on her—surprises he didn't have at his disposal, this time. No, he'd do better to sneak away, instead, and pray—pray hard—that Zelia would finish her business at Riverboat

Landing and depart without ever knowing that their paths had crossed.

At least, Arvin thought, he had one thing in his favor if Zelia did find him: the power that Tanju had taught him, shortly before Arvin had departed for Sespech. Using it, Arvin could link the fates of any two individuals. While it was active, if one was injured, the other would be, too. If one died, so would the other. Or, at the very least—in the case of extremely powerful spellcasters or magical creatures—the other would be seriously reduced in power.

Knowing that Zelia would be severely debilitated or even die if she killed him was cold comfort, but it was the best he could do. Her powers were vastly superior to his; the defenses he'd learned would only hold her off for so long. But if he could link their fates, it would at least give him some bargaining time.

Keeping a wary eye on the Eelgrass Inn, Arvin made his way to the inn farthest from it to book a room for the night. He'd have to rise just before dawn in order to sneak aboard the riverboat, but he didn't think he was going to have any problem with that.

He doubted he was going to get much sleep.

CHAPTER 3

With a lurch that caused the hard, lumpy ingots of iron Arvin had been lying on to shift, the riverboat got under way. The cargo hold was nearly full; the deck was a mere palm's width above Arvin's face. Footsteps thudded across it, loud above the constant rush of water past the hull. Arvin, lying in darkness, shivered and tried to flex numbed fingers and toes. The temperature had hovered around the freezing point even after the sun came up, and he was chilled to the bone.

He lay just below one of the smaller hatches, its edges outlined with thin morning sunlight. As footsteps passed over him once more, making the deck creak, he awakened the energy that lay coiled at the base of his scalp and manifested the power he'd used the night before.

Silver sparkles flared around him then disappeared. He sent his awareness upward, through the deck, and sent it questing through the minds of the people who were aboard the boat. He dipped briefly into the thoughts of a sailor who was gripping the riverboat's tiller—how much better it was, this fellow was thinking, to sail aboard a boat as a free man—and into those of a second sailor who was serving as lookout. Perched high on the mast, this second fellow was awed by the speed at which the riverboat was traveling. It was only his tenth trip south, and yet he'd been chosen as lookout, due to his keen eyesight. The thought filled him with pride.

There were also two guards on board—one half-asleep as he leaned on one of the deck-mounted crossbows, the second tense as a spring and gleefully visualizing sending a bolt into attacking slavers. Idly watching them was the captain, a man whose mind wasn't on his duties. Instead his thoughts were lingering on the woman he'd lain with last night as he tried to recall her name.

The thoughts of the next man were much more interesting. His mind was focused intently upon the wind that was driving the boat along. He was controlling its intensity with a spell. Unlike the others on board, he thought in terms of sound and tactile sensation. Though he was directing the wind against the sail, there was no accompanying picture in his mind. He thought of the sail in terms of a taught canvas under his hand, of the creak of its yard as it shifted under the wind. He must, Arvin realized with some surprise, be blind.

There were three passengers on board: a merchant who was fretting over a delay that had nearly caused him to miss the boat, and a husband and wife on their way to Ormpetarr to attend a relative's wedding. She was eagerly anticipating it; he was dreading the tedium of being cooped up in a room with her boring kinfolk.

Arvin continued searching, but found no sign of Karrell. He wondered why she wasn't on board. Had she chosen not to travel to Ormpetarr after all? The thought disappointed him. At the same time he felt relief to have found no sign of Zelia. There were only nine people aboard the riverboat, all of them strangers to Arvin. All were just what they seemed to be. None were mind seeds.

Arvin drew his awareness back inside himself, ending the manifestation. He slid a hand under the small of his back, grasped the dagger that was sheathed there, and vanished it into his glove. He wouldn't use his weapon unless he had to. For now, his plan was to present himself as a stowaway with good reasons for sneaking on board—the captain's thoughts had given him an idea—and offer to pay for his passage.

He shoved open the hatch and clambered up onto the deck, dragging his pack behind him. Two people who must have been the husband and wife—he a sour look-ing man with a heavy black beard, she a narrow-faced woman wearing a white fur hat, her hands shoved into a matching muff—had been standing next to the hatch. They started at Arvin's sudden appearance. The mer-chant, a portly, balding fellow in a gold-thread cloak, was a few paces away. As Arvin appeared from the hold, he blinked in surprise.

One of the guards—a wiry fellow with a hook nose and tangled black hair—whipped a glance over his shoulder, shouted, "Slaver!" and immediately tried to swing his crossbow around to point inboard, only to find that it wouldn't swivel that far. The other guard—the older, gray-haired man Arvin had distracted last night when he crept aboard—looked startled but wasn't yet awake enough to react.

Arvin glanced up at the raised rear deck, searching for the captain. Three men stood there: a dark-skinned human with short, dark hair tarred flat against his head and a shadow of stubble on his chin; a barrel-chested man with a beard that didn't quite hide the faded S-brand on his cheek, holding the tiller; and an elf clad head to toe in white, his eyebrows furrowed in a **V** of concentration and his silver hair twisting in the magical wind like fluttering ribbons. The elf's eyes were unfocused, identifying him as the blind spellcaster.

Though both of the other men looked like ordinary sailors, the dark-skinned one was clearly in command. He stared a challenge at Arvin, fists on his hips.

Arvin gave the captain a grin and opened his mouth to begin his explanation, but before he could get a word out, he saw a motion out of the corner of his eye. The hook-nosed guard had yanked a sword from the sheath at his hip. He tensed, about to attack.

So much for explanations, Arvin thought. Quick as a blink, he summoned energy from points deep in his throat and his third eye and sent it down into his right foot. A droning noise filled the air as he stomped the deck, sending a flash of silver shooting through the planks toward the guard holding the sword. The deck below hook-nose's feet bucked, sending him staggering. He grabbed at the rail and managed to steady himself, but lost his weapon overboard. "My sword!" he shouted. Cursing, he stared at the dark water that had swallowed it.

The gray-haired guard by now had a hand crossbow leveled at Arvin's chest, but Arvin's chief worry was the spellcaster at the stern. The elf, however, seemed oblivious to what was happening on the main deck. His attention remained focused on the riverboat's main sail. By feel alone, he was directing the magical wind, his fingers moving in complicated patterns as if he were knotting a net.

Arvin bowed to the captain and manifested a second power—this one coercive rather than confrontational. "Sorry to have startled you, sir," he said. The base of his scalp prickled as energy coiled there. He let it uncoil in the direction of the captain and saw the fellow tilt his head as if listening to something as the power manifested. "I'm no slaver, but a simple stowaway. I snuck aboard to avoid a woman who...ah...thinks I should marry her."

The captain's lips quirked in a smile. "Got her in the family way, did you?" He walked down the short flight of steps to the main deck, motioning for the gray-haired guard to lower his crossbow.

As the guard complied, Arvin sighed with relief. His charm had worked. He reached into his boot, pulling out his coin pouch. "I'll gladly pay for my passage to Ormpetarr."

The hook-nosed guard stomped over to where the captain was standing, muttering under his breath. "What about my sword, then? Who's going to pay for that?"

"Do not worry," a female voice said from the bow. "This man is on his way to a meeting with Ambassador Extaminos. If he does not compensate you, the ambassador surely will."

Arvin whirled around. "Karrell!"

"Hello, Vin." She stood, smiling, a pace or two behind him. She'd obviously been aboard all along; she must have been wearing or carrying a magical device that protected her from mind-probing magic. That would explain how he'd missed her last night, when he sifted the thoughts of those at the inn. She'd been standing up on the bow until a moment or two ago, screened from view by the sail, which was why Arvin hadn't seen her. The wind of the boat's passage had tangled her hair. Somehow it made her even more beautiful.

The captain tilted his head slightly in her direction and spoke to Arvin in a low voice. "Is she the one you're—"

"No," Arvin said firmly. "She's not. We met on the wagon to Riverboat Landing. I got to know her during the journey."

The gray-haired guard smiled knowingly. "Lucky man," he said, a chuckle in his voice. "I can see why you wanted to slip the other woman."

The wife clucked her tongue in disapproval and tucked one of her hands possessively into the crook of her husband's arm. The merchant rolled his eyes.

"What about my sword?" the hook-nosed guard complained. "It was dwarven-forged steel."

The captain gave him a disdainful stare. "It was a standard trade sword, and cheaply made."

Hook-nose lowered his eyes.

"But I'm sure this man—Vin, his name was?—will pay for it," the captain continued. Then, to Arvin, in a low voice, "Five plumes is more than enough. And nine more, for your passage."

Arvin nodded, rummaged in his pouch for the gold coins, and handed them to the captain, who counted five of them into the hand of the guard.

Karrell, meanwhile, moved closer to Arvin. "I am glad you are aboard, Vin," she said, taking his arm. "Come. We will talk."

Arvin picked up his pack and followed her to the bow. As they passed the sail, the wind of the ship's passage hit them full force, whipping Arvin's cloak. They were traveling up the broad, open river at the speed of a galloping horse; already the cluster of inns that made up Riverboat Landing was far behind.

The windblown bow was empty; the closest person was the lookout, who sat on a swinglike perch that had been hoisted to the top of the mast. He was a teenager, judging by the cracking of his voice as he called out hazards on the river ahead. Cupping his hands to his mouth, he shouted back at the captain. "Snag! Snag dead ahead, two hundred paces!"

The yard creaked as the sail shifted, swinging the bow slightly to port. Arvin glanced over the bow and saw a submerged log, its tangled root mass just below the surface and barely visible. The roots were wound around something round and gray, probably a large stone that had been uprooted with the tree when the wind blew it over. Arvin heard a thump and scrape as the hull grazed the snag, and the riverboat continued on its way, having avoided the worst of the hazard thanks to the lookout's keen eyes.

Arvin set his pack at his feet and turned to Karrell. "I'm surprised to find you on the boat," he said. "I didn't, ah . . . see you come aboard."

Karrell's lips twitched. "I did not see you board, either."

"I slipped into the hold this morning, just before dawn," Arvin said. He lowered his voice so the sailors wouldn't overhear. "I told the guard the truth—there was a woman, back at the Eelgrass Inn, who I'm trying to avoid. A woman with red hair and green scales that look like freckles. And a blue forked tongue. Did you notice her?"

"So that is why you left so hastily." Karrell thought a moment. "She is yuan-ti?"

"Yes. But she can pass for human, at a distance."

"I saw her. Twice. Last night, when I first arrived at the inn, and this morning, when she was talking to the innkeeper."

Arvin leaned forward, tense. "You didn't say anything about me, did you? Anything she might have overheard?"

"No."

Arvin relaxed a little. "Did you hear what she said to the innkeeper?"

"That she would stay another night."

Arvin nodded, thankful that Zelia hadn't chosen to catch this morning's riverboat. He'd been terrified by the prospect of being trapped in the cargo hold, unable to emerge on deck, and slowly freezing to death during the long voyage. Even if she did set out for Ormpetarr on the next riverboat, he would reach that city a full day ahead of her.

Karrell stared at him. "Why do you fear her?"

Arvin swallowed. Was it that obvious? He gave Karrell a weak grin. "She dislikes me. A lot. She wants me dead. Fortunately, she believes I *am* dead. I'd prefer to keep it that way."

"Did you quicken her egg?" Karrell asked.

"Her what?"

"She is yuan-ti. The snake people lay eggs. And the captain said—"

"Oh," Arvin said, understanding at last. He laughed at the absurdity of it and shook his head vehemently. "We didn't have *that* kind of relationship. We were . . . close, for a time. But not that close. She's a. . . ." He paused, shuddering. He'd been about to tell Karrell that Zelia was a psion, but she probably wouldn't know what that was.

He saw that Karrell's lips were pressed together in displeasure and decided to change the subject. Like most humans, she was probably appalled at the thought of a yuan-ti and human mating. "What was it you wanted to talk to me about?" he asked.

The displeased look vanished instantly from Karrell's face. She leaned forward and placed her hand upon his arm. Her touch sent a thrill through him but nothing near the rush of desire he'd felt after she'd charmed him. "You never said whether you would introduce me to Dmetrio Extaminos."

Ah. So it was that again, was it? He wondered why she wanted to meet him so badly. Was she an assassin, after all?

Karrell reached for her cloak, one hand curling as if she were about to draw it closed at her neck. Odd—she didn't look cold. Suddenly Arvin remembered where he'd seen the gesture before. It was the same one she'd used yesterday when she'd charmed him. Even as her lips parted to whisper the spell, Arvin awoke the psionic energy at the base of his scalp and manifested a charm of his own. Karrell halted in midwhisper, her eyes shifting to the side as if she'd heard something in the distance, over the creak of the riverboat's rigging.

Arvin suppressed his smile. The shoe would be on the other foot, this time around.

Above them, the lookout shouted. "Disturbance in the water, one hand to port, three thousand paces ahead!"

The boat swung slightly to starboard and slowed.

Arvin glanced over the bow. The boat would soon be passing a small, rocky island near the center of the river; between this island and the boat was a circular patch of disturbed water about two paces wide. It looked as though a boulder had splashed into the river at that spot, sending out ripples. Arvin searched the island, but didn't see anything. The island was rocky and flat—devoid of vegetation that would offer concealment, and low enough that a ship wouldn't be able to hide behind it, which ruled out a catapult.

"What's causing it?" the captain called up at the lookout.

The young man at the top of the mast chewed his lip. "I don't know. Maybe a dragon turtle?" he asked nervously.

"Do you *see* a dragon turtle?" the captain asked in a tense voice.

"No."

The gray-haired guard snorted. "It was probably air escaping from a wreck. Or a fish fart."

The lookout twisted around to glance down at him. "Do fish fart?"

The guard chuckled.

Red-faced, the young lookout went back to his duties.

Arvin turned back to Karrell. "I'll introduce you to Ambassador Extaminos," he told her. "But I'd like to know more about you, first." He lowered his voice and caught her eye. "You can trust me. Is it Chondath you serve?"

Karrell gave a slight frown. "Who?"

Arvin was surprised by her response. Chondath, directly to the east of Sespech, was a country, not a person. Either she was playing dumb—really dumb—or she was what she claimed, a traveler from the Chultan Peninsula. "Tell me," he urged. "What's the real reason you're going to Ormpetarr?"

Karrell's voice dropped to a whisper. "I'm looking for—"

"Disturbance three hands to starboard, two thousand four hundred paces ahead!" the lookout shouted, interrupting her. This time, his high-pitched voice had an edge to it.

The riverboat turned a few degrees back to port, and slowed still more. Karrell glanced in the direction the lookout was pointing, a slight frown on her face.

Arvin touched her arm—and felt her move into his touch. "What are you looking for?" he prompted.

"Something that was entrusted to the people of Hlondeth many years ago. It—"

"Disturbance one hand to starboard, one thousand paces ahead!" the sailor shouted.

The riverboat slowed momentarily then picked up speed and turned sharply to port.

"Yes?" Arvin prompted.

Karrell opened her mouth to speak but was interrupted a third time.

"Disturbance dead ahead, four hundred paces!"

Arvin glanced up as the lookout repeated his cry, his voice breaking. "Disturbance dead ahead!" he shouted at the guards. "Something's breaking the surface!"

Arvin glanced back at the guards. They stood tensely behind their crossbows, fingers on triggers as their eyes searched the river ahead. The merchant, the husband, and the wife milled uncertainly on the main deck. At the stern, the elf and barrel-chested sailor awaited the captain's orders. The elf's hands were raised, ready to redirect the wind. The captain glanced back and forth between the low island—much closer now—and the bubbling patch of water, his face twisted with indecision. At last he gave an order; the sailor responded instantly, leaning into the tiller.

The boat heeled sharply to port, causing Karrell to stumble. She blinked, gave Arvin a sharp look, and took a quick step back from him, withdrawing her arm from his hand. The charm Arvin had manifested on her seemed to have broken. "What is happening?" she asked, glancing warily around.

"I don't know," Arvin answered. "But I don't think it's goo—"

"Naga!" the teenaged lookout shrilled. "Gods save us, it's a naga!"

"This far north?" the captain shouted. "Are you *sure?*"

The lookout mutely nodded, white-faced. Arvin stared at the spot he was pointing at—a frothing patch of water a few dozen paces to starboard. A serpentlike creature had risen from the center of it. The creature looked like an enormous green eel with blood-red spines running the length of its body. Its head was human-shaped, its face plastered with wet, kelp-green hair that hung dripping from its scalp. Its eyes were dark and malevolent as it stared at the riverboat.

"Shoot it!" the captain shouted.

Arvin heard a twang as the gray-haired guard loosed a crossbow bolt. In that same instant, the naga withdrew under the surface of the water with astonishing speed. Even as the bolt plunged into the river, the naga was gone, leaving only a spreading circle of lapping waves behind.

A moment later, over the shouting of the crew, Arvin heard a loud thud as something struck the underside of the hull. The boat canted sharply up, its stern leaving the water entirely, throwing Arvin and Karrell together into the point of the bow. Timbers groaned as the boat was forced upward by the naga rearing up beneath it; Arvin heard wood splintering as the tiller was torn away. Something splashed into the water near the stern, and someone amidships screamed—either the wife or the merchant, he wasn't sure. From above came the crack-voiced, terrified prayers of the lookout.

Then the stern slammed back down into the water. The riverboat rocked violently from side to side, water sloshing over the gunwales and its sail wildly flapping. A wave nearly carried Arvin's pack over the side. As he grabbed for it, he heard Karrell whispering urgently in her own language. From behind them came the shouts of the captain and the terrified screams of the other passengers.

A thud came from the starboard side as the naga rammed the boat a second time. The riverboat rolled sharply to port, a yardarm brushing the water. The lookout screamed as his swing-seat cracked like a whip, throwing him into the water. Clinging to the rail, Arvin heard thumps and curses as the other crew and passengers tumbled across the now-vertical deck, and a groan and cracking noises as the mast struck the water. Karrell flew past him and fell headlong into the river; Arvin shouted her name as she sank from sight. Then something hit him from behind, and he was underwater.

The first thing he noticed was the water's terrible chill; it would have taken his breath away had there been any air in his lungs. The second was the fact that the strap of his pack was loosely tangled around his left wrist. Clinging to it, he fought his way back to the surface in time to see the deck of the riverboat rushing down at him. It slammed into his face, tearing open his cheek and forcing him under again.

When he came up for the second time, he tasted blood on his lips; warm blood was flowing down his cheek. Karrell was treading water nearby. "Are you all right?" Arvin shouted.

Karrell grimly nodded, her wet hair plastered to her face. Like Arvin, she appeared to be unhurt, aside from a few scrapes and bruises. Her dark eyes mirrored Arvin's concern. "And you?" she asked, staring at the blood on his face.

Arvin took stock. He ached all over, but nothing seemed broken. "Fine." He touched the crystal at his neck, silently thanking Tymora for her mercy. "Nine lives," he whispered to himself.

The lookout floated facedown a short distance away. Arvin swam over to him and tried to flip him over then saw that the young crewmember's neck was broken.

The riverboat was turned completely over, its splintered keel pointing skyward. A tangle of lines surrounded it like a bed of kelp. Four people treaded water within this tangle: the gray-haired guard and the three passengers. The merchant was closest to the boat; he clambered onto the overturned hull, water streaming from his hair and sodden cloak, then clung to the broken keel, dazedly shaking his head. The gray-haired guard immediately followed, dragging a hand crossbow behind him, then turned to help the husband and wife out of the water. The wife was sobbing but seemed unhurt; the husband grunted with the effort of trying to kick his way out of the water with an injured leg.

There was no sign of the rest of the crew, save for the hook-nosed guard. He was swimming determinedly toward the tiny island without a backward glance.

Arvin heard a third thump as the naga struck the bottom of the overturned boat; it rocked violently, prompting a whimper from the merchant. Arvin turned to stare at the hook-nosed guard—the fellow had already reached the island, which was no more than a hundred paces away—then caught Karrell's eye. "Let's go," he told her.

She stared at the overturned boat. "But the passengers—"

"There's no room for us on the hull," Arvin said. "And we can do more on solid ground."

At last Karrell nodded. They swam.

Karrell reached the island first. Arvin was still dragging his pack; it slowed him down, but he couldn't afford to lose the dorje inside it. He nearly let it go when he heard a splashing noise behind him, but when he glanced over his shoulder, he saw it was the husband. The fellow had slipped back into the water and was trying to scramble out again.

Arvin reached the rocky shore and climbed out, gratefully accepting Karrell's hand. He'd only been in the river a short time but was shivering violently. Noticing this, Karrell chanted softly in her own language then touched his hand. Warmth flooded through Arvin, banishing the cold from his body. He nodded gratefully, understanding now why she hadn't needed the blanket during yesterday's wagon ride. Though a chill wind had started to blow, he felt as comfortable as if he were in a fire-warmed room. His abbreviated little finger didn't even ache. A useful spell, Arvin thought, wondering if there was a psionic power that might do the same.

"Hey," the hook-nosed guard protested, his teeth chattering. "What about me?"

Karrell was turning toward him when the wife's scream made her whirl toward the river instead. The naga had burst out of the water next to the boat, no more than a pace or two away from the battered hull. Its slit eyes ranged over the four humans who had taken refuge on top of the overturned boat: the merchant, cowering with a horrified expression on his face; the wife, trying to pull her husband out of the water; and the gray-haired guard, loudly cursing as he fumbled one-handed with his crossbow. The guard was injured, Arvin saw; the fingers of his other hand stuck out at odd angles and his face was drawn and pale.

The naga's eyes settled on the merchant. Its tongue flickered out of its mouth, tasting the man's fear. Then it opened its mouth, baring its fangs.

The merchant screamed.

The naga lashed forward. Its teeth sank into the merchant's shoulder, injecting a deadly dose of venom. Then it reared up. The merchant, hanging from its jaws, gave one feeble kick then slumped. The naga dropped his lifeless body. It splashed into the river then bobbed back to the surface facedown.

Arvin tossed down his pack and summoned his dagger into his glove. Before he could throw it, however, the gray-haired guard raised his crossbow and shot. The bolt struck the naga in the neck. The naga jerked and lashed its head from side to side, trying to shake the bolt loose. Then it glared at the guard. It opened its mouth and flicked its tongue four times in rapid succession. Four glowing darts of energy streaked toward the guard, striking him in the chest. He grunted, slumped down onto the deck, and slid into the river.

"Tymora help us," Arvin whispered. He'd heard tales of nagas. They were said to be as cunning as dragons and as slippery as snakes, with a bite as venomous as that of a yuan-ti. He hadn't realized they also were capable of magic.

Realizing his dagger would do little against such a fearsome monster, Arvin vanished it back into his glove. He glanced at the hook-nosed guard, hoping the fellow might also have a crossbow, but the fellow had lost his weapons during the swim to the island.

Karrell took a step toward the water's edge; it looked

as though she were about to dive back into the river. "Don't," Arvin urged, catching her hand. "Wait."

"For what?" she said fiercely. "Someone else to die?"

Despite her angry rebuke, Karrell halted. She began chanting what sounded like a spell.

The naga, meanwhile, gave a loud hiss and turned its head back and forth, as if trying to decide who its next victim would be.

Arvin had to do something—and quickly, before the naga struck again.

Sending his awareness inward, he manifested one of the attack forms Tanju had taught him—the mind blast. A psion targeted by this attack would crumple emotionally as his self-esteem and confidence were flayed away by the blast of psionic energy. A creature incapable of psionics, like the naga, would only be briefly stunned. But perhaps it would be enough.

Arvin imagined the form as Tanju had taught it to him—a man standing braced and ready, his hands held out in front of him with forefingers and thumbs touching to form a circle. When the visualization was clear, Arvin imagined the man—himself—drawing the circle toward his forehead. As power coiled tightly behind his third eye, he threw it outward at the naga. Silver sparks spiraled out from this third eye as the energies contained in the blast swept toward the creature. As they struck, the naga swayed. Its eyes rolled back in its head.

"Swim for the island!" Arvin shouted at the couple. "It's stunned—now's your chance!"

The husband tried to get into the water, but his wife clung to him. "Lie still!" she cried. "Lie still, and it won't see us!" As they struggled together, the naga blinked and shook its head. It glared down at them, its tongue flickering in and out of its mouth as its jaws parted in anticipation.

Arvin swore. The naga had recovered from the mind

blast with surprising speed. Arvin wished, belatedly, that he'd chosen a different power to manifest. If he'd linked the naga's fate with that of the merchant—or the guard—their deaths would have weakened the naga, perhaps even killed it. He could still manifest a fate link—but not until he knew for certain that another death was both imminent and unavoidable.

Arvin's eye was caught by a flash of white above his head; craning his neck, he saw that it was the elf, walking through the air as if on solid ground. He held his hands out in front of him, as if half expecting to bump into something. "What happened?" he shouted. "Where is everyone?"

The hook-nosed guard stood. "Over here!" he shouted, waving his arms.

The elf turned toward the sound of his voice and started to descend. Each step carried him forward several paces at a time. But he wasn't going to reach them in time. Not before someone else died.

Karrell finished her spell. She shouted at the naga it in a language Arvin didn't recognize. The naga whipped its head around, staring at her, and made a series of strangled cries that sounded almost like words. Then it gave a long, menacing hiss.

Arvin groaned. Karrell had distracted the naga's attention from the couple—but her spell seemed to have angered the monster. Would a glowing bolt of magical energy follow?

Just then, however, the husband at last wrenched himself away from his wife. He balanced unsteadily on the hull, preparing to dive, but then his injured leg slipped on the wet wood. Spotting the sudden movement, the naga lashed down, catching the husband's arm in its jaws. The wife screamed in horror. The husband cursed, striking the monster with his free hand. But his blows were feeble; the poison was swiftly sapping his strength.

That decided it.

Arvin sent his awareness deep into his chest, unlocking the energies stored there. As he exhaled through pursed lips, a faint scent filled the air—the power's secondary display. To Arvin, it smelled of ginger and saffron, spices his mother used to cook with, but each person catching a whiff of it would interpret it differently. To some, it might be the scent of a flower; to others, the tang of heated metal.

Arvin directed the energy first at the husband, then at the naga. The monster continued to hold the husband's arm in its jaws, oblivious to the fact its fate had just been linked with the human. The husband, meanwhile, grew increasingly weak. When his eyes began to glaze, the naga at last released him. The husband collapsed in a heap on the hull, next to his ashen-faced wife.

Arvin stared at the naga in anticipation. It shook its head and swayed loosely back and forth, part of its body sliding back under the water. It stared with dull eyes at the humans who were proving so much of an annoyance, and for one hope-filled moment Arvin thought the injuries the fate link had inflicted might cause it to retreat back into the river. But then it gave a loud, angry hiss. Whatever had prompted its attack on the riverboat, it wasn't giving up.

Arvin heard the sound of panting just above. Turning, he saw the elf had reached them at last.

"The naga's by the boat!" Arvin shouted at the elf. "Use your magic against it—quickly!"

"Where?" The elf cocked his head, trying to pinpoint the naga by sound alone. The monster, however, was no longer hissing. And the wife was wailing as she clutched her husband's lifeless body, masking any sounds the naga was making.

Arvin made a quick mental calculation. "About a hundred and fifteen paces away," he called over his shoulder. "And. . . ." He glanced at the naga and took a wild guess. It was slightly to the left. "And one hand to port?"

The elf immediately cast a spell. Pointing a finger at the sky, he shouted in his own lilting tongue, and whipped his hand down so that it was pointing at the naga. As he did, a bolt of lightning streaked down from the overcast above, momentarily blinding Arvin. Thunder exploded directly overhead.

When Arvin opened his eyes again—blinking them to clear away the white after-image of the lightning—he saw that the bolt had missed. Instead of striking the naga it had struck the overturned boat, tearing a huge hole in the riverboat's stern. Smoke rose from the blackened planks.

"Did I hit it?" the elf cried.

The naga gave a humanlike scream, which ended in a fierce hiss of anger. Then it retaliated. Its tongue flicked out, hurling a glowing dart of energy toward the elf. He gave a sharp cry as it struck him in the shoulder and he immediately tried to cast a counter spell. But even as his lips parted, a second magical missile struck him in the chest, then a third, and a fourth. The elf faltered, fell to his knees, and began sinking through the air toward the island.

Arvin tried to manifest a second fate link—this time, between elf and naga. The monster wouldn't suffer the effects of the damage the elf had already taken, but if it continued to attack, the pain it would suffer would give it pause for thought. Though he felt a slight tingle in his chest, nothing happened. His psionic energies were too depleted to manifest that power.

The wife's wails were increasing in volume. Releasing her husband's body at last, she rose unsteadily to her feet and shook her fist at the heavens, one hand gripping the keel. "Why him?" she screamed. "Why?"

The naga's head whipped around. It lunged down, sinking its teeth into her upraised arm. She gave a choked cry and staggered backward as the naga released her. She collapsed into a seated position, supporting herself with one hand.

"Stay where you are," Karrell called to the woman. "I am coming to help." Then, before Arvin could stop her, she dived into the water. What Karrell thought she could accomplish, Arvin had no idea. The woman would be dead within a few heartbeats from the naga's venom. Even if Karrell reached her in time to cast a preventive spell, she'd be the next to fall.

"Karrell, no!" Arvin cried. "Come back!"

She ignored him, swimming steadily on toward the boat.

He had to do something—but what? His energies were almost depleted, but there was one small thing he could do. Sending his awareness down into his throat, he chose one of his lesser powers—one that caused its target to become momentarily distracted by an imagined sight or sound. A low droning filled the air as it manifested. The naga had been lashing back and forth, but as the power manifested, its head turned sharply to stare at a distant spot on the river.

As Karrell at last reached the boat and climbed up to help the injured woman, Arvin used his power to distract the naga a second time. "Karrell!" he shouted. "Swim with her back to the island! Get away from there!"

Karrell, however, wasn't listening. She crouched beside the woman, touching her arm.

The naga glanced down at her and parted its jaws.

Arvin distracted it a third time.

"Hurry up," Arvin gritted under his breath. "Finish the spell."

The naga recovered—more quickly than before.

Arvin distracted it a fourth time.

Karrell still hadn't completed her spell.

The naga loomed above her, hissing furiously. It was almost as if the monster realized it was being hit with psionics—and blamed the attacks on the woman who was crouched on the overturned boat, within easy striking distance.

Arvin tried to distract the naga a fifth time.

Nothing happened. The energy stored in his *muladhara* had run dry. "Leave her!" he shouted at Karrell.

She ignored him.

"Where . . ." a faint voice asked, ". . . is it?"

Arvin glanced around. The elf was kneeling on the rocks behind him, his head drooping.

"Give me your hand," Arvin said. "I'll show you." He grabbed the elf's hand and aimed it at the spot where the naga was. "There," he said. "About. . . ."

Seeing that Karrell was also in a direct line with the elf's hand, he hesitated. If he judged the distance or angle incorrectly, she would die.

The naga bared its venomous fangs. Its eyes were locked on Karrell.

"One hundred and seventeen paces away!" Arvin urged. "Quick! Cast your spell."

The elf's lips drew together in a determined line. He pointed at the sky with his free hand and chanted the words of his spell. Guided by Arvin's hand, his arm swept down—

The naga lunged forward; Karrell jerked to one side. The naga reared back, preparing to lash out at Karrell a second time—

The lightning bolt struck. This time, the aim was true. The bolt lanced into the naga's head, exploding it. This time it was bits of skull and brain that splashed down into the water, rather than splinters of wood. The suddenly headless naga swayed back and forth for a moment longer then crumpled into the water. It disappeared from sight, leaving behind ripples that sloshed against the overturned boat, staining the river red.

The elf turned his head, listening. "Did I—"

"Yes," Arvin answered. "It's dead." Dropping the elf's hand, he dived into the water and swam rapidly toward Karrell. She was hunched over the injured woman, unmoving. But as he crawled up onto the hull, he saw Karrell straighten. Her movements seemed steady enough.

"Thank the gods it missed you," he started to say. "For a moment there, I thought—" As he climbed up onto the hull, his eyes fell on her trouser leg and the twin puncture marks in it. A dark stain surrounded each puncture: blood.

Karrell glanced at the wound. "Yes. It bit me. But the wound is small." As she turned back to comfort the injured woman, Arvin saw her wince.

"But the venom?" he asked. "Why didn't it kill you?"

"My magic halted it."

Her hands, Arvin noticed, were bare. She'd yanked off her gloves to lay hands on the injured woman. Arvin saw now what had caused the bulge under her glove—a wide gold ring, set with a large turquoise stone, on the little finger of her right hand. It was probably the source of the magic that shielded her thoughts.

"You're a cleric?" Arvin guessed.

Karrell nodded. She reached for her gloves and began pulling them on.

"Of what god?" Arvin continued.

"You will not have heard of him, this far north. He is a god of the jungle."

"Your wound is still bleeding," he told her. "We've got to staunch the blood." He reached for her leg.

"No," Karrell said sharply.

Arvin drew his hands back. "No need to take offense," he told her.

"I can heal it myself." She laid a palm over the punctures and chanted a brief spell in a language Arvin had never heard before—her native tongue, he guessed. The words were crisp and short, as abbreviated and staccato as her accent.

The riverboat creaked, listing slightly as it settled deeper into the river. Glancing down at the water, Arvin saw a dark-skinned body, surrounded by a stain of red, tangled in the submerged rigging. That explained where the captain had gone. The body of the husband floated nearby. The man's head had suffered the same fate as the naga's; it had ruptured like a smashed melon. Pinkish chunks floated in the river next to it.

Karrell, wisely, had turned the wife's head away from the gruesome sight.

The boat shifted, releasing a bubble of air half the size of a wagon. Arvin was forced to grab the keel as the boat tilted still further. "It's going to sink," he told Karrell. He glanced down at the injured woman. "Let's get her to the island."

The wife had fallen silent now; she stared straight ahead with dull eyes. Together, Arvin and Karrell eased her into the water and dragged her between them as they swam back to the island where the guard and elf waited.

Karrell immediately went to the elf, despite the guard's protests that he was "freezing to death" and in need of one of her warming spells. Kneeling beside the elf, she cast a healing spell. Arvin, meanwhile, stared at the riverboat. Its bow rose slowly into the air at an angle, and it sank, borne down by the weight of its cargo.

The injured woman sat up and stared at the spot where it had gone down, crying. Karrell's spell had saved her life, but the woman's heart was still wounded. "My husband," she keened. "Why ... ?"

Karrell, meanwhile, cast a warming spell on the

hook-nosed guard. Instead of thanking her, he spat. "So many dead—and for what? A few lousy ingots of iron."

The elf turned toward him. "The barony needs steel; that iron would have forged new shields, armor, and weapons to keep Chondath at bay." He turned blind eyes toward the water. "Did the boat sink? Was the cargo lost?"

"All but this pack, here," the guard muttered, giving Arvin's pack a kick. The pack rolled over, spilling a length of trollgut rope. Horrified, Arvin realized that the main flap had been torn. Had his dorje fallen out during his swim to the island?

The guard frowned. "That's a strange-looking rope."

Arvin hurried to his pack and began rummaging inside it, searching frantically for the dorje. He breathed a sigh of relief as his fingers brushed against the cloth-wrapped length of crystal.

"What I don't understand is what the naga was doing this far north," the guard continued, turning back to the elf. "Nagas *never* come north of the barrier. And why did it attack? We did nothing to provoke it."

"Yes, we did," Karrell said softly. "We crushed her nest."

The guard snapped his fingers. "That snag," he said. "The one we grazed."

Karrell nodded. "She had laid her eggs in its roots."

Startled, Arvin looked up at Karrell. He'd seen the "rock" in the snag—but Karrell hadn't. "How did you know that?"

"I asked her."

"*That* was the spell you cast?" he asked, incredulous.

Karrell shrugged. "I thought I could talk to her. But she was too angry."

Arvin shook his head. "You can't reason with a

gods-cursed *serpent*," he told her. He gestured at the weapon that still hung from her belt. "Next time, use your club."

Karrell's face darkened, but before she could snap back at him, Arvin turned to the elf. "What now?" he asked. He wanted to pull the dorje out of his pack and check it, but not in front of the others. "Do we wait here for the next riverboat?"

"There won't be another until tomorrow morning," the elf said. "But I can air walk back. With a magical wind to push me, I'll be swift."

Arvin stared at the elf's unfocused eyes. "How will you find your way back?"

"Hulv will guide me," the elf said, gesturing in the general direction of the hook-nosed guard. "I can cast the spell on him, as well."

Karrell nodded down at the injured woman. "Can you take her with you?" she asked. "She needs more healing than I can provide."

The elf nodded. "Hulv will carry her."

"What about my husband?" the woman asked in a trembling voice. She stared at the spot where his headless body floated, next to that of the merchant. The lookout and gray-haired guard floated a short distance away, but the captain's body was nowhere to be seen; it must have been dragged below by the boat. As for the barrel-chested sailor, he had completely disappeared.

"Lady, your husband's body will be recovered later, together with the others who died," the elf told her. He tilted his face in the general direction of Arvin and Karrell. "I don't have enough magic to cast the spell on all of us, so you two will have to wait here. I will get them to send another riverboat—it should reach you by midday."

"Fine," Arvin said. He pulled his cloak tighter as a breeze started to blow—a natural wind, this time. Arvin squinted up at the overcast sky, hoping it wasn't going to start snowing again. If it did, the riverboat would have a hard time locating them.

The elf cast the spell on himself then on the sailor. Hulv picked up the injured woman and followed the elf into the air, as if climbing an invisible staircase. They walked swiftly away and soon were no more than specks in the distance.

Arvin glanced at Karrell, who had her back to him. She was staring at the bodies, which were slowly drifting away from the island, back in the direction of Riverboat Landing.

"We should recover them," she said. "Before the current carries them away."

"I suppose," Arvin agreed reluctantly. Despite the fact that the spell Karrell had cast on him was keeping him warm, he was nervous about entering the river again. "But what if another naga happens along?"

"None will come," Karrell said. "The naga was alone—an outcast, hiding from the others of her kind. She thought this would be a safer place to lay her eggs."

"Ah," Arvin said. He glanced again at the bodies. The river had only a sluggish current; it wasn't as if they were going to vanish in the next few moments. "I need to check something in my pack first. Just give me a moment; then I'll help."

Karrell didn't reply. She seemed to still be smarting from his critical remark about the spell she'd used on the naga. Arvin gave himself a mental kick for being so sharp with her—especially after she risked her own life to save that of the woman—and tried to stammer out an apology, but she dived into the water alone.

"Uh ... I'll be right there," Arvin called to her.

He pulled the dorje out of his pack—then stiffened as he felt something shift inside the cloth in which it was wrapped. He tore the cloth open with fumbling fingers and groaned as he saw what lay within. The dorje had snapped cleanly in half. The lavender glow of psionic energy that had once filled it was gone.

Cursing, he slammed a fist against his leg. Now that the dorje was broken, Arvin would have to rely on his own, limited, psionic powers.

Finding Glisena wasn't going to be easy.

He shoved the broken crystal back into his pack, together with his ropes. As he tied the torn flap shut, he wondered how long it would take the second riverboat to reach them. Thinking about that, he realized the broken dorje wasn't his only problem. When the riverboat came to rescue them, it would also recover the bodies Karrell was so diligently recovering. Its crew wouldn't want to travel with these all the way to Ormpetarr. Instead they would return to the closest town—to Riverboat Landing ...

Which was the last place Arvin wanted to go ...

Especially if Zelia was still there.

CHAPTER 4

As the dark shape that had been moving upriver drew closer, resolving into a riverboat, Arvin waved his arms above his head. This boat had neither sail nor rudder. Instead it was drawn by a giant eagle whose talons gripped a crossbar attached to the end of the bowsprit. The bird was enormous, with a wingspan nearly as wide as the riverboat was long. The eagle let out a *screee* as it spotted the pair of humans on the island, and the boat slowly turned until its bow was pointed toward them.

"They've seen us," Arvin said, lowering his arms. Warming his back at the fire they'd built from wood salvaged from the wreck of the first riverboat, he watched as the boat draw nearer. He tried to pick out the figures on board, hoping he wasn't going to see an all-too-familiar face.

He'd wrapped a scarf around his face so that only his eyes showed and had disappeared his dagger into his glove. If Zelia was on board, these crude preparations might give him a chance to catch her off guard. He just wished he hadn't used up his store of psionic energy. He couldn't even manifest a simple distraction, let alone shield himself from whatever Zelia might hurl at him.

Karrell stared at the approaching boat. "Is it dangerous?"

It took Arvin a moment to realize she was talking about the eagle. "I'm sure we'll be fine," he said. "They wouldn't use a bird that wasn't tame. They probably raised it from a hatchling."

Karrell seemed unconvinced. As the riverboat drew up to them, dropping anchor next to the island, she took a step back. The eagle—taller than a human and looming even larger from its perch on the bowsprit—flapped its massive wings in agitation, stirring up ripples in the water on either side of the boat. It must have sensed Karrell's uneasiness, for it snapped its beak in her direction. The driver—a human with close-cropped brown hair—gave the reins a quick yank, jerking the bird's head back. He stood on the bow, just behind the bowsprit.

"Sorry," he called out. "She usually isn't this skittish."

Arvin's mind was on other things. By now, the elf would have told everyone at Riverboat Landing about their narrow escape from the naga—and the role that "Vin" had played in it. The chances were slight that the sailor would have mentioned Arvin's pack and the "strange-looking rope" that had spilled from it. But if he had, and Zelia had overheard....

Arvin glanced quickly over the boat's open deck. Besides the driver, the crew included two sailors—one working the tiller at the rear of the boat and one amidships—and two guards. As before, they were stationed at rail-mounted crossbows on either side of the boat. Their eyes ranged warily over the river.

Zelia wasn't on board. Arvin breathed a sigh of relief.

The sailor lifted a gangplank over the side of the boat; Arvin caught the end of it and placed it firmly on the island's rocky shore. Then he made his way across it. Karrell followed, keeping him between her and the eagle. "Don't worry," Arvin said over his shoulder. "I'm sure the driver will hold it in check."

The eagle turned, keeping a baleful eye on Karrell as she approached the boat.

Arvin climbed aboard and turned to help Karrell, but the sailor was there first, handing her a woolen blanket. She took it but ignored his urgings that she wrap it around her shoulders. Arvin, whose clothes were also still sodden, wasn't offered a blanket.

"Will we be continuing to Ormpetarr?" Arvin asked.

The sailor—a man with calloused hands and uncombed hair—shook his head. "Nope. Back to Riverboat Landing to finish loading." His eyes lingered appreciatively on Karrell.

Arvin fought down his uneasiness. "But I need to get to Ormpetarr quickly," he protested. "I have important business there that mustn't be delayed."

The sailor grunted. "Where we go next depends on how much coin you've got. Speak to the captain." He jerked his head in the direction of the man on the bow. Then, together with the second sailor, he crossed the gangplank to the island and surveyed the five bodies Karrell and Arvin had recovered from the river. Karrell had laid them out in a neat row, arranging their arms at their sides and closing their eyes before the bodies stiffened.

Arvin approached the captain. The eagle had settled

down, allowing him to slacken the reins. Arvin repeated his plea to journey directly to Ormpetarr, but the captain shook his head.

"She's only half loaded," he said, nodding at the deck beneath his feet. He glanced at the two sailors, who were carrying the first of the bodies to the ship. "It's not worth my while, unless...."

Arvin took the hint. He dug his coin pouch out of his boot and jingled it. "How much?"

The captain gave the pouch a brief glance then shook his head. "More than that can hold, even if every coin in it is a plume."

Arvin lowered his pouch. Normally, he'd have manifested a charm to help things along, but he'd expended every bit of energy his *muladhara* could provide. Not until after tomorrow morning's meditations and *asanas* would he be able to manifest his powers. "When we reach Ormpetarr, I'll be meeting with Dmetrio Extaminos, prince of Hlondeth and ambassador to Sespech. He will reimburse you for your losses."

The captain thought about this. "I'd need some sort of security. Something of value. Do you have any magical devices?"

Arvin hesitated. He'd no sooner give up his glove, bracelet, or knife than he would another fingertip, and while he did have magical ropes, he didn't want word of them reaching Zelia's ears. If she was still at Riverboat Landing when this crew returned in a few days' time, she'd quickly realize who "Vin" was.

The captain grew impatient. He glanced at the sailors, who were struggling to lift the last of the bodies on board—that of the husband. The headless corpse was as stiff as a beam of wood. They angled it down through a hatch and into the hold, on top of the other bodies, then closed the hatch and hauled up the rope ladder.

"Bodies stowed," one of the sailors reported. "We're ready to go."

"Right," the captain said, gathering up his reins. "Back to Riverboat Landing, then."

Arvin decided to take the chance. "I do have a magical device," he said, shrugging the pack from his shoulders. The captain of a riverboat would surely recognize the value of the trollgut rope. "It's a valuable one. Here, let me show you."

"Sure you do," the captain scoffed.

Karrell touched Arvin's arm, startling him—she'd come quietly up behind him during the conversation. "Allow me," she murmured. She said something in her own language then turned to the captain, making a pleading gesture. "I, too, must reach Ormpetarr quickly," she told him. "My mother is ill, and I have magic that can cure her. If I am delayed even one day...."

Arvin was impressed with the quaver she managed to inject into her voice.

The captain gave a hesitant frown. "I don't know. I—"

"I can compensate you for your losses," Karrell said. She reached into the pouch at her belt and pulled from it a grape-sized, multifaceted gem the color of new grass. Normally, Arvin wouldn't have had the first idea of what it was—or its value. But a little of the knowledge he'd gleaned from Zelia's mind seed remained—enough to tell him it was a spinel, and valuable due to its unusual color.

"Please," Karrell continued. "Won't you accept this? It is all I have left—it cost me everything else I had to get this far. But if this will help me to reach my mother before it is too late, I will gladly give it to you."

"Keep it," the captain said gruffly. "You'll need it." He turned to Arvin and held out a hand. "You, on the other hand, can pay for your passage. Twenty plumes."

It was more than twice the amount normally charged, but Arvin handed over the coins without complaint.

The captain shouted down to his crew. "Make ready. We're making for Ormpetarr."

When the riverboat was underway, Arvin walked with Karrell to the stern, where they seated themselves on a raised hatch. "Nicely done," he said, nodding in the direction of the captain. "You're handy with a charm spell."

Karrell tilted her head. "As are you. But I would advise you not to cast one on me a second time."

"What makes you think I charmed you?" Arvin asked, feigning innocence.

Karrell just stared at him.

Arvin shrugged. "Well, you charmed me first, so that makes us even."

Karrell tossed her head. "I never—"

Arvin raised a finger. "Yes, you did. I wouldn't have . . . made such a fool of myself, otherwise."

"All men are fools," she said. Then, as Arvin drew himself up to protest, she smiled. "And so are some women, at times."

Arvin nodded. To a woman as beautiful as Karrell, the men constantly gaping at her must indeed seem fools. Drawn by the eagle, the riverboat traveled swiftly. The wind of its passage swept through Karrell's hair, drawing it back and revealing her jade earring and the smooth curve of her neck. Even without the charm spell, Arvin felt a rush of longing for her.

She leaned toward him. "When we get to Ormpetarr—"

"I know," Arvin said. "You want me to introduce you to Ambassador Extaminos." He folded his arms across his chest. "Tell me why you want to meet him so badly. The real reason. Is it connected with whatever it is you're looking for?"

Karrell was silent for several moments. The only sounds were the steady *whup-whup* of the eagle's wings and the creak of the hull timbers.

"Yes," she answered at last. "Dmetrio Extaminos may know where it is. I simply want to ask him a few questions."

"That's all?" Arvin asked.

Karrell met his eye. "That is all. I do not intend harm to the ambassador."

"I see." Arvin wanted to believe Karrell, but everything pointed to her being a rogue, out to steal something of Dmetrio's. A rogue armed with clerical magic, as well as natural beauty—but even so, she needed someone to help her earn Dmetrio's trust, to get her inside. Arvin sighed, wondering if he would ever be free of rogues and their schemes.

"You're going to charm Dmetrio," he said. It was an easy enough guess—that was the tactic Arvin had planned to use. "And get him to give you ... whatever it is you're looking for."

Karrell's silence was answer enough.

Arvin pictured her luring the ambassador into her bed—once there, any man would gladly give her whatever it was she wanted. The image of the ambassador's scaly body coiled around hers repulsed Arvin.

"How about this," he offered. "I'll be meeting with the ambassador in his residence. Just tell me what it is you're looking for, and I'll try to find out where it is. I'm ... pretty good at spotting things."

Karrell tilted her head. "You are asking me to trust you."

"Yes."

Her eyes narrowed. "What is it *you* are looking for? Or rather ... who?"

"I can't tell you that."

Karrell stared at him, waiting.

Arvin sighed. "Point taken."

Karrell shifted her gaze to the captain. "I am helping you to reach Ormpetarr—and to avoid the woman you so fear. Without my assistance...."

"Fine," Arvin sputtered. "I'll introduce you to the ambassador. But not until after my business in Ormpetarr is concluded."

He was hedging, of course. The last thing he needed was a member of House Extaminos's royal family linking him with a theft. One yuan-ti wanting him dead was trouble enough. But Karrell seemed to accept his offer; after giving him a long, measuring look, she nodded.

"In the meantime, no more charm spells," Arvin insisted. "Agreed?"

"Agreed." She touched a hand to her heart and looked sincere, but Arvin vowed to be careful, even so.

The rest of the journey passed too swiftly—and too slowly—for Arvin's liking. Too swiftly, because once they reached Ormpetarr, he would probably never see Karrell again. Too slowly, because, despite his best efforts to pass the time in conversation, he kept saying things that irritated her—that made him wish the journey were already over. When the riverboat stopped for the night at Halfway Station, a hamlet even smaller than Riverboat Landing, he'd struck up a conversation about Hlondeth over dinner, telling her how pleased he was to be away from the city of serpents. He cautioned her that the yuan-ti were a devious and cruel race that cared little for humans. It was merely intended as a warning that the members of House Extaminos were dangerous folk to anger, but she seemed to take this to imply that she couldn't take care of herself. After the meal, she curtly declined Arvin's offer of a mug of mulled wine and his invitation to linger at their table beside the fire, and turned in to bed.

The next day, when their journey resumed, she spoke little. She stared over the rail, watching the riverbank slide by. Arvin tried once more to engage her in conversation, asking if it ever snowed in the Chultan Peninsula, but though she smiled at him as they chatted, the smile never quite reached her eyes. After a while, he gave up on conversation and instead stared at .the passing scenery, watching as the riverboat left the river behind and slid out onto a broad, open lake.

It was well after sunset before they caught sight of their destination. Like the other cities of the Vilhon Reach, Ormpetarr had been built centuries ago and had long since outgrown its walls. A scattering of buildings spread for some distance up and down the lake. Most appeared to be connected with the fishing industry; the small amount of moonlight that penetrated the clouds gave Arvin a view of racks used for drying fish, and a number of boats that had been drawn out of the water for the winter. The buildings themselves were little more than blocks of darkness from which squares of light shone—windows, Arvin realized after a moment, square, rather than round.

As the riverboat drew closer to the city proper, these squares of light became numerous and clustered closer together.

At last Ormpetarr's harbor came into view. The city was walled even on the side that fronted the lake; the stout stonework was punctuated by a series of heavy wooden gates, each lined up with a pier that ran out into the river. More than a dozen riverboats were tied up there. Most were empty, their sails furled, but a few were disembarking passengers and unloading freight.

The city seemed dark to Arvin, who was used to the constant glow of Hlondeth's magically quarried stone, but somehow he found that comforting. In Ormpetarr there would be plenty of shadows, plenty of places to hide from Zelia. And what light there was—the glow of street lanterns and the light that shone out of the windows—was warm and yellow and welcoming, rather than an eerie green.

The riverboat drew up to one of the piers. Once the sailors had tied the boat fast, Arvin gathered up his pack and climbed down onto the pier. Karrell immediately followed. The planks underfoot were treacherous with half-melted ice; at one point she slipped, and he caught her arm. She smiled her thanks to him and continued to cling to his arm as they walked up the pier.

"Which inn are you staying at?" she asked.

Arvin gave her a wry look. Was she going to suggest they share a room? "I won't be staying at an inn," he told her. "I have accommodation elsewhere."

"At the ambassador's home?" Karrell guessed. "Or perhaps at the palace?"

They reached the small group of people who were passing through the gate at the end of the pier. On either side of the gate was a watchful soldier. Each wore a brightly polished steel breastplate, embossed with the eye of Helm, over a padded leather coat that hung to his knees. Unlike the clerics in Mimph, these soldiers carried visible weapons—maces with knobbed heads. Their open-faced helms were decorated with purple plumes.

Each person passing through the gate was asked his or her business in Ormpetarr. Arvin and Karrell repeated the stories they'd told each other earlier: he saying he was a rope merchant's agent; she claiming to be an artist.

When they were through the gate, Arvin plucked Karrell's hand from his arm. "Well, goodnight," he told her.

Karrell raised an eyebrow. "Surely you do not think to be rid of me so easily?"

"I'm not trying to get rid of you," Arvin told her. "When my business here is done, I'll send for you. I'll introduce you to the ambassador then."

Karrell snorted. "You have not even asked what inn I am staying at."

"I was just about to."

"No you were not."

Arvin sighed in exasperation. "Goodnight," he said firmly. He strode up the street. The shops on either side were closing for the night, their merchants busy shuttering windows and locking doors. The roads ran in straight lines and were hundreds of paces long—a far cry from the mazelike streets of Hlondeth—and were illuminated along their length by lanterns. It would be more difficult to hide here—or to lose someone who was following you—than he'd expected.

He glanced over his shoulder. Karrell was a few paces behind him, following like a shadow.

Arvin picked up his pace, sidestepping around the other people on the street.

Karrell did the same.

After several blocks, Arvin realized the futility of trying to leave her behind. He could hardly run through the streets. She'd only chase after him—and gods only knew what the local folk would think of that. At the middle of a wide square dominated by one of the silver gauntlet statues, he rounded on her. "Look," he said, irritated. "You'll just have to trust me, and wait until I send for you. Unless you back off, I'm going to warn the ambassador about you—tell him *not* to meet with you."

Karrell's eyes narrowed. "You think you can threaten me?" she asked. "That dagger cuts both ways. What if I were to tell that woman at Riverboat Landing about you?"

Arvin felt his face grow pale. With an effort, he steadied himself. "Riverboat Landing is two days downriver. By the time a message got there—"

Karrell smiled. "A spell can always be used to speed a message on its way."

Arvin shivered. She might be bluffing, but he didn't want to take the chance. "It seems we've reached a stalemate."

Karrell started to whisper something in her own

language. Before she could finish, Arvin slapped a hand onto the gauntlet. The cold metal chilled his bare fingers, making him shiver. "Don't try to charm me," he warned her. "It won't work. Not here. This statue is magical. It will turn the charm back on you, instead."

He had no idea, of course, if the statue's magic would even protect him from a spell that did no actual injury. But presumably, neither did Karrell.

She stared at him. "You will not stand here all night."

"I will if I have to," Arvin said.

"So will I."

They stared at each other for several moments. Then Arvin heard footsteps behind him. He turned—his hand still on the gauntlet—and saw one of the red-cloaked clerics approaching. The man hadn't been there a moment ago; the gauntlet seemed to have summoned him.

"Is there a problem?" the cleric asked, his eyes on Karrell. "Did this woman threaten you?"

Arvin let his hand fall away from the gauntlet and raised it to his lips, blowing on it to ward off the metal's chill. For a moment, he considered answering yes. Having Karrell detained was a tempting thought—it would keep her out of the way until he'd accomplished his mission. But subjecting her to the magical punishments the innkeeper in Mimph had described was something Arvin just couldn't do. He shook his head.

"No," he told the cleric. "I was just leaning against this statue while we talked. But she is pestering me—she keeps trying to solicit me and won't leave me alone. Do you have a law against that?"

The cleric scowled at Karrell. "Helm's Sanctuary is not a place for solicitation."

Karrell's face flushed. Her mouth opened then closed. "I apologize," she said at last. "It will not happen again." Chin in the air, she turned and strode away.

The cleric turned his scowl on Arvin. "The gauntlet is intended to be used only in times of true danger."

"Sorry," Arvin said. "I'm a stranger here. I've got a lot to learn about your customs." He paused. "Could you direct me to the home of Ambassador Extaminos? I came to Ormpetarr to meet with him."

The cleric gave Arvin a skeptical look. Then he raised his left hand and held it, palm out, toward Arvin. "State your business with the ambassador."

"I'm. . . ." Arvin started to say that he was a rope merchant's agent who hoped for a formal introduction to the baron, but other words spilled out of his mouth. "I'm here to question Dmetrio Extaminos about the disappearance of—" With an effort that brought beads of sweat to his brow, he choked off the rest of what he'd been about to say. The magical compulsion the cleric had just placed on Arvin was one he recognized; he had once been forced to wear a ring that compelled him to speak the truth.

The truth, fortunately, could be told selectively. "I'm here on state business," he told the cleric. "I'm meeting with the ambassador at the baron's request. Baron Foesmasher will not be pleased if you force me to reveal state secrets."

"Ah. My apologies." He lowered his hand, gave Arvin directions, and strode away.

After a quick glance in the direction Karrell had gone, Arvin started on his way. It took him a while to figure out what "blocks" were, but after he started walking, it became obvious. He was used to the directions they gave in Hlondeth—a series of "fork rights" and "fork lefts." Here in Ormpetarr, the intersections were composed of four streets, not three. Each intersection offered three choices—straight ahead, right or left, but instead of saying "fork straight" the people of Ormpetarr grouped all of the straights together and simply gave a total. Arvin lost his way more than once but eventually got himself pointed in the right direction. He peered over his shoulder several times, making sure that Karrell was not following. Though he did catch sight of the same man twice—a tall man with gaunt, beard-stubbled cheeks—he saw no sign of Karrell.

The tall man, however, was cause for concern. Arvin had noticed him down on the docks earlier; it seemed improbable that the fellow would have taken exactly the same route as Arvin through the city. Convinced the fellow was a rogue, out to tumble a newcomer to the city—and well aware that where there was one rogue, there might be others—Arvin took an abrupt turn into a side street and activated his magical bracelet. He scuttled up a wall like a lizard, jogged across the rooftop and climbed down the other side of the building. Peeking around the corner, he spotted the tall man hesitating at the side street Arvin had just vanished from. As the fellow started down the street, Arvin hurried back up the main thoroughfare then turned into another street two blocks from the one the tall fellow was searching.

He continued for several blocks, sometimes walking with his cloak hood up, other times with it down. On streets where others were walking, he positioned himself immediately beside or behind them, giving the appearance that he was part of a larger group. On streets that were empty, he turned into doorways, pretending to be opening the door with a key but all the while keeping an eye on the street, searching for the tall man—or anyone who might be one of his accomplices.

At last, satisfied he'd given the rogue the slip, he started again for the ambassador's residence.

It took him some time to find it, despite the cleric's directions. Losing the rogue had thrown Arvin off; he had to double back and recount the blocks. It was quite late before he found the right section of town;

the darkened streets were empty, and the temperature had dropped below freezing, making the streets slippery with ice.

Eventually he located the building he was looking for: a three-story residence that stretched from one street to another, the length of one of Ormpetarr's blocks. He knew it must be the ambassador's residence when he saw two members of Hlondeth's militia—recognizable by their distinctive helmets, which were flared in the shape of a cobra's hood—standing just inside the wrought-iron fence that surrounded the building. Arvin hailed them and explained that he'd come to meet with the ambassador.

"This late at night?" one of the men asked from behind the gate. He was an older, stocky man with a neat gray beard and hands crisscrossed with faded white scars: a career soldier.

Arvin spread his hands apologetically. "I was delayed." He held up the letter of introduction Tanju had given him. Written by one of Lady Dediana's scribes, the folded letter bore a dab of wax impressed with the insignia of House Extaminos: a mason's chisel and a ship on either side of a wavy line that represented a serpent.

"Could you at least show Ambassador Extaminos this and ask if he'll see me?"

The bearded militiaman held out a scarred hand; Arvin passed the letter through the bars. As he carried the letter inside the building, the second militiaman—a thin, young man with a prominent nose that was red with cold—stood by the gate, waiting. Arvin heard his teeth chattering.

"An unpleasant night to be stuck outside," Arvin said. "I've never seen a winter this cold."

The militiaman nodded. "It's better than crewing a galley, though." He glanced at Arvin's face. "What happened to you?"

Arvin touched the wound on his cheek. The flesh was tender and bruised under the scab. He hadn't shaved this morning and probably wouldn't for the next few days, at least. "A riverboat accident," he answered. "We were attacked by a naga."

The young militiaman's eyes widened. "*That's* what delayed you?" Before he could comment further, however, the other militiaman returned. "The ambassador will see you in the morning," he announced, passing Arvin's letter back.

"But I've traveled far," Arvin protested. "And my business is urgent."

"In the morning," he said firmly.

Silently, Arvin cursed the thief who had delayed him. Baron Foesmasher was expecting Arvin to show up at the palace tomorrow morning, and—so Arvin had heard—the baron wasn't a man who liked to be kept waiting. Arvin had hoped to question Dmetrio this evening. If Dmetrio was sleepy, so much the better. It would be easier for Arvin to manifest a charm on him.

"I realize it's late," Arvin said, manifesting a charm on the bearded militiaman even as he spoke. "But I won't have time to come back in the morning. I just need a quick word with the ambassador, and I'll be on my way." He smiled and drew the coin pouch from his boot. "I realize he'll be angry at you for annoying him a second time, but I can make it worth your while. Please let me speak with him. Tonight."

The bearded militiaman tilted his head—then shook it, like a man shaking himself awake. "No," he said firmly.

Arvin swore under his breath. The bearded man's mind must have been as tough as the rest of him.

The younger man stared greedily at Arvin's coin pouch. "Sergeant," he said in a low voice. "Couldn't we just—"

"That's enough, Rillis," The sergeant placed a hand on his sword hilt and stared at Arvin through the gate. "The merchant can come back at a civilized hour of the morning ... or not at all."

Arvin let his hand fall away from his pouch. "In the morning, then," he said with a sigh. Then, "Could you at least tell me where to find a reputable inn?"

CHAPTER 5

The next morning, Arvin rose well before dawn. He dressed in his better clothes and ate a quick meal of fried cheese and thick-crusted bread. He waved away the ale the innkeeper offered; he wanted a clear head for this morning's work.

As he stepped outside the inn, the air bit at his lungs, crisp and cold. The sky to the east was turning a faint pink behind the clouds. It had snowed overnight; a few flakes were still falling from the sky. Snow crunched beneath Arvin's boots as he strode past merchants opening the shutters of their shops, boys kindling fires in the stoves of their mulled-wine carts, and men carrying heavy sacks on their backs as they made early-morning deliveries to the shops and homes in this part of the city. These men were doing the work of slaves, yet not one of them had an S-brand on his cheek.

Arvin had heard that, while slavery existed in Sespech, it was an uncommon practice. Those slaves who did exist within the barony had been brought to Sespech by their masters. Hearing this and seeing it with his own eyes, however, were two different things. It felt odd to be walking along streets populated by free men. It was odder still to have no viaducts arching above—to be on a street that was open to the sky. For perhaps the first time in his life, Arvin walked without the slight hunch that a human in Hlondeth automatically adopted—the tensing of shoulders and neck that came with the constant awareness of the yuan-ti slithering along the viaducts overhead. He felt lighter, somehow, more sure of himself, relaxed.

He smiled.

The smile vanished as something sharp pricked through the fabric of his cloak and shirt, jabbing his back. A hand on his shoulder turned him toward a doorway.

"Inside," gritted the man behind him.

Arvin risked turning his head slightly. The tall rogue from last night had the hood of his cloak pulled up, but Arvin recognized him by his gaunt, stubbled cheeks. "My pouch is in my boot," Arvin told him, gesturing at his coin pouch; as soon as the fellow bent for it, Arvin would draw his dagger and stab backhanded through his cloak, giving the rogue a nasty surprise. He put a quaver in his voice. "Please don't hurt me. Just take my coin and go."

The rogue pressed the sharp object—most likely a dagger—into Arvin's back. The blade was icy cold; the flesh around the wound immediately began to ache.

"One thrust, and it will freeze your flesh," the man promised in a grim voice. "I don't think you'd survive long with your entrails turned to ice." He gave Arvin a slight shove. "Now ... inside."

"Listen, friend," Arvin began, raising his hands so the rogue could see them. He'd use silent speech to show the fellow that he, too, was Guild, albeit from Hlondeth, then hit him with a charm. "I'm one of—"

The dagger pricked harder, drawing a gasp of pain from Arvin. It felt as though a needle of ice were being driven into his back.

"No tricks," the rogue gritted. "There's others watching—others with weapons who will take you down if I fall. One suspicious move, mind mage, and you're a dead man."

Arvin blinked. How did the rogue know he was a psion? Arvin knew better than to look around. The threat would be genuine; rogues almost never worked alone. "What do you want?" he asked.

"To talk," the rogue answered.

"All right," Arvin said. "Let's talk." He reached for the handle of the door and opened it.

As he stepped inside what turned out to be cooper's workshop, he braced himself for what was to come. Someone in the local rogues' guild must have heard that a member of the Hlondeth Guild was in Sespech. The locals probably wanted to learn what Arvin was doing here—to make sure he wasn't planning on thieving on their turf. Arvin balled his left hand into a fist and felt the familiar ache of his missing fingertip. He didn't intend to lose another.

The rogue removed the dagger from Arvin's back and stepped quickly away from him, closing the door. The weapon was an odd-looking one, made of metal as white as frost and with a spike-shaped blade that tapered to a point, like an icicle. The rogue sheathed it—a bad sign. It meant that the room held other, more potent threats.

Arvin glanced around. The workshop looked ordinary enough; half-finished barrels stood on the floor, next to loose piles of metal hoops. The smell of fresh-sawn wood lingered in the air, suggesting the workshop had been used recently. Chisels, saws, and mallets were scattered about; Arvin could have turned any one of them into a surprise weapon using the power that allowed him to move objects at a distance. He refrained, however, realizing that the tall man probably wasn't the only rogue in the room. His guess was confirmed a moment later when some sawdust on the floor shifted slightly; a second person, cloaked by invisibility, was also present. The tall man confirmed this a moment later, with two words in the silent speech, directed at his invisible companion: *None followed.*

Arvin shifted his eyes away from the spot where the invisible person stood, looking at the tall man instead. "What do you want to talk about?"

"We know the baron's daughter is missing and that you've come from Hlondeth to find her," the rogue said.

Only through years of practice did Arvin manage to prevent his eyes from widening. This wasn't what he'd expected.

"We want to make you an offer," the rogue continued.

Arvin raised an eyebrow. "One that's just too good to refuse?"

The rogue nodded. He pointed at one of the finished barrels; a small leather pouch sat on top of it. "Look inside."

Arvin stepped over to the pouch and loosened its ties. Something glittered inside: gems—dozens of them. Seeing the way they sparkled, even in the dim light of the shop, Arvin realized what they were: diamonds. Small, easily portable and immensely valuable, they were a currency that could be spent anywhere in Faerûn that Arvin might care to go.

Assuming they weren't just an illusion, which gave him an idea. "How do I know they're real?" he asked.

"Inspect them as closely as you like," the rogue offered.

"May I use magic to evaluate their worth?"

The rogue hesitated. "No tricks," he warned. "Or—"

"I know, I know. Or I'm a dead man," Arvin continued. "Don't worry. There will be no tricks."

He bent over the pouch and stirred the gems with a finger. They seemed real enough. Then he braced himself; it was now or never. He picked up the pouch and manifested the power that would allow him to listen to the thoughts of those in the room. Silver sparkles erupted from his third eye and streamed toward his hand, dissipating as they hit the gems; if his bluff held, the rogue would think the spell was targeting them. Out of the corner of his eye, Arvin saw the rogue frowning, as if listening to a distant, half-heard sound. Arvin wondered if the invisible person was doing the same thing.

An instant later, his question was answered. Two separate voices whispered into his mind: the thoughts of the rogue and the invisible person. Ignoring the former—he would be an expendable member of the guild, one who'd been told as little as possible—Arvin concentrated on the latter. The thoughts were those of a man who stood with his finger on the trigger of a crossbow, loaded with a bolt whose head was smeared with a poison more lethal than yuan-ti venom. Worse yet, the trigger was a dead man's switch: if the invisible man relaxed his finger, even a little, the crossbow would shoot.

Arvin hid his shudder and gestured at the gems. "What do I have to do to earn this?"

"The girl," the rogue answered. "When you find her, give her to us."

Arvin nodded, concentrating on the thoughts of the second man. The fellow was worried about the diamonds, which were real enough. If he killed the psion, they'd scatter on the floor, and some might be lost in the cracks. If even one went missing, someone named Haskar would have his head.

"What will you do with Glisena?" Arvin asked.

"Ransom her," the rogue answered. He gestured at the pouch. "For a *lot* of coin. What we're going to demand from the baron will make that look like the contents of a beggar's cup."

Arvin nodded, still listening to the thoughts of the second man. The guild wasn't going to ransom Glisena to the baron. No, that would be too dangerous. They'd sell her, instead. Lord Wianar would pay well for the girl—and there would be no need for dangerous exchanges or worrying about those damn clerics.

Arvin nodded to himself. Alarmed though he was at the thought that the local rogues' guild knew who he was—they must have a spy in the baron's court—he was relieved to find that their plan was so simplistic. He let his manifestation end, satisfied he'd learned everything he could.

Somewhere outside, a horn sounded three times: the morning call to prayer for Helm's faithful. The rogue ignored it.

"How do I contact you?" Arvin asked.

"Enter any tavern and make this sign," the rogue instructed. With a finger, he rubbed first the inside corner of his right eye, then the outside corner.

Arvin smiled to himself. It was one of the first words in silent speech the Guild had taught him.

"When you see someone make this sign," the rogue continued, making a V with the first two fingers of his right hand and drawing them along his left forearm from elbow to wrist, "you'll know you've found us." He paused. "Do we have an agreement?"

Arvin nodded. "It's certainly a tempting offer," he said. "I'll let you know." He set the pouch back on the barrel—carefully, so none of the diamonds spilled.

"May I go now?"

The rogue opened the door and stepped away from it. As Arvin walked past him, he moved his hand to the hilt of his dagger. "Just remember," he warned in a low voice. "We'll be watching you. Don't cross us."

Arvin nodded. The rogue wasn't telling him anything new. If Sespech's rogues' guild was anything like Hlondeth's, Arvin's every move would be marked.

It had been bad enough, finding Zelia in Sespech. Now he had a second reason to watch his back.

❧ ❧ ❧ ❧ ❧

Arvin went directly to Dmetrio's residence. There was no need to be secretive about his destination—not when the local rogues' guild knew who he was. The meeting with its two representatives had taken only a short time; the sun had risen, painting the winter sky a dull white, but it was still early in the morning. The same two militiamen were still on guard duty outside the residence. The younger man was yawning widely—and being glared at by his sergeant.

"Good morning, Rillis," he called to him. "Don't they ever let you sleep?"

Rillis grinned through chattering teeth. "Soon, I hope. The watch change—"

The sergeant jabbed him with an elbow. "Quiet, soldier," he snapped. Then, to Arvin, "I suppose you expect to see the ambassador now?"

Arvin nodded and pulled out his letter of introduction.

The sergeant took it. "I'll let him know you're here."

After a few moments, he returned and opened the gate. "This way," he instructed.

As Arvin stepped through the gate, he heard rapid footsteps behind him.

"Vin! I am so sorry!"

Startled, Arvin turned and saw Karrell hurrying toward him. She slipped her hand under Arvin's arm, grasping him firmly by the elbow. "Please do not be angry with me, Vin," she said, tugging him toward the front door of the residence. "I did not mean to sleep so late. When I saw that you had left without me, I hurried here as quickly as I could." She tugged Arvin toward the residence.

The sergeant quickly blocked their way. Rillis was slower to react; he'd been gaping at Karrell. Belatedly, he stepped forward and held up a hand.

Karrell beamed a smile at him. "Was Ambassador Extaminos kept waiting?" She loosened her cloak, as if to cool down from her run. Rillis's eyes lingered on her breasts, which rose and fell as she panted. "No, lady. He has only just been summoned."

Arvin glared at Karrell.

She gave him a coy smile. "Come, Vin. Be thankful it's me who is accompanying you, and not that blue-tongued she-demon. She'd only embarrass you in front of the ambassador."

Arvin tensed at the thinly veiled reference to Zelia. He wished he'd had the cleric lock Karrell up last night, when he had the chance. What now? If he protested, she would alert Zelia to his presence in Ormpetarr.

"It's all right," he told the sergeant. "She's with me." He pinched Karrell's arm, however, as they walked toward the door. "An introduction," he gritted under his breath. "No more. Then you go."

She nodded.

Rillis unlocked the front door with cold-stiffened fingers and ushered them through. He was about to close it again when the sergeant motioned him inside. "Go ahead, Rillis," he said. "Warm up a bit."

Rillis grinned then followed Arvin and Karrell inside. They stepped through the door into a wide, semicircular hall whose floor tiles glowed with a soft green light. A ramp, its stonework also glowing, curved up the wall on the right to doors on the building's second floor. The wall to the left had a fireplace in which a fire was roaring; a rolled-up carpet and several boxes lay against the wall next to it. The air in the hall was uncomfortably hot and stank of spice and snake. Arvin unfastened his cloak and wiped his face with a sleeve, blotting away the sweat that was beading on his forehead. Another member of the militia—this one with wide shoulders and watchful eyes—stood just inside the door, dressed in full armor. Arvin wondered how the fellow could stand the oppressive heat.

As Rillis warmed his back at the fire, sighing his relief, Karrell moved toward what Arvin had at first taken to be a painting that rested on the mantle. He saw that it was a hollow pane of glass, filled with viscous red, turquoise, and indigo liquids that rose and fell in a swirl of ever-changing patterns.

"It's a slitherglow," Rillis said. "I don't suppose you've seen one before."

"It is beautiful," Karrell answered. She held out her hands to the fire, warming them, and stared at the slitherglow as if mesmerized. Arvin shook his head. She certainly wasn't acting like a rogue casing the residence. Her eyes should have been darting around the room, noting the exits and appraising its contents. The larger boxes, for example, probably held breakables, judging by the sawdust packing that had trickled out of the corner of one of them—ceramics, perhaps, or statuettes. And the rug was bulged slightly; something was rolled inside it. Judging by the boxes and the bare appearance of the room, the ambassador was planning a move from the residence, probably in a few days' time. Arvin wondered where he was going.

A door at the top of the ramp opened. The militiaman standing next to Arvin stiffened, and Rillis ushered

Karrell back to Arvin's side then stood flanking her. Neither had a weapon in hand, but Arvin didn't want to make any sudden moves. Rillis was probably new to the militia, but the second man looked tougher, more experienced—and the House Extaminos bodyguards were rumored to coat their weapons with yuan-ti venom.

A man in a red silk robe stepped through the door and began making his way down the ramp. He appeared human, at first glance. He had dark hair that swept back from a high forehead; a long, narrow nose; and a thin, muscular body. His walk, however, immediately gave him away as yuan-ti. Instead of stepping, as humans did, he turned each footstep into a slither, sliding his slippered feet along the stone. His body swayed as he walked, his head moving gently from side to side. As he drew closer, slit pupils and a flicker of a forked tongue confirmed his race. Despite these attributes, he was a handsome man, full of poise and self-confidence. No wonder the baron's daughter had fallen for him.

In one slender hand, he held Arvin's letter of introduction. The other hand was hidden by a silk sleeve that hung past his fingertips.

Arvin bowed. "Ambassador Extaminos."

Dmetrio stared at him. "Vin of Hlondeth," he hissed, his voice as devoid of emotion as dry leaves. "Agent of the Mariner Mercantile House."

Dmetrio shifted his gaze to Karrell, who also bowed. He stepped closer to her as she rose, his tongue flickering in and out of his mouth as he drank in her scent. "And who is this?"

Arvin rose. "An ... acquaintance of mine," he said slowly. Threat or no threat, he wasn't going to call Karrell more than that. "We met on the journey here, and she insisted on meeting you. Her name is Karrell. She—"

Out of the corner of his eye, Arvin saw that Karrell's hand had curled in what was, by now, a familiar gesture to him. She was whispering her charm spell. Arvin thought about grabbing her hand and putting a halt to the spell, but she finished it before he could react.

"I'd like to show you something," Karrell said to Dmetrio, reaching under her cloak.

"Guards!" Dmetrio hissed.

The militiaman behind Karrell reacted with the speed of a striking snake. He grabbed Karrell's arms, yanking her elbows behind her back.

Karrell yelped. She dropped a piece of parchment she'd been holding; it fluttered to the floor. It landed faceup, revealing a rendering, done in ink and charcoal, of the cathedral in Hlondeth.

Arvin stared at it. The drawing was good—really good. Maybe Karrell was an artist, after all.

That, or she'd stolen the picture.

Belatedly, Rillis reacted, yanking out his sword and stepping back to give himself room to swing it, if need be. He glanced between Arvin—who carefully stood with his hands open and away from his sides—and Karrell.

Karrell tossed her head. "I simply wanted to show you a drawing," she said. Her face was flushed—she was obviously angry that Dmetrio had not succumbed to her spell. She had to nod at the picture on the floor, since the militiaman held her arms. "A sample of my work. I also do portraits. I have drawn a number of members of noble yuan-ti houses."

Dmetrio stared at her, unblinking. "Name one."

"Mezral Ch'thon, *ssthaar* of the Se'sehen."

Dmetrio's eyebrows rose. "You are from Tashalar?"

Karrell nodded.

"Are you Se'sehen?" Dmetrio asked. He added something in a language filled with soft hisses.

"*N'hacsis*—no," Karrell said, shaking her head. "I speak only a little Draconic. The language is difficult for me. It requires a serpent's tongue."

"You are *human?*" Dmetrio asked, giving the

word a derisive sneer. He flicked his fingers, and the militiaman holding Karrell released her. Rillis reacted a moment later, sheathing his sword.

Karrell gave a slight bow in Dmetrio's direction then gathered up the parchment. "It is true that I invited myself here today, but I could think of no other way to meet with you. I had hoped to do your portrait."

"And gain a healthy commission from House Extaminos, no doubt." Dmetrio gave a hiss of laughter. "Your trip to Ormpetarr was a waste of time. I'm leaving—and have no time for portraits."

Arvin raised his eyebrows. Dmetrio was leaving Ormpetarr? That was interesting. "Ambassador Extaminos," he said, wresting the conversation away from Karrell, "my letter of introduction included a request that you—"

Dmetrio's upper lip twitched, revealing just the points of his fangs, a subtle sign of irritation. "I have no time for meetings, either," he said. He thrust the letter of introduction in Arvin's direction.

Arvin caught it just before it fell. "But I was told you would introduce me to the baron," he protested. "My merchant house is counting on me to—"

"Introduce yourself," Dmetrio said curtly.

Karrell stepped forward. "Your Excellency, I—"

"Show them out," Dmetrio hissed.

As they were hustled back to the street, Arvin fumed. This wasn't the way it was supposed to have gone. If Karrell hadn't butted in, he would have been talking to Dmetrio still, subtly nudging the conversation around to Glisena as he talked about his "trade mission" to Sespech. Now, in order to question Dmetrio, Arvin would have to be blunt. He'd have to reveal his real reason for coming to Ormpetarr. If Dmetrio was involved in Glisena's disappearance, he would be on his guard. Charming him would be that much more difficult—maybe even impossible.

As the wrought-iron gate clanked shut behind them, Karrell turned to Arvin. "It seems you are a merchant's agent, after all, and I have ruined your chances to—"

"Not another word," Arvin said, a quiver in his voice. He pointed down the street. "Go."

Karrell opened her mouth to say something more then thought better of it. She turned and walked up the street.

Arvin closed his eyes and sighed. Karrell had really gotten under his skin. He wished he'd never started that conversation with her in the sleigh in the first place. He'd been stupid—and had shown a pitiful lack of self-control.

When he opened his eyes, she was gone. He stared at her footprints, which were starting to fill with falling snow.

"All for the best."

Arvin turned. It had been Rillis who had spoken—he was still standing just on the other side of the wrought-iron gate. The sergeant was at the far corner of the building, making his rounds.

"You're better off not having the ambassador introduce you," Rillis added in a confiding tone.

Arvin turned. "What do you mean?"

Rillis rubbed a thumb and forefinger together. The gesture was the one word in silent speech that was understood even by those not in the Guild: coin.

Arvin nodded and pulled his pouch out of his boot. He counted two silver pieces into the militiaman's outstretched hand.

Rillis quickly pocketed them. "The ambassador and the baron had a falling out," he told Arvin. "It's been more than a month since Ambassador Extaminos visited the palace. I don't think they've even sent a message to one another, in all that time."

"Why is that?" Arvin asked. Carefully, he probed for information, under the pretense of sarcasm. "Did the baron's daughter pay him a visit and forget to go home one night?"

Rillis laughed. "You obviously haven't met her chaperones. She never sets foot outside the palace without them. Baron's orders." He winked. "He didn't want any little ones slithering out from under the woodpile. Not without a formal joining of the houses."

Arvin nodded. "Is a joining likely?"

"Not now that the ambassador's being withdrawn from Sespech." He paused to draw his cloak tighter across his chest.

"When is he leaving?"

Rillis stared pointedly at Arvin's pouch. Taking the hint, Arvin handed him another silver piece.

"As soon as the new ambassador arrives," Rillis continued. "Meanwhile, the house slaves can't seem to pack fast enough for Ambassador Extaminos. He's been hissing at them for nearly a tenday."

Arvin nodded. Interesting, that was roughly the amount of time that had elapsed since Glisena's disappearance. He glanced up at the windows of the ambassador's residence, saw slaves bustling about in each room, and wondered why Dmetrio was in such a hurry to leave. Was the baron's daughter hiding somewhere nearby, waiting to depart with him?

Arvin sighed and stared down the street, in the direction Karrell had gone. After what Rillis had just told him, Arvin realized that he probably wouldn't have gotten anything out of Dmetrio, anyway. The ambassador had shrugged off Karrell's charm like a duck shedding water. Arvin's attempt to charm Dmetrio probably would have been equally futile.

"Thanks for the information," Arvin told Rillis.

The militiaman patted his pocket. "My pleasure."

Bidding Rillis good day, Arvin set out for the palace.

CHAPTER 6

Baron Thuragar Foesmasher sat at one end of
the council chamber, his broad hands resting
on the arms of the heavy wooden chair. The
man exuded both power and confidence. He was
large, with dark eyes, hair cut square just above
his eyebrows, and a blockish chin framed by a
neatly trimmed beard. He wore a purple silk
shirt; black trousers tied at the ankle, knee,
and groin; and leather slippers embroidered
in gold thread with the Foesmasher crest: a
clenched fist. A heavy gold ring adorned the
forefinger of his right hand; a silver brooch in
the shape of a beetle was pinned to his shirt
front. Arvin had no doubt that both pieces of
jewelry were magical.

On a table next to the baron sat a helmet
chased with gold and set with a single purple

plume. Foesmasher had entered the room wearing it, but had taken the helm off after Arvin submitted to a magical scan by the baron's chief advisor, a cleric named Marasa. She stood to the left of the baron's chair. She wore a knee-length blue tunic over trousers and fur boots with gold felt tassels. Her hair was steel-gray and hung in two shoulder-length braids, each capped with a silver bead shaped like a gauntlet. On each wrist was a thick bracelet of polished silver bearing the blue eye of Helm. A mace hung from her belt.

The baron had dismissed Marasa from the chamber earlier, when he'd sent the servants away, but she had refused to leave. She was obviously an old friend—a supporter, rather than a vassal.

"Both clerical magic and wizardry have failed to locate my daughter," the baron told Arvin. "But Lady Dediana has informed me that you can work a different kind of spell—one that requires neither spellbook nor holy symbol. She said it might circumvent whatever is preventing Glisena from being found."

Before Arvin could respond, Marasa interrupted. "I doubt a sorcerer can part a veil that Helm himself has failed to rend." She stared at Arvin, a challenge in her eyes. It was clear from the derisive way she'd used the term that she disapproved of sorcery.

Arvin met her eyes. "I'm not a sorcerer," he told her. "I'm a psion."

"What's the difference?" she asked.

"A sorcerer casts spells that draw upon magic that is woven into the world. A psion uses mind magic. We tap the energies of the mind itself. If the magic of the Weave were to unravel tomorrow, sorcerers and wizards would lose their spells, but psions would continue to manifest their powers."

Marasa nodded politely but appeared unconvinced.

"What spell will you cast?" the baron asked.

Arvin was acutely aware of the broken dorje in his

pack. Without it, he had to rely on his wits—and the one psionic power that just *might* be of use—in order to find the baron's daughter. "We call them 'powers,' not 'spells,' Lord Foesmasher. There are many I could choose from," he continued, waving his hand breezily in the air, "but I'll need to know more about the circumstances of your daughter's disappearance in order to determine the best one to use. When was the last time you saw Glisena?"

The baron sighed heavily. He stared the length of the room, past the tapestries that commemorated his many skirmishes with Chondath, past the trophy shields and weapons that hung on the walls. His eye settled on a half dozen miniature ships that sat on a table near the far wall, models of the galleys Hlondeth was helping him build. For several moments, the only sound was the crackling of the fire in the hearth behind him.

"A tenday ago," he said at last. "We dined together, spent the evening listening to a harpist, and Glisena took her leave and retired to bed. The next morning, her chamber was empty. High Watcher Davinu was called in to recite a prayer that should have discerned her location but was unable to. It's as if Glisena was spirited away to another plane of existence." His voice crackled. "Either that, or she's. . . ."

Marasa touched his arm. "Glisena is still alive," she said. "Davinu's communion told us that much, at least." She turned to Arvin. "But she seems to be shielded by powerful magic, which leads me to believe she didn't leave willingly. She was kidnapped, most likely, by agents from Chondath. They—"

"There have been no demands," Foesmasher interrupted, "from Wianar, or anyone else. My daughter left here of her own accord." He stared broodingly at the wall.

The cleric gave an exasperated sigh. It was clear she

had ventured this theory to the baron before—with the same result.

"Lady Marasa, I believe Baron Foesmasher is right," Arvin said, breaking the silence. "Lord Wianar does not have Glisena."

"How do you know this?" Marasa asked.

The baron, too, turned to stare at Arvin.

Arvin took a deep breath. "Does the name Haskar mean anything to you?"

The baron's eyes blazed. "Haskar!" he growled. "Is *that* who has my daughter? By Helm, I'll have his head."

Arvin raised a hand. "Haskar doesn't have Glisena. But he knows that she's missing. He'd like to find her so he can sell her to Lord Wianar." He turned to Marasa. "So you see, lady, it appears that Lord Wianar doesn't have Glisena. If he did, Haskar wouldn't have made him the offer."

"How do you know all this?" the baron asked.

Arvin told him about the events of that morning. He emphasized the reward he had been offered, adding that he'd rather receive "honest coin" for his work. He was careful, however, to avoid any mention of his ability to listen to others' thoughts, making it sound instead as though he had tricked the man into giving him the information. The baron seemed like a straightforward, honest man, but there might come a time when Arvin needed to know what he was really thinking.

Marasa listened carefully to Arvin's report then shook her head. "The fact that Haskar's rogues want to offer Glisena to Chondath means nothing," she said. "Lord Wianar might have kidnapped her without the rogues' knowing it."

"The fact remains," the baron interrupted, "that there have been no demands. Chondath is silent." He turned to Arvin. "You've done a good morning's work, but now comes the true test. Can you find my daughter?"

Arvin took a deep breath. "Of course, Lord Foe-smasher," he said in a confident voice. "But I need to know just a little more about what happened on the night of her disappearance. Did you entertain any guests that evening?"

The baron's eyes bored into Arvin's. "If you mean to ask if Ambassador Extaminos was here, the answer is no. Nor were any other guests present. It was a . . . quiet evening. Just Glisena and myself."

"And the harpist," Marasa noted. "She may have been a—"

"The harpist is a regular guest of this household and well trusted," the baron growled, "as are the servants who attended us that evening."

Arvin knew little of royal households, but he'd spent two months in the home of the wealthy uncle who had cared for Arvin briefly after his mother had died. There had been a constant flutter of servants around his uncle—servants to help him dress and undress, to carry his parcels, to turn down his bed and place a draught of fortified wine on his bed table each night. In summer a servant stood over his bed while he slept, waving a fan to keep him cool. Arvin's uncle had little privacy—a princess of a royal household would have even less.

"Have you questioned Glisena's servants?" Arvin asked. "The ones who attended her bedchamber that night?"

"No servants attended her on the evening she disappeared," Foesmasher said. "Glisena's head pained her. She said she could not bear even the slightest noise and dismissed them from her chamber."

"Her head pained her?" Arvin echoed. A wild notion occurred to him—that Zelia might have planted a mind seed in the baron's daughter. Arvin had stripped that power from Zelia six months ago, but she may have regained it since. That would explain what she was doing in Sespech—she may have been stopping at Riverboat Landing on her way *back* from Ormpetarr, rather than on her way to the city. It would also explain Glisena's sudden disappearance.

Then again, he reminded himself, it might be a simple elopement he was dealing with, after all. No need to jump to conclusions . . . yet. "Was this the first time your daughter complained of a headache?" he asked.

Foesmasher shook his head. "Glisena had been feeling unwell for several days."

"How many days?" Arvin asked sharply. A mind seed took time to blossom. If her headache had begun seven days before her disappearance . . .

"Several days," Foesmasher repeated. He gave an exasperated sigh. "What does it matter? Her illness had nothing to do with her disappearance."

"Glisena had been unwell for nearly a month," Marasa told Arvin. She turned to the baron, "You should have summoned me."

"Her illness was minor," Foesmasher said. There was a testy edge to his voice. It sounded, to Arvin, that the baron and his advisor had gone through this argument at least once before. "It was a slight upset of the stomach. Nothing that required magical healing."

"A stomach upset?" Arvin asked, confused. "I thought you said she had a headache."

Neither the baron nor Marasa was listening to him. Marasa bristled at Foesmasher. "A simple laying on of hands would have saved Glisena much discomfort."

"The headache was an excuse to dismiss the servants!" the baron growled. "Glisena *ran away*."

Marasa glared right back at him. "How can you be so sure? Wianar's agents may have infiltrated the palace and kidnapped her. Whether the headache was feigned or not, if you'd summoned me that night—"

"That's enough, High Watcher Ferrentio!" Foesmasher shouted. He looked away, refusing to meet the cleric's eye. He glared at the far wall, visibly composing himself.

Marasa gently touched his hand. "You and Glisena were arguing again, weren't you?"

Foesmasher sighed. "Yes."

Arvin's eyebrows rose. A "quiet evening," the baron had said. Given the baron's propensity for shouting, it had probably been anything but. No wonder Glisena had fled to her chamber. "So the headache had only come on that evening?" he asked.

The baron turned to Arvin, a suspicious look in his eye. "Why are you so interested in my daughter's health?"

Arvin paused, considering whether to tell the baron about Zelia. Foesmasher was a powerful man, with an army at his disposal. That army included clerics of Helm—clerics who had proven themselves capable of dealing with the yuan-ti. They could arrest Zelia and throw her in prison. On the other hand, Zelia's presence in Sespech might be mere coincidence; she might not be searching for Arvin, after all. If she was hauled before the baron for questioning and was able to probe his thoughts, she'd be alerted to the fact that Arvin was alive, and in Sespech. If she later escaped....

Arvin decided it was worth the risk. Perhaps Zelia would resist capture, and the clerics would kill her. The thought made Arvin smile.

"There is a power that psions can manifest," he told the baron, "one that plants a seed in the victim's mind that germinates slowly, over several days. During that time, the victim suffers head pains and experiences brief flashes of memory—the memories of the psion who planted the seed. On the seventh day...." He paused, revisiting the dread he'd felt at slowly losing control of his mind. For six days and nights, Zelia's mind seed had warped his thoughts and slithered into his dreams, turning them into nightmares. Under its influence,

Arvin had lashed out at people who tried to help him, had even killed an innocent man. Only on the seventh day, when he'd been within heartbeats of having his own consciousness utterly extinguished, had the mind seed at last been purged.

"On the seventh day?" the baron prompted.

Arvin chose his words carefully; he was about to impart what might be very bad news, indeed. "On that day," he said slowly, "the victim's own mind is destroyed, and replaced it with a copy of the psion's mind, instead."

Marasa's face paled. "Helm grant it is not so," she whispered.

The baron leaned forward, his eyes intent on Arvin. "You know someone who can cast this spell," he said. "Someone here, in Sespech."

Arvin met his eye. "Yes."

"Name him."

"It's her, not him," Arvin answered. "Her name is Zelia. I spotted her three days ago, at Riverboat Landing. She's a yuan-ti."

Arvin expected the baron to immediately demand a description, but Foesmasher seemed disinterested. Beside him, Marasa looked visibly relieved.

"Aren't you going to arrest Zelia?" Arvin asked. "If she planted a mind seed in your daughter—"

"She couldn't have," the baron said. "Glisena has had no contact with yuan-ti for ... some time."

"How can you be so sure?" Arvin asked. "Yuan-ti can assume serpent form. Zelia could have slithered into the palace undetected and—"

Marasa interrupted him. "Tell him, Thuragar," she said, giving the baron a hard look.

Baron Foesmasher sighed. "You will, no doubt, have heard that I disapproved of Ambassador Extaminos's courtship of my daughter?" he said.

Arvin nodded.

"A little over a month ago, I forbade my daughter from seeing Ambassador Extaminos again. I took precautions against him . . . contacting her. It is no longer possible for a yuan-ti to enter certain sections of the palace. The hallways, doors, and windows—every possible entrance to those parts of the palace that Glisena would have any cause to enter—have been warded to prevent serpents from entering. All serpents. Even yuan-ti in human form."

He gave a heavy sigh before continuing. "Glisena has not . . . *had* not," he corrected himself, "set foot outside those sections of the palace since this was done. She's had no contact with serpents since that time. *That* is how I know this Zelia person could not have planted a mind seed in my daughter."

"I see," Arvin said. He understood, now, why the baron was so certain his daughter had run away. Anyone would, after being placed under what was, essentially, a prison sentence, however sumptuous and comfortable the prison might be. Arvin was starting to have second thoughts about the baron. If he ruled his own daughter with such a domineering hand, how did he treat his hirelings?

"You're certain the wards were effective?" Arvin asked.

It was Marasa who answered. "I oversaw their placement myself." The look she gave the baron suggested she'd been unhappy with this task.

Arvin nodded. Even if Zelia had relearned the mind seed power, it wouldn't have been possible for her to plant a seed in Glisena—she wouldn't have been able to get close enough to the princess.

Marasa leaned closer to the baron and spoke, interrupting Arvin's thoughts. "This 'mind seed' could be used to create the perfect spy," she told him in a voice that was pitched low—but not quite low enough that Arvin couldn't overhear.

"Yes," the baron agreed. "It could." He gave Arvin a level stare. "Is that why you told us about Zelia? Is this a warning from Lady Dediana—that she has ears within my court?"

Arvin met the baron's eyes. "I didn't come to Sespech to play at politics, Lord Foesmasher," he answered. "I'm here for one purpose only: to find your daughter. Whether Zelia has seeded anyone in your court is a question that's best put to her. But be careful; Zelia's dangerous. This I know, from personal experience."

"She's your enemy," the baron observed. "Yet you serve the same mistress."

Arvin took a deep breath. Now was the moment he'd been waiting for, the moment to make a commitment— one that would affect everything that was to follow in his life. He reminded himself that this wasn't like his incarceration in the orphanage, or his obligation to the Guild. He was *choosing* this alliance.

"I don't serve Lady Dediana," he told the baron. "I'm a free agent; I choose who I work for. It is my belief that working for a human—especially a man of your stature—will be much more ... rewarding."

The baron gave a low chuckle. "I see." He exchanged a look with Marasa. "I think that, after Arvin has found my daughter, he and I will have a chat about mind seeds and spies ... and rewards."

"Will you arrest Zelia?" Arvin asked.

"That wouldn't be expedient at the moment," Foesmasher replied. "There was an ... unfortunate incident a few days ago. It seems that the new ambassador from Hlondeth had an altercation with one of the less reputable citizens of Mimph—an altercation that resulted in his arrest. If I simply order his release, it will appear that certain people are above Helm's law. Yet if I allow the Eyes to place Helm's mark on him, it may fracture the alliance. I have to tread carefully, where yuan-ti are concerned. I can't afford to ruffle any more scales."

Arvin realized at once who the baron was talking about: the yuan-ti who had attacked the young pickpocket. He shook his head in disbelief. The yuan-ti had a lot to learn about diplomacy.

Foesmasher continued speaking. "If you provide me with a description of Zelia, I will see to it that she is watched. If she comes to Ormpetarr, you'll be alerted."

Arvin murmured his thanks. It was time to get back to business. "You said that, on the night of Glisena's disappearance, she retired to her chambers and dismissed her servants. Presumably after that, she slipped out her door—"

"No," the baron said. "The guard in the hall was questioned under Helm's truth. He did not see her, and he was awake all night."

"Did she climb out a window?"

"Her chamber has no window."

Glisena was sounding more like a prisoner by the moment.

"Does your daughter know any magic?" Arvin asked.

Foesmasher shook his head. "Not so much as a cantrip. Yet she must have used magic to flee the palace. Someone aided her."

"Or kidnapped her," Marasa muttered under her breath.

Wanting to stave off another argument, Arvin interrupted. "I'm ready to manifest my power," he told them. "Could I see Glisena's chamber?"

"High Watcher Davinu already examined it," Marasa said. "There was nothing—"

"And now the psion will examine it—with mind magic," Foesmasher told her sternly. "Come," he said to Arvin, rising from his chair. "I'll take you there."

❖ ❖ ❖ ❖ ❖

Glisena's bedchamber was even more ornate than Arvin had imagined. The bed, side tables, and wardrobe were painted white and trimmed with gilt. The rug on the floor was also white, with a border of prancing centaurs. Arvin's feet sank into its softness as he entered the room. The windowless walls were divided into panels, painted with scenes of noblewomen waving silken favors at jousting knights. The ceiling was of molded white plaster, the pattern an ornate spray of bouquets and tree boughs.

The chamber gave the appearance of still being occupied. A fire crackled in the hearth, and a brazier filled with scented oil perfumed the air. A gown had been laid out on a clothing rack and fresh water stood in a pitcher beside a floral-print wash bowl. Next to these were a comb and brush. The bed was turned down for the night.

"I felt it wise to keep up appearances," the baron explained. "None of the servants know that Glisena is gone."

Marasa, standing a little behind him, shook her head sadly but made no comment. "What do you hope to find here?" she asked Arvin.

"There is a psionic power that allows me to view emotionally charged events that have occurred in this room," Arvin explained. "Whether Glisena ran away or was kidnapped, she's certain to have been highly emotional at the time. I hope to catch a glimpse of something that will provide some clue as to where she went." He glanced around the room, wondering where to begin. "The manifestation will take some time," he told them over his shoulder. "Please don't interrupt until—"

The baron placed a heavy hand on Arvin's shoulder and turned him around. "You said you were going to use mind magic to track her—not to spy on her private moments. What my daughter does in her chamber is her own affair."

"What are you so concerned about, Thuragar?" Marasa asked. "That he might catch a glimpse of Glisena undressing for bed?"

The baron's face flushed. "He will not cast that spell."

"Thuragar!" Marasa said in an exasperated voice. "Your daughter is missing. Surely a chance at finding her, no matter how slim it might be, is more important than—"

"Lord Foesmasher," Arvin interrupted. "Be at ease. I assure you that, whatever I might see, I will be ... discreet."

"For Glisena's sake, Thuragar," Marasa said. "Let him cast the spell."

Arvin smiled to himself. Marasa, so doubtful of his powers at first, now seemed willing to believe in them.

The baron stood in silence for several moments, conflicting emotions in his eye. At last, reluctantly, he nodded. "Very well." His hand fell away from Arvin's shoulder. "Begin."

Arvin looked around the chamber, sizing up its contents. Though the power could provide glimpses into the past of any event that happened in the immediate area—up to three dozen paces away from the manifester—it was most effective if it was concentrated on a specific item—a bed that an angry young woman might have flopped down onto after an argument with her father, for example.

Touching one of the lace-trimmed pillows, Arvin manifested the power. Psionic energy awoke within two of his power points: his throat vibrated, and a coil of energy slowly unwound within his abdomen, tickling the area around his navel. The baron and Marasa glanced uneasily at each other as a low droning filled the air—part of the secondary display. As the power manifested fully, Arvin felt the pillow dampen with ectoplasmic seepage where his fingertips touched it.

The vision came almost at once. Suddenly the bed was occupied by two people thrashing against one another—a man and a woman making love. The figures were transparent, almost ghostly, and seemed to be writhing on the neatly folded-down sheets without ever mussing them.

The woman was young and somewhat plain in appearance; her face was a little too square to ever be pretty, though her naked body was sensuously curved. Her head was thrown back in rapture, her long loose hair splayed against the pillow Arvin was touching. Arvin felt a blush warm his face as he realized he was looking at the baron's daughter, soon to peak in her passion.

The man on top of Glisena had his back to Arvin. His lower torso was hidden by the bedding. But when he tossed back his long, dark hair, Arvin caught a glimpse of slit pupils and snake scales, and a face he recognized at once. Dmetrio ran the forked tip of his tongue along Glisena's breast, and as her mouth fell open in a low, shuddering moan, he began to laugh. The look in his eyes was harsh, triumphant. He suddenly withdrew from her, levering himself up off her body, and spoke in a sneering hiss. "If you want more," he taunted, "you'll have to beg for it."

"Please," Glisena gasped, clutching at Dmetrio and trying to draw him back down to her. "I'd do anything for you. Please."

"That's a good start," Dmetrio said, a look of triumph in his slit eyes. His feet were visible now, protruding out of the bedding. They were rounded and scaly and looked like snake tails; each foot ended in a single large, blunt toe. Dmetrio wrenched himself free of Glisena and sat up in a kneeling position, then twined his fingers in Glisena's hair and yanked her forward. Dmetrio, like many yuan-ti males, had a slit at the groin, inside which his reproductive organs rested. Arvin, staring, was horrified to see emerging out of it not one, but two....

With a shudder, Arvin yanked his fingers away from the pillow. He felt sullied by what he'd seen. If he did manage to find the baron's daughter, it would be hard to look her in the eye.

"Well?" the baron asked. "What did you see?"

Arvin hesitated. The baron had closed the gate long after the horse had bolted from the stable—or rather, into the stable, in this case. The wardings on the palace had been in vain, but how to tell the baron that diplomatically?

"Your daughter was quite . . . passionate about Dmetrio, wasn't she?" Arvin began.

The baron's face purpled as he realized what Arvin was implying. "Here? In this room?"

Marasa glanced sharply at the baron.

"I saw Glisena and Dmetrio kissing," Arvin said. "The vision must have been more than a month old— from before the wards were set. It wasn't the one I was hoping for. I'll try again."

Before the baron could reply, Arvin retreated into a second manifestation. As the droning of his secondary display filled the air once more, he looked around the room, this time trying to pick up general impressions. As he glanced at the baron, he once again saw a double image—a ghostly baron standing just behind the first, his face also twisted with rage. He was shouting something. Curious, Arvin extended his hand in that direction, willing the vision to come into focus.

It did, with a volume that startled him.

"You will never see him again!" the ghostly image roared.

Arvin heard the sound of weeping behind him. He turned and saw Glisena—fully clothed, this time, and sitting on a neatly made bed—wringing a lace-trimmed handkerchief in her hands. Tears were sliding down her cheeks and a strand of her dark hair had fallen out of the pearl-studded net that held her hair in a bun at the nape of her neck. "But we're in love," she sobbed.

The baron snorted. "*You're* in love. That ... *snake* is as cold-hearted as any of his race. He cares nothing for you, girl. Nothing."

Glisena shook her head fiercely. "That's not true. You'll see. When I tell him about—"

"You'll tell him nothing." The baron strode forward and loomed over Glisena. "Nor will you tell anyone else what's happened. We're going to take care of this ... quietly."

Anger blazed in Glisena's eyes and flushed her cheeks. "You only care about your stupid alliances. If Dmetrio marries me—"

"He won't."

"Yes, he will," Glisena shrilled. "And when he does, your hopes of an alliance with Turmish are over. You can't force me to marry Lord Herengar's son. He's as stupid as he is ugly."

"At least he's *human*," the baron spat back.

"What do you think I am?" Glisena wailed. "A child? I'm a grown woman. You can't do this to me."

The baron's voice dropped dangerously low. "You did this to yourself," he growled. "And now you'll face the consequences." Turning on his heel, he wrenched open the door, startling the guard who stood in the hallway outside. "Make sure she doesn't leave," he snapped at the guard then slammed the door behind himself.

The vision—and Glisena's faint sobbing—faded.

"What did you see this time?" the baron asked. His voice startled Arvin; it took a moment for Arvin to realize that he was back in the here and now. A fine sheen of ectoplasm shimmered in the baron's hair. He didn't seem to notice it.

Arvin swallowed nervously. The last thing he wanted to report was that he'd listened in on a family argument—a very private family argument.

"I didn't see much this time," he said, "just Glisena sitting on her bed, crying. But I think I'm getting closer to the night of her disappearance. I'll try again."

The baron gave a brief nod. His hands, Arvin noticed, were white-knuckled. What was it he was so afraid of?

Arvin manifested his power a third time, scanning the room, and out of the corner of his eye saw a movement near the hearth. There were two ghostly women there, one standing, the other kneeling in front of her. Concentrating on these, he brought them into focus.

The standing woman was Glisena. She held her night robe slightly open, revealing her stomach. The look on her face was one of acute apprehension.

The woman who knelt in front of her touched Glisena's stomach with a forefinger and chanted in a language Arvin couldn't understand. Her finger moved back and forth across the bare flesh as if sketching, but left no visible marks. She was casting a spell of some description, but Arvin had no idea what its purpose might be.

This second woman had her back to Arvin; all he could tell was that she was large and was wearing a dark green cloak. He moved across the room—closer to the hearth, which began to sweat a sheen of ectoplasm—and got a view of her face.

The spellcaster had heavy jowls, a double chin, and brown hair with a streak of gray at one temple. Her small eyes were screwed shut as she concentrated on her magic. Arvin looked for a brooch or pendant that might be a cleric's holy symbol, but saw none. The only item of jewelry the woman wore was a ring, a band of brownish-red stone around her pudgy little finger. A band carved from amber, Arvin thought, identifying the stone from the lingering bits of gem lore Zelia's mind seed had left him with.

When the spell was done, the woman stood. Glisena closed her robe and stood with her palms lightly pressing against her belly. "When will it take effect?" she asked.

The spellcaster gave her a motherly smile. "Some time tomorrow." She tugged at the ring on her little finger. "This," she said, working it back and forth to pull it free. "Will convey you to me." She held the ring out to Glisena. "Use it as soon as you feel the magic of the spell begin."

Glisena took the ring with what looked like reluctance. A tear blossomed at the corner of one eye and trickled down her cheek. "Did he really tell you to end it?" she asked.

"He did." The spellcaster said in a grim voice. Then she patted Glisena's cheek. "But all's well now. We'll fool him." Glisena nodded and clenched her hand around the ring. "Yes."

"Now listen closely, and I'll tell you how the ring works," Naneth said.

The vision shifted then. The spellcaster disappeared, and Arvin had a palpable sense of leaping forward in time to a moment when Glisena stood in just the same spot in front of the hearth. As before, the moment was emotionally charged. Tears were streaming down her face. She wore clothes instead of a night robe, as well as a heavy cloak pinned at the shoulder and high leather boots. And her stomach was no longer flat. It bulged, visibly pregnant. *Very* pregnant.

Arvin whistled under his breath. No wonder Glisena and her father had argued. Glisena was carrying Dmetrio's child. A child that was only partly human. He watched as the ghostly Glisena toyed with something she held in her hands—the spellcaster's amber ring. A knock at the door caused her to startle, nearly dropping it.

"Glisena?" a muffled male voice called. "I'm sorry we argued. Can we talk?"

Glisena's eyes flew open wide. She glanced down at her belly then back at the door, and she drew her cloak around herself, as if to hide her pregnancy. Then her lips pressed together in a determined line. Tossing the ring on the floor, she spoke a word: *"Ossalur!"* As the ring hit the floor, it grew, expanding into a hoop fully two paces in diameter within the space of an eyeblink. Glisena jumped into the center of it—an awkward hop while holding her belly—and vanished. The ring contracted to its normal size then disappeared.

The door to her chamber opened. Baron Foesmasher poked his head tentatively into the room. "Glisena?" he called softly. He glanced at the empty bed—then looked wildly around the chamber. "Glisena!" he shouted. "Glisena!"

The vision faded.

Arvin let out a long, slow sigh and stood for several moments with his eyes closed. Then he turned to the baron. "I have news," he reported. "I've seen how Glisena esca—ah, that is, how she fled from the palace."

The baron ignored Arvin's slip of the tongue. "Tell me," he said.

"Your daughter was given a ring," Arvin said. "One that gave her the ability to teleport."

"Who gave it to her?" Marasa asked, her voice low and tense.

"A spellcaster," Arvin said. He started to describe the woman, but Marasa interrupted him after he'd barely begun.

"The midwife?" she asked. Then, to the baron, "What was she doing here, in the palace?"

Arvin was wondering the same thing. What *had* the spellcaster been doing to Glisena?

The baron stood rigid, his shoulders tense. The words jerked out of him. "Glisena was pregnant. By that ... serpent. By Ambassador Extaminos."

Marasa's mouth dropped open. "Pregnant?" she whispered. Then she nodded to herself. "Was *that* why she'd been feeling unwell?"

The baron stared at the far wall, not answering.

"And Naneth?" Marasa prodded.

"She came to cast a spell," the baron began. "A spell that. ..." His voice trembled. He sank onto the bed, head in his hands, unable or unwilling to say more.

Marasa's face paled. "Naneth came to end the pregnancy, didn't she?"

The baron refused to look up.

Marasa flushed with anger. "Killing an innocent is a grievous sin! And nothing is more innocent than an unborn child." She pointed a trembling finger at the baron. "Helm will never countenance this. Never! He will demand retribution. He—"

The baron looked up, his face twisted with remorse. "Helm has punished me already. Glisena is gone. *Gone.*"

Marasa lowered her accusing hand. "Oh, Thuragar," she said, her voice anguished. "What were you thinking?" She turned her back on him and paced across the room to stare at the hearth, shaking her head.

Arvin shifted uncomfortably, wishing he were someplace else. He stood in silence, debating whether to tell the baron what he'd seen in that last vision. The spell Naneth had cast on Glisena hadn't ended her pregnancy. Instead, it had hastened it to term. In that first vision, Glisena had not been visibly pregnant—she was at most two to three months along. And in the second vision, the one in which she'd used the ring, she'd been full-bellied, close to giving birth. Yet only a day had passed.

The spell must have taken effect on the evening that Glisena disappeared. That was why she'd dismissed her servants that night—she could feel the spell starting to work its magic. That was why she'd hidden her belly from view when her father knocked at her door.

The baron didn't know that Glisena was still pregnant.

But he would, once Arvin found her.

Sickened, Arvin stared at the carpet, unwilling to look at the baron. The last thing he wanted to do now was return Glisena to him.

Foesmasher balled his fist. "She's with Naneth," he said in a low voice. He sprang to his feet and crossed the room, wrenching the door open. "Stand aside," he shouted at someone as he stomped down the hall.

Marasa had whirled at the sudden motion. As the baron's heavy footsteps faded down the hall, she ran after him. "Thuragar! Wait!"

After a moment's hesitation, Arvin hurried after her. He caught up with Marasa as she was passing a guard who had a puzzled expression on his face. The baron was nowhere to be seen. Somewhere down the corridor, a door slammed.

Marasa grabbed Arvin's arm and dragged him down the hall with her. "He'll go to Naneth's house," she said in a low voice. "I'm worried. If he finds Glisena there...."

Arvin nodded grimly. "Indeed. And when he learns she's still pregnant—"

Marasa jerked to a halt. "She's what?"

"Still pregnant. Naneth didn't end the pregnancy—she cast a spell that hurried it along instead. In that last vision, Glisena looked ready to give birth at any moment. She may even have had the child by now."

Marasa looked grim. "We must find her, then. Quickly, before Thuragar compounds his sin."

Arvin's eyes widened. "He wouldn't harm the child ... would he?"

"No," Marasa said. "He wouldn't. Not *Thuragar*," she said, sounding as if she were trying to convince herself.

"But I do fear for Naneth's safety."

"What can we do?"

"Does your mind magic allow you to teleport? Could you reach Naneth's house ahead of Thuragar?"

Arvin shook his head. "No. But I can send a warning to her"—shoving a hand into his pocket, he pulled out the lapis lazuli—"with this." He touched the fingernail-sized chip of stone to his forehead. It adhered at once as he spoke its command word. Drawing power from the magical stone, he manifested a sending. He imagined that he was looking at Naneth and felt a prickling at the base of his scalp. A heartbeat later her image solidified, and he was staring at the midwife. She was leaning over, placing a saucer filled with water inside something that Arvin couldn't see. As the connection between her and Arvin grew stronger, she jerked upright, spilling the water. Her mouth moved in a sharp question, but Arvin couldn't hear what she was saying.

"Naneth," he said, speaking the words aloud. "I know you have Glisena. If she's at your home, move her. Hide her. The baron is on his way there now. He knows what you did."

The sorcerer repeated her question; this time Arvin could hear it. "Who are you?" she said, staring intently at his face. Her eyes were narrow with suspicion. "I don't recognize you."

She paused, waiting for an answer, but Arvin couldn't give one. That was how the lapis lazuli worked—he could send a brief message, and receive one in return. A few heartbeats later, the sending reached the limits of its duration. Naneth faded from view.

"It's done," Arvin said. "What now?"

"Are you quick on your feet?" Marasa asked.

Arvin nodded.

"Then let's get moving. I know where Naneth lives."

CHAPTER 7

They arrived at Naneth's residence just as the baron stormed out the front door, sword in hand. "Glisena's not here," he gritted. "Neither is Naneth. But the Eyes will round her up, soon enough."

Two of Foesmasher's soldiers emerged from the building, one of them holding the arm of a frightened-looking woman whose long black hair was starting to gray at the temples. She looked vaguely familiar, but Arvin couldn't place her.

"I've done nothing wrong," she protested.

"We just want to question you," the soldier holding her arm said.

"I simply came to pay Naneth for her services," the woman continued, drawing her cloak protectively around herself with her free hand as the soldiers led her away. "I don't *know* where she is." She turned to the baron, a pleading look in her eyes. "Lord Foesmasher, please. Whatever quarrel you have with the midwife, I have no part in it."

Foesmasher ignored her. "Have one of the Eyes question her," he said. "Find out if she does know where Naneth is. And send a detail of soldiers to secure this house."

The soldiers nodded and led the woman away.

"Baron Foesmasher," she pleaded. "Please don't imprison me. I've done nothing wrong."

Foesmasher stood, hands on his hips, scowling as she was led away.

Marasa, still panting from the run through the streets—the residence was more than two dozen blocks from the palace—exchanged a look with Arvin then hurried after the baron. "Thuragar," she said in an ominous voice. "You face Helm's wrath for what you ordered Naneth to do. You must atone before he—"

"I have other matters to attend to, first," Foesmasher snapped. Turning on his heel, he strode away.

Marasa hurried after him. "Thuragar, wait! Hear me out."

Arvin, only half listening, stared at the residence. It was a narrow building, two stories tall and sharing a wall with the building on either side. All of the windows were shuttered against the cold. His eyes ranged from one window to the next as he calculated the distance between them. If there was a wall that was a little thicker than it should be—enough to conceal a person— he'd find it when he counted off the paces inside.

The front door was open. Arvin walked up the short flight of steps that led to it and knocked—loudly.

"Naneth?" he called out, hoping that, if she was still here, she might recognize his voice.

No one answered.

A long hallway ran the length of the first floor.

On the left was a kitchen; on the right, a sitting room. A flight of stairs at the rear of the hall led to the second floor. He stepped inside and shut the door behind him.

The kitchen was warm and steamy; water boiled in a large pot on the stove. Bundles of drying herbs hung from the kitchen's ceiling beams, filling the air with their aromatic scents. Arvin moved the pot to the table, setting it beside a stack of neatly folded squares of white cloth, and the bubbling noise slowly calmed. He listened, but heard only the hiss of dried grain spilling from a sack that had slumped over inside a pantry cupboard. The doors of the pantry stood ajar, as if they'd been yanked open.

The sitting room also showed signs of the baron's intrusion. A tapestry lay on the floor beneath a broken curtain rod; a chair was on its side; and a shelf had been yanked away from one wall, spilling books onto the floor. One of them was on the hearth, its pages starting to curl from the heat of the fire. Arvin picked it up. Flipping idly through it, he saw that the book contained a number of illustrations: male and female pairs of various humanoid creatures—orcs, two-headed ettins, cloven-hoofed satyrs, lizardfolk, and several other races. Next to each figure was an enlarged drawing of that creature's genitals; the female illustrations were accompanied by a drawing showing a baby growing within the womb.

He had no idea what the text of the book said, but here and there he spotted a line that he recognized as Draconic. The spine of the book was deeply creased, as if it had been referred to many times, and one of the pages was marked with a ribbon. Flipping to it, Arvin saw an illustration of a male and female yuan-ti. Dmetrio Extaminos, it seemed, had been no aberration. It was common for a male yuan-ti to carry two swords in his scabbard . . . so to speak.

Closing the book, he set it back on the shelf.

A quick pacing of the first-floor rooms and a few knocks on walls determined that neither the kitchen nor the sitting room had any hiding places. There was a cupboard under the stairs at the back of the hall, but a glance inside revealed nothing but dust and cobwebs.

"Glisena?" Arvin called. "Are you here?"

There was, as he expected, no answer.

The stairs led to a landing with three doors. All were open. The one to Arvin's right looked as though it had been kicked open, splintering the door frame; it must have been locked when the baron arrived. Arvin glanced into the other two rooms first—a small washing-up room and a bedroom, its bed dragged to one side and its wardrobe open and spilling clothes—then turned his attention to the third room. He eased open the broken door.

"Glisena?" he called. "Naneth?"

As the door swung open, the stench struck him. Small and shuttered tight against the cold outside, the room reeked of snake. The walls were lined with tables; on these stood square containers made from panes of leaded glass, each with a wooden lid that had been drilled with holes. A different type of snake slithered around inside each container. One was a brown-scaled boa, coiled tight around a feebly twitching rat. Its body flexed, and the rat stopped moving. In the container next to it was a clutch of small green snakes, tangled together in a mating ball. Next to these was a flying snake from the southern lands, its body banded in light and dark green, its wings a vivid shade of turquoise. It fluttered inside its glass-walled container, hissing.

Arvin shook his head. Naneth certainly had odd taste in pets.

As he stepped into the room, a reddish-brown viper with a thick band of black at its throat reared up and spat a spray of venom onto the glass. Arvin eyed it warily, glad that the lid prevented it from getting out. The container next to it, however, was open; its lid sat on the table beside it. A saucer lay upside down inside the glass-walled cage, next to the gold-and-black-striped snake that was coiled there; this was where Naneth had been standing when Arvin contacted her with his sending.

Arvin picked up the lid and set it cautiously back in place, closing the cage. The snake inside, he saw now, was coiled on top of a clutch of eggs. Its body covered most of the small, leathery ovals, but as the snake shifted, Arvin caught a glimpse of something strange—it looked like a symbol, painted in red, on the egg that was closest to the glass. Squatting down for a closer look, Arvin saw he was right. The symbol was in Draconic. What it signified, he had no idea. He touched a hand to the glass the egg rested against, and it happened. Just as it had on the ship. For the space of several heartbeats, he stared, with naked eyes, into the future.

A pool of blood spread around someone's feet. And a finger-thin stream of red flowed away from the pool, toward a dark shape Arvin couldn't quite make out. Yet somehow he knew that it was something evil, something *monstrous*. The creature looked down then lifted the stream of blood from the ground with one hand—the hand of a woman—and began drawing the blood toward itself like a fisher hauling in a line.

Arvin's ears rang with an anguished scream—a woman's scream. Startled by it, he jerked his hand away. Only after his heart had pounded for several moments did he realize the sound had been part of his vision.

The snake shifted, covering its eggs once more. It looked at Arvin through the glass, tongue flickering in and out of its mouth, and gave a soft, menacing hiss.

Shaken by the premonition, Arvin stood.

Someone was going to die. Naneth?

He forced his mind back to the job at hand. Had

Naneth still been in this room when the baron kicked the door in? If so, the room might hold a clue as to where she'd gone.

For the fourth time that evening, Arvin manifested the power that made him sensitive to psychic impressions. The snakes hissed as a low droning noise filled the air. Allowing the energy that lay just behind his navel to uncoil, Arvin held out a hand and turned in a slow circle, scanning the room. Ectoplasm blossomed in his wake on the containers that held the snakes, covering their glass with a translucent sheen.

Arvin focused on the saucer Naneth had dropped. A vision flashed before his eyes—of Naneth, startled, releasing it. The image was faint and ghostly, at first, but grew in detail and solidity as Naneth listened and responded to the warning Arvin had sent. By the end of the sending, the midwife was visibly agitated. She ran from the room, into the bedroom across the landing, and returned an instant later with something tucked in the crook of one arm. Slamming the door behind herself, she quickly locked it. She shoved aside one of the glass containers, ignoring the agitated hissing of her snakes, and placed the item on the tabletop. It turned out to be a wrought-iron statuette of a rearing serpent holding a fist-sized sphere of crystal in its mouth.

Arvin felt the blood drain from his cheeks. He'd seen a crystal ball identical to it once before. It had belonged to a yuan-ti named Karshis—a yuan-ti who had served Sibyl.

Sibyl, the abomination who had killed Naulg, Arvin's oldest friend.

Painful memories swam into Arvin's mind—of Naulg, barely recognizable as human, his body hideously transformed by the potion Sibyl's minions had forced him to consume. Driven insane by his transformation, Naulg had glared at Arvin after his rescue, frothing and snapping his teeth, not recognizing his friend. And

Arvin, staring down at one of the few people to have shown him kindness without wanting something in return, had realized that there was only one thing he could do for his old friend, one final kindness.

He could still hear Naulg's final choked gasp as the cleric's prayer took effect ... and the silence that followed.

Together with Nicco and the others in the Secession, Arvin had thwarted Sibyl's plan to turn the humans of Hlondeth into mindless semblances of yuan-ti. But the abomination herself was still at large. Though the Secession had been searching for her, these past six months, they'd turned up no trace of her. Arvin had bided his time, hiding from Zelia and slowly learning new psionic powers from Tanju. He'd told himself that, when Sibyl did rear up out of her hole again, he'd be ready to avenge himself on her. That was something he'd sworn to do—sworn in the presence of a cleric of Hoar, god of retribution.

The god must have been listening. Why else would he have placed another of Sibyl's followers in Arvin's path?

As if in answer, thunder grumbled somewhere outside, rattling the shutters of the windows.

Arvin swallowed and nervously touched the crystal that hung at his throat.

The vision his manifestation had conjured up was still unfolding. In it, Naneth raised a hand to her mouth and pointed her forefinger at the crystal ball. "Mistress," she said in a tight, urgent voice, one hand stroking the crystal. "Mistress, heed me."

A figure took shape within the sphere—a black serpent with the face of a woman, four humanlike arms, and enormous wings that fluttered above her shoulders. The abomination twisted to look at Naneth with eyes the color of dark red flame, her forked tongue flickering.

"Sibyl," Arvin said in an anguished whisper, speaking the name at the same time the ghostly figure of Naneth did.

"Speak," the abomination hissed.

Arvin watched, horrified.

"I have just received word, mistress," Naneth said, addressing the figure that stared at her from inside the sphere. "The baron has learned of our plan."

Sibyl's eyes narrowed. "Who told you this?"

"A man I've never met before. A spellcaster—he used magic to deliver his message."

"Describe him."

Arvin's breath caught.

"He was human. With collar-length brown hair, and. . . ." Naneth paused, frowning. "And an oval of blue stone attached to his forehead."

"Do you have any idea who he might be?"

"None."

Arvin laughed with nervous relief. The description Naneth had just given was vague enough that it might have been anyone—aside from the lapis lazuli, which he'd be careful to keep out of sight from now on.

"What, precisely, did the spellcaster say?"

Naneth frowned. "Only this: 'He knows what you did.'" She paused. "It's a ruse, isn't it? One designed to get us to tip our hand."

"You humans are not always as stupid as you seem," Sibyl answered, her tongue flickering in and out through her smile.

From behind the closed door came the sounds of a man shouting. Then footsteps pounded up the stairs. For a moment, Arvin thought the baron had returned, but then he realized that this was part of the vision. To his eyes, the door was still closed and locked—and shuddering as the baron pounded on it and shouted at Naneth to open it.

The midwife gave a quick glance over her shoulder

then turned back to the sphere. "The baron is here," she whispered in a tight voice. "Should I—"

Sibyl's wings flared. "Do nothing rash," she hissed. "Do not go to the girl; if this is a ruse, they will have a means of following you. Avoid the baron, for now. Continue your preparations."

Naneth bowed her head. "I am your servant, oh Sibilant Death."

As the baron shouted what sounded like a final warning, the image of Sibyl vanished from the sphere. Scooping up the crystal ball, Naneth spoke several words in a foreign language. Then she vanished, leaving only swirling dust motes behind.

A heartbeat later the door crashed open, propelled by the baron's boot. He stormed into the room and glared around it, nose crinkling as he caught the odor of snake. Then he whirled and stomped out of sight.

Devoid of emotion to feed it, the manifestation ended.

Arvin knocked a fist against his own forehead, chastising himself in the silent speech. Stupid. If only he hadn't sent that warning to Naneth, they might have learned where Glisena was—but now Naneth was gone.

It was no consolation to Arvin that, until a few moments ago, Naneth had seemed nothing more than a helpful midwife. Marasa had been right all along. Glisena *had* been kidnapped, albeit without her realizing it. The baron's daughter had unwittingly placed herself—and her unborn child—in the hands of servants of an utterly ruthless and evil abomination. What terrible scheme was Sibyl up to this time?

Whatever it was, it had to involve the child.

Six months ago, Sibyl had attempted to install Osran Extaminos, youngest brother of Lady Dediana, on Hlondeth's throne. She would have succeeded, had Arvin not thwarted her plan to turn Hlondeth's humans into Osran's private slave army. This time around, Sibyl must have been planning to use Lady Dediana's grandchild.

That this was a scheme of opportunity, Arvin had no doubt. There was no way for Sibyl to have known that Glisena was pregnant by Dmetrio, or that the baron would summon a midwife to the palace to end that pregnancy. That it had been Naneth the baron had chosen had been mere ill fortune.

Unless—and here was a chilling thought—Dmetrio was somehow involved. Had he gotten the baron's daughter pregnant on purpose?

Another talk with Ambassador Extaminos was in order. It would have to be a very private talk, one in which Arvin would listen both to what was said—and what wasn't being said.

In the meantime, he needed to send a warning. He stepped out into the hallway, pulled the lapis lazuli from his pocket, held it to his forehead, and spoke the command word. He concentrated, and the face of his mentor became clear in his mind—a deeply lined face framed by short gray hair, the eyes with a curious fold to the eyelid that marked Tanju as coming from the East.

Tanju blinked in surprise as the sending connected them then turned to listen to what Arvin had to say.

"Glisena is pregnant with Dmetrio's child," Arvin told him. "A midwife named Naneth helped Glisena hide. Naneth serves Sibyl. Sibyl hopes to use the child."

Tanju nodded thoughtfully. He ran a hand through his hair as he composed his reply. "Learn what Sibyl intends. I will warn Lady Dediana."

The connection faded. *"Atmiya,"* Arvin said, letting the lapis lazuli fall into his palm. He tucked it carefully back into his pocket and turned toward the stairs. Just as he was about to descend, he heard a creaking noise from below: the front door opening. Then a male voice called out. "Naneth?" The voice sounded hesitant, uncertain. Something moved in the hallway downstairs. It sounded like the clomping of a horse, though softer, like the footsteps of a foal.

Remaining motionless, Arvin peered down the stairs. A short, slender man wearing a forest-green hooded cloak stood in the hallway, staring nervously into the kitchen. At first Arvin took him to be an elf, but then he realized that those weren't goat's-fleece trousers but the fellow's own thickly furred legs. Each ended in a black cloven hoof. As the man turned, Arvin saw his face. It was narrow and had pointed ears, like those of an elf, but a black horn curled from each temple. The chin was sharp and covered in a tuft of black hair.

A satyr.

What was a satyr doing in a city, far from any forest?

"Naneth?" the fellow called again. "Come now, woman, are you here?" He spoke with a high, soft voice, with a lilt that made it sound as if he were reciting poetry.

Was the satyr also one of Sibyl's servants? There was one way to find out—by probing his thoughts. Slowly, Arvin drew back from the staircase, intending to manifest the power from hiding, but the satyr's senses were keen. His eyes darted to the spot where Arvin stood. He bleated in surprise then bolted.

He was out the door before Arvin could react. Cursing, Arvin pounded down the stairs and out the front door himself. He glanced right, left . . . and saw the satyr disappearing around a corner. Arvin charged after him, elbowing his way through the people on the street and summoning his dagger from his glove as he ran. If need be, he would use it, but only as a threat—he had less lethal ways of bringing the satyr down.

The satyr sprinted up the street, darting nervous

glances behind himself as he ran. His hood had fallen away from his head, revealing his ramlike horns and dark, flowing hair. He skidded around a corner, slipping a little on the snow, and Arvin narrowed the gap between them. Arvin pelted around the corner.

A hoof lashed out, narrowly missing his groin. Pain shot through Arvin's thigh as the hoof gouged into it—and the satyr was off and running again, this time down an alley.

Biting his lip against the throbbing of his thigh, Arvin stumbled after him. He shoved his ungloved hand into his pocket and pulled from it a fist-sized knot. He skidded to a stop and threw the monkey's fist at the satyr, shouting the command word that activated its magic.

The ensorcelled knot unraveled in flight, splitting into four trailing strands. The main part of the monkey's fist struck the satyr in the side as he rounded another corner, and immediately two of the strands of twine wrapped around his waist. The others encircled his legs. The twine yanked his legs together, immobilizing them, and he tumbled to the ground.

Arvin approached cautiously, dagger in hand. He halted just outside the flailing arc of the satyr's bound legs. He glared down at the fellow, manifesting the power that would allow him to listen in on the satyr's thoughts. "Who...are you?" he panted, a spray of silver sparkles erupting from his forehead as the power manifested. He turned his dagger so that its blade caught the light. "Do you serve Sibyl?"

The satyr's ears twitched. He tossed his head. "Leave me be, thief. I carry no gems—not a single sparkle." Behind the words was a faint, panicky echo: his thoughts. They were in his own language, but Arvin heard them as if they'd been spoken in the common tongue. *What has he done to Naneth? If he has caused her harm....*

"Sibyl," Arvin repeated sternly. "The abomination. Do you serve Sibyl?"

Who? The satyr struggled against the twine and tried to rise to his feet, but tripped and fell backward. His thoughts tumbled over one another. *What game does he play? What does he want of me?*

Arvin sighed and vanished the dagger back into his glove. "I made a mistake, it seems," he told the satyr. "I thought *you* were the thief."

The satyr paused in his struggles. "You were not the mischief-maker who trampled Naneth's home?" *Who is he, then?*

Arvin shook his head. "I came to consult Naneth," he said, answering the unspoken question. "I found her door open, her home disrupted."

"Ah." The satyr relaxed. *That is why he was there. His woman is with child.*

Arvin knelt beside the satyr and grasped the monkey's fist firmly. He repeated the command and the twine instantly unwound from the satyr's limbs and reknotted itself back into a monkey's fist.

A sorcerer, the satyr thought. *They are thick as brambles here.*

"Was that why you came to Naneth's house?" Arvin asked, extending a hand to help the satyr up. "Is your woman also pregnant?"

A troubled look crept into the satyr's eyes. *The female,* he thought. *She is unwell. If Naneth does not attend her, she may lose her child.* "Yes," he answered aloud.

Arvin barely masked his startle. The satyr was thinking in his own language, but the power Arvin was manifesting allowed him to understand the subtle nuances of each word. "Female," he'd said, not "woman." He wasn't referring to one of his own kind—he was talking about a woman of some other race.

Glisena?

"Is the birth not going well?" Arvin probed. "Is that why you came to fetch Naneth?"

The satyr nodded.

"Perhaps I could help. When my first child was born, I assisted the midwife. I know some healing spells—I used them to help my wife." He paused, pretending to think of something. "Of course, my wife is *human....*"

Might he help? the satyr wondered. *He may have a spell that will banish fever from humanfolk.*

Arvin felt his heart quicken. The satyr *was* talking about Glisena. He was certain of it.

The satyr considered, for the briefest of moments, accepting Arvin's offer—then decided against it. "The midwife would be more suited," he said. "Do you know where she might be?"

"I wish I did," Arvin answered truthfully. He paused. "If I do see Naneth, where should I send her? Where is the woman who needs help?"

A brief thought flickered through the satyr's mind— a mental picture of a hut made from a mud-plastered lattice of woven branches, its bark-slab roof draped with brambles. It stood at the base of a tree in a snow-dappled forest.

"Is your forest far from here?" Arvin prompted.

"Why ask you this?" the satyr asked suspiciously.

"That is, I'm assuming you live in a forest," Arvin added hurriedly, realizing he'd almost given himself away. "For all I know you have a house here in Ormpetarr. If your woman was ill with a fever, you would naturally seek out the closest midwife who could—"

The satyr's eyes narrowed. *I never told him the female had a fever.*

Arvin had only the briefest flicker of a warning before the satyr leaped forward and up—just enough to let Arvin twist aside as horns slammed into his forehead. Hot sparks of pain exploded across Arvin's vision as he was knocked backward. Stunned, barely conscious, he dimly heard the satyr running away. He rolled over onto his stomach and pressed his face into the snow. The cold revived him a little, took away some of the sting. But when he sat up, the alley spun dizzily around him. By the time he was able to stagger to his feet, the satyr was long gone. Arvin stood, one hand against a wall, the other holding his pounding head. For the second time in a single evening, he'd seriously misjudged someone.

The monkey's fist lay in the snow near his feet. He picked it up, brushed it clean, and shoved it back into his pocket. His finger brushed against a small, hard object: the lapis lazuli, tucked safely inside a hidden seam. He considered using it to ask Tanju for advice, but he knew what the psion would say. He'd tell Arvin to use the dorje to track the satyr—and Arvin would be forced to admit that the magical item had broken. Hearing this, Tanju might insist on coming to Sespech and conducting the search for the baron's daughter himself. And Arvin would be out of a job.

There was, however, still a chance that the situation could be salvaged. If the satyr could be found and questioned, Arvin might yet learn where Glisena was.

Touching the stone to his forehead, he formed a mental image of Baron Foesmasher. It took only a moment for the baron to become solid in his mind's eye; he was leaning over a table, barking orders and gesturing at something that was spread out on the table before him. He started as Arvin interrupted whatever it was he'd just been saying.

The sending allowed Arvin only a few words. He chose them carefully. "A satyr knows where Glisena is. He just fled from Naneth's house. He's wearing a green hooded cloak. We need to find him."

The baron regained his composure instantly. "Return to the palace," he ordered. "At *once*."

Arvin nodded his acknowledgement then tucked the lapis lazuli back in his pocket. Now that he knew that Sibyl's minions were involved, he felt a newfound resolution. He would find Glisena. He wouldn't allow Sibyl to claim another victim.

Rubbing his aching forehead—a lump was already starting to rise over his right eye—he turned and trudged back to the palace.

CHAPTER 8

Arvin lay on the floor of the practice hall with his arms extended and upper torso bent back like that of a rearing snake. His palms, hips, and feet pressed against the floor as he craned his neck back to stare with unfocused eyes at the ceiling. He wore only his breeches, despite the chill in the hall. Snow fell outside the narrow leaded-glass windows that reached from floor to ceiling, muffling the sounds from the city.

His breathing was slow and deep, his mind focused entirely on his meditations. With each breath in through his nose, he drew in strength, courage, and confidence. With each breath out through his mouth, he blew away weakness, uncertainty, and doubt.

Picturing his mind as a net, he sent his consciousness down the strand that twined around his spine and located the *muladhara* that lay at the base of it. When he was ready, he activated his power points one by one, following this line. The "third eye" in his forehead emitted a flash of silver sparkles; a vibration deep in his throat filled the hall with a low droning noise; the base of his scalp prickled, causing the hair on the back of his neck to rise; his chest filled with crackling energy, which he exhaled in a breath scented with ginger and saffron; and a spiral of energy uncoiled from his navel, dewing the floor around him with a fine sheen of ectoplasm.

The energies coiled around his *muladhara*. The spiral grew tighter and stronger as Arvin wove strand after mental strand into it, replenishing it.

Arvin let out one last slow exhalation, ending his meditation. But he wasn't finished yet. Rising gracefully to his feet, he completed his morning routine, flowing through the motions that Tanju had taught him. The five combat and five defensive modes each had a pose associated with them, designed to focus the mind of the novice. Arvin had learned how to manifest just seven of them, but he ran through all ten poses, flowing from one to the next in what looked like one long, continuous motion.

When he was done, he yawned. He'd had very little sleep this past night; upon his return to the palace, Foesmasher had demanded a full report of what had transpired with the satyr. Arvin had been forced to admit that he could lift private thoughts from the minds of those around him, but the baron hadn't seemed alarmed by this revelation. Instead he'd been overjoyed to at last have some indication as to where his daughter had gone.

"So that's where she is," he said, "the Chondalwood." One heavy hand clapped Arvin's shoulder. "Well done. Now we just need to find that satyr and learn where his camp is." He paused. "You said the satyr was worried about Glisena's health. What was it, exactly, that he said?"

Arvin met the baron's eye. "That she was ill. He was worried she would lose her child."

"There is no child," the baron said with a catch in his voice. "Naneth saw to that, may Helm forgive me. You said that the satyr didn't actually use Glisena's name?"

"No, but—"

"Then it must have been someone else who needed the midwife's ministrations. Some other girl. Glisena is no longer with child."

"Yes, she is, Lord Foesmasher," Arvin said quietly. "Naneth didn't do as you ordered. She tricked you." Choosing his words carefully, he summed up what the visions had shown him—both in Glisena's chamber and at Naneth's house. He omitted any mention of the warning he'd given the midwife.

"When you charged into Naneth's home, she must have realized you'd learned of her treachery," Arvin concluded. "She teleported away."

"Gods willing, she'll have gone to wherever Glisena is," the baron said. His forehead puckered with worry. "I shudder to think of my daughter alone in the forest, giving birth in some dirt-floored shack with only *satyrs* to aid her. At least some good has come of my actions: I sped the midwife on her way."

"That . . . would not be a good thing," Arvin said.

"What do you mean?" the baron asked sharply.

Arvin took a deep breath then gave the baron the bad news. Naneth wasn't just a midwife. She served one of Lady Dediana's enemies—Sibyl. The yuan-ti abomination must be hoping to use Glisena's child as a playing piece in her bid for Hlondeth's throne. Once she had the child in hand. . . .

The baron's eyes widened. "After the child has been born, Glisena is no longer of any value to them," he said in a strained voice. "She will be ... disposed of."

"There may still be hope," Arvin said. "The satyr said the child hadn't been born yet. Until Glisena gives birth, Naneth won't harm her. Sibyl *wants* this baby. And once the baby is born, they will need Glisena to nurse the child." He paused. "Have your clerics found any trace of Naneth yet?"

The baron shook his head. "She has shielded herself, it seems, with the same magic that is preventing us from finding my daughter." He sighed. "It all hinges, now, on finding the satyr."

That was when things had become awkward. Foesmasher had demanded that Arvin use his psionics to find the satyr, and Arvin had been forced to do some quick talking. He'd drained his energies, he told the baron. He needed to sleep, then to meditate, before he could manifest any more powers. Like a wizard consulting his spellbook, or a cleric praying to her god, he needed to restore his magic.

Grudgingly, the baron had agreed to the delay. Marasa and her clerics would search for the satyr while Arvin rested.

If only the dorje Tanju had given Arvin hadn't broken, finding the satyr would have been an easy matter, Arvin thought. Without it, he would be forced to rely on his own, limited, powers. The only one he had that might be of use was one that gave him an inkling of whether a given course of action was good or bad. By manifesting it, he might get a sense of whether it would be better to search *this* section of the city or *that* one for the satyr. But the inklings weren't always accurate, and the power could be manifested only so many times. And now it was morning, and his meditations were over—and the baron would expect him to perform a miracle.

Hunger grumbled in his stomach, reminding him that he hadn't eaten yet. He should get dressed and find some food. He lifted his belt from the rack that held wooden practice swords and buckled it around his waist, adjusting it so his dagger was snug at the small of his back. His trousers and shirt were draped over one of the battered wooden posts that served as man-sized targets; his boots lay on the floor nearby. He dressed then crossed the room to a table on which stood a bowl of cold water. He splashed some of it onto his hair, combing it away from his eyes with his fingers. He flexed his left hand—his abbreviated little finger always ached in cold weather—then pulled on his magical glove. Then, just to see if he could do it, he drew his dagger, closed his eyes, and suddenly spun and threw the weapon, relying on memory to guide his aim. He heard a *thunk* and a creaking noise and opened his eyes. The arm of the quintain was rotating slowly, the dagger stuck fast in the center of the small wooden shield that hung from one end of it. Arvin smiled.

Applause echoed from above. Glancing up, Arvin saw the baron standing on the spectator's gallery that ran along one side of the practice hall. He had entered it silently, his footsteps muffled by the gallery's thick carpet. Arvin wondered how long he'd been standing there. The baron had changed into fresh clothes, but his eyes were pouchy; he hadn't slept. A sword was at his hip, and he was wearing his helmet. Its purple plume swayed as he descended the stairs to the floor of the practice room.

"The satyr has been found," Foesmasher announced.

"Excellent!" Arvin exclaimed, relieved. "If we ask the right questions, his thoughts will tell us where. . . ." Belatedly, he noticed that the baron's lips were pressed together in a grim line. "What's wrong?"

"When I received your warning last night, I ordered the city's gates sealed," Foesmasher said. "The Eyes began a block-by-block search of Ormpetarr; their spells flushed the satyr out a short time ago. He scaled the city wall. One of my soldiers gave chase along the battlements. The satyr slipped and fell to his death."

"That's terrible news," Arvin said.

"Yes. The soldier responsible has been punished."

Hearing the grim tone in Foesmasher's voice, Arvin cringed, thankful he hadn't been the one to cause the satyr's death. He didn't want to ask what had been done to the soldier; his imagination already painted a vivid enough picture.

The baron walked over to the quintain and pulled Arvin's dagger from it. "You've rested and replenished your magic." It was a statement rather than a question.

Arvin gave what he hoped was a confident-looking nod.

"What will you do next?"

Arvin was wondering that, himself. Even with the dorje intact, he might not have been able to locate Glisena. Whatever was preventing her from being located by wizardry and clerical magic might very well block psionics, as well. There was one person, however, who wasn't shielded by magic.

"I'm going to pay a visit to Ambassador Extaminos," Arvin told the baron.

Foesmasher frowned. "To what end?"

"It's possible that Sibyl plans to use the child as a means to force Dmetrio to do her bidding," Arvin explained. "Demands may already have been made—and if they have, and it's Naneth who's making them, Dmetrio may be our way of finding her. And through her, Glisena."

"Excellent," the baron said. "Let's go there at once. If he doesn't tell us what we want to know—"

"That might not be such a good idea, Lord Foesmasher," Arvin said in a careful voice. "Your presence might . . . agitate the ambassador. And an agitated mind will be harder for my psionics to penetrate. The best chance we have of learning more is if I meet with the ambassador alone."

The baron toyed with Arvin's dagger, considering this. "Was it mind magic that allowed you to find the target with your eyes closed," he asked, testing the dagger's balance, "or the magic of this dagger?"

"Neither," Arvin said, surprised by the change of subject. "I've worked as a net weaver and rope maker since the age of six. It makes for nimble fingers—you learn to be quick with a knife. Target practice does the rest."

The baron handed him the dagger. "Helm grant that the questions you put to Ambassador Extaminos also find their mark."

❧ ❧ ❧ ❧ ❧

Arvin paced impatiently in the reception hall, angry at having been kept waiting an entire morning. Dmetrio's house slaves had provided him with wine and food—roasted red beetles the size of his fist, precracked and drizzled with herbed butter—but Arvin waved away the yuan-ti delicacy. He'd already blunted the worst of his hunger at the palace and was too restless to eat. He ignored the smooth stone platform the slaves urged him to recline on and instead paced back and forth across the tiled floor, staring at the locked door of the basking room. At last it opened and a slave, bent nearly double under the weight of the jug of oil he carried, stepped through. Arvin strode toward the door.

"Wait!" the slave cried through the scarf that covered his mouth. "There's *osssra* inside. You mustn't go in there!"

"Too late," Arvin muttered as he pushed past the slave. "I'm already in."

The air in the basking room was thick with smoke that smelled like a combination of mint tea, singed moss, and burning sap. It hit Arvin's nostrils like a slap across the face, leaving them watering. As he breathed in the smoke, the room swayed and his legs began to tremble. He staggered, catching himself on one of the pillars that held up the domed ceiling. He clung to it, shaking his head, fighting the waves of dizziness.

A low chuckle helped him focus. Still clutching at the pillar, he turned toward the sound.

Dmetrio Extaminos lay in a shallow pool in the floor a few paces away. His naked, scaled body was coiled under him; it gleamed from the oil that filled the pool. His upper torso rose from it, bending back like a snake's. He looked up at Arvin with a languid expression, slit eyes wide and staring, his dark hair slicked back from his high forehead. A forked tongue flickered out of his mouth, tasting the smoke-filled air.

"Ah," he said. "The rope merchant's agent. Are you really here . . . or just part of my dream?"

Smoke drifted slowly from the half dozen lidded pots that surrounded the pool, drawing Arvin's eye. He watched, fascinated, as amber-colored tendrils twisted toward the ceiling. Only when he heard the slither of Dmetrio shifting position was he able to wrench his eyes away from the smoke. He shook his head violently, trying to concentrate. The smoke, he thought. He should have listened to the servant's warning. He tried to manifest the power that would allow him to overhear Dmetrio's thoughts, but his own thoughts were too sluggish; they drifted like the smoke. A glint of silver sparked in his vision then was gone.

"Ambassador Extaminos," he said thickly, his words slurred. "Glisena is in danger. Her child—"

"What child?"

"The one you fathered," Arvin continued. "The midwife, she. . . ." He paused, blinking slowly. What was it he'd wanted to ask?

"Glisena is pregnant?" Dmetrio asked. A slow hiss of laughter escaped from his lips.

Arvin tried to shake a finger at him and nearly fell over. "She's also missing," he said when he'd righted himself. "She's been kidnapped."

"So?" Dmetrio curled into a new position in the oil, his scales leaving glistening streaks on the tiled edges of the pool.

"Do you know where she is?"

Dmetrio slowly arched his neck, stretching it. Oil trickled down one cheek. "No. I don't. Nor do I care."

"She's with child. *Your* child," Arvin protested. "She might die."

"Human women die in childbirth all the time," Dmetrio said. "Bearing live young is messy. Laying eggs is a much more efficient way of doing things." He rolled over in the oil, coating his scales with it. "Glisena has grown tiresome. I'll be glad to be away from here."

Arvin let go of the pillar. He meant to take a step toward Dmetrio, but he reeled sideways. "But the child," he said. "You must care about...." His mind wandered. It was getting more difficult to concentrate by the moment. His thoughts were like bugs, caught in sap and struggling to get free. The smoke.... His gaze drifted up to the ceiling again. He wrenched his mind back.

"But the child," Arvin repeated. "Won't you take it ... with you?"

Dmetrio let out a loud hiss of laughter. "Why would I want to do that?"

"Because it's *your* child. You can't just *abandon—*"

Dmetrio waved a hand. Someone seized Arvin's arms from behind—two someones, wearing armor and helmets flared like cobra hoods. "Rillis?" Arvin asked, peering at them through the smoke.

Neither was the guard Arvin had bribed for information the day before. They dragged him backward out of the basking room. A servant—the one who'd been carrying the jar of oil—closed and relocked the door behind them. Arvin found himself being dragged through the reception hall, down a corridor, out a door, and down a snow-covered ramp. His heels skidded through the snow, leaving two drag marks. He stared at them, fascinated. They were like the trails left by snakes. If he moved his feet from side to side, they slithered....

A gate creaked open and the militiamen lifted him up. Then he was floating through the air. No, not floating ... he'd been thrown, tossed out by the militiamen. He landed on his back in the snowy street. As people drifted past him, shrinking back from the spot where he lay, he stared, intrigued, at the snowflakes falling out of the sky. He watched them while the snow soaked through his cloak, trousers, and shirt. They started off so small and got so big. Like that one ... it was *huge*.

No, that wasn't a snowflake. It was a woman's face, looking down at him. She had dark eyes, wide cheekbones, and black, wavy hair that reached toward him like snakes.

Heart pounding, Arvin tried to crawl backward through the snow, to escape the snakes. Then he spotted the frog hiding behind them. The notion of a frog sitting on a woman's earlobe seemed so *silly*, somehow, that he had to laugh. It came out like a croak.

"Vin?" the woman asked. "Are you all right?"

Arvin stared dreamily up at Karrell for several moments, tracing the curve of her lips with his eyes. He tried to raise a hand to touch them, but his arm flopped into the snow above his head. He needed to tell her something—that he'd breathed in something called *osssra*—but his lips wouldn't form the word. "Sssraaa," he slurred.

Karrell bent down and lifted his arm from the snow. "Vin," she said, her voice low and serious. "You need help. Please try to stand."

His arm drifted up around her shoulder, and his legs were scrabbling under him, messing up the snow. Yanked along the street by Karrell, he stumbled after her, staring at the pattern his feet made, oblivious to the people staring at them. There were so *many* footsteps... and not a one of them from a satyr's cloven hoof.

Why that mattered, he couldn't say.

❧ ❧ ❧ ❧ ❧

Arvin sat up, rubbing his head. His mind was his own again, but his head ached, and he felt shaky; it was difficult to coordinate his movements. He took it slow, swinging first one leg, then the other, off the side of the bed. When he stood, his legs trembled. He was naked, save for his breeches and the braided leather bracelet around his right wrist. And—he touched the crystal that hung at his throat—the now-depleted power stone his mother had given him, all those years ago.

He was in a small, simply furnished room with a door and one window. Through the shutters he could see that the snow had at last stopped falling; the street was three stories below. It was dark and a horn was sounding elsewhere in the city, signaling the evening prayer. He must have been unconscious for some time.

The room's furnishings included a bed, a narrow wardrobe by the fire, and a wooden table and chair. He was relieved to see his belt hanging on the back of the chair, his dagger still in its sheath. His magical glove lay on the table, next to a drawing of his sleeping face, rendered in charcoal on parchment. It was an amazingly good likeness; Karrell must have drawn it. A fire burned in the grate; his damp clothes and cloak hung, steaming slightly, on the fire screen in front of it. Noise wafted up from somewhere below—the overlapping sounds of voices, a stringed instrument, and the clatter of crockery. With it came the smell of food, a mouthwatering blend of stew and baking bread. Arvin's stomach growled.

He walked toward the fire—slowly, so he wouldn't stumble—and searched the pocket of his shirt. Inside the false seam was a familiar bulge: the lapis lazuli. Pulling it out, he affixed it to his forehead and tried to concentrate on Tanju, but the psion's face kept slipping out of focus. Realizing he was simply too tired to manifest a sending, Arvin removed the lapis lazuli and tucked it back inside his pocket. He'd contact Tanju later. All he really had to report, anyway, was that Dmetrio wasn't involved in Glisena's disappearance.

As he was making his way back to the bed, the door opened. Karrell came in, carrying a platter on which stood a bowl of stew, some bread, and a mug of ale. She set the platter down on the table then took Arvin's arm, guiding him toward the table. "You're still unwell," she said. "You should rest."

Arvin sank into the chair. "How long have I been here?" The savory odors of carrots, potatoes, and beef rose to his nostrils. He licked his lips and picked up a spoon from the platter. "And where am I?"

"I found you at midday, outside the ambassador's residence," Karrell answered, closing the door. "You are at the Fairwinds Inn, a short distance from there."

Arvin nodded and tore a chunk off the bread, following it up with some stew. As the flavors washed over his tongue, he closed his eyes and sighed. He took a drink of ale then tucked into the stew in earnest. "Thanks," he said, nodding at the bowl. "And thanks for helping me."

"You were fortunate," Karrell said. "*Osssra* can be fatal to humans."

"What is it?"

Karrell walked to the fire screen and lifted Arvin's cloak from it, turning it so the other side was to the heat. "*Osssra* are oils," she told him over her shoulder.

"When burned, they have special properties. Some *osssra* clear the mind, while others heal the body. Some purge enchantments, while still others—like the one whose odor lingers on your hair and skin—stimulate dreams and memories."

"The only thing it stimulated in me was dizziness," Arvin said, talking around a mouthful of bread. The food was helping; he was starting to feel better already. "It made me as stupid as a slug."

"Be thankful it only enfeebled your mind. Some *osssra* are fatal to humans. They are intended for yuan-ti."

"You know a lot about these magical oils," Arvin noted between spoonfuls of stew.

Karrell shrugged and continued turning his clothing. "You came from the direction of the palace. Did you manage an audience with the baron, after all?"

"You were watching the ambassador's residence, weren't you?" Arvin asked between mouthfuls of food.

"Yes," she admitted. "Was he just as rude as before?"

Arvin's fist tightened on the spoon. "Worse. He's an arrogant, unfeeling bastard. Just like all the rest of—"

Karrell's eyes narrowed. "All the rest of *what?*"

Arvin shrugged. He might as well say it. This wasn't Hlondeth; he could say what he liked.

"House Extaminos."

"Ah." Karrell walked back across the room and sank onto the bed—the only other place to sit. She toyed with the collar of her dress, which was white and hemmed with intricate turquoise embroidery. The dress was made from a soft, thin fabric unsuited to a winter climate, a fabric that hugged her breasts. She tossed her hair with a flick of her head, revealing her jade earplug and the soft curve of her jaw and throat. Arvin found himself losing interest in his food. He really *was* feeling better—much better. Even without the benefits of a charm spell, Karrell looked amazing.

She smiled and said something in a low voice. Arvin leaned forward. "Excuse me?" he asked, sopping up the last of the stew with his bread. "What did you just—"

He realized that she'd slid one hand behind her, as if to lean back on it. He caught sight of her fingers moving in an all-too-familiar gesture. Before she could complete her spell, he manifested a charm of his own. The base of his scalp prickled as psionic energy rushed from it. Break her promise, would she? Well he wasn't about to let her get the better of him this time.

He saw Karrell tilt her head slightly.

Arvin felt a rush of warmth flow through him. He could see, by the sparkle in her dark eyes and the way she looked at him, that she cared for him—*really* cared for him—as much as he did for her. She'd just saved his life, hadn't she? Karrell was someone he could count on, trust in, confide in. Setting down the piece of bread, he turned toward her. "He doesn't care," he told her.

She gave a slight frown. "Who does not care—and about what?"

"Dmetrio Extaminos." Arvin shoved the empty bowl away. "I tried to tell him that the woman carrying his child might be in danger, and he just laughed. He's not even going to try to look for Glisena; he's just going to walk away. To abandon his own child. Just like. . . ."

He looked away.

Karrell laid a hand on his knee. "Just like what, Vin?"

"It's Arvin," he said.

"Just Arvin?" she asked. "No clan name?"

"My father didn't live long enough to marry my mother. He died before I was born. Or at least, that's what my mother told me."

"Some fathers are not worth knowing," Karrell said.

Arvin caught the look in her eye, and saw that it would be better not to pursue this comment. He tried to lighten the mood. "The yuan-ti have that advantage," he said. "Their women lay their eggs all together in a brood chamber. None of them know their fathers." He chuckled. "It's a wonder they know who their mothers are."

"The yuan-ti of Tashalar have a similar custom," said Karrell. "So I hear." She flipped her hair back, showing off her jade ear plug. "I am of the Tabaxi, of Clan Chex'en."

"Check . . . shen," Arvin repeated, trying to capture the same inflection. "Was that your father's clan?"

Karrell smiled. "My mother's. The humans of Chult, like the yuan-ti, pay little attention to who sired them." Her smile faded. "In most cases."

"The Tabaxi don't have husbands?" Arvin asked.

"We do not use that word. We call them *yaakuns*," She paused, searching for the translation. "Lovers."

Arvin nodded. "What about you? Do you have—"

"Brothers and sisters?" she interrupted. "No. And you?"

Arvin had a feeling she'd deliberately misinterpreted his question. He let it drop. "I was my mother's only child."

"Was?"

"My mother died of plague when I was six."

"You must have been very lonely afterward."

Arvin shrugged. "There were plenty of other kids in the orphanage." Only one of them, however, had been his friend: Naulg. And Naulg was dead.

"Orphanage?" Karrell repeated. The word was obviously unfamiliar to her.

"It's something like a brood chamber," Arvin said, "for human children who have no parents. The priests run it."

"Priests of what god?"

"Ilmater," Arvin said, his lips twisting as he spoke the name. "God of suffering. His priests made sure we got plenty of it."

"This orphanage of yours sounds ... unpleasant."

"It was," Arvin agreed grimly.

Karrell stared into the distance. Her hand was still resting on his knee. Arvin glanced at the ring on her little finger. He'd love to know what she was thinking right now. Just as well that the ring was shielding her thoughts; otherwise he might be tempted to listen in on them.

She must have sensed his unwillingness to talk further about his childhood, for she changed the subject abruptly. "That woman you came to Sespech to find," she asked. "Was it Glisena Foesmasher?"

A tiny warning voice sounded in the back of Arvin's mind. One look into Karrell's dark eyes, and it was extinguished. Arvin nodded. "The baron's daughter ran away a tenday ago; I came to Sespech to help find her. A midwife helped her flee the palace. Glisena thinks the midwife was helping her, but Glisena is being used. They want her child—Dmetrio's the father. They hope to use it in a grab for Hlondeth's throne. Once it's born, the gods only know what Sibyl will do with—"

"Sibyl?" Karrell asked sharply. Her grip on Arvin's knee tightened.

"She's a yuan-ti," Arvin explained. "The midwife is one of her followers. They believe that Sibyl's an avatar of the god Sseth."

"She's no avatar," Karrell whispered.

Arvin blinked. "You know who I'm talking about?"

Karrell's eyes bored into his. "How do you know about Sibyl?"

Arvin's jaw clenched. "She killed my friend. I swore I'd do whatever I could to avenge his death. Even if it meant taking on an avatar."

Karrell took his measure for several moments before speaking. "Sibyl is mortal, though that was not always the case. For a time—during the Time of Troubles, when the gods walked Faerûn—her body was possessed by Sseth. But when the Time of Troubles ended, the god withdrew from her body. That was fifteen years ago; she has been mortal since. But she hopes to become a god, just as did Sseth, who himself was once no more than an avatar of Merrshaulk."

Arvin stared at Karrell. He had only the barest notion of what she was talking about. The only god he knew much about was Ilmater; the priests at the orphanage had drilled every painful, gory detail of the sufferings of the Crying God's martyrs into the children under their care. Arvin didn't even know Hoar's history, despite the fact that he had sworn an oath of vengeance to that god—an oath the Doombringer seemed bent on forcing Arvin to keep.

"How do you know all this stuff about Sibyl?" Arvin asked Karrell.

Karrell gave him a hard, level look. "To defeat an enemy, one must learn her ways."

Outside the window, thunder grumbled in the distance: the voice of Hoar. Arvin whistled softly. "I think the gods have thrown us together for a reason."

"I, too, believe this," Karrell said. She leaned closer and spoke in a confiding voice. "The yuan-ti of the south still believe Sibyl to be Sseth's avatar. Only a handful see her for what she really is—a power-mad mortal out to resurrect the empire of Serpentes at any cost."

Arvin had heard of Serpentes. It was an ancient yuan-ti empire that had stretched across the whole of the Chultan Peninsula—an empire that the yuan-ti still talked about, even though it had fallen nearly fourteen centuries ago. "I thought it was Hlondeth that Sibyl was after," he said.

"Only as a means to an end," Karrell said. "Nearly two years ago, Sibyl vanished from our lands. We were relieved to hear that she was gone, until we learned that she had traveled north. When we learned that she had gone to Hlondeth—"

"Who's we?" Arvin interrupted.

"The *K'aaxlaat*," Karrell said.

He gave her a blank look.

"Protectors of the jungle. We walk in the footsteps of Ubtao."

Arvin nodded, though he was no closer to understanding. It sounded like some sort of druidic sect.

"We realized," Karrell continued, "what Sibyl must be looking for: an artifact that had been given, long ago, to House Extaminos for safekeeping. It was hidden, then forgotten as the centuries went by. But Dmetrio Extaminos found it."

Despite himself, Arvin was intrigued. "And you came north to Hlondeth to find it. To steal it."

Karrell's eyes blazed. "No. To *recover* it. To prevent it from falling into Sibyl's hands. To ensure it would never be used again."

"What is it?"

"Do you know the Story of Sseth?" Karrell asked.

Arvin shrugged. "Not really. Those of us of the 'lesser race' aren't exactly encouraged to learn about the serpent god. I've never even set foot inside the Cathedral of Emerald Scales. Except once. By proxy."

The memory rose, unbidden, from those that lingered on from Zelia's mind seed. He'd seen the temple through her eyes as she genuflected before a statue of the god in winged serpent form. He nodded to himself; no wonder the yuan-ti believed Sibyl to be Sseth's avatar. She had the wings—even for an abomination, that was rare. And her eyes glowed red—they flickered like the flames that had surrounded Sseth's statue.

Arvin dredged up the last of Zelia's memory. "There's

a prophecy about Sseth rising from the flames, isn't there?"

Karrell nodded, visibly impressed. "From the Peaks of Flame—volcanoes on the Chult Peninsula. There is a door there, one Sibyl hopes to open. She thinks it leads to Sseth's domain. She hopes to convince the god to claim her as his avatar once more. But the door does not lead to the Viper Pit. It leads to a cave on the Fugue Plane occupied by one of the eternal evils—Dendar the Night Serpent. Should the door be opened, and the Night Serpent escape, thousands will die—perhaps hundreds of thousands. A giant is a mere morsel to her; she can swallow an entire village in one gulp. Those she swallows are utterly destroyed; not a shred of their souls remain for the gods to claim. And the more souls she consumes, the larger she grows—and the more she feeds. According to the prophecies, if released and unchecked, she will grow until she is capable of swallowing the very sun—of plunging the world into eternal night. A night in which no plants will grow, all of the waters of Faerûn will freeze, and the gods themselves will fade as their last worshipers die."

Arvin felt his eyes widen. Normally he would have blown off such an exaggerated story. But to hear Karrell tell it—to hear the tremble in her voice as she spoke of the end of the world—shook him. "This thing you came north to find," he said. "It's a key, right?"

Karrell's eyes bored into his. "It is called the Circled Serpent. It is made of silver, in the shape of a serpent biting its own tail and has a diameter about so." She held her hands about two palms' widths apart. "It was fashioned in two halves—one with a head, the other with a tail—which must be fitted together for its magic to work."

She lowered her hands. "I know this much: that Dmetrio Extaminos found the Circled Serpent when he was restoring the old section of Hlondeth. I believe he may have brought it with him to Sespech, but I am unable to locate it with my magic. During your last visit to the ambassador's residence, did you see anything like I have just described?"

Arvin shook his head.

"I did not expect so," Karrell said. "He will have it hidden. He fears another attempt by Sibyl's followers to steal it."

"The Pox?" Arvin asked, alarmed. "Did some of them survive?"

"Who are The Pox?"

"Followers of Talona, goddess of plague and disease," Arvin's heart was beating quickly. "And servants of Sibyl. They're the ones who killed my friend."

Karrell frowned. "No. The ones I am speaking of worship a different deity: Talos, god of storms and destruction. They, too, have formed an alliance with Sibyl. At her bidding, they tried to steal the Circled Serpent after Dmetrio Extaminos discovered it inside the ancient tower."

Suddenly, Arvin realized what she was referring to. Last summer, a gang of rogues had attacked the workers who were restoring the Scaled Tower, killing the project's yuan-ti overseer. The attack had been the talk of Hlondeth's thieves' guild for tendays; the rogues had not belonged to the Guild, and retribution was called for. The theft had taken place while Arvin was busy battling The Pox, and so he had not paid it much attention. Even when he'd met Tanju, and the militiaman accompanying him had let slip that Tanju was tracking someone who had committed a theft, someone called the "stormlord," Arvin hadn't put the pieces together. But now he understood. And he had bad news for Karrell. According to Tanju, the "rogues" had succeeded in getting what they came for.

"You're too late," he told Karrell. "Sibyl already has the Circled Serpent." Quickly, he recounted for her the events of last summer, and what he'd overheard.

Karrell's face paled. After a long moment of strained silence, she shook her head fiercely. "That is not possible," she said. "The workers I questioned said that Dmetrio Extaminos still had the artifact they had dug up in his possession. They even described the container it was in: a round wooden box, coated with lead to prevent magic from revealing the contents."

"Perhaps they lied," Arvin suggested.

"That would not have been possible."

"You charmed them," Arvin concluded. He thought a moment. "The people I spoke with were equally certain that the followers of Talos *did* manage to steal whatever had been found in the tower. Maybe they only got half of it."

"Yes. That must be what happened." She twisted the ring on her finger, a worried look on her face. "Do you know where Sibyl is now?"

Arvin shook his head. "If I did, I would have tried to avenge my friend's death. I've been looking for her for the past six months, but even the Guild can't find her."

"It is more vital now than ever that I recover the second half of the Circled Serpent," Karrell said. "The half Dmetrio still has."

"Do you think he knows what it is?" Arvin asked. "Perhaps if we told him what was at stake. . . ." Remembering who he was talking about, Arvin shook his head. Dmetrio Extaminos was arrogant, cruel, and callous. He cared nothing for Glisena and even less for his own child. He wasn't the sort to be moved by the fate of hundreds of thousands of strangers.

"What's next?" Arvin asked. "Are you going to try to speak to Dmetrio a second time?"

"I have already questioned his house slaves," Karrell answered. "None of them have seen the Circled Serpent. Nor have they noticed a lead-coated box among the household goods they have been packing. I am starting to suspect that he did not bring the Circled Serpent with him, that he left it behind, in Hlondeth."

"Will you return there?" Arvin asked, starting to miss her already.

Karrell sat in silence for several moments. "Perhaps." Then she straightened, a look of determination in her eye. "No. I will search for Sibyl, instead. Finding her should prove easier than trying to locate a small box lined with lead."

Arvin leaned forward. "I can help you with your search," he said. "But I'll need your help in return. I've promised the baron that I'll find his daughter. She's somewhere in a forest called the Chondalwood. She can't be located using magic; she's shielded against all forms of detection. But you have a spell that might be able to help—the one that allowed you to communicate with the naga. If you used it to question the animals of the forest, we might find one who has seen Glisena. If we can find her, we stand a good chance of also locating Naneth; the midwife will certainly be on hand for the baby's birth. And once we have Naneth. . . ."

"We can force her to tell us where Sibyl is," Karrell said.

"Then I'll have my revenge. And you'll have a chance to recover the Circled Serpent. Or half of it, anyway." He extended a hand. "What do you say? Partners?"

Karrell stared into his eyes for several heartbeats, ignoring his hand. Then she leaned forward and kissed him—passionately. Her fingers twined in his hair; her lips pressed against his. Excitement coursed through his body with a fire so fierce it left him trembling. Karrell was everything he'd dreamed of, everything he'd ever hoped to find in a woman. Her kiss left him as dizzy as the *osssra* smoke—and it showed no sign of ending. She pulled him toward her and he tumbled, landing on top of her on the bed. His hands brushed against her waist, her breasts—then found their way inside her dress. Still kissing her fiercely, he tried to stroke her breast, but for some strange reason the dress had gotten in the way. Its fabric felt rough under his fingertips.

No, that wasn't the dress. It *was* her breast. That wasn't skin his fingertips were caressing, but . . .

Scales?

Her charm spell—which only now did he realize she'd been successful in casting—abruptly ended. He broke off the kiss, jerking his hand out of her dress. Suddenly, everything made sense. Her strange comments, her taking offense when he'd tried to warn her about the yuan-ti of House Extaminos.

Karrell was—

She sat up. "You have just realized that I am half yuan-ti," she said. Her expression was a strange mixture of hurt and defiance.

Arvin nodded, mute. "That's not why—" he stammered. "It's just. . . ." Conflicting emotions surged through him. He wanted Karrell, he *ached* for her, even without the benefit of her charm spell—but now she reminded him of Zelia.

Her cheeks flushed. With a quick, angry motion she jerked at her dress, straightening it. "I am used to it," she snapped. "It is just one of the barriers in the maze of life—a barrier that I must overcome, if I am to find my true path. But it is hard. People are always mistaking me for human. How do you think it feels, to hear their comments about how 'cold-hearted' and evil the yuan-ti are, knowing that it is you they are talking about? The yuan-ti, also, are unkind. To them I look too human to ever be considered. . . ." She glanced away.

"Beautiful?" Arvin asked. "Desirable?" He reached out with a hand and lifted her chin. "You are. Believe me." He sighed. "It's just that, for a moment, you reminded me of someone. Another yuan-ti woman—a psion. She used her psionics to plant a seed in my head. If it hadn't been removed, it would have stripped my mind from my body and left me an empty husk for her to fill with a copy of herself. She *used* me."

Karrell's eyes softened. "The woman at Riverboat Landing?"

Arvin nodded.

"Not all yuan-ti are so cruel."

"I realize that," Arvin said. "And now that I look at you—really look at you—I see that you're not like Zelia at all. Not one bit."

He leaned forward—slowly—and kissed her.

Karrell didn't resist. Instead, at first hesitantly, she kissed him back.

Arvin broke off the kiss. "How do you say it?" he asked. "'Kiss'—in your language."

"Tsu."

Arvin smiled. The word puckered Karrell's lips beautifully as she spoke it. "And 'beautiful'? How do you say that?"

"Kiichpan."

"'Woman?'"

She gave a slight frown, obviously wondering what he was up to. *"Chu'al."*

Arvin returned it with a frank stare. "Keech-pan choo-hal," he said haltingly. "May I be your *yaakun?*"

She tossed her hair, mischief dancing in her dark eyes. Then she slapped him—lightly—across the cheek. "You charmed me," she said in an accusing voice.

Arvin chuckled. "And you charmed me." He rubbed his cheek, pretending the slap had stung the cut on his face, and saw her eyes soften in apology. "But I'm not under your spell anymore. Not that one, anyway."

"Your spell, also, has ended," Karrell said. Then she smiled. "Yet somehow, I still find you . . . intriguing." She hesitated then began unlacing the front of her dress.

As Arvin unlaced his breeches, removing them, his eyes were drawn to her breasts. Her scales, he saw, were small and fine, and a delicate shade of reddish-brown that nearly matched her skin, giving it a flushed appearance. He was, he realized, about to find out if the stories about yuan-ti women were true.

When she let her dress fall to the bed and moved toward him, encircling him in one graceful motion, he decided they might be, after all.

CHAPTER 9

Where have you been?" the baron growled. "My daughter is ill—she may be *dying*—and instead of finding her, you—"

Arvin bowed. "I apologize, Baron Foesmasher. I was poisoned."

The baron blinked. "Poisoned?"

"The ambassador kept me waiting all day. I decided to confront him in his basking chamber. I didn't realize it was filled with poisonous smoke. I only recovered from its effects a short time ago."

That wasn't strictly true, of course. His interlude with Karrell had followed. It had been brief—both of them felt the urgency of what was now a shared goal. But time had been lost; it was now nearly the middle of the night.

The room in which they stood—a chapel with

one of the enormous, silver gauntlets of Helm standing on a dais near one wall—was lit by a single lantern. The baron had been standing in prayer, his left hand raised and head bowed, when Arvin was ushered in. Karrell had been detained outside the room by the soldiers who served as palace guards. She stood at the end of the hallway, waiting.

Baron Foesmasher glanced at her. "Who is the woman?"

"Another tracker," Arvin said. "She's going to help in the search for your daughter."

The baron's eyes narrowed. "You have told her Glisena is missing?"

"Yes," Arvin acknowledged.

"What else have you told her?"

Arvin met the baron's eye. "Only that Glisena has run away," he said. "And that she is most likely hiding in the Chondalwood, among the satyrs. *And* that her flight from the palace was aided by minions of Sibyl, who hope to exploit your daughter for their own, ill purposes."

"By the sound of her accent, she's from Chult," Foesmasher said. "Is she yuan-ti?"

Arvin met the baron's eye. "Yes."

The baron grunted and turned back to Arvin. "You promised to be discreet. And now I find you've told a complete stranger. Another *serpent*."

"If you want me to find your daughter, Lord Foesmasher, you'll have to trust my judgment," Arvin told him. "I trust Karrell. It was a stroke of Tymora's fortune that she turned up here, in Sespech. Karrell knows a great deal about Sibyl; the abomination has had her people under her thrall for some time. Karrell was already investigating what Sibyl's minions are up to in Sespech. She would have learned, eventually, of your daughter's disappearance. By including her now, we gain some valuable assistance."

The baron glowered. "You assured me your mind magic would locate Glisena."

"It's already narrowed the search," Arvin countered. "We've learned she's in the Chondalwood."

"That tells us very little," the baron said. "The Chondalwood is enormous. It's nearly as wide as Sespech is long. Were I to send an entire garrison into it to search for Glisena, they could wander for a tenday and never meet a soul, let alone find a band of reclusive satyrs. And ordering in a garrison is something I can't do. Lord Wianar has laid claim to the Chondalwood; he hopes to cut off the supply of wood I need to build my navy. Sending troops into it would only give him the excuse he needs to invade." His eyes bored into Arvin's. "One man, however, would slip into the Chondalwood unnoticed. But that brings us back to the central problem—we don't know where to look."

Arvin thought a moment. "How close is the nearest edge of the Chondalwood to Ormpetarr?"

"Nearly two days' ride to the north, just across the river from Fort Arran."

"The satyrs seemed quite worried about Glisena's health," Arvin said. "They wouldn't have come to Ormpetarr to fetch Naneth unless their camp was a reasonable distance from the city."

"Naneth gave a teleportation ring to Glisena," the baron pointed out. "She may have also given one to the satyr."

"If she had," Arvin countered, "surely he would have used it to flee Ormpetarr, instead of trying to scale the walls."

"Indeed," the baron said, nodding in agreement. "But even if you are correct in your guess about what part of the forest the satyr came from, how do you propose to find his camp?" He nodded at Karrell. "And why do you need her help? Is your mind magic not up to the search?"

"It is," Arvin assured him. "But it won't be able to cover enough ground in the limited time we have left before Glisena . . . becomes more unwell. Karrell knows a spell that can help find the camp quickly. One that gives her the ability to communicate with animals."

The baron frowned. "Asking questions of a handful of animals in one tiny corner of the forest will accomplish nothing." He shook his head. "And I thought you were an expert tracker."

"We won't ask just *any* animals," Arvin countered. "We'll ask wolves. They're swift runners, capable of traveling a distance as far as that between Ormpetarr and Mimph in a single day. Their territories span even greater distances than that. And their sense of smell is keen enough to pick out the scent of a human from an entire camp of satyrs. If anyone can locate the satyr camp Glisena is staying in, it's wolves."

The baron nodded, grudgingly impressed.

"The only problem," Arvin continued, "will be in getting to the Chondalwood quickly enough."

The baron picked up his helmet, which had been sitting on the floor next to him. "You'll be in the Chondalwood tonight," he said, pulling it on. The purple plume bobbed as he spoke. "Naneth isn't the only one with a teleportation device."

"Can yours teleport two people at once?" Arvin asked.

"It can," the baron answered. "But that brings up an important question." He gestured at Karrell. "If it's her spell that will find my daughter, what further use are you?"

Arvin had anticipated that question. "In order for Karrell to use her spell, the wolves need to be close enough for her to speak with them," he said.

"Any hunter can find a wolf," the baron countered.

"I'm not just going to *find* wolves," Arvin said. "I'm going to call them to me. With this." He pulled the lapis lazuli from his pocket and displayed it on his palm. "This is what I used to send you the message about the satyr. With it, I can contact anyone. Human . . . or wolf. It has magic that only a psion can use."

Though he spoke with confidence, Arvin wasn't actually certain what he was proposing would work. He could definitely send a message that would catch a wolf's attention—the whine of an injured pup, for example—but a sending wasn't like a shout; it sounded inside the recipient's head. Arvin might be able to say "come here," but only by putting the sending to the test would he find out if he could convey where "here" was. But it was worth a try.

"The stone will also allow me to report to you—'at once'—the moment we find Glisena," Arvin added, deliberately using one of the baron's favorite phrases.

The baron nodded, satisfied. "You're a man who uses his head," he said. "I like that." He reached into a pouch that hung from his belt and pulled from it a shield-shaped brooch. It was made of polished steel and no larger than a coin, with Helm's blue eye on the front of it. Foesmasher handed it to Arvin.

"Pin this somewhere it won't be seen," he instructed.

"What is it?"

"Something that will assist me in locating you, once that message is sent," Foesmasher explained.

Arvin pinned the brooch to the inside of his shirt. "You'll come to the Chondalwood in person?" he asked, surprised.

"Yes." The baron stared at Arvin. "My teleportation magic is limited, so be certain that you are with Glisena—at her side—before you summon me."

"I will."

Foesmasher turned to the soldiers in the hall then paused, as if remembering something. "Oh yes, that yuan-ti you mentioned: Zelia."

Arvin tensed.

"She's in Ormpetarr. She arrived by riverboat last night."

Arvin gave a tight nod. Zelia in Ormpetarr was bad news. But he'd soon be out of the city. Tymora willing, Zelia would be gone by the time he got back. Or she'd do something that would give Foesmasher an excuse to arrest her.

Foesmasher gestured to the soldiers, indicating they should bring Karrell into the room.

Arvin caught her eye as she entered. "Lord Foesmasher has agreed," he told her. "You'll be joining the search."

Foesmasher waved his guards away then clapped one hand on Arvin's shoulder, the other on Karrell's. "Shall we go?"

"This teleportation device," Arvin asked "Is it a portal, or—"

The floor suddenly fell out from Arvin's feet, and the walls of the chapel spun crazily around him. He dropped about a palm's width through the air, landing unsteadily on the floor of a room with thick stone walls and arrow-slit windows. Two officers wearing armor bearing the baron's crest who were sitting at a table, deep in discussion, leaped to their feet, startled, then bowed deeply.

"Lord Foesmasher," one said. "Welcome."

Foesmasher removed his hands from Arvin's and Karrell's shoulders. "These two," he announced, "are en route to the Chondalwood. Make sure they reach it without Lord Wianar's patrols spotting them."

The officers exchanged a glance.

"Is there a problem?" Foesmasher demanded.

"We're not sure," one of the officers replied. "Wianar's men seem to have drawn back from the river. There hasn't been a sighting of them all day. But there may have been an incident."

Foesmasher frowned. "*May* have been?"

"One of the patrols we sent across the river this morning didn't return," the second officer said. "Nor did the one we sent to find it. Until we know what happened to them, it wouldn't be prudent to—"

"These two must reach Chondalwood," The baron growled. "Tonight."

The officer gave an obedient bow. "As you command, sir."

❧ ❧ ❧ ❧ ❧

They crossed the Arran River in a wagon drawn by a centaur. The wagon had no driver, nor was the centaur fitted with reins; he seemed to be draft animal and driver in one.

Arvin was amazed to see such a magnificent creature in harness. Centaurs were creatures of the wild, untamed and proud. This one was the size of a warhorse, his upper torso more muscular than any human's could ever be, his arms nearly as thick as a man's thighs. Coarse, almost woolly hair covered his lower torso, but his chest and arms were bare to the elements. He seemed not to mind the cold as he trotted on enormous hooves that thudded heavily on the massive timbered bridge that spanned the river. Every now and then he snorted, his breath fogging the night air, and tossed back his black, tangled mane, exposing pointed ears. Around his waist he wore a belt; from it hung a sheathed knife the size of a small sword. Hanging from the sheath was a purple feather, like the ones Foesmasher's soldiers wore on their helms.

Two of Foesmasher's soldiers had been assigned to accompany Arvin and Karrell; each man was armed with a crossbow and sword. The first—Burrian, a burly fellow with a black beard and enormous, calloused hands who said he had been a woodcutter before joining the militia—would serve as their guide in the Chondalwood. The second—Sergeant Dunnald, a man with a narrow face and long blond hair—would return to Fort Arran with the wagon. Burrian was watchful as they left the bridge, turned right off the main road, and started toward the Chondalwood. Dunnald, however, seemed confident, even a little bored. Arvin hoped that boded well for their journey. Perhaps the two officers they'd met earlier had been alarmists. There were any number of reasons that soldiers might fail to return from a patrol. Even so, Arvin found himself touching the crystal at his neck, for luck.

It didn't comfort him.

The forest lay some distance ahead, a dark, bumpy line against an even darker sky. Behind them, the bridge across the River Arran fell steadily away into the distance. Fort Arran dominated the far side of the bridge, its crenellated wooden towers keeping watch over the timbered arch that spanned the narrows and the road that led north from it to Arrabar. For now, this road was open, linking the two capitals of Chondath and Sespech. Come daylight, it would be dotted with merchant wagons and travelers. But if war broke out between the two states, Fort Arran would act as a gate, barring entry to any army that Lord Wianar might send marching south.

Arvin glanced up at the sky. The moon was half full, haloed by a thin layer of clouds. At least it wasn't snowing. The air was cold, but Karrell had cast another of her spells upon him, making him feel cozy and warm. He yawned, exhausted. It must have been well past middark by now. He leaned back, trying to make himself comfortable. Lulled by the thud of the centaur's hooves and the warmth of Karrell seated next to him at the rear of the wagon under a thick wool blanket, he dozed.

A while later, something poked Arvin's side—Karrell's hand. Instantly, he was awake. "What is it?" he asked.

Karrell pointed at something ahead. Arvin tried to peer past the centaur but could see only the dark line of the woods, drawing steadily closer. Between the forest and wagon was a flat expanse of snow-covered ground that sparkled in the moonlight.

"I don't see anything."

"Was it the movement near the woods you spotted?" Dunnald asked Karrell. "It's just a herd of wild centaurs, out for a moonlit trot. There's nothing to be frightened of."

Burrian called out to the centaur who drew the wagon. "Some of your old pals, Tanglemane?"

The centaur ignored him.

"I did not mean the centaurs," Karrell told the sergeant, an indignant edge in her voice. "And I am *not* frightened." She stood and pointed. "There is something up ahead. A dark line on the ground."

Dunnald continued to smile indulgently. "That's nothing to fret about, either," he told her. "Just the trail left by the centaurs through the snow."

Karrell sat down again and turned to Arvin. "Do they always travel in such complicated paths?"

Arvin stood and peered ahead. The line in the snow Karrell had spotted ran in a broad arc from left to right, paralleling the curve of the woods at a more or less constant distance from the forest. But instead of following a direct path, the centaurs seemed to have paused at several points along their journey to loop back upon their own trail. "Looks like they doubled back the way they came, crisscrossing their path," Arvin told Dunnald, who obviously didn't take anything a woman said seriously. "Several times. What would make them do that?"

Burrian looked to his sergeant for an answer, but

Dunnald only shrugged. "Who knows? Maybe they were playing follow the leader."

"Tanglemane?" Arvin asked. "What do you think?"

The centaur shook his head. "It is unusual," he said in a voice as low as the wagon's rumble.

As the wagon drew closer to a spot where the hoof-prints formed a loop, Arvin's frown deepened. Now that they were about to cross the trail through the snow, its complicated meanderings reminded him of something.

"Stop the wagon!" he shouted.

Startled, the centaur skidded to a stop, his four legs stiff and ears erect. The wagon jerked to an abrupt halt, jostling its passengers and causing Dunnald to drop his crossbow.

"What are you doing?" Dunnald snapped, picking up the weapon. "Why did you order the beast to halt?"

Arvin glanced over the side. He had called out a moment too late; the wagon was already inside one of the loops that had been stamped into the snow. "Don't move, Tanglemane," he instructed, reaching for his pack.

"What is wrong?" Karrell asked.

Burrian scanned the open ground around them, his crossbow at the ready. "Yes, what's the matter?" he echoed. "I don't see anything."

Arvin pulled a sylph-hair rope out of his pack. Soft as braided silk, it shimmered in the moonlight. "I'll know in a moment." He tossed the rope into the air, and smiled at the faint intake of breath he heard from Burrian as the rope streaked upward then hung, motionless, as if attached to thin air. He passed the lower end of it to Karrell. "Hold this, will you?"

Karrell took the rope, a curious look in her eye.

Arvin climbed. As he did, the meandering trail through the snow came increasingly into view. From a height, it was possible to see the intricate loops that had been stamped into the snow. The centaurs had not been wandering randomly; there was a design below—one that had been deliberately done. The wagon had halted inside one of its loops.

"The centaurs weren't playing follow the leader," he called out to the others. "They were making an arcane symbol in the snow."

The soldiers, Karrell, and the centaur all stared up at him.

"What kind of symbol?" Dunnald asked.

Arvin, studying the design below, shook his head grimly. "I think it's a death symbol."

Dunnald scowled. "You *think?* You're not sure?"

Beside him, Burrian looked nervous. "So *that's* what got our patrols."

Arvin slid down the rope. "I saw a symbol just like this one, years ago," he told the others as he recoiled his rope. "It was the central motif on an old, threadbare carpet from Calimshan. The carpet supposedly once had the power to fly; the noble who owned it thought that repairing it might restore its magic. He hired me to do the job. The day after I completed the work, he must have decided to try the carpet out. His servants found him sitting on it later that day, dead. He was slumped at the center of the carpet, without a mark on him. The spot he was sitting on was blank—the symbol I'd restored had vanished."

Karrell glanced nervously over the side of the wagon. "We are inside the symbol," she observed.

"Yes," Arvin answered.

"But not fully inside it?"

"We're not at the center of it, no," Arvin began. "But I'm not sure if that—"

Dunnald abruptly stood. "This is getting us nowhere," he said. "We can't just sit here all night." He clambered down from the wagon and walked toward the line in the snow, then squatted down next to it.

"Don't touch it!" Arvin warned.

Dunnald drew his sword and used it to prod at the symbol. "It's a trick," he announced. "A feint, to frighten us away from the woods. I'm touching it, and nothing's happening."

"You're touching it with your sword," Arvin noted, wondering if the sergeant would be stupid enough to touch a foot to the line.

He wasn't.

"If it is a magical symbol, it's not very effective, is it?" Dunnald commented as he straightened up. "It's narrow enough to step right over." He gave Burrian a meaningful glance. "If this *is* what waylaid our two patrols, we need to get a report back to the fort."

Burrian's eyes widened. He wet his lips. "Sir, I...."

Dunnald cocked his head. "Are you refusing my order, Burrian?"

Burrian shook his head. "No, sir.. It's just...."

Dunnald gestured at the track in the snow. "Tanglemane walked across it without harm. Look here—one of his hooves actually touched it."

"He's a centaur," Arvin interjected. "Perhaps centaurs are immune to it and humans aren't."

"*Humans* crossed the symbol once already," Dunnald countered. He glowered at Burrian. "Get down from that wagon, Burrian."

The soldier swallowed. "Yes, sir." He glanced at Arvin, lowering his voice to a whisper. "What do you think?"

"I don't know," Arvin said, less certain now. "The sergeant's right about one thing: we did pass across it once already in the wagon. But I'm no wizard. I don't know how these things—"

"Trooper Burrian!" the sergeant snapped. "Now!"

Reluctantly, Burrian climbed down from the wagon. He started to walk up to the track in the snow, then turned around again and came back to wrench a board off the wagon. He laid this across the track, visibly screwed up his courage, and took a long step across, taking care to keep both feet on the board. As his foot touched the board on the far side of the track, however, he crumpled to the ground.

Karrell gasped then leaped out of the wagon. Arvin shot to his feet, calling out a warning to her, but Karrell had the presence of mind to stay well back from the line in the snow. She dragged Burrian away from the dark line in the snow, lifted his arm, tugged up his sleeve, and pressed her fingers to the inside of his wrist. "He's dead," she announced, staring accusingly at Dunnald.

Dunnald's eyes narrowed. He wheeled on Arvin. "This is *your* fault. You said the center of the symbol was what killed, not the—"

Arvin leaped out of the wagon and caught Dunnald by the collar of his cloak. The sergeant tried to draw his sword, but Arvin batted his hand aside. "Not another word," Arvin growled. Shoving the sergeant aside, he stared at the dead man who lay facedown in the snow, feeling sick. Then he squatted to study the symbol. The line was darker than it should be—blacker than the shadows that filled it. Though both Burrian's body and the board he'd tried to use as a bridge had been drawn back across it, scuffing deep gouges in the snow, the line itself remained intact.

"Can you dispel it?" Arvin asked Karrell.

She looked doubtful as her eyes ranged up and down the symbol in the snow. "It is so large. But I can try."

Spreading her hands, she began to pray. As she did, Arvin watched the line in the snow. When Karrell completed her prayer, there was no visible change. The darkness was just as intense.

The sergeant, meanwhile, rotated his hand in a circle. "Tanglemane! Turn the wagon around and go back across the line. Return to the fort and fetch one of the clerics. We need someone who can dispel this thing."

The centaur snorted, his ears twitching.

"There's nothing to be afraid of," the sergeant said. "You crossed it once already. Go on—move! What's the matter—what are you afraid of?"

"Afraid?" the centaur snorted, his breath fogging the air. His eyes narrowed. "You're the one who's afraid, human. Cross it yourself."

Arvin was still staring thoughtfully at the line in the snow. He noted the ruts the wagon wheels had made as they traversed it and the spot where one of Tanglemane's hoofs had touched the symbol. Perhaps the captain was right about Tanglemane being immune to its magic. Then again, perhaps he wasn't.

Arvin stood and pulled out his lapis lazuli. "Sergeant, there's no need to send another person across. I can use mind magic to send a message back to the fort."

Dunnald wasn't listening. His face red, he glared at the centaur. "That's an order, Tanglemane," he said in a low voice. "Don't forget, you are one of the baron's soldiers now. Shall I report to Lord Foesmasher that you broke your vow by failing to carry out your duties?"

Tanglemane shook his head, a pained look in his eye.

"Then return to the fort," Dunnald ordered, pointing back at the distant bridge.

"As you order ... sergeant." Tanglemane began to turn the wagon.

Arvin rushed forward and grabbed the harness. "Tanglemane, wait." He turned to the sergeant. "We don't know how the symbol's magic works. Maybe trying to *leave* is what activates it."

"Leaving it is what we need to do," said Dunnald. He pointed. "And quickly. The centaurs are headed this way."

Arvin glanced in the direction the sergeant had just indicated. The herd that Karrell had spotted earlier had turned around and was moving toward them at a brisk trot. Arvin glanced at Tanglemane. "Are they hostile?"

"Of course they're hostile," Dunnald snapped. "They're wild things. Not like Tanglemane, here."

"They will be angry, if they see me in harness," the centaur said in a low voice. He started to unbuckle the straps across his chest. "Already they have drawn their bows."

"The centaur's right," Dunnald said. "We need to get moving." He offered Karrell his hand, as if to help her into the wagon. "We'll be right behind you, Tanglemane, in the wagon," he told the centaur. He gave Karrell a sly look. "Won't we?"

Karrell took a step back, folding her arms across her chest.

"We're not moving," Arvin said. "Nor is Tanglemane," he added. "We'll take our chances with the centaurs."

Dunnald climbed into the wagon, muttering under his breath. Then, louder, "You'll all see in a moment there's nothing to fear."

Tanglemane continued to unfasten his harness.

"Stop that," the captain ordered. "Get moving."

One of the harness straps fell away from the centaur's broad chest.

"Move!" Dunnald shouted, drawing a crossbow bolt and slapping it against the centaur's flank.

At the sting of the improvised whip, Tanglemane's eyes went wide and white. He slammed a hoof against the wagon, splintering its boards. The wagon shot backward, yanking the partially unfastened harness from his shoulder.

Dunnald sprawled onto the floor of the wagon as it rolled away. "You stupid beast!" he shouted from inside the wagon. "When we get back to the fort, I'll have you—"

As the wagon rumbled to a stop just beyond the line in the snow, Arvin suddenly realized the shouting had stopped. Karrell took a hesitant step forward. Arvin caught her arm, holding her back.

Beside them, Tanglemane whickered nervously. "I have killed him," the centaur said. "Killed the sergeant. When the baron hears of it...."

"It was an accident," Karrell said softly. "You didn't mean to."

Behind them, Arvin heard the sound of pounding hooves. Glancing in that direction, he saw a dozen centaurs racing toward them across the open plain. They skidded to a stop just outside the symbol and aimed powerful composite bows at Arvin, Karrell, and Tanglemane.

One of the centaurs—a male with a white body and straw-colored mane—snorted loudly and stared at them. "Soldiers of Sespech," he said in heavily accented Common. "You yet live?" He tossed his mane then pulled a white feather from a leather pouch that hung at his hip and waved it over the line in the snow. The magical darkness that filled it seeped away and the trail through the snow became just that: an ordinary trail of hoofprints. The centaur put the feather away and gestured curtly. "Come you with us."

❧ ❧ ❧ ❧ ❧

"What are they saying?" Arvin whispered to Tanglemane.

The centaur swiveled an ear to listen to the combination of whinnies, snorts, and whickers that made up the centaur language. Thirteen centaurs surrounded Arvin, Karrell, and Tanglemane, herding them along through the ankle-deep snow north along the river, toward Ormpetarr. The Chondalwood lay to their right, but it was falling farther behind with each step. The forest was still close enough that they could have reached it by dawn at a walking pace, even hindered by the snow. But it might as well have been a continent away. Six of the centaurs had their bows in hand with arrows loosely nocked; if the prisoners tried to flee, they'd quickly be shot down.

When the centaurs had first captured them, they had confiscated Karrell's club and Tanglemane's knife, giving the centaur several swift kicks when he didn't surrender it quickly enough. They'd taken an intense dislike to Tanglemane, perhaps because he'd allowed himself to be harnessed to a wagon. Tanglemane, however, showed a stoic indifference to the kicks the other centaurs had aimed at him, bearing them with only the slightest of winces.

The centaurs had also forced Arvin to turn out the contents of his pack. They seemed to have an aversion to rope—they'd tossed aside his magical ropes and twines as if they were poisonous snakes, and declined to search the pack further. Fortunately, they'd made no protest when Arvin gathered the ropes up again and returned them to his pack. Nor had they confiscated his glove, which he'd managed to vanish his dagger into.

The centaurs finished speaking. Tanglemane bowed at the waist to speak in Arvin's ear. "They serve Lord Wianar," he said. "They will turn us over to his soldiers."

Arvin had been afraid of that. Chondath wasn't officially at war with Sespech . . . yet. But the larger state was overdue for another attempt to oust Baron Foesmasher and reclaim lands they had never given up title to. Lord Wianar would be keen to question "soldiers from Sespech" to learn the current strength of Fort Arran's defenses. The questioning would no doubt be brutal and long.

Arvin swallowed nervously. "Would you tell them we're not soldiers?" he asked Tanglemane.

Tanglemane's eyes blazed. "I *am* a soldier," he said. Then his voice softened. "I tried to convince them earlier that you and the female are not the baron's vassals, but it was no use. They say you are spies."

Arvin swallowed. "That's worse than being a soldier, right?"

Tanglemane nodded. He lowered his voice. "You are not the first spies to cross the river. Last night, our soldiers took another across. These centaurs spotted him as he slipped into the woods. They laid the symbol in retaliation; they claim the woods as their own."

Arvin blinked. Foesmasher, it seemed, hadn't been content to wait for Arvin to reappear. There were others searching the Chondalwood for Glisena. The search had become a race.

Arvin glanced at the big white centaur. "What's their leader's name?" he asked.

"You could not pronounce it."

"In Common," Arvin said. "What would it translate as?"

"Stonehoof."

Arvin caught Karrell's eye then tipped his head at the centaur leader. "We need to talk him into letting us go," he whispered. "Let's see how ... persuasive we can be. If I don't manage to convince him, perhaps you can."

"I cannot help you," she whispered back. "That ... ability comes to me only once a day."

"Looks like it's up to me, then," Arvin said. Leaving Karrell, he jogged ahead to a position closer to the centaur leader. Stonehoof was even more powerfully built than Tanglemane, his massive hooves hidden by a fringe of hair. His upper torso was as pale as the rest of his body, covered with the same short white hair. His eyes were ice-blue.

Stonehoof glared at Arvin. "Return you to center of herd," he said sternly.

Arvin spread his hands in a placating gesture. "Stonehoof," he said, feeling energy awaken at the base of his scalp as he spoke. "You've got the wrong people. We don't serve the baron—we're not even from Sespech."

"Came you across river in soldier wagon." Stonehoof said. One of his ears swiveled, as if he'd heard something in the distance.

"That's true," Arvin agreed. "But we were only getting a ride with the soldiers. We're actually from Hlondeth. We were just passing through Sespech on our way to—"

One of the centaurs let out a loud, startled whinny. Instantly, the herd halted. They formed a circle, facing outward with bows raised. Stonehoof planted one of his massive hooves in Arvin's chest and shoved. Arvin stumbled backward, landing on his back in the snow beside Karrell and Tanglemane. He sat up, rubbing his bruised chest.

"The charm did not work?" Karrell whispered as she helped him to his feet.

"Apparently not," Arvin said.

Tanglemane stood next to them, listening. He lifted his head, his nostrils flaring as he sampled the breeze, then snorted.

A moment later, Arvin's less sensitive ears picked up the sound the centaurs had reacted to: the thud of hooves.

"Who is it?" Arvin whispered to Tanglemane. "Soldiers?"

"No." Tanglemane said. "A lone centaur."

As the centaur loped into view, Stonehoof and his herd relaxed. Most lowered their bows—though two kept arrows loosely nocked as they returned their attention to their captives.

The newcomer slowed to a trot and tossed his head. He was black from mane to tail, save for a blaze of white on each of his front hooves. Unlike the other centaurs, whose manes flowed freely down their backs, this one wore his hair pulled back with a thong. A wide leather belt around his waist held his quiver and bow case, as well as a large pouch.

As the black centaur approached, Stonehoof charged out to meet him. When only a pace or two separated them, Stonehoof reared up on his hind legs, forelegs flailing in the air. It looked to Arvin like a challenge of some sort, but a moment later Stonehoof bowed his head, and the two powerful males were slapping each other's backs in greeting.

"Who is he?" Arvin asked.

"They greet him by the name Windswift." Tanglemane answered.

"Is he their leader?"

Tanglemane stared appraisingly at the newcomer. "No. But he *will* lead the herd, someday soon, judging by the way Stonehoof submitted to him."

Windswift turned and trotted toward them, followed by Stonehoof. The other centaurs parted to let him through their circle. Windswift said something to Tanglemane in the centaur language and received an answer, then turned his attention to Arvin and Karrell. After studying them a moment, he spoke. "You're not soldiers." His Common was flawless, save for a slight lisp on the final word. He swayed slightly, causing Arvin to wonder if the centaur was as exhausted as he was. Steam rose from Windswift's back; he must have traveled some distance.

"You're right: we're not soldiers," Arvin agreed, relieved to be speaking to someone who might prove sympathetic. He manifested his charm a second time. This time, Tymora willing, there would be nothing disrupt it. "We're from Hlondeth. I'm a rope merchant's agent, and this—" He reached for Karrell's hand. "Is my wife."

One of Windswift's ears twitched, as if to catch a distant sound, and Arvin smiled. But then Windswift tossed his mane, and his eyes cleared. Arvin's heart sank. Windswift had shaken off his charm.

The centaur's eyes narrowed. "A psion?" he said in a voice barely above a whisper.

As Arvin stood stupidly, blinking—how had Windswift known?—Karrell gave his hand a quick squeeze and pressed something into his hand: her ring. He hid his surprise and slipped a finger into it, using her hand to shield the action. And just in time. A heartbeat later Windswift manifested a psionic power. Shielded by Karrell's ring, Arvin no longer had cause to fear Windswift listening in on his thoughts. What did send a shiver of fear through him, however, was the power's secondary manifestation.

A hiss.

By the gods, Arvin thought, feeling his face grow chill and pale, Windswift isn't just any psion.

He's one of Zelia's mind seeds.

Arvin's hands trembled, and his thoughts stampeded in all directions. Should he throw up a defensive mental shield? Launch a psionic attack? Had the centaur-seed realized who he was yet? Arvin had just identified himself as a rope merchant from Hlondeth, and Windswift had heard Arvin's own, unique secondary manifestation, and yet the centaur-seed hadn't attacked him. He didn't seem to know who Arvin was.

Arvin's racing heart slowed—a little. Zelia must have planted the seed in Windswift more than six months ago, *before* she'd met Arvin.

The hissing of the centaur-seed's secondary display faded. One hoof pawed the snow-covered ground in irritation.

Arvin nodded to himself. Windswift must have been the person Zelia had been waiting to meet at Riverboat Landing; the centaur-seed must have been spying, on Hlondeth's behalf, on Chondath.

It all fit. The centaur-seed couldn't have come into

the inn without giving himself away; his appearance was too distinctive. And the fact that he hadn't reacted to Arvin must mean one of two things. Either he hadn't made it to his meeting with Zelia—or Zelia *hadn't* come to Sespech in search of Arvin, after all.

If the latter, Arvin's secret was safe. Zelia still thought he was dead.

Arvin could see only one way out of his current predicament, and it involved taking a gamble—a big gamble. He caught the centaur-seed's eye and lowered his voice. "Zelia."

Windswift drew in air with a sharp hiss.

"I, too," Arvin said. "Three months ago." He nodded first in Karrell's direction, then toward Tanglemane, turning the motion into the sort of motion a yuan-ti would make: swaying, insinuative. The mannerisms came to him easily—disturbingly so. "We three," he continued in a low, conspiratorial voice, "must reach the Chondalwood."

Karrell, thankfully, kept her silence. The gods only knew what she was thinking about the odd turn the conversation had taken, but she had the good sense not to interrupt. Tanglemane also stood quietly, a puzzled frown on his face. The other centaurs, however, were getting restless. Stonehoof took a step closer to Arvin and Windswift, only to prance back when the centaur-seed launched a warning kick in his direction.

"Why was I not told?" Windswift hissed. "I was just. . . ." He glanced out of the corner of his eye at the other centaurs, whose ears were twitching as they strained to listen, and thought better of continuing.

Arvin smiled to himself. So Windswift *had* met with Zelia. "I was at Riverboat Landing recently, too," he answered in a low voice. "And I was not told about *you*, either. We like to play our pieces behind our hand, don't we?"

Windswift tossed his head. "That we do." He arched one eyebrow. "You're not as handsome as we usually pick," he chided.

Arvin gave a mental groan. What *was* Karrell thinking of all this? He returned the centaur-seed's coy look. "We needed someone less ... distinctive for this mission, this time. A mission I should be attending to." He glanced pointedly at the Chondalwood. The sky was brightening over the forest; it was almost dawn.

"Yes. You've been delayed long enough." Windswift turned and addressed the other centaurs in their own language. There was more than one murmur of protest, and Stonehoof reared up, challenging the centaur-seed a second time, but an instant later he clapped Windswift on the back, as he had before.

This time, Arvin was close enough to the centaur-seed to hear the hiss of the charm power's secondary display.

Stonehoof whinnied an order, and the centaurs lowered their bows. They handed Karrell's club back to her—and very pointedly ignored Tanglemane when he held out his hand for his knife—then allowed a gap to form in their ranks. Tanglemane stiffened then, eyes darting back and forth and tail lashing, trotted through it. Arvin and Karrell followed.

When they were well away from the centaur-seed, Arvin slipped the ring off his finger and pressed it back into Karrell's hand. "Thanks," he whispered. "Now let's get out of here before Stonehoof changes his mind."

CHAPTER 10

When they reached the edge of the Chondalwood, Arvin glanced back the way they'd come. Stonehoof and his herd of centaurs were disappearing around a bend in the river, headed south. Across the river to the west, smoke rose from the chimneys of Fort Arran, white against the gray winter sky, as the soldiers started their day. A patrol would no doubt soon be sent out; Arvin had used the lapis lazuli to send a message to one of the officers he'd met last night, warning about the death symbols in the snow. The bodies of Sergeant Dunnald and Burrian—and those of the missing patrols—would be recovered. And the centaurs—including Zelia's seed—would be tracked down and dealt with.

In the meantime, the centaurs wouldn't be laying out any more death symbols in the snow, which had been gradually melting as Arvin, Karrell, and Tanglemane had walked toward the wood. Soon there would be nothing on the ground but slush.

Tanglemane, who had been trudging along behind Arvin and Karrell, also turned to look at the departing herd.

"What now?" Arvin asked. "Will you return to the fort?"

Tanglemane shook his head. "You'll need a guide." He smiled. "It will be good to be out of harness, for a time."

Karrell tipped back her head, looking up at the trees. "It looks so odd," she said. "Trees, without leaves. This forest seems so ... lifeless."

"I assure you, it is not," Tanglemane replied. "The Chondalwood is filled with life—though only the strongest will have survived this harsh winter."

Arvin stared at the forest. The Chondalwood was a gloomy place, indeed. Tendrils of withered, brown-leafed ivy clung to bare branches, and dark moss hugged the trees. The slushy ground was an impassible-looking tangle of fallen logs, wilted ferns, and bushes dotted with blackened lumps that had once been berries. Dead boughs, snapped by the previous night's cold and hanging by a thread of bark, groaned in the breeze. As Arvin glanced up, an icicle fell from a branch and plunged point-first into the slush at his feet. He hoped it wasn't an omen of things to come.

He touched the crystal at his throat for reassurance then turned to Tanglemane. "I need to find a landmark," he told the centaur. "One that would be easily recognized by the animals that live in this part of the forest. Is there one nearby?"

Tanglemane thought a moment. "There is Giant's Rest, a stone that looks like a slumbering giant. Everyone knows it, and it's no more than a morning's trot from here."

Arvin stared at the tangle on the forest floor. "Even through that?"

"I will carry you."

Arvin's eyebrows rose. From all he'd heard, a centaur would rather cut off a hoof than allow a rider on his back.

"You saved my life," Tanglemane said, answering Arvin's unspoken question. "Not once, but twice. I repay my debts. Both to you . . . and to the baron."

"What put you in the baron's debt?" Arvin asked.

Tanglemane snorted. "Nearly two years ago, he spared my son's life. I vowed to serve him until that debt had been repaid. To serve in harness, if need be." He spoke in a level voice, but his whisking tail gave away his agitation.

Arvin smiled. "Gods willing," he told Tanglemane, "you're finally going to get the chance to pay off that debt. We came to these woods to find something for the baron. Something he holds dear. It's in a satyr camp we believe is nearby."

"A worthy task, indeed," Tanglemane said. He flashed broad white teeth in a grin. "Much better than pulling a wagon." He knelt. "Climb aboard."

        ❧   ❧   ❧   ❧   ❧

During their ride through the forest, a wet snow began to fall. It lasted only a short time, but by the time they reached Giant's Rest, Arvin was both soaked to the skin and utterly exhausted. The only thing keeping him awake was the constant ache of his legs, spread too wide across Tanglemane's broad back. Arvin didn't see the massive stone at first—he was too busy wincing. Only when Karrell, seated behind him with her arms tight around his waist, pointed it out did he realize they'd arrived at the clearing.

Arvin studied the stone through the dripping

branches. It did, indeed, look like a sleeping giant lying on his back with an arm draped over his eyes. Fully fifteen paces long, the enormous rock was a variety of hues. A darker patch of brownish-gray began at the "waist" of the giant and ended just short of the "feet," and the knob of stone that looked like a head bore veins of quartz that streaked the stone white, giving the impression of hair.

"That is no natural rock," Karrell said. "Nor even a fallen statue. Something turned a giant to stone." She glanced around nervously.

"Whatever happened here took place centuries ago," Arvin said. "Just look at how weathered he is."

Tanglemane knelt, and first Karrell, then Arvin, slid from his back. Arvin winced; it felt as if his legs would never straighten. The insides of his calves and thighs had been chafed raw by the wet fabric of his pants, and his lower back ached. It was already highsun, and he still hadn't performed his morning meditations. He needed them as much as he needed to rest, and to sleep. But Glisena was somewhere in these woods. The more time that passed, the less chance they had of finding her before she gave birth to her child—and became expendable.

Arvin lifted his arms above his head, stretching. He twisted first right, then left, trying to loosen tightly kinked muscles. Then he reached into his pocket for the lapis lazuli. "I should get started," he told Karrell. "If I manage to summon a wolf, it might be some time before it gets here."

Karrell nodded. "When it comes, I will be ready."

Tanglemane whickered. "You're summoning wolves?" he asked, his voice rising.

"Only one," Arvin reassured him. "That's how we'll find what we're looking for. Karrell will speak to the wolf. It can tell us if there's a satyr camp nearby."

Tanglemane's nostrils flared. "Wolves run in packs.

How can you summon just one? It is winter, and they will be hungry. You must not do this. Summon an eagle, instead. Their eyes are keen."

"I can't summon an eagle," Arvin said. "I couldn't possibly imitate its cries, and it wouldn't be able to see through the trees. What we need is a keen sense of smell. If you're afraid of the wolves. . . ." Belatedly, he realized what he was saying; the lack of sleep had left him irritable. "Sorry," he told Tanglemane.

The centaur turned, his tail whisking angrily back and forth. Without another word, he trotted away into the forest. Arvin sighed, hoping Tanglemane would come back when his temper cooled.

He touched the lapis lazuli to his forehead. He spoke its command word and felt tendrils of magical energy fuse with his flesh. Then he walked to the head of the stone giant and knelt beside it on the muddy ground. Pressing his cheek against the cold, wet stone, letting the weathered face fill his vision, he linked his mind with the power inside the lapis lazuli. Psionic energy slowly awakened at the base of his scalp; the power point there was as sluggish as his thoughts. Eventually, it uncoiled. Arvin sent his mind out into the forest, questing, and slowly the creature he was seeking materialized in his mind's eye. For a heartbeat or two, several wolves blurred across his vision. He selected one of them: a lean, gray wolf with a muzzle white as frost, its ears erect and nostrils flaring. To this wolf, Arvin sent out not words, but a wolf's howl. He imitated it from memory, drawing upon his recollections of the wolf he'd spotted, years ago, while walking past a noble's garden in Hlondeth. The animal had been straining at the end of a short length of chain—a prisoner. Intrigued by its cries, Arvin had returned to the garden the next night to stare at the wolf through the wrought-iron fence. And the night after that saw him at the garden again. Moved to compassion, he had slipped into the garden to set it free. His reward had been a sharp bite on the arm; two tiny white scars remained where the wolf's teeth had broken the skin. But he'd smiled and bade the wolf Tymora's luck as it bolted into the night.

Now, in his mind, he repeated one of the howls that had prompted him to free the creature: a long, wavering, mournful cry.

The wolf cocked its head and gave Arvin a questioning look. It would see him for what he was: a human who had just howled like a wolf. Then it threw back its head. Its reply startled Arvin; it sounded as if the wolf were right next to him, howling in his ear. The cry ended, the wolf cocked its head a second time, following Arvin's gaze as if it, too, were looking at the stone. Arvin could hear it panting . . . and the sending ended.

Exhausted, Arvin rose to his feet.

"Did it work?" Karrell asked.

"I made contact with a wolf, but I don't know if it will come," Arvin said. "We'll have to wait and see." He left the lapis lazuli in place on his forehead. If a wolf didn't arrive in a reasonable amount of time, he'd try again.

Tanglemane returned then, carrying an armful of dead branches. He cleared a bare spot on the ground near the stone giant then dumped the branches onto it. "We need fire," he announced. "To keep warm. And to keep the wolves from coming too close."

Arvin nodded. Tanglemane needed something to drive away his fear of the wolves while they sat and waited. Arvin slipped his pack off his shoulders and rummaged inside it for the wooden box that held his flint and steel. The moss and shavings that were nestled inside were still dry, he was glad to see. He offered the fire kit to Tanglemane, who took it with a nod of his head.

The centaur soon had a small fire burning, despite the dampness of the wood he'd collected. He fed it until it blazed. Arvin felt its heat as no more than a dull warmth, thanks to Karrell's spell, but soon his wet clothes were steaming. He stripped down to his breeches and hung his shirt, pants, and cloak on sticks near the fire. He even pulled off his glove; it might be magical, but the leather had become as soaked as the rest of his clothes by the fall of sleet.

Karrell hesitated a moment—unlike other yuan-ti, she seemed to be shy about her body—then stripped off her own clothes. Something that glinted reddish-brown in the firelight fell to the ground: loose scales.

Arvin glanced at them, wondering if he should say anything. Curiosity won out. "Do you shed your skin?" he asked.

Karrell stared at the scales that lay on the ground at her feet. "Not normally at this time of year," she said. Then she shrugged. "Perhaps it is the change in the weather. Or perhaps the wet clothing chafed them off."

She settled cross-legged by the fire, naked, combing her long, dark hair with her fingers. Her breasts and hips were full and rounded, her mouth soft and inviting.

If Tanglemane hadn't been with them. . . .

Arvin decided to channel his energy elsewhere, into something productive. He stood and kicked away fallen branches and dead leaves, expanding the bare patch around the fire. "I need to meditate," he told Tanglemane and Karrell. "Let me know if the wolf shows up."

He lay prone on the cold, wet ground, assuming the *bhujanga asana.* He still found it the most effective pose for replenishing his *muladhara;* sitting cross-legged, as his mother had done, never worked quite as well. The rearing-serpent pose gave his meditations an edge that the comfortable, seated position did not.

When his *muladhara* was replenished, he rose and

flowed through the ten forms Tanju had taught him. Tanglemane was still keeping a close eye on the surrounding woods, but Karrell watched Arvin, her eyes ranging up and down his body. Her frank interest distracted him, causing him to lose his concentration and falter slightly on the final pose.

He sank down beside her and held his hands out toward the fire, even though her spell had made warming them unnecessary.

Karrell reached out for his left hand and turned it, looking at his abbreviated little finger. "An accident?"

Arvin shook his head. "I was young and on my own and hungry. I made the mistake of stealing on someone else's turf. The Guild cut it off as a warning." He picked up his glove, which had dried, and started to pull the stiff leather over his hand, but Karrell stopped him. She raised his hand to her lips and kissed it.

"You have had a difficult life," she said.

Arvin eased his hand from hers. "No more difficult than some. I'm sure your life hasn't been easy."

"It became much more pleasant after I pledged myself to the *K'aaxlaat*. They helped set my feet on the path I was to follow through the maze of life. They have become like broodmates to me."

"Do you miss your home?" Arvin asked.

"Often," Karrell said. Then she smiled. "But not at the moment."

Tanglemane stood suddenly.

"What's wrong?" Arvin asked, reaching for his dagger.

"All is well," Tanglemane assure them. "I simply go to find more firewood." Without another word, he trotted into the woods.

Karrell gave a soft laugh. "He realizes we would rather be alone."

"Does he think we want to—"

Before he could finish the question, she kissed him, answering it.

Arvin could hear the sound of Tanglemane's footsteps growing fainter. Collecting firewood, indeed. As the fire crackled beside them, filling the air with the sharp tang of smoke, he returned Karrell's kiss, wrapping his arms around her. Before his meditations, he'd been exhausted. But now....

Easing her onto the ground, he kissed his way down her throat.

❧ ❧ ❧ ❧ ❧

A rustling in the woods startled Arvin awake. It was dark, but the fire was burning brightly. Tanglemane must have stoked it while Arvin and Karrell slept. The centaur stood next to the fire, head lolling on his chest, fast asleep.

Karrell lay beside Arvin. Like him, she was still naked; they had fallen asleep, tangled together, after their lovemaking. She stirred, lost in a dream. It must have been an unpleasant one; she gasped and jerked her hand, as if trying to free it from something.

Arvin nudged her awake.

She blinked then sat up. "What is it?" she asked.

"I'm not sure," Arvin said. "I heard something in the woods. I think it's—"

Eyes glinted at him from the edge of the clearing—eyes that were low to the ground and shone red from reflected firelight.

"A wolf," Arvin finished.

Tanglemane must have heard the word in his sleep. That, or he caught the wolf's scent. Instantly, his head was up, nostrils flaring. Tail flicking back and forth, he started to reach toward the empty sheath at his hip then changed his mind and turned his hindquarters to the wolf, lifting one massive hoof in readiness to kick.

Karrell sat up, fully awake now. "Tanglemane, wait. I will speak to it." She murmured something in her own language then gave a series of yips, half-barks, and growls. She was answered in kind by the wolf, which padded into the clearing. It proved to be an older animal, with a white muzzle and a lean, hungry-looking face.

"Has the wolf seen any satyrs?" Arvin asked. "Is there a camp nearby?"

"She does not know. She will ask her pack."

"Are they—" Before Arvin could complete the question, the wolf threw back its head and howled. A second wolf answered it from just inside the forest on the opposite side of the clearing. Then a third answered, from slightly deeper in the forest. Within moments, howls came from the woods on every side, both from close at hand and from a great distance. There must have been a dozen voices or more. The chorus lasted for several moments, rising and falling like a song, then one by one the wolves fell silent.

Arvin glanced at Tanglemane, who stood stiff-legged and trembling. He placed what he hoped was a reassuring hand on the centaur's flank. "Steady, Tanglemane," he told the centaur. "You were right; they're afraid of the fire. They're not going to come any closer."

The wolf who had answered Arvin's sending stared at Karrell and gave a series of yips and barks.

"A satyr camp lies to the east of here," Karrell translated, her voice tight with excitement. "There is a human in it. A female human."

"Tymora be praised," Arvin whispered. Touching the crystal at his throat, he whispered a quick prayer of thanks to the goddess of luck, promising to throw a hefty handful of coins in her cup—coins that would come from the baron's reward. "Can the wolves lead us there?" he asked Karrell.

She translated his question and received a reply. "They can. But they are hungry; the winter has been hard. They want something in return: meat. They want our 'horse.'"

"Our horse?" Arvin echoed.

Tanglemane gave him a wild-eyed look.

"Tell them that's of the question," Arvin said, placing a protective arm across Tanglemane's broad back. He glanced at the rock behind them then spoke in a low voice to Karrell. "Too bad we didn't have a way to turn the rock back into a giant. We'd have enough meat to feed a dozen packs of wolves."

"Could you summon another animal for them to eat?" Karrell asked. "An elk, or. . . ."

"Not without knowing how it 'talks,'" Arvin said. "A wolf's howl is the only animal sound I could imitate reliably. Other than a snake's hiss, of course."

Tanglemane's nostrils flared. His eyes were wide, with white showing around the edges as they darted back and forth, following the shapes that flitted through the darkness. "They're coming closer," he whinnied.

Arvin manifested his dagger into his glove. "Then we'll fight them," he said.

"Wait," Karrell said, laying a hand on Arvin's arm. "Let me try something else."

Abruptly, she transformed into her serpent form—a sleek reddish-brown snake with a band of gold scales around the tip of its tail. One moment she was standing in the firelight; the next, she was slithering along the ground, circling around the fire. Tanglemane startled, rearing up, and for several moments Arvin frantically tried to calm him, terrified that the centaur would crush Karrell under his hooves. By the time Arvin turned around, Karrell was between them and the wolves, swaying back and forth. She hissed softly, slit eyes turning to stare first at one patch of darkened forest, then another. Arvin found himself swaying slightly as he watched her and felt Tanglemane doing the same.

The first wolf—the one with the white muzzle—padded closer. It stopped several paces from Karrell and stared at her as if mesmerized. Then another wolf walked out of the woods, then two more. Within moments, six shaggy gray beasts were sitting in a circle, surrounding Karrell. All were thinner than they should have been: hungry.

Something flashed out of the darkness—a seventh wolf that hadn't succumbed to her trance. Releasing the near-panicked Tanglemane, Arvin raised his dagger, but before he could throw it, Karrell turned and confronted that wolf with a spitting hiss. The wolf immediately flattened on the ground, ears back and tail tucked between its legs. Whimpering, it crawled back to the woods. As soon as it reached the safety of the forest, it fled, crashing away through the undergrowth.

Karrell, meanwhile, had resumed her dance. The six remaining wolves continued to sit and stare at her, swaying in time with her motions. She drank in their scent with her flickering tongue then opened her mouth. What emerged wasn't a hiss, but a series of yips, followed by a long howl.

One by one, the wolves threw back their heads and howled with her.

Arvin felt a shiver run through him. It suddenly came home to him that Karrell was something utterly non-human. It hadn't fully struck him when he'd first seen her scales. But seeing her in serpent form—watching as she reduced one wolf to a quivering bundle of fear and ensnared the remaining wolves in her trance—was a different matter. He'd been thinking of her as a human with a hint of serpent about her. He'd refused to fully acknowledge that she was yuan-ti—and everything that came with it. Those charms she'd cast on him were only a small fraction of her powers.

The sight of her in serpent form terrified him. Yet he cared for her—even admired her. She could be kind, selfless, and brave. Just look at how she'd risked her own life to save the woman who had been bitten by the naga. These were qualities that simply didn't occur in a yuan-ti.

And yet she was yuan-ti.

Karrell twisted, still swaying, to face Arvin and Tanglemane. "They have agreed," she announced in her human voice—a strange thing, indeed, to hear coming out of a serpent's mouth. "They will lead us to the satyr camp *before* we give them the meat."

"What meat?" Tanglemane asked, his eyes rolling.

Karrell turned to Arvin. "You said that Foesmasher would teleport to us, once we have located—" She paused as Tanglemane gave her a sharp look. "Once we have found what we are searching for. He can bring meat with him."

Arvin nodded. It was a sound plan—as long as the wolves' hunger didn't make them impatient.

Tanglemane glanced back and forth between Arvin and Karrell. "Lord Foesmasher will teleport into the *Chondalwood?*" he asked, incredulous. "This . . . 'thing' that he holds dear. It must be very precious."

"It is," Arvin assured him.

"As precious as my son is to me?" Tanglemane guessed.

"Yes," Arvin said, meeting his eye.

The centaur nodded then slowly smiled. "I will pray to Skerrit, lord of the herds, that we find her, then."

Arvin glanced at the hungry wolves then spoke in a low voice to Karrell. "If Glisena isn't at the camp, we're in trouble."

"She will be there," Karrell said. "The wolves said so."

Unless, Arvin silently added, Glisena gave birth before they reached the satyr camp. If she had, all they would find would be her corpse—a report that wouldn't please the baron.

And the wolves *would* feed.

⊙ ⊙ ⊙ ⊙ ⊙

They walked all night, following the white-muzzled wolf through the forest. Arvin and Karrell walked on either side of Tanglemane, soothing him with reassuring words. Yet when dawn brightened the sky to the east, illuminating the trees with wintry light, Arvin could see that fully two dozen wolves surrounded them. They padded through the forest, tongues lolling, casting hungry glances at Tanglemane. Occasionally one would veer closer, and White Muzzle would growl and bare her teeth, warning it away. As the sun rose, these challenges became more frequent. And now that Arvin could see the wolves clearly, he realized they weren't eyeing just the centaur. They were looking hungrily at him and Karrell, too.

For the last little while, they had been climbing a low hill. The top of it was crowned with a tangle of brambles that extended for several hundred paces to the left and right. The pack halted before reaching it and White Muzzle turned and gave a series of bark-yips. Karrell recast her spell and spoke to the wolf.

"The satyr camp lies upwind, at the heart of these brambles," Karrell said.

"Is the human female still in the camp?" Arvin asked.

Karrell translated. White Muzzle sniffed the air and yipped once.

"Yes," Karrell said.

Arvin started to move toward the brambles, but White Muzzle planted herself in front of him, blocking his path, and growled. Glancing around, Arvin saw wolves in every direction, hunkered down as if ready to charge. He looked to Karrell for the translation, even though he really didn't need one.

"She has done as she promised," Karrell said. "She led us to the satyr camp. Now she wants her meat."

"Tell her she'll have to wait just a little longer," Arvin said. "Tell her the meat is at the satyr camp; that we'll return in a little while with it."

Karrell did then listened to White Muzzle's reply. "They want their meat now," she translated. "They want Tanglemane."

Arvin flexed his gloved hand. He'd disappeared his dagger into it earlier; at a whisper it was back in his hand.

Karrell tensed and laid a hand on her club. "We will fight?" she whispered.

"No," Arvin answered. "I have something else in mind."

One of the wolves moved in closer. Tanglemane whinnied nervously. Arvin laid a hand on his back. "Don't run," he urged. "It's what they want you to do."

Tanglemane nodded but remained tense. Arvin could feel him trembling. "Tanglemane," he said. "I'm going to cast a spell on you. Don't resist it."

That said, Arvin awakened the psionic energies that lay deep inside his chest. The wolves sniffed as the scent of ginger and saffron filled the air, and White Muzzle's hackles rose. But a moment later, it was done: the fates of Tanglemane and the pack leader were linked.

Arvin manifested his dagger into his gloved hand and passed it to Tanglemane. "When I tell you to," he instructed, "use this to prick the palm of your hand."

Tanglemane hesitated for only a heartbeat then took the dagger. Arvin, meanwhile, spoke to White Muzzle while Karrell translated.

"I have just cast a spell," he told the pack leader. "Whatever happens to the centaur will also happen to you. If the centaur is wounded, you will suffer the same injury." He nodded at Tanglemane, cueing him, and the centaur poked the dagger into his palm.

White Muzzle yelped and started to lift a paw. The other wolves tensed, and she immediately lowered it again. She growled at them, her legs firmly braced to meet any challenge.

"If the centaur dies, then *you* will die," Arvin continued, taking his dagger back from Tanglemane. "Tell your pack to stand aside and let us enter the satyr camp. After we've finished our business there, you'll get your meat. As promised."

White Muzzle's eyes narrowed as she heard this, but she quickly turned and spoke to her pack in a series of threatening growls. One or two growled back at her, but when she bared her teeth, they parted, letting Arvin, Karrell, and Tanglemane through. For several paces, Arvin walked with tense shoulders, expecting an attack to come at any moment—but none did. By the time the three of them had reached the edge of the brambles, the wolves had melted away into the forest.

"Well done," Karrell said.

Arvin nodded his acknowledgement. His eyes were on the brambles; they formed a near-impenetrable mass. Clumps of mushy berries, blackened by the earlier frost, hung from a tangle of vines studded with finger-long thorns.

"What now?" Arvin asked.

"There will be a path through them, somewhere," Tanglemane answered. "Let's circle around."

Before long, Arvin spotted hoofprints in the snow. Squatting down, he saw a tunnel leading into the heart of the tangled vines.

"This must be the way in," he said. He glanced up at Tanglemane then down again at the hole. He and Karrell could follow the path on their hands and knees, but Tanglemane would never be able to fit.

Tanglemane nodded, as if hearing his thoughts. "I will have to wait here."

"What about the wolves?" Karrell asked.

Tanglemane held up his bloody palm. "I'll have to trust in Arvin's magic to hold them back."

"The fate link will last at least until sunset," Arvin said. "Tymora willing, we'll be back before then—with some meat for the wolves. And the baron can teleport us all away."

He turned to Karrell. "The next part is up to you," he told her. "We need to make sure Glisena is here—and that Naneth isn't. In your serpent form, you could slip in and out without being seen. Will you do it?"

Karrell nodded and started removing her shirt.

"Be careful," Arvin added. "I don't want to lose you."

Karrell dropped her shirt to the ground, gave Arvin a kiss that sent a rush of warmth through him, and shifted. She slithered away into the brambles.

Arvin waited. While Tanglemane kept a wary eye on the forest, watching for wolves, Arvin stared at the brambles. After what seemed like an eternity, Karrell returned. Still in her serpent form, she coiled her body at his feet and lifted her head. "Glisena is there," she said. Her tongue flickered in and out of her mouth, which was curved into a smile. "She is in one of the huts. There is no sign of Naneth."

Relief washed through Arvin. He touched the brooch that was still pinned to the inside of his shirt. "I need to get close to Glisena," he announced. "Close enough that Foesmasher can teleport in. I'm going to go openly into the camp; I'll charm the first satyr I meet and tell him that Naneth sent me. If that doesn't work, I might need a distraction." He stared down at Karrell. "Follow me, but stay out of sight. If I run into trouble, I'll use my stone to call you. Use your own judgment about whether to intervene."

He turned to the centaur. "Stand fast, Tanglemane. Don't let the wolves spook you."

Then he dropped to his hands and knees. As he crawled into the brambles, keeping low to avoid snagging his pack, he saw Karrell slither off to the right.

The tunnel through the brambles twisted this way and that, branching several times and coming back together again. Wary of getting lost in what was obviously a maze, Arvin consistently chose the left fork, hoping this would eventually lead him to the center of the tangle. Every now and then he saw what was probably a satyr's hoofprint in the slush, but the wet ground was too soft to hold a firm outline. There was no way to tell which direction the satyr had been traveling in. A thorn plucked at his cloak, snagging it and preventing him from going forward until he yanked it free. Other thorns jabbed at him through the fabric of his clothes. Soon his arms and legs were covered in tiny scratches. He crawled on, ignoring these pinpricks of pain.

At last the brambles thinned up ahead, and he was able to see a clearing. From it came the murmur of voices and the sounds of satyrs going about their daily chores. Unfortunately, the tunnel through the brambles at this point bent sharply to the right. Arvin followed it, but after going a short distance, it led back to another path. He'd just looped back the way he'd come. Frustrated at being so close yet so far from his goal, he tried another route, turning right, this time. He crawled quickly, angry at the waste of time. The next fork, if he remembered correctly, was just ahead.

Glancing up, he saw a satyr squatting in the tunnel, pan pipes raised to his lips. Startled, Arvin manifested a charm, but even as he did, the satyr blew into his pipes. Music swirled around Arvin like falling leaves, lulling him to sleep.

CHAPTER 11

Arvin's eyes fluttered open. He lay on his back in the middle of a clearing, surrounded by at least a dozen satyrs. All were standing with their bows at full draw, arrows pointed at him. The satyr with the pan pipes—a fellow with eyebrows that formed a V over his nose, and a pointed tuft of beard on his chin—stood next to Arvin's pack, peering at something he held cupped in one hand. Arvin frowned, and pain lanced through his forehead. Something warm and sticky—blood—trickled down his temple, and his hair felt matted. Moving his hand slowly, so the satyrs wouldn't shoot him, he touched his forehead and felt an open wound the size of a thumbprint. Realization dawned: they had cut the lapis lazuli from his flesh. The charm he'd manifested when the satyr had first startled him obviously hadn't worked.

"Is this how you treat a friend?" Arvin asked.

The satyr with the pan pipes tipped the lapis lazuli into a leather pouch that hung from his belt and wiped his hand on his furry leg. "Friend?"

"Naneth sent me," Arvin said, watching for a reaction. A couple of satyrs holding bows glanced at each other; one said something in the satyr tongue. The other shrugged and slackened the draw of his bow, just a little.

Arvin eased himself into a sitting position, keeping a wary eye on them. Blood from his forehead trickled into his eye; he wiped it away with his hand. As he did this, he took stock. The satyrs had taken his pack—it lay on the ground a short distance away—but they'd overlooked the brooch Foesmasher had given him; Arvin could feel its cold metal against his chest. They'd also overlooked his magical bracelet and glove. He'd vanished his dagger into the latter, but it would do him little good at the moment, with a dozen arrows pointed at him.

He debated whether to attempt one of his psionic powers. He longed to know what the satyr with the pan pipes was thinking, but was hesitant to use the power that would allow him to read thoughts. As soon as the first sparkle of light erupted from his third eye, the satyrs would feather him with arrows.

"I'm one of Naneth's assistants," Arvin continued. "When your friend arrived with the news that the human woman was feverish and ill, Naneth asked me to take a look. She had urgent business elsewhere, and wasn't able to come herself."

As he spoke, Arvin wondered just where Naneth *had* gone. Three nights had passed since the baron had stormed into her home, causing her to flee.

As the satyrs talked in their own language Arvin glanced around. There were three tunnels through the brambles leading away from the clearing; drag marks through the slush showed the one they had hauled Arvin out of. Around the edges of the clearing stood a dozen huts like the one he had glimpsed while reading the thoughts of the satyr in Ormpetarr; it was impossible to tell which one Glisena was inside.

"Where *is* the human?" he asked. "I have healing magic that can help her."

The satyr with the pan pipes motioned with his hand; the others lowered their weapons. Then he tipped his horned head toward one of the huts—the only one that had smoke rising through the vent hole in its roof. "Follow me."

Arvin scrambled to his feet, wondering where Karrell had gone. There was no sign of her. Out of habit, he reached to touch the crystal that hung at his throat, to steady himself.

The crystal was gone; the satyrs must have taken it.

Arvin glared at the satyr who was leading him to the hut. Arvin's mother had given him the crystal just before she died; he'd worn it faithfully for two decades. Through the long years at the orphanage, it had been the one reminder that he'd once had a parent who loved him. Arvin was damned if he was going to let the satyrs keep it.

The satyr opened the door of the hut—an untanned hide hung from crude wooden pegs—and motioned for Arvin to enter. Arvin stepped inside and felt excitement course through him as he spotted the object of his search.

Glisena lay on a sheepskin near a fire pit. She stared up at the ceiling, hands on her enormous belly, her long hair damp with sweat. Even over the smell of wood smoke, Arvin caught the odor of sickness; a fly circled lazily in the air above her head. Glisena still wore the dress she'd had on when she used Naneth's ring to teleport away from the palace; her winter cloak and boots lay in a heap against the far wall. Through the fabric of the dress, Arvin saw Glisena's stomach bulge momentarily: the baby kicking. Glisena gave a faint groan.

At least mother and baby were both alive.

Arvin should have felt elation. Instead he felt sadness and a grim sense of foreboding.

The satyr gave Arvin a shove from behind. "Heal her."

Arvin stumbled forward. Kneeling beside Glisena, he saw that the object circling above her was not a fly, after all, but a small black-and-white stone, ellipsoid in shape. That it was magical, he had no doubt. It was probably what had kept the spellcasters from finding Glisena. He left it alone; grabbing it would only alarm the satyr.

Gently, Arvin turned her face toward him. Her skin felt hot under his fingers. "Glisena?" he said. "Can you hear me?"

She blinked and tried to focus. "Dmetrio?"

Arvin's jaw clenched. Dmetrio Extaminos had cast this woman aside like spoiled fruit, long ago. Arvin longed to tell Glisena the truth—that Dmetrio was the last person she should expect. That he would soon be departing for Hlondeth without giving her a second thought. But that would hardly be a kindness.

"No, Arvin said gently. "It's not Dmetrio."

He snuck a glance at the satyr. The fellow stood near the door, scowling at Arvin, pan pipes still in hand.

"Naneth sent me," Arvin announced in a louder voice.

"Where ... is she?" Glisena asked weakly. "Why hasn't she come?"

Once again, Arvin said nothing.

As she finally focused on him, Glisena's eyes widened in alarm. "Your face," she whispered. "It's bloody."

That one, Arvin had an answer for. "There was a misunderstanding," he said, glancing at the satyr as he spoke. "The satyrs didn't recognize me. Now be still. I need to figure out what's wrong with you."

He went through the motions of checking Glisena as a healer would, drawing upon his memories of how the priests at the orphanage had inspected children in the sick room. He held a finger to her throat, feeling her lifepulse; peered into her eyes; and sniffed her stale-smelling breath. Then he laid the back of his hand against her forehead as if measuring the heat of her fever. "When did you last see Naneth?" he asked.

"The night I . . . left," Glisena said. "She brought me here."

Arvin lifted each of Glisena's hands, pressing on the fingernails as if checking their color. Her fingers were bare; she no longer had Naneth's teleportation ring. Naneth must have taken it from her to prevent Glisena from leaving the satyr camp.

Glisena looked at Arvin with worried eyes. "Is it supposed to hurt so much? Naneth said the baby would be born soon after the spell. But it's been more than . . . a tenday. And still it won't come. Do you think my baby is. . . ." Her words choked off and her hands tightened on her stomach protectively. Tears puddled at the corners of her eyes and trickled down her cheeks.

Arvin wiped them away. "I'll check," he told her.

He laid his hands on Glisena's distended stomach. It felt taut as a drum beneath his palms. Was the child in distress? There might be a way to find out . . . and to learn what the satyrs intended, as well.

"I'm going to cast a spell," Arvin told the satyr. "One that will tell me what is causing the fever."

The satyr stared suspiciously at him a moment then raised his pan pipes to his lips. "Cast your spell. But remember that the others outside will kill you, should I fall."

Arvin nodded. He sent his awareness deep into himself, awakening the power points at the base of his scalp and in his throat. Silver sparkles erupted from his third eye as the power manifested, momentarily obscuring his vision. Then the thoughts of those inside the hut crowded into his mind. Glisena's were filled with anxious worry—she feared for her own life, as well as that of her child. She also clung to a desperate hope that Dmetrio would come for her. Naneth had promised to tell Dmetrio where she was. What could possibly have delayed him? Had something bad happened to him? Maybe he—

Unable to listen further, Arvin turned his attention to the satyr's thoughts.

The satyr—whose name turned out to be Theyron—didn't believe Arvin's story. Naneth had warned him that one of the baron's men might show up and try to fetch Glisena home. The baron's man might even use Naneth's name, in an attempt to trick the satyrs and take Glisena away—just as this human had done.

But maybe this human did have healing magic, as he claimed. If he *was* the baron's man, he would want to heal Glisena; a dead female wasn't worth stealing. And it was important that Glisena remain alive. Naneth had promised the satyrs much wealth, in return for watching over the female for a few days. As to why Naneth had asked them to hide the baron's daughter, Theyron didn't know—and didn't care. When Naneth returned to claim the female, his clan would reap its reward.

As for the human, well, as soon as the baron's man completed the healing, Theyron would kill him. One note from the pipes, and the human would slumber. And his throat could be slit.

Unsettled by the callousness of the satyr's thoughts, Arvin disengaged from his mind; he doubted he was going to learn much more, and his manifestation would end soon. He turned his attention to the third source of thoughts within the hut: the unborn child. He focused on them, letting the thoughts of Glisena and the satyr fade to the background....

Rage.

Boiling, inarticulate, all-consuming rage.

The thoughts of the child pounded into Arvin's mind like a hammer smashing against his skull. *Out!* snarled a voice as deep and hollow and devoid of humanity as a bottomless chasm. *Release me!* The thing inside the womb began kicking, fists, and feet pounding against Glisena's flesh, jolting Arvin's hand up and down. *Let ... me ... OUT!*

Shocked, Arvin jerked his hand away and ended the manifestation. He stared at Glisena in horror.

Whatever was inside her wasn't human.

It wasn't yuan-ti, either.

Naneth had changed the unborn child in Glisena's womb into something ... else.

The thought sickened Arvin to the point where he felt physically ill. This was even more monstrous than what Zelia had done to him. This time, the victim had been an innocent babe. But it was an innocent babe no longer.

"Something's ... wrong, isn't it?" Glisena asked in a trembling voice.

Belatedly, Arvin composed his expression. "I don't know yet," he said. Then, acting on a hunch, he added, "I'll need to take a look."

Easing Glisena's hands aside, he unfastened the lacings of her dress nearest her stomach. Even without opening her dress, he could feel the heat radiating from her belly. He lifted the fabric to glance at her stomach and saw something that disturbed him: a series of crisscrossing lines. They looked like the faint whitish scratches fingernails would leave on skin. Remembering his glimpse of Naneth casting her spell on Glisena, Arvin was certain that the midwife had drawn them. That certainty solidified when he recognized the symbol the lines formed. It was the same one he'd spotted on the egg that one of Naneth's pet serpents had been sitting on.

Arvin had no idea what the symbol signified. But he was certain it wasn't good.

He refastened the lacings of Glisena's dress and took her hand. "Something *is* wrong," he told her. "But I'm here to help."

Theyron tapped a hoof impatiently. "Well? Can you heal her?"

Still squatting beside Glisena, holding her hand, Arvin brought his gloved hand up to scratch his head—a gesture a man would make when thinking. "The fever has held her in its grip for many days," he said. "It won't be easy to break its hold." As he spoke, the power he was manifesting filled the air with a low droning noise: its secondary display. Theyron didn't notice it, however; he had already turned to stare at the distraction Arvin had just manifested. His eyebrows pulled into an even tighter V as he frowned, trying to figure out what had just caught his attention.

With a whisper, Arvin summoned the dagger from within his glove. It appeared in his hand as he had been holding it when he'd vanished it: point between his fingers, ready to throw. His hand whipped forward. At the last instant, Theyron turned his head back and tried to blow into his pipes, but before he could exhale, the dagger buried itself in his throat.

Arvin leaped to his feet, manifesting a second power. A glowing line of silver energy shot out of his forehead, wrapped itself around the pan pipes, and yanked. The pipes flew out of Theyron's hands. Arvin caught them in his gloved hand and vanished them into his glove. He spoke the word that sent the magical dagger back to his other hand then rushed forward, plunging the weapon to the hilt in the satyr's chest. Slowly, with a faint gurgling noise, Theyron slumped to the floor, pulling free of the dagger.

Arvin felt a twinge of remorse at having taken Theyron's life but shook it off; if the playing board had been turned, the satyr would have killed him without a moment's pity. He peeked outside the flap that covered the doorway. The other satyrs stood a few paces away. Some were staring at the hut, but they didn't seem to have heard anything. Two were rummaging through his pack. When one pulled out a piece of the broken dorje, the other made a grab for it. An argument broke out. The first satyr wrenched it out of the second one's hand and bellowed a challenge. The other satyr glared back and said something. The first nodded, and placed the broken dorje back in Arvin's pack. Then, slowly, each backed away from the other. Suddenly they charged forward, horns lowered. Their foreheads slammed together with a loud crack. Each staggered back then lowered his head a second time, like duelists bowing at each other, ready to repeat the charge. As the combatants pawed the earth with their cloven feet, the other satyrs cheered in anticipation.

Arvin breathed a sigh of relief. That should keep them busy for a while.

When he turned around, Glisena had forced herself up off the sheepskin. Eyes wide and terrified, she held herself in a seated position with trembling arms. As Arvin took a step toward her, she bleated and tried to crawl back, but only managed to collapse. She opened her mouth to scream.

Arvin leaped forward to clamp a hand against her mouth. "Don't," he said. "I'm not here to hurt you. I've come to rescue you."

Glisena's lips moved under Arvin's palm. Cautioning her with a look, he lifted them slightly, allowing her to speak.

"From what?" she gasped.

"Naneth tricked you," Arvin said. "Her spell didn't just hasten your pregnancy along. It affected the child inside you in other ways. The child was transformed into something . . . else."

"No," Glisena whispered.

Arvin couldn't tell if she was hearing his terrible news—and denying it—or simply reacting with horror to his words. "I'm afraid so," he said. As he spoke, he plucked the stone that was circling her head from the air. It resisted him for a moment, straining to free itself from his palm. Then it went still.

"Naneth wouldn't—"

"Yes she would," Arvin said, tossing the stone aside. "Naneth isn't just a midwife. She's an agent of a powerful yuan-ti who is an enemy of House Extaminos. Naneth used you; she only pretended to help you after your father asked her to—"

"To kill my child," she said in a flat voice. Her hands cradled her belly.

"Yes."

She stared at her stomach a moment, groaned as the thing within kicked, and gave Arvin a defiant look. "I won't let him hurt my baby."

Arvin sighed. She was forcing him to be blunt. "Whatever's inside you isn't your baby anymore. We need to get you back to Ormpetarr. Someone there will know what to do."

Glisena's jaw tightened. "I won't go back." Exhausted as she was, with dark circles under her eyes, she had the determination—and stubbornness—of her father. "Dmetrio—"

"Isn't coming," Arvin said, finishing the sentence for her. "He's leaving for Hlondeth. Without you."

"That's not true," she whispered again. "He loves me. He'll take me with him."

"He won't."

"He will." The determination was still in her eyes,

but something else had joined it: exhaustion. Fresh beads of sweat broke out on her forehead. She sank back onto the sheepskin, trembling. "My *father* sent you . . . didn't he? You're lying. About Naneth. And Dmetrio. So I'll . . . go back."

"I'm telling you the truth," Arvin insisted. "Much as I hate to do it."

Glisena turned away, not listening to him. Even when she was down, she wouldn't admit to defeat. Arvin had to admire that.

He'd been naive, to think that he could convince Glisena of the truth. It was simply too much, too hard. He peeked outside again—the satyrs were still butting heads, Tymora be praised—then turned his attention to the dead satyr's belt pouch. Opening it, he found his mother's crystal inside. He tied it around his neck with a whispered, "Nine lives," then recovered his lapis lazuli, which still had a jagged, coin-sized flap of his skin clinging to it. He spoke the stone's command word, and the skin fell away. Then he touched the stone to the raw wound on his forehead and spoke the command a second time. The lapis lazuli sank into the wound, attaching itself to the lacerated flesh. Fresh blood trickled from the wound; he wiped it away from his eye.

Not knowing how much time he had before the satyrs ended their contest, he decided to manifest a sending. He started to imagine the baron's face then changed his mind. Instead he pictured Karrell.

Nothing happened.

Arvin's heart thudded in his chest. He could visualize Karrell's face clearly, but he couldn't contact her. Was she dead?

Then he realized what was wrong. He was visualizing her human face. He shifted his mental picture of her, imagining her snake form instead. Instantly, the image solidified.

I'm with Glisena, he told her. *I'm inside her hut. Slip in through the back, where the brambles touch the wall. I'll contact Foesmasher.*

Karrell stared back at him, tongue flickering in and out of her mouth. Arvin couldn't read her expression—it was impossible, with that unblinking stare—but he could hear the concern in her voice as she stared at his forehead. *You are wounded! I am sorry; I fell to a magical slumber. I will come.* Her mouth parted in what might have been a smile. *At once.*

Her image faded from his mind.

Immediately, Arvin concentrated on the baron's face. When it solidified in his mind, Foesmasher was talking to someone, emphasizing his words with a pointing fork; Arvin must have interrupted his midday meal. From the scowl on his face, he was issuing a reprimand, or arguing with Marasa again. He halted abruptly in mid-sentence as he recognized Arvin.

I found Glisena, Arvin told him.

Relief washed across the baron's face. His eyes closed a moment; when he opened them, he blinked rapidly, as if clearing away tears. He whispered something Arvin couldn't hear; probably a prayer of thanksgiving.

Arvin chose his next words carefully. Even with the brooch for Foesmasher to home in on, Arvin needed to pack as much information as possible into the brief message the lapis lazuli would allow. *I'm with her inside a hut. Satyrs armed with bows are outside. And wolves. Bring—*

I'm on my way, the baron said.

Arvin silently cursed. Now that Foesmasher had replied, there was no way for Arvin to interrupt, to tell him to bring meat for the wolves. Foesmasher continued speaking as he yanked on his helmet and drew his sword. *Tell Glisena I'll be there at ...*

"... once," said a low voice from Arvin's immediate left.

Arvin couldn't help but be startled, even though he'd been expecting the baron. He raised a finger to his lips. "Quietly, Lord Foesmasher," he cautioned. "The satyrs are just outside."

The baron immediately fell to his knees beside his daughter. "Glisena," he said in a choked voice. "Father's here. My little dove, I'm so sorry. May Helm forgive me for what I've done."

The thing inside Glisena kicked, bulging her stomach. She screwed her eyes shut and groaned.

"What's wrong?" the baron asked, looking up at Arvin. "Is the child coming?"

"It's . . . not a child," Arvin said. Quickly, he told the baron his suspicions. He expected the baron's face to blanch, but Foesmasher proved to have more mettle than that. "Why would Naneth do such a thing?" he asked in a pained voice.

Arvin didn't answer.

The baron stared at his daughter. "Marasa will tend to it," he said firmly. "Whatever it is."

Arvin nodded, relieved.

Outside, the satyrs had resolved their argument. One of the combatants lay unconscious on the ground; the others stared at him, shaking their heads disdainfully. One, however, was staring suspiciously at the hut, his ears perked forward, listening. He turned to the others and said something to them. Arvin, watching, tightened his grip on his dagger.

Foesmasher must have seen Arvin tense. He sheathed his sword, lifted Glisena into his arms, and stood. He gestured for Arvin to come closer.

Arvin was still staring outside. He'd spotted a movement across the clearing in the brambles, well behind the satyrs: a snake, slithering along the ground.

Karrell was circling around the clearing to reach the hut.

"Wait," Arvin said. "Karrell's coming. I don't want to leave her behind."

"I can teleport no more than three people at a time," the baron whispered back. "Myself, Glisena . . . and one other."

Arvin's jaw clenched. Foesmasher had neglected to tell him this important detail. "Teleport us just outside the brambles, then," Arvin whispered back. "There's a centaur waiting there for us: Tanglemane."

The baron's eyebrows rose at the name.

"He and I can watch over Glisena while you come back for Karrell," Arvin continued.

The baron shook his head. "I am also limited to teleporting no more than three times per day. If I return for you, it will be a day before I can get back to Ormpetarr." He nodded at Glisena. "My daughter needs me."

Arvin's eyes narrowed as he realized what Foesmasher was saying. "You won't be back."

"No."

"Send someone else then," Arvin insisted. "One of your clerics. I know they have teleportation magic; I've seen them use it."

"Only the most powerful of them can teleport without the gauntlets to aid them—and Glisena will need their prayers." He held out his hand. "Come with me—or stay. Choose."

Arvin folded his arms across his chest. There really was no choice. Arvin couldn't just abandon Karrell, or Tanglemane. "I'm staying."

"I'll send help as soon as I can," Foesmasher promised. "In the meantime, Helm be with you." Then he teleported away.

The other satyrs had started walking toward the hut. One of them called out—to Theyron, Arvin presumed—and nocked an arrow when he received no reply. The others did the same, fanning out and training their arrows on the doorway. Arvin, trapped inside a hut with only one exit, tried feverishly to decide what to do. There were too many satyrs for him to charm. And it would only take one arrow to kill him.

What was keeping Karrell?

Arvin moved to the side of the doorway, readying his dagger.

A hairy hand gripped the door flap. It started to open.

A new voice sounded outside the hut: a woman, speaking the satyr tongue. She barked what sounded like an angry question at the satyrs—one they answered with a babble of voices.

Arvin peeked outside. As he saw who the newcomer was, his mouth went dry.

Naneth.

CHAPTER 12

Arvin's heart pounded as he stared out of the satyr hut at Naneth. For the moment, the satyrs were busy talking to her—which was bad. They'd be telling her about the human who claimed to be her assistant. Arvin had to act quickly. Energy awakened at the base of his neck, sending a prickling through his scalp as he manifested a charm. The midwife, however, didn't cock her head; the power seemed to have had no effect on her.

She turned toward the hut and gestured.

The inside of the hut filled with an explosion of color. Arvin was still staring at Naneth and saw the swirling colors only in his peripheral vision, but his eyes were drawn to them like moths to a flame. He turned to watch the rainbows that danced and rippled in the air then took a step closer. It was like standing inside the crisscrossing rays cast by a thousand prisms. "Beautiful," he whispered, reaching up to touch one of the rainbows. It twisted away through the air like a snake, leaving a blur of red-violet-blue in its wake. "So beautiful," he breathed.

Dimly, he was aware of the door flap opening and Naneth stepping inside. She glanced around the hut—at Theyron's body, the empty sheepskin where Glisena had lain, and Arvin—and her lips pressed together in a thin line that made her mouth all but disappear in her heavy jowls. Fear flickered in her eyes. It was clear what she was thinking: she'd lost Glisena, and now would have to face Sibyl's wrath. Whatever punishment Sibyl dreamed up would probably make the suffering Naulg had gone through look trivial.

A distant part of Arvin's mind screamed at him that this was the moment to throw the knife he held loosely at his side, to manifest a different psionic power, to *run*, but the colors held him. His gaze drifted back and forth, watching the rainbows.

Naneth ignored the shifting lights. Above and behind her, Arvin saw a snake peering in through a gap in the rear wall of the hut. It, too, was staring at the beautiful lights, tongue flickering in and out of its mouth as if it hoped to taste them. For some reason, that concerned Arvin, but only briefly. The lights were fascinating, scintillating, and *beautiful*.

More beautiful than any snake.

Naneth reached into a belt pouch at her hip and pulled out an egg painted with a blood-red symbol. She held it out toward Arvin, but he barely glanced at it; the shimmering colors still held his eye. Then she spoke a word in what sounded like Draconic.

The rainbows disappeared.

So did the hut.

Arvin found himself curled in a ball inside something smooth and leathery that pressed against him on every side. Warm, sticky fluid surrounded him, soaking his clothes and hair. With a start, he realized he was breathing it in and out like air; it felt thick and heavy in his lungs. His mind was his own again, but he was unable to move. He couldn't even lift his chin from his chest. Suddenly claustrophobic, he kicked at the wall of his prison. It didn't give. He jabbed it with his knife. The blade bounced off it without making a dent. Trapped—he was trapped in here! It took all of his will to keep himself from panicking.

Karrell was out there somewhere, he told himself, in the hut, with Naneth. She'd do something to rescue him.

Unless she was still staring at rainbows.

A muffled voice came from outside Arvin's prison. "Where is the girl?"

"Naneth!" Arvin exclaimed. "You got my warning. Let me out of here, and I'll tell you what's going on." His voice sounded only slightly muffled, despite the fact that he was exhaling liquid. The cloying taste of raw egg lingered on his tongue.

The egg shook violently. Arvin, dizzy, tried not to throw up.

"Where's the girl?" Naneth repeated.

Arvin tried to manifest the power that would let him listen in on Naneth's thoughts, but though silver sparkles erupted from his third eye, briefly illuminating the liquid that surrounded him, the link could not be forged. Whatever magic had protected Naneth from being charmed was also preventing Arvin from reading her mind.

Arvin groaned. He'd have to rely on his wits alone to convince Naneth to let him out of this prison. He thought frantically, trying to come up with a story that would sound plausible. Should he drop Sibyl's name and claim to be working for one of the factions allied with her? Claim to be one of Talos's worshipers? Neither was likely to work. He had only the vaguest of ideas of what Sibyl was up to; he'd probably say something that would give him away.

Suddenly, he realized there was one story that would make sense—and that would throw Naneth off track, way off track.

"You're too late," he told Naneth. "Chondath has claimed Glisena."

"You're one of Lord Wianar's men?" Naneth asked.

Arvin smiled. She'd taken his hook. Now to set it.

"I'm Wianar's eyes and ears within the Sespech court. Three days ago, Baron Foesmasher captured a satyr who had come to Ormpetarr to fetch you; the satyr told him his daughter was in the Chondalwood. It wasn't in Chondath's best interests that Glisena be found, so I sent you the warning. Just in case you didn't heed it, I made my way here. I was surprised to find the girl had not been moved. I was ordered to take advantage of that oversight."

"Where is Glisena now?" Naneth asked. "In Arrabar?"

"All you need to know is that Wianar has her."

For several moments, Naneth was silent. Then she replied—in a strained voice that instantly told Arvin how desperate she was, and how willing to bargain. "Tell your master that keeping the girl would be a terrible mistake. One that could prove fatal for him."

"What do you mean?" Arvin asked.

There was a long pause. When Naneth at last spoke, her voice sounded reluctant. "The child in Glisena's womb is ... dangerous," she began.

"Go on," Arvin prompted. He held his breath, praying that Naneth would expound upon what she'd done to the baron's daughter—that she'd reveal the nature of the *thing* she'd put in Glisena's womb. "What is it?"

"A demon."

"A demon?" Arvin gasped, horrified. "How—"

"Magic," Naneth said smugly. "A unique form of binding no other sorcerer can perform."

"But why?" Arvin asked, still struggling with his horror at what Naneth had done. He felt queasy, as though he were going to be sick.

A gloating smile crept into Naneth's voice. "Lady Dediana is anxious to see the birth of her first grandchild," she said. "What a surprise it will be when she sees the new heir. The shock alone will kill her—and if it doesn't, the 'child' will. *Now* do you understand why it's in Chondath's best interests not to keep the girl? Wianar has much more to gain by letting us place someone more . . . agreeable on Hlondeth's throne. Someone who would turn her back on Sespech, and instead form an alliance with Chondath."

Arvin's eyebrows rose. At last he understood what Sibyl had planned. The thing inside Glisena was part of an elaborate assassination attempt against Lady Dediana. Sibyl, once again, was making a bid for the throne—and this time, she was going to claim it herself, instead of merely installing a puppet. Naneth must have been in Hlondeth, these past three days, setting the whole thing up.

"Glisena will give birth soon," Naneth continued. "When she does, she'll need a midwife. One who knows how to deal with what's inside her. Lord Wianar's best interests lie in turning the girl over to me."

"Who do *you* serve?" Arvin asked, knowing full well what the answer would be.

"Sseth's avatar," Naneth answered. "In this incarnation, he is known as Sibyl."

"Where is this Sibyl?" Arvin asked, hoping that Karrell was listening. "In Hlondeth?"

"Why?" Naneth asked—suspiciously enough that Arvin's guess might have been on the mark.

"Lord Wianar will insist on dealing with her personally."

"That won't be necessary. Deliver the girl to me, and I'll convey her to Sibyl."

"Why should Lord Wianar trust you?" Arvin asked.

"The hiding place you chose was compromised; be thankful that I found it before Foesmasher did. No, I think he will want to deal with Sibyl, in person."

There was a long pause. "What is it Wianar *wants*?" Naneth asked.

"What do you mean?" Arvin asked.

The egg shook, making Arvin dizzy. "Don't play with me," Naneth spat. "Wianar wants something from Sibyl, in return for the girl. But he doesn't realize the consequences of the delay he's causing—or of angering Sibyl. Only a fool would dare to blackmail a god. And you are a greater fool, to serve him."

"I may be a fool, but I know where Glisena is, and you don't," Arvin countered. "And unless you want to face the wrath of your god, you'll have to do something other than threaten me. What can *you* offer, in return for Glisena?"

"I'm not so foolish as you think," the midwife growled. "I held a playing piece back from Sibyl—one that will prove valuable, if Dediana survives. I'm willing to offer it in trade for the baron's daughter. But I'm obviously wasting my time with you. I'll talk to Lord Wianar myself."

Arvin's breath caught. Would she kill him now? Then he realized that Naneth was bluffing—trying to make Arvin sweat a little. As if being trapped in an egg wasn't doing that readily enough.

"Lord Wianar knows better than to trust you," he countered. "But he trusts me." He paused. "What can you offer *me,* if I help you?"

"Your life," Naneth said, relief evident in her voice, "and the gratitude of a god."

"That's a good start," Arvin agreed. He rapped on the inside of the egg with the hilt of his dagger. "But

I'm not going to negotiate from inside an egg. Let me out of here, and we'll talk."

Arvin was jostled back and forth, and a seam of light shone in through a rip in the egg. He saw Naneth's pudgy fingers—impossibly large—tear the egg, widening the rip, and felt the liquid drain away. Suddenly he was breathing air once more. The egg parted into two halves, and he fell. The floor of the hut rushed up to meet him. . . .

Before it struck him, he returned to his full size. His feet hit the floor with a thud. He staggered then regained his balance. As he looked up, he saw that the rainbows were gone—and that Karrell was hanging from the ceiling, just behind Naneth. She was swaying back and forth, hissing softly. No, not hissing, whispering the words of her charm spell.

A spell that, Arvin knew, would have no effect whatsoever on Naneth.

Reacting to the hissing, Naneth whirled to face Karrell.

"Naneth," Karrell hissed. "I have an urgent message for Sibyl from the *ssthaar* of the Se'sehen. Where is she?"

Naneth's eyes narrowed. One hand was behind her back; with it, she began a complicated gesture that could only have been the start of a spell. Karrell, under the impression that Naneth had been charmed, didn't seem to have noticed. She just hung there, swaying, about to take the brunt of whatever spell Naneth was going to cast.

The time for bluffing was over.

Arvin leaped forward, seizing the midwife's hand and clamping a hand over her mouth, but Naneth twisted her head aside and spat out a one-word incantation. Electricity shot into Arvin's hands and surged through his body, throwing him backward. He landed heavily on the floor, heart rattling in his chest, gasping for breath.

Naneth turned away, ignoring him. "Tell me your message. I'll convey it."

Karrell's head swayed back and forth. "My message is for Sibyl's ears alone. Where is she?"

Arvin, listening, knew that Karrell's attempt to pry information from Naneth was doomed. Under the compulsion of a charm spell, the midwife might have overlooked the extremely coincidental arrival of a messenger from Tashalar, asking exactly the same question "Lord Wianar's spy" had just asked. Without the charm, everything Karrell said was an obvious lie. Naneth was toying with Karrell, buying time to cast a spell. Once again, her hand was behind her back, her fingers working.

Forcing himself up off the floor, Arvin threw his dagger. It spun through the air, striking Naneth in the back. But instead of penetrating, the weapon fell harmlessly to the floor, deflected by magic. The midwife spun and leveled a pointing finger at Arvin.

Karrell hissed sharply, glanced between Naneth and Arvin, and sank her teeth into Naneth's shoulder.

Naneth's eyes widened. She jerked away, clamping a hand to her injured shoulder. Barking out a two-word incantation, she vanished.

Arvin clambered to his feet.

Karrell dropped from the ceiling, shifted into human form, and rose gracefully to her feet. Despite the urgency of the moment, the sight of her, naked, took Arvin's breath away. Her words, however, were harsh. "Why did you do that? In another moment she would have told me where Sibyl was."

"No she wouldn't; your charm spell didn't work," Arvin said, rising to his feet. "Naneth is shielded against spells that affect the mind. She knew you were lying and was about to cast a spell on you. I was afraid you'd be killed."

Karrell's eyes softened. "I thought the same...about you."

"I know," Arvin said, touching her cheek. He let his hand fall. "I'm sure whatever spell Naneth was about to cast wouldn't have been very pleasant. But at least we won't have to worry about her anymore. Yuan-ti venom is . . . pretty potent stuff, right?"

"My bite is not venomous."

"Oh," Arvin said. He frowned. "We'd better get out of here, then. As soon as Naneth figures out she hasn't been poisoned, she'll be back. And she won't be happy— with either one of us." He peered outside the door. The satyrs had obeyed Naneth's instructions and were waiting outside, but they looked agitated. They were talking in low voices, and pointing toward the hut.

Arvin beckoned Karrell to the doorway. "Do you have all of a yuan-ti's usual magical abilities?" he whispered.

She nodded.

"We need to get out of here," Arvin continued. He pointed at his pack, which lay on the ground near the satyrs. "If you cast a magical darkness just outside the hut, I should be able to grab my pack. I'll make for the nearest tunnel and keep going. In the meantime, use your magical fear on the satyrs; I hope I'll be out of the maze before they've gathered enough courage to follow me. As soon as you've done that, assume snake form and get out yourself. We'll meet back where we left Tanglemane and figure out some other way of finding Sibyl. Agreed?"

"Agreed." She planted a kiss on his lips. "For luck."

"Thanks," he said, smiling. His lips tingled where she'd kissed them. Dagger in hand, he readied himself, calculating the number of paces it would take to reach his pack. "Do it."

As utter darkness filled the clearing outside the hut, Arvin flung the door flap aside. He sprinted for his pack, keeping low. From his left, he heard the thrum of a bow, followed by the hiss of an arrow over his head.

The satyrs shouted at each other in confusion. Then Karrell loosed her second wave of magic, and the shouts turned to bleats of fear. Arvin scooped up his pack on the run, slinging it over a shoulder by one strap and praying that its contents weren't spilling out behind him. Then he reached the edge of the darkness. He burst into daylight a dozen paces or so from the edge of the brambles. The tunnel the satyrs had dragged him out of was to his left. He raced for it then flung himself prone and started to crawl. Behind him, he heard shouts and the *thrum-thrum* of a bow being shot twice in rapid succession; at least one of the satyrs had shaken off the magical fear. His shots, though aimed at random from inside the darkness, passed uncomfortably close to Arvin. One struck a vine just above his head.

Crawling rapidly, pack still slung awkwardly over one shoulder, Arvin followed the drag marks. They led to the spot where he'd been ambushed by the satyr with the pan pipes; from this point on he followed his own trail. All the while he prayed that the satyrs wouldn't figure out where he'd gone—that they wouldn't know a quicker route through the bramble maze. The fear seemed to have worn off; Arvin could hear them in the clearing, shouting at one another.

Tymora must have been with him, however; the satyrs didn't catch up. Soon he could see Tanglemane through the thicket of thorny vines. The centaur's ears were twitching; when he spotted Arvin, he gave a snort of delight. Arvin crawled out of the brambles, leaped to his feet, and was relieved to see Karrell slither out after him a moment later. As she shifted into human form, he turned to Tanglemane. "We need to get out of here fast," he told the centaur. "We've got a hornet's nest of angry satyrs behind us. Will you carry us?"

"I would," Tanglemane said. Then he glanced into the forest nervously. "But there's a problem. The wolves are still waiting for their meat."

Arvin turned and saw the wolves. They had been sitting, waiting, but when White Muzzle rose to her feet, the rest followed her lead. Tongues lolling, they stared at Arvin and Karrell. White Muzzle growled—and even without Karrell to translate, Arvin understood. The wolves were hungry.

And the satyrs' shouts were growing closer. They would be through the brambles at any moment.

Arvin glanced at Karrell. "Magical fear?" he asked.

She shook her head. "Not again. Not so soon."

An arrow careened out of the brambles behind them, narrowly missing Arvin. "What about darkness?" he asked Karrell.

"Not yet. But I have other magic that may help." Turning, she gestured at the brambles. As her fingers wove complicated patterns in the air, the vines constricted, closing off the tunnel like a net being pulled shut. The satyrs, trapped inside and pierced by thorns, bleated angrily.

Karrell cast a second spell, and their bows twisted into knots. No more arrows were fired.

"That's one problem down," Arvin said. The wolves, however, continued to pad closer to Arvin, Karrell, and Tanglemane. They were working up their courage with a series of low growls. Any moment now, they would rush forward and attack.

Arvin eyed the trees. He and Karrell could climb to safety, but not Tanglemane.

The centaur's ears twitched wildly. "We should run."

"No," Arvin said. "That's what they want." He glanced once more at the vine-trussed satyrs then turned to Karrell. "Speak to the wolves. Tell them we've brought their meat: the satyrs. The moment your spell wears off, the wolves can rush them. Then they'll have all the meat they like."

Karrell nodded then rapidly barked this out to White Muzzle. The wolf growled something at her pack then yipped a question back at Karrell, who answered it.

"I told her I broke the satyrs' bows, but she is still fearful," Karrell translated. "The satyrs are fierce fighters, even without weapons."

Arvin chuckled in reply. "Not when they're asleep." He spoke his glove's command word, and the pan pipes he'd vanished into it reappeared. "Plug your ears," he instructed. Tanglemane and Karrell did as instructed. Arvin, praying the pipes wouldn't affect the person playing them, lifted them to his lips and blew.

A shrill noise squealed from the pipes, but nothing happened. Neither the satyrs nor the wolves fell asleep. The nearest satyr, however, did twist around in the brambles, earning himself several scratches, to say something to his fellows. His voice sounded worried.

Arvin lowered the pipes. Only a satyr could evoke their magic, it seemed. But if that was the case, why did the satyrs sound concerned? He glanced closely at the pipes, noting for the first time that they were made from individual reeds, bound together with twine in a series of intricate knots.

Magical knots?

Grinning, Arvin slid the point of his dagger under one of the knots. He held the pan pipes out where the satyrs could see them. "Do as I say!" he shouted. "Or I'll destroy them."

A babble of voices broke out as the satyrs conversed in their own tongue. Then one of them shouted. "What want you?"

White Muzzle had begun to slink forward again, the rest of the pack following.

Arvin spoke quickly to Karrell. "Can you loosen just a few of the brambles?" he asked. "Enough to let one of the satyrs go?"

She nodded.

"Translate what I say for the wolves," Arvin told her. Then he turned his attention back to the satyrs. "We're going to release one of you," he shouted. "That one will go back to the clearing and fetch Theyron's body, and bring it to me."

Karrell translated, and White Muzzle gave a satisfied growl. The satyrs, however, seemed reluctant. Arvin held the pan pipes a little higher, and started to saw with his blade.

"Stop!" one cried. "We shall bring him."

Arvin smiled. He tipped his head in the direction of the satyr who had spoken. "That one," he told Karrell in a low voice. Loosen the brambles around him."

As the vines untwined themselves from him, the satyr leaped to his feet. He gave Arvin a fierce glare, then trotted back in the direction of the satyr camp. While he was gone, the brambles around the other satyrs began to loosen. Karrell recast her spell.

The satyr returned a short while later, dragging Theyron's body. He paused just before leaving the brambles, catching his breath, then readjusted his grip on the body and continued dragging it toward Arvin. The wound in the dead satyr's neck was still leaking blood; it left a trail of red. The wolves moved forward, licking their lips in anticipation. Then, at a yip from White Muzzle, they moved forward in a rush. The satyr bleated and scurried back into the brambles. The wolves converged on the corpse, growling at one another as they tore bloody chunks from it.

"Let's get moving," Arvin said in a low voice, eyeing the wolves. "Before they finish eating and decide they're still hungry."

Tanglemane nodded and knelt, motioning for Arvin and Karrell to get on his back. Arvin started to climb on then heard the creak of a bow being drawn. He turned his head just in time to see one of the satyrs—the one who had dragged Theyron's body back—standing inside the brambles with a bow held at full draw. Arvin ducked as the satyr let his arrow fly.

The satyr wasn't aiming at Arvin however, but at the wolves. One of them yelped as the arrow struck it.

"Let's go," Arvin shouted, boosting Karrell onto Tanglemane's back.

Tanglemane, however, crumpled to his knees, spilling her to the ground. The centaur staggered to his feet a moment later, clutching his chest. A thin line of blood trickled out from beneath his hands.

"Tanglemane," Karrell said, alarmed. "What's wrong?"

Even as she asked the question, Arvin realized the answer. The arrow had struck White Muzzle, and the fate link had caused Tanglemane to suffer an identical wound.

The satyr shot another arrow. This one struck another wolf in the head, instantly killing it.

The pack bolted, White Muzzle in the rear, limping.

Arvin silently cursed his stupidity; he should have guessed that the satyr would pick up another bow when he returned to the camp.

The satyr nocked another arrow. This time, he turned toward Arvin as he drew his bow.

"Wait!" Arvin shouted. "If you shoot me, you'll never get these back." He flourished the pan pipes then vanished them into his glove.

"The pipes are inside my glove," he told the satyr, splaying his fingers wide to show that they had truly vanished. "And I'm the only one who can work the glove's magic. Kill me, and you'll lose the pipes forever." He paused to let that sink in then added, "Let us leave the forest, and I'll give the pipes back to you. They're useless to me—I have no interest in keeping them. I'll leave them at the forest's edge for you. Do we have an agreement?"

The satyr lowered his bow a fraction and turned to speak to his fellows. Low murmuring followed. As the satyrs conferred, Arvin glanced at Tanglemane. The centaur's face was pale; his legs trembled. Only a trickle of blood seeped from the wound; the arrow must have still been buried in White Muzzle's flesh. Given her limited, animal intelligence, she would probably flee from the pain until she dropped, until she died.

"Agreed!" the satyr shouted back. "You may leave."

Cautiously, Arvin and Karrell backed away from the brambles, leading the injured Tanglemane. The satyr held his fire.

Tanglemane was able to walk, but he gasped with each breath.

Arvin touched the crystal at his throat. "Nine lives," he pleaded.

Tanglemane was going to need them. Even if the satyrs kept their end of the bargain, the centaur was unlikely to make it out of the woods.

CHAPTER 13

Arvin squatted beside Tanglemane, gently repositioning the blood-soaked bandage he'd made earlier from pieces torn from his shirt. The centaur had proved stronger than Arvin expected; he'd walked for some distance through the forest before crumpling to his knees. Karrell had cast a healing spell on him just after they'd left the satyr camp, but it had only helped a little bit. The wound in the side of his chest was still open, still seeping blood. It was a hollow hole that, on White Muzzle, would have been filled with an arrow shaft. It was a wonder the wolf had survived this long, with an arrow still in her. Every now and then the flesh around the puckered hole quivered; Arvin realized that White Muzzle must have been licking her wound, jostling the arrow around.

He hoped that meant she had found somewhere safe to hole up—somewhere predators wouldn't find her.

"Hang on, Tanglemane," Arvin urged, one hand on the centaur's shoulder. "It's almost sunset. The fate link will end soon." For the hundredth time, he wished he could dispel the power, but once manifested, a fate link endured for its full duration.

The centaur's breathing was labored now. He sat with head bowed and eyes screwed shut, as if trying to block out the pain. Had he been human, Arvin and Karrell might have carried him, but the centaur must have weighed three times their combined weight.

Karrell beckoned Arvin to her and nodded at the darkening forest. "The satyrs are still following us."

"It's not the satyrs I'm worried about," Arvin said. "I keep wondering where Naneth is—why she hasn't teleported back to squeeze more information out of me."

"She would have to find us first."

Arvin jerked a thumb in the direction of the dark shapes flitting through the forest. "Easily done. She just has to ask them where we are."

"Perhaps," Karrell said in a low voice, "that is what she is doing. She must hope we will lead her to Glisena."

Arvin nodded. It made sense for Naneth to allow them to think they had escaped. While the satyrs kept an eye on them, she could check up on the story Arvin had told her. But for all Naneth knew, Arvin might have teleportation magic—magic he'd used to spirit Glisena away. She was taking a big risk—for all she knew, Arvin might just vanish from the forest.

He paused to rub his forehead; his wound was itching again. The lapis lazuli was still in place; he'd used it just after they left the satyr camp to let Tanju know that Glisena had been found, that there was a demon inside her—and that Sibyl's plans had been thwarted. Tanju had commended Arvin for a job well done. After speaking to his mentor, Arvin had left the lapis lazuli where it was; removing it would have meant tearing open the scab that had already formed over it. Now he wondered if that had been wise. On two other occasions during their flight through the forest he'd felt a peculiar sensation behind the stone, deep in his "third eye"—a soft fluttering, like an eyelid rapidly blinking. He felt it again now. It was almost as if his third eye were trying to focus on something it couldn't quite see.

Along with it came an uncomfortable sensation of being watched. Arvin had assumed this was because the satyrs were following them, but now he began to wonder if there was something more to it. Was someone trying to manifest a sending?

No, that wasn't quite right. A sending created, in the recipient's mind, a mental image of the person dispatching the image. A failed sending produced no sensation at all. It simply . . . failed. This was somewhere between the two. It was almost as if someone had manifested the link that made a sending possible . . . without conveying any message.

Suddenly, Arvin realized the cause: Naneth was using her crystal ball to spy on them.

A chill ran through him as he wondered what he'd already given away. Had he said anything that would indicate the baron had teleported Glisena back to Ormpetarr while Naneth had been scrying on them? He hoped not.

Karrell was staring at Arvin, her brow creased. "What's wrong?" she asked.

"The satyrs," Arvin told her in a low voice—one just loud enough for Naneth to also hear. "They're listening. Say nothing, or Wianar will have our heads. And keep up the pretense in front of the centaur. Pretend that we're headed for Ormpetarr; if the satyr lives, he'll help throw Foesmasher off the scent."

Karrell's frown deepened, and for a moment Arvin worried that she was going to blurt out something that would give the game away. Then she nodded—though there was still a hint of confusion in her eyes.

A moment later, Arvin felt the fluttering in his forehead fade away. He waited, making certain it was gone, then whispered urgently to Karrell. "Naneth was just scrying on us. I can sense when she's doing it. If it happens again, I'll signal you. If I do this"—he formed a V with the first two fingers of his right hand and touched his shoulder: the sign, in silent speech, that someone was spying—"it means Naneth is listening. Be careful what you say."

"I will."

Behind them, Tanglemane gave a loud groan and tried to rise to his feet. Arvin and Karrell hurried to his side.

"What's wrong?" Arvin asked.

Tanglemane's nostrils flared. "Giant," he gasped. "Coming this way."

Arvin's jaw clenched. That was all they needed—another hostile creature to contend with. No wonder humans avoided these woods. Already he could feel the ground trembling and hear the snap of branches.

He caught Karrell's eye. "Shift form," he urged her. "Hide."

Her dark eyes bored into his. "And you?" she asked. She gestured at Tanglemane. "And him?"

Arvin drew his dagger. "Tanglemane doesn't have that option—and I can't just leave him. Fortunately, a little of my psionic energy remains." He grinned. "Perhaps the giant will find me . . . charming."

"Be careful," Karrell urged. She shifted into snake form and slithered under a bush.

Arvin, meanwhile, laid a hand on Tanglemane's shoulder, steadying him, and turned toward the direction the crashing sounds were coming from.

A moment later he spotted the giant lumbering through the woods. The giant was more than twice the height of a man and had skin as gray and pitted as stone. His head was nearly level with the tops of the trees, which he parted with massive hands as he shouldered his way through the forest. He wore a tunic that had been crudely stitched together from the skins of a dozen different animals, and a wide belt into which was tucked an enormous stone club. His bare feet crushed bushes and snapped deadfall branches with each step.

Arvin watched nervously. That club looked heavy enough to crush him with a single blow.

The giant spotted Arvin and Tanglemane and came to an abrupt halt.

"Hello!" Arvin called, waving up at him. Swiftly, he manifested a charm. "It's good to see you, friend."

The giant cocked his head. "Baron Foesmasher told you I was coming?" he asked.

Arvin's eyebrows rose. "The baron sent you?"

The giant shrugged. "One of his clerics sent word to find you. She said you might be having trouble with the satyrs, and by the smell of it, she was right." He glanced down at Tanglemane then rested massive fists on his hips. "What can I do to help?"

Karrell reassumed human form and rose to her feet, clothing in hand. She gestured at Tanglemane. "Can you carry him?" she asked. "Gently?"

The giant grinned, revealing teeth that glinted like quartz. "I can, snake-lady." He dropped to his knees, and the earth trembled. Slipping broad hands under Tanglemane, he lifted the centaur as easily—and gently—as a man lifting a kitten. "Where to?"

"Fort Arran," Tanglemane gasped. "There are healers there."

Arvin stared at the centaur and whispered a prayer that Tanglemane would be able to hold on that long.

❧ ❧ ❧ ❧ ❧

The fate link wore off just after darkness fell, as they were leaving the woods. Tanglemane gasped as his chest suddenly started to bleed again, and the giant lowered him to the ground. Arvin stripped off what remained of his shirt and tore it into pieces, tying a fresh bandage against the wound to staunch the bleeding and Karrell cast a healing spell that partially closed the wound. Then the giant picked the centaur up once more.

Before following, Arvin summoned the pan pipes into his gloved hand. The satyrs had kept their side of the bargain by not attacking—though the giant's presence probably had a lot to do with that decision—and now Arvin would keep his. He set the pipes down on a rock, where they would be easy to spot.

They walked toward the bridge that spanned the river, Arvin and Karrell leading, followed by the giant. Arvin kept looking nervously around, hoping the centaur herd wouldn't return. He didn't want to face the centaur-seed a second time. Even in proxy, Zelia was formidable.

Karrell took his hand and gave it a squeeze. "Stop worrying," she said. "We are nearly there."

They walked on, holding hands. The air had turned colder as night fell; here and there puddles of water had developed a thin skin of ice that crunched underfoot. Moonlight glinted off the broken shards, making them sparkle like a scattering of diamonds. "I had heard about ice before I came north," Karrell said. "But I never knew it could be so beautiful."

Arvin nodded. He snuck a glance at Karrell, remembering the serpent form that lay beneath her human skin, then fixed his eyes on the far shore. In the distance he could see a wagon setting out from Fort Arran. It was moving across the bridge; the two horses drawing it were running at a good clip. The giant cradled

Tanglemane in the crook of one arm and waved at it. Figures in the wagon waved back.

"What will you do, once we reach the fort?" Karrell asked.

Arvin touched his forehead. "Contact the baron, as soon as I'm able. Find out how Glisena is doing. Hopefully, the clerics have been able to ... purge ... what's inside her."

Karrell gave him a startled look. "They will kill her child?"

"It's no child," Arvin said. There hadn't been time, until now, to tell Karrell everything he'd learned. When he did, her face paled.

"Helm's clerics will deal with the demon," Arvin reassured her. "Lord Foesmasher seemed confident that they could. And once they have, we won't have to worry about Naneth looking over our shoulders anymore. In fact, we can turn her scrying to our advantage. If we let it 'slip' that Glisena's womb is empty, Naneth will realize her scheme has failed. Glisena will be safe from her."

And, Arvin added silently, he would be able to collect his reward. The baron would no doubt be pleased with his work; Arvin had done everything he'd promised, and more. Not only had he located Glisena, he'd provided vital information that would help the clerics save her. The baron's emotions ran high when it came to his daughter. No doubt he would be as generous with those who had saved her as he was merciless against those who threatened her.

He realized that Karrell hadn't answered. She walked in silence, one arm wrapped protectively across her stomach. Arvin supposed it only natural; what had been done to Glisena would hit a woman harder.

"I too have been thinking about what we might say the next time Naneth scries on us," Karrell said at last. "I think it would be a mistake to reveal that Glisena is no longer pregnant. If we choose our words carefully—make her think that Glisena is in a location of our choosing—we can lure Naneth to us."

"Are you sure that's wise?" he asked. Naneth was a powerful sorcerer—he wasn't keen on facing her spells a second time.

"I must find Sibyl and recover the Circled Serpent," Karrell said. "Naneth is the one thread that will lead me through the maze. I must follow it." She leveled a challenging look at Arvin. "If, however, you no longer wish to help me. . . ."

Arvin stared at the approaching wagon, wishing he could just board it, return to Ormpetarr, and collect his reward. Then he thought of what Sibyl's minions had done to Naulg and to Glisena's unborn child. He met Karrell's eye. "You kept your end of the bargain," he told her. "I'll keep mine. Whatever I can do to thwart Sibyl, I will."

Karrell gave him a long look. "If we find that Sibyl is in Hlondeth, will you return there with me?"

"Hlondeth isn't a healthy place for me to be," Arvin said. He clenched his left hand, remembering. By now, the Guild would be wondering where he'd gone . . . and asking questions—questions that might lead them to a realization that he'd been feeding Tanju information on their activities over the past six months. Arvin had been forced to trade his mentor *something,* in return for the lessons in psionics. If the Guild found that out, they'd cut out Arvin's tongue. "I have enemies there."

"You have enemies here," Karrell said softly. "Zelia."

"True," Arvin agreed. Then he smiled. "And Zelia, according to the baron, is in Ormpetarr—which makes my decision easier."

He expected Karrell to smile at his faint attempt at humor, or to ask what his decision was, but her face had a distant look, as if she were lost in thought.

"The centaur Windswift," she said abruptly. "You addressed him as Zelia. Was he one of her seeds?"

Arvin's jaw clenched. "He was. Zelia must have created him to spy on Chondath."

"Zelia is an agent of Hlondeth?" Karrell asked.

Arvin nodded.

"She serves House Extaminos?"

"Yes," Arvin answered. "Why?"

Karrell countered with a question of her own. "Why did she try to seed you?"

Arvin gave a bitter laugh. "You'll appreciate the irony, I'm sure. Zelia hoped to use me to infiltrate The Pox—the clerics who were allied with Sibyl during her first attempt at Hlondeth's throne. Zelia needed a human who had...." His voice faltered as he remembered the terrible transformation Naulg had undergone—and the final kindness Arvin had been forced to pay him. "Who'd had the misfortune of falling into their hands. They wouldn't have accepted anyone else into their ranks."

Arvin was thankful that Karrell didn't ask him to elaborate.

"What other psionic powers does Zelia have?" she asked.

Arvin gave her a sharp look. "Don't even think about it," he snapped. "Zelia's dangerous. And untrustworthy. She's as slippery as a—" He realized what he was saying, and stopped himself just in time.

Karrell's eyes narrowed. She yanked her hand out of his. "As what? A serpent?"

Arvin's face flushed. That was exactly what he'd been about to say.

The giant, seeing that they had stopped walking, halted. "Is something wrong?" he rumbled. Tanglemane lifted his head slightly; his face looked pale.

"It's nothing," Arvin said. He pointed at the wagon, only a few hundred paces from them now. Behind the driver sat two soldiers and a third man, identifiable as a cleric of Helm by his eye-emblazoned breastplate and deep red cloak. "Get Tanglemane to the wagon. We'll follow in a moment."

The giant shrugged then continued with heavy footsteps toward the wagon. It pulled to a halt as he drew near it, and the cleric hopped out. The giant lowered Tanglemane to the ground. The cleric crouched beside him and started removing the centaur's crude wound binding.

Arvin turned back to Karrell. "Zelia's dangerous," he repeated. "Perhaps as dangerous as Sibyl herself."

"And she is Sibyl's enemy. And she has mind magic beyond what you possess. Magic that may force Naneth to tell us where Sibyl is."

"True," Arvin agreed, bristling. "But she's the last person I'd ever ask for help from. As soon as she found out I'm alive, she'd kill me. Quick as spit. It's bad enough that Windswift knows what I look like. The next time he reports to Zelia. . . ." He shook his head, amazed at the complicated net he'd managed to weave around himself, hoping he could keep it from drawing any tighter.

"I was not suggesting that *you* speak with Zelia," Karrell said. She raised her right hand and nodded at the ring on her finger. "And she will not learn that you are alive. Not from me."

Arvin shook a finger at her. "Don't do it. Gods only know what Zelia will do to you. She's dangerous," he repeated again, grasping at straws. "She's—"

"A yuan-ti," Karrell said. "As am I." She glared at him. "And do not presume to give me orders. I am not human, and you are not my. . . ." She paused, searching for the word. "Not my husband. Even if you did quicken my eggs." Tossing her hair angrily, she turned her back.

Arvin's mouth gaped open. "Your *what?*"

She touched her stomach. "My eggs," she repeated softly.

Arvin stared at Karrell. "You're pregnant?" he asked in a strained whisper. "But it's only been"—he did a quick tally in his head—"two days—no, three—since we first...." He shook his head. "How could you possibly know so soon?"

"My scales," she said. "They are shedding out of season—it is one of the early signs." She touched a hand to her belly. "And the way I ... feel. I *know*."

Arvin was stunned. He didn't know what to say. What to think. If Karrell was right, he was a father. Or soon would be. The thought terrified him; he knew nothing about children. "How long until...." He swallowed hard, and rubbed his forehead. His wound was bothering him again.

Beside Arvin, someone cleared his throat hesitantly—the cleric. He had completed his healing; Tanglemane was back on his feet, his color restored. The cleric had walked over to where Arvin stood without Arvin even noticing.

"Are you Arvin?" he asked.

Arvin nodded. Eggs, Karrell had said. Plural. How *many* eggs?

"I'm to convey you to Ormpetarr at once," the cleric continued. "The baron needs your mind magic. There's someone at the palace who's ... not well. Will you come? You must be willing, in order for me to teleport you."

"I don't have any healing powers," Arvin protested. Absently, he rubbed at his forehead. The itching was getting worse.

"The baron needs you to ... listen to some thoughts," the cleric said.

"Whose?" Arvin asked absently. He stared at Karrell, realizing he hardly knew her. Yet she bore his child. His *children*.

"A ... demon's," the cleric whispered, shooting a worried glance at Karrell.

Arvin rubbed his itching forehead. No, not itching. Tickling. The flutter was back—had been back, for some time.

Naneth was listening.

"It is all right," Karrell assured the cleric. "I know all about Glis—"

Arvin sprang forward and clapped a hand across her mouth. With his free hand he signaled frantically, jerking two V-splayed fingers over his shoulder.

Karrell's eyes widened.

Pretending that he was worried about the cleric overhearing, Arvin whispered fiercely at Karrell in a voice he hoped was loud enough for Naneth to hear. "The cleric isn't one of us. Don't say anything that will give the game away. Don't mention Lord Wianar. Or the fact that it's not . . . not really Glisena that Foesmasher has, but a . . . an illusion. If they find out Glisena is really in . . . in Arrabar, they might find her."

The tickling in his forehead faded. Arvin stared at Karrell, stricken by the knowledge that they had probably just given the game away, despite his feeble attempt to lay a false trail. He let his hand fall away from Karrell's mouth.

Her eyes asked a silent question.

"Too late," he croaked. "She heard all of it."

Karrell's mouth tightened.

As the cleric looked back and forth between Arvin and Karrell, obviously confused. "Are you willing to come?" he asked. "Can I teleport you?"

"Teleport both of us," Karrell said. "To wherever Glisena is. As quickly as you can."

She held out a hand for Arvin. He took it.

"Let's hope Naneth doesn't beat us there," he said.

Karrell nodded grimly. "Yes."

❂ ❂ ❂ ❂ ❂

When they arrived at the palace, the baron was waiting. His face was haggard as he strode across the reception hall to meet them. His hair was uncombed, and the odor of nervous sweat clung to him. There were dark circles under his eyes.

"You're here," he said, clasping Arvin's hand as the cleric who had teleported them there hurried away. "Helm be praised."

"Be careful what you say, Lord Foesmasher," Arvin warned. "Naneth has a crystal ball. She's using it to scry on me. I tried to mislead her, but it might not have worked. If she learns ... what's going on ... she may—"

"Don't worry about Naneth," Foesmasher assured Arvin. "Marasa has placed a dimensional lock on Glisena's room. Nobody is going to teleport into it—or out. The room has also been warded against scrying. Come."

Foesmasher shifted his grip to Arvin's elbow and steered him toward a door that was flanked by two soldiers. Karrell started to follow, but the soldiers blocked her way, one of them rudely thrusting a hand against her chest.

Arvin stood his ground as Foesmasher wrenched open the door. "Karrell's a healer," he told the baron. "Her spells—"

"Come from a serpent god," Foesmasher said in a low voice. "My daughter needs *human* healing."

Arvin gave Karrell an apologetic look. She returned it with a shrug, but he could see the bitterness in her eyes. "Go," she said. "I will wait."

The baron led Arvin through another reception hall; up a flight of stairs; and through a room in which several soldiers stood, armed and ready. Foesmasher gestured, and they stepped away from a locked door. Foesmasher placed his palm on the door; a heartbeat later, magical energy crackled around the lock. The door swung open, revealing a chamber in which nine of Helm's clerics stood. They were gathered in a circle, praying in low voices, their gauntleted hands extended toward a bed where Glisena lay. Nine shields, each embossed with Helm's eye, floated in the air behind their backs, forming a circle that turned slowly around them. Marasa sat on a stool next to the bed, holding Glisena's hand. She glanced up, kissed Glisena, and rose to her feet, motioning for the baron to take her hand. He crossed to the bed, a strained smile on his face as he kneeled at his daughter's side. "Little dove," he whispered. "Father is here."

Glisena turned her head away from him.

Marasa's face was grim as she approached Arvin. "Helm be praised," she said. "The giant found you."

Arvin stared at Glisena. She was still pregnant—and looked even worse than before. Despite the ministrations of the clerics, her face had a sickly yellow pallor. She had been bathed—a ceramic tub filled with scented water stood in a corner of the room—and was wearing fresh night robe, but the odor of vomit lingered in the room. She twisted restlessly on the bed, her free hand scrabbling at the blankets, shoving them aside. Her stomach was an ominous bulge.

Arvin swallowed nervously. There was a *demon* in there. He met Marasa's eye. "Does she know?" he asked. "About—"

"We told her," Marasa said. Her expression grew pained. "But I don't know if she believes us. Not after what her father tried to do." She sighed heavily, not looking at Foesmasher.

"The cleric who teleported us here said you wanted me to listen to the demon's thoughts," Arvin prompted. "Are you going to try to banish it?"

"We can't," Marasa said, her voice low. "It is linked to Glisena by the blood cord. If we banish it, Glisena will be drawn into the Abyss with it. We will have to try to kill it, instead."

Arvin, suddenly remembering the vision he'd had in Naneth's home—of a woman, linked by a thread of blood, to her own death—felt his face grow pale. "That might kill her," he whispered. Quickly, he told Marasa of his vision.

Marasa listened quietly, a strained look on her face. Then she gave a helpless shrug. "There is nothing else left to try," she said. She stared at Glisena. "The demon is small, and Helm willing, will succumb to High Watcher Davinu's holy word. It can then be birthed—or removed—in the same way as a stillborn child. But if the demon does not succumb—if it tries to trick us by feigning death—we need to know what it is thinking. Perhaps it will give us some clue that will tell us what *will* harm it."

"I see," Arvin said, not wholly convinced. His eyes remained locked on Glisena's distended belly. It was taut as a drum—one that might tear open at any moment.

"Prepare yourself," Marasa said. "And we will begin."

Arvin took off his cloak and draped it over a chair. Sending his awareness down into his *muladhara,* he was relieved to see that it contained enough energy to manifest the power Marasa had requested. He walked across the room, steeling himself for what he was about to experience. The thought of contacting the demon's mind a second time terrified him, but—he glanced at Glisena's pale face—if it would help, he would do it.

He crossed the room and stood at the foot of Glisena's bed. "I'm ready," he told Marasa.

She nodded at one of the clerics—an older man with pale blue eyes and hair so white and fine that the age spots on his scalp could clearly be seen through it. He seemed hale enough, however; he wore the suit of armor that was the priestly vestment of Helm's clerics with the upright posture and ease of a much younger man.

"Give High Watcher Davinu a signal, Arvin, when you have made contact," Marasa said. "Once you have, he will begin."

Arvin smiled to himself. Using the silent speech, he could have described, moment by moment, exactly what was happening as he manifested his power. But he didn't want anyone to know he was Guild . . . ex-Guild. "I'll raise my hand," he said.

As he prepared to manifest his power, Glisena caught his hand. Startled, Arvin looked down at her. She was straining to speak, her eyes imploring him. Concerned, he moved to the side of the bed and leaned over to hear what she was saying.

"Where did it go?" she whispered.

"Where did what go?" Arvin asked.

Glisena glanced warily at her father then continued to whisper in Arvin's ear. Her breath was fever-hot. "My baby," she said. "Naneth had to take my baby out before she put the demon in. She had to put her *somewhere*. Find my baby for me. Promise you will. Please?"

Arvin blinked. It hadn't occurred to him, until now, to wonder what had happened to the child Glisena had been carrying. He'd assumed it had died or been subsumed when Naneth summoned the demon into Glisena's womb. Either that, or teleported elsewhere— the Abyss, perhaps—and had died a swift death outside the womb.

But what if it had been teleported into *another* womb?

If it had, Glisena's unborn child might still be alive. And Naneth would have an extra playing piece to haggle with.

An extra playing piece she had offered to trade for Glisena earlier, when she thought Arvin was Lord Wianar's man.

Foesmasher leaned forward, stiff with tension. "What is Glisena saying?"

Arvin straightened, shaking his head. "She's delirious," he said, trying to ease his hand out of Glisena's. She clung to it with a grip tight as death. Her eyes begged a silent question of him.

He nodded. "I'll do it," he promised her.

Glisena's hands relaxed.

"Do what?" the baron growled.

Arvin didn't answer.

Glisena sighed and released his hand, closing her eyes. When she opened them again, she nodded at High Watcher Davinu. "I'm ready," she announced in a faint whisper. Then, in a stronger voice, she said, "You may begin."

Arvin smiled. Despite Glisena's faults, she was her father's daughter.

As Davinu prepared to cast his spell, Arvin sent his awareness down into the power points at the middle of his forehead and base of his scalp. Linking them, he manifested his power. Sparkles of silver erupted from his eyes and drifted gently down toward Glisena's stomach; as they settled there, vanishing, the thoughts of those in the room swam into his mind. Marasa was relieved that Arvin was finally here, and praying for Helm's mercy on the innocent Glisena. High Watcher Davinu was concentrating on the spell he was about to cast. He would channel Helm's glorious might into a single word so powerful that it would snuff out even a demon's life. The other clerics were focused on their prayers.

And the demon—dark, malevolent, seething, and gloating. *Soon,* it thought, the words reverberating like the growls of a dragon in its cave. *I will be free soon. The bindings . . . fade.*

Arvin shuddered. He raised his hand and signaled for Davinu to begin.

Davinu raised one gauntleted hand above his head. Praying now—evoking Helm in a low chant as the other clerics whispered their own prayers in the background—he slowly closed his hand into a fist. He caught Marasa's eye—she nodded—and that of the baron. Foesmasher squeezed Glisena's hand. His free hand was clenched in a white-knuckled fist and trembling.

Soon, the demon thought, its voice an evil chuckle.

"Do it," Foesmasher croaked.

Davinu's hand swept down toward Glisena's stomach, creating a sound like that of a sword sweeping through the air. *"Moritas!"* he cried.

Glisena's eyes flew open. She gasped, arching her back.

Foesmasher's eyes squeezed shut; his lips moved rapidly in silent prayer.

Soon, the demon whispered. *I will be—*

Arvin heard a wet thud—a sound like a blade striking flesh. For the space of a heartbeat, everyone in the room was silent, their minds blank with suspense. Even the demon was still. Arvin searched desperately for its mind, hope bubbling through him.

He found only silence. He closed his eyes in relief.

Stupid mortal, the demon suddenly roared. *You thought you could kill me?* Its mind erupted with laughter: a sound like thick, hot, bubbling blood.

Arvin opened his eyes. Davinu, Marasa, and Foesmasher were staring at him expectantly, their faces filled with cautious hope.

"It's . . . not . . . dead," he croaked.

Their faces crumpled into despair.

I hear you, the demon growled into Arvin's mind. *I will remember your voice.* It gave a mental shove . . . and the manifestation ended.

Arvin sagged.

Marasa caught his arm, steadying him. "Did you overhear anything?" she asked. "Anything that might help?"

"The demon is bound," Arvin said. "But the bindings

that hold it are fading. It thinks it will be free. 'Soon' was the word it used."

Marasa looked grim. She stared at Glisena's distended stomach. "Does that mean it will be born?" she asked softly. "Or...."

Foesmasher dropped his daughter's hand and rose to his feet. "Abyss take you!" he gritted at Davinu, his fists balled. "And you," he said, pointing at Marasa. "You assured me the prayer would work."

"I don't understand why it didn't, my lord," Davinu protested, backing away. "Something so small ... yet so powerful? We expected a minor demon—a quasit, given the size—but it appears we were wrong. Naneth seems to have reduced a larger demon—many times over—without diminishing its vital energies in the slightest."

Marasa stood her ground before the baron's verbal onslaught. "Thuragar," she said, her voice dangerously low. "If Helm has forsaken your daughter, you have only yourself to blame."

Foesmasher glared. His hand dropped to the hilt of his sword.

Marasa glared back.

The other clerics glanced warily between baron and cleric, waiting for the storm to break.

When it did, it came as a flood of tears. They spilled down Foesmasher's cheeks as he stared at his daughter. His hand fell away from his sword. He turned away, his shoulders trembling with silent sobs.

Davinu turned to Marasa. "What now?" he asked in a weary voice.

Marasa sighed. She looked ready to collapse herself. One hand touched Glisena's forehead. "We wait," she announced at last, "until it is born. And banish it then."

"The birth will be ... difficult," Davinu said, his voice a mere whisper.

Marasa's eyes glistened with anguish. "Yes."

Arvin shuffled his feet nervously.

Marasa turned to him. "Go," she said in a flat voice. "Rest and meditate—but do not leave the palace. We may have need of your mind magic later."

Arvin nodded. He wanted to wish Marasa and the other clerics luck, but if Helm had forsaken Glisena, so too might Tymora. His heart was heavy—could he do *nothing* to stop Sibyl's foul machinations? Giving Glisena one last sorrowful glance, he left the bed chamber and walked wearily down the corridor, back to the reception hall where he'd left Karrell.

She wasn't there.

Arvin turned to the soldiers. "The woman I came here with," he said. "Where did she go?"

The soldiers exchanged uncomfortable looks.

"What?" Arvin snapped.

"She left a message for you," one of them answered at last. "She said she had to talk to someone, and for you to stay here, at the palace. She'll return when she was done."

Arvin felt his face grow pale. "Did she mention a name?"

The second soldier chuckled. "Looks like he's been stood up," he whispered to his companion.

The first soldier nodded then answered. "It was Zeliar . . . or Zelias. Something like that."

Arvin barely heard him. A chasm seemed to have opened at his feet. Nodding his thanks for the message, he stumbled from the room.

Zelia.

CHAPTER 14

Arvin sat in Karrell's room at the Fairwinds Inn, staring at the cold ashes in the fireplace, exhausted in mind and body. His limbs were heavy with fatigue and his wounds ached; even thinking was as difficult as wading through deep water.

What was Karrell doing, speaking to Zelia? She was putting not only Arvin's life in danger by doing so, but her own life, as well. The two women might share the same goal—finding Sibyl—but Zelia was utterly ruthless in that pursuit. She'd allowed Arvin and Naulg to fall into the hands of The Pox then subjected Arvin to one of the cruelest psionic powers of all in order to achieve her goal. Why would Karrell ever want to ally herself with such a person?

Because, Arvin thought heavily, Karrell was also a yuan-ti. She didn't fear that race, the way a human would.

And because—and with this thought, Arvin sighed heavily—Zelia was a far more powerful psion than he was, far more capable.

Had Karrell decided to abandon him?

The drawing Karrell had done of him was still lying on the table. He picked it up. She'd drawn him as he lay sleeping; in the portrait, his face looked relaxed, at peace, which was hardly how he felt right now.

Everything had gone right, yet everything had gone wrong. He'd done what Tanju had demanded of him—found Foesmasher's daughter—even without using the dorje. But what good had it done? Glisena was about to give birth to a demon; her chances of survival weren't high. And once again, those who had committed this foul crime—Naneth and the abomination Sibyl—would go unpunished.

Thunder grumbled in the coal-dark sky, a distant echo to Arvin's thoughts.

If Glisena did die, Foesmasher would be devastated. The baron didn't think clearly where his daughter was concerned. He was bound to take his frustrations out on those who were "responsible," in however oblique a way, for any harm that came to her. He demonstrated that when he'd lashed out at the soldier after the death of the satyr. Arvin might be the next one on the chopping block—especially if his absence from the palace were discovered. Marasa had instructed him to stay close at hand, and he'd disobeyed her. That alone would be enough to rouse the baron's wrath.

Arvin clenched his gloved hand until his abbreviated little finger ached. It was like serving the Guild, all over again.

He'd been wrong to think he could make a new home for himself in Sespech; wrong in putting his faith in the baron; and most of all, wrong about Karrell.

He stared at the bed in which they'd made love—in which they'd conceived a child—then he looked back at the portrait, still in his hand. He crumpled it and tossed it onto the cold ashes in the fireplace.

He leaned forward and drummed his fingers on the table. If he knew where Zelia was, he might have tried to head Karrell off, to talk some sense into her. But the baron had been too preoccupied—to say the least—for Arvin to ask him where Zelia had been spotted. All Arvin knew was that she was somewhere in Ormpetarr ...

... Which was all Karrell knew about Zelia, as well. And yet the message she'd left with the soldiers sounded as if she knew where Zelia was. How? Karrell was a stranger here; she knew less about Ormpetarr than even Arvin did. She'd have no idea which inn Zelia might have chosen to stay at—

Arvin stiffened. Zelia was an agent of House Extaminos, a trusted employee of Lady Dediana. She wouldn't stay at an inn.

She'd stay at the ambassador's residence.

That was where Karrell went.

His exhaustion suddenly forgotten, Arvin hurried from the room.

❀ ❀ ❀ ❀ ❀

Arvin approached the ambassador's residence warily, his feet squelching on melting snow. If he was right in his guess that Zelia was staying here, he didn't want to run into her in the street. He pulled his hood up and tugged it down over his forehead to hide his wound. The lapis lazuli was still in place over his third eye; if Naneth scried on him again, he wanted to know it. Besides, removing the stone wouldn't accomplish much. Though the cut on his forehead had scabbed over completely, hiding the stone from view, Zelia would quickly realize what had prompted such a wound. Even with several days' worth of stubble shadowing Arvin's face, she'd recognize him.

He stared at the ambassador's residence from the shadow of an arched gate down the street. Several lights were on inside the building, and figures moved busily back and forth, their silhouettes passing across the draped windows. A large cargo wagon was pulled up in front of the main gate. The wagon was already half filled with boxes, rolled-up rugs, and furniture; slaves hurried back and forth from the residence, loading it.

It looked as though Ambassador Extaminos was beating a hasty retreat from Ormpetarr. Had he heard what was happening at the palace?

Four militiamen in cobra-hood helmets stood guard over the wagon. Arvin recognized one of them by his prominent nose. He touched the crystal at his neck, whispering a prayer of thanks to Tymora for sending him good fortune. He still had a little energy left in his *muladhara,* but he didn't want to spend it on a charm unless he had to. Rillis, fortunately, responded to more mundane prods.

Arvin fished two silver pieces out of his coin pouch then walked toward the front gate of the residence, hailing Rillis by name. "I'm looking for Karrell—the woman who was with me when I spoke with Ambassador Extaminos. Have you seen her?"

The young militiaman shook his head.

Relief filled Arvin. Maybe Karrell had second thoughts about talking to Zelia. Then again, maybe Rillis hadn't been in a position to spot her. "How long have you been on watch?"

"All night," Rillis said with a wry look. "As usual."

"Always at the front gate?"

"Mostly," he said. He kicked at the slush. "The snow

might be melting, but it's still been a damp, chilly night," he added with a wink.

Arvin noticed that Rillis wasn't shivering. He'd obviously been inside at least part of his watch, warming himself at the fire.

Rillis stared at the wound on Arvin's forehead. "What happened this time?" he asked. "Another naga?"

Arvin shook his head. "Nothing so exciting as that," he lied. "A thief tried to grab my coin pouch. He cut me."

Rillis nodded sympathetically. "Good thing he wasn't aiming lower," he said, drawing a hand across his throat.

Arvin nodded gravely. He stepped closer and opened his hand just enough to reveal the two coins. "There's another woman I'm also looking for. A yuan-ti who serves House Extaminos, named Zelia. She has red hair, green scales, and a blue forked tongue. Have you seen her?"

Rillis arched an eyebrow. "One gorgeous woman isn't enough?" He started to laugh but faltered when he saw the glower in Arvin's eye. "The red-headed yuan-ti is here," he said quickly. "She's a guest of the ambassador."

Arvin glanced up at the residence. "Is she here now?"

Rillis rubbed his finger and thumb together. Arvin passed him the coins.

"Yes."

"Which room is she in?"

"Second floor. At the back. The second to last suite on the right." Rillis gave Arvin a tentative glance, his expression a mixture of greed and fear. "Do you . . . need me to get you inside?"

"That won't be necessary," Arvin answered.

Rillis looked relieved.

Arvin took two more coins from his pouch and passed

them to Rillis. "If Karrell does show up and asks for Zelia," he instructed, "tell her that Zelia's *not* here. That she's somewhere else."

Rillis grinned as he took the coins. "Consider it done. But I'm only on duty until dawn. The ambassador has finally risen from his dream sleep, and he's in a hurry to leave; I'll be part of the escort accompanying him to the morning riverboat."

"Will Zelia be going with him?" Arvin asked. "Or will she be staying on at the residence?"

Rillis shrugged. "That's up to the new ambassador. He'll decide which slaves and militia—and which house guests—he wants to stay on."

"Thanks," Arvin said. "You've been a big help."

He walked down the street, turned a corner, and circled around the block to the street at the rear of the ambassador's residence. He walked the length of the building, glancing up at the residence only when the two militiamen who were standing out back weren't watching. The last two windows of the second floor were dark, but light glowed through the next two; that must have been Zelia's suite. The curtains on one of the windows had been drawn but not quite all the way; a slight gap remained. It was impossible, however, to see inside from this angle.

The militiamen watched Arvin as he walked the length of the block but lost interest in him as he turned the corner. Making his way to the rear of the building that was directly behind the ambassador's residence, he walked up a short flight of stairs to one of its doors. Pretending to be fitting a key into the lock, he glanced up and down the street. No one was watching. Then he activated the magic within his bracelet and climbed the wall.

Arvin swung himself up onto the roof. Crawling to the far side through patches of wet snow, he stared across the street at the window that had caught his attention a moment ago. Through the gap in its curtains he spotted Zelia. She was seated in a chair that had its side to the window. She was leaning forward in hungry anticipation, her forked tongue flickering through a smile that sent shivers through him. She'd smiled at Arvin in just the same way when she gloatingly told him about the seed she'd planted in his mind. She leaned forward more, gesturing at someone who sat opposite her.

A sudden dread filled him. Who was Zelia talking to?

He crawled farther along the rooftop, ignoring the discomfort of the slush that had soaked through his pants and shirt. No matter what angle he viewed the window from, however, he couldn't see the second person. Working his way back to his original position—a spot directly opposite the window—he sent his awareness into his third eye. He was taking an enormous chance by manifesting a power—if Zelia detected his psionics, he would give himself away—but he had to know if Karrell was inside.

As the energy stored in his third eye uncoiled, a thread of silver light spun out into the night, toward the window. It penetrated the glass and touched the curtain inside, weaving its way into the fabric. Then, one tiny tug at a time, it began to pull.

Slowly, the curtain eased back. After each tug, Arvin waited for several heartbeats, terrified that Zelia might hear the soft slide of the curtain on its rod or notice the gradually widening gap between the curtains. She didn't.

Finally, Arvin got a glimpse of the person she was talking to. It wasn't Karrell.

It was Naneth.

Arvin blinked in surprise. He'd expected Naneth to come to Ormpetarr in an attempt to recapture Glisena, but he'd also expected her to show up at the palace. He did not expect her to be here, inside the ambassador's home.

He had to find out what was going on.

With all that remained of the energy in his *muladhara*, he manifested one last power. Sparkles of light streamed out of the center of his forehead then curled around his head. With them came a heightened awareness. The lighted windows in the ambassador's residence became a babble of overlapping sounds; the lights elsewhere in the city, a distant hum. Even the stars in the night sky emitted a faint, crackling hiss.

Those, however, weren't the sounds Arvin was interested in.

He curled both of his hands into loose fists then held both of them up to his left eye, forming a tube. Through it, he peered at Zelia's window with his other eye shut. The waves of noise that had been pouring into his mind were stopped down to a trickle; now he "saw" only the sounds emanating from Zelia's room. He had to shift, slightly, to screen out the light from the hearth, which filled his mind with a sharp crackle. The fire had been well stoked; like all yuan-ti, Zelia liked her rooms at basking temperature. At last he managed to narrow his field of view to include just Zelia and Naneth. As he did, their voices sprang into focus.

"... to be done tonight," the midwife said.

"Why?" Zelia asked.

"Because Foesmasher has summoned his clerics," Naneth said urgently. "He's convinced *them* to do his dirty work. This time, the child will be killed."

Zelia arched an eyebrow. "Surely he wouldn't slay his own grandchild?"

Naneth snorted. "He doesn't have the same respect for life that Lady Dediana does. To him, the child is just a serpent. I've heard it said that he refers to it as 'the demon.'" She shook her head in a parody of sadness, sending a ripple through her double chin.

Zelia lounged in her chair, her expression confident. "I'll get the girl out."

"How?" Naneth asked. "Glisena's chamber is warded against serpents."

Zelia smiled. "There are ways of getting around wards."

Naneth leaned forward, pudgy hands on her knees. "Just so long as you can do it. Remove her from the palace, and I'll teleport her to Hlondeth."

"Directly to the House Extaminos compound?" Zelia asked.

Naneth nodded. "Yes. Tell your mistress the girl will be delivered, as promised."

Arvin waited, tense with anticipation.

"I'll contact you as soon as I have her," Zelia promised.

"This needs to be done sooner, rather than later," Naneth urged. "As swiftly as you can."

"Swift as a striking serpent," Zelia agreed with a hiss of laughter. She leaned forward as she spoke, playing with a strand of her long red hair. It parted, revealing a finger-long chunk of crystal that hung from a silver hoop in her ear. Judging by its faint glow, it was a crystal capacitor or power stone—which was strange, since Zelia had always before scorned the use of psionic "crutches."

Something must have made Naneth nervous; the midwife raised a hand to her temple to wipe sweat from her forehead.

Zelia settled back into her chair, staring at Naneth through slit eyes. Her tongue flickered out of her mouth, as if she were savoring the midwife's discomfort.

Naneth wiped her temple, glanced in the direction of the hearth, and moved her chair a little farther from it. Arvin gave a mental nod; he felt the same discomfort in the yuan-ti's overheated rooms.

"Will you be staying on in Sespech once our business is concluded?" Naneth asked.

Zelia smiled. "Only for a few days," she said. "Then we really must leave."

"Who is 'we'?" Naneth asked.

Zelia smiled. "You'll find out—seven days from now." A soft, satisfied hiss of laughter followed.

Arvin's eyes widened as he realized what he'd just witnessed. Naneth hadn't been wiping sweat from her brow. She'd been wiping away a sheen of ectoplasm. Zelia had just seeded her. The earring—a power stone—must have contained a copy of the mind seed power.

The power that Arvin thought he had stripped from her for good, six months ago.

Arvin closed his eyes, blocking out both sight and sound. Bile rose in his throat; he swallowed it down. He could guess what must have happened. He'd relayed his warnings about Naneth being one of Sibyl's minions to Tanju, who in turn had conveyed them to Lady Dediana. And she, in turn, had passed the information along to Zelia, her agent in Sespech. Together, no doubt, with an order: that Zelia try, once again, to plant a spy within Sibyl's ranks.

Thunder grumbled from a clear sky: the laughter of Hoar. Naneth had placed a demon in Glisena's womb, and Zelia had just planted a mind seed in the midwife. The god of poetic justice was, beyond a doubt, pleased.

Arvin shuddered.

He watched as the two women in the room exchanged good-byes. Zelia promised to use another sending to contact Naneth the instant Glisena was out of the palace. Naneth nodded then teleported away.

Zelia turned and stared out the window, her eyes flashing silver as she manifested a power. Fearful that she would detect him, Arvin immediately ended his power. For several terrible moments he held his breath, bracing himself for her attack. Then he saw Zelia shiver.

An annoyed look on her face, she swayed to the window and yanked the curtains shut.

Slowly, Arvin let out his breath. Then he scrambled to the far side of the building and climbed back down to the street. He hurried up the road, casting several glances behind him, but saw no signs of pursuit. Relieved, he turned his steps toward the Fairwinds Inn.

As he walked, he pondered what he'd just seen and heard. He didn't believe for a moment that Zelia would attempt to remove Glisena from the palace—she'd just wanted to distract Naneth while she seeded her. That seed, however, would take seven days to blossom. And long before those seven days ended, Naneth would face Sibyl's wrath for having failed to deliver the pregnant Glisena to Hlondeth. What good would Zelia's mind seed be then?

He reached the inn and—after one more careful glance around—let himself in through the back door. He climbed the three flights of stairs that led to the attic room that Karrell had rented. As he reached the landing, he heard sounds of movement behind her door. Karrell had at last returned, it seemed. He prayed she'd been unsuccessful in finding Zelia. As he started to reach for the latch, he heard a wooden clatter that sounded like a chair falling over inside the room. It was immediately followed by a whispered oath, spoken by a male voice.

Arvin summoned his dagger into his glove and flattened himself against the wall beside the door. With his free hand, he reached into his pocket for the monkey's fist he'd used to waylay the satyr. A heartbeat later, the latch turned. The door eased open and a man started to back through it. Arvin recognized the fellow at once: the gaunt-faced rogue with the ice dagger who had waylaid him four days ago. The rogue was bent over, carrying something: an unconscious woman. A second man, still inside the room, held her feet. Even though both the room and hallway were in darkness, Arvin recognized their victim at once by her long hair and hugely pregnant belly.

Glisena. What in the Nine Hells was she doing *here?*

Arvin sprang forward, simultaneously slamming the hilt of his dagger into the temple of the rogue while hurling the monkey's fist in through the door at the second man. The intricate knot unraveled as it flew through the air, strands of it lashing the second man's arms against his sides. The skinny rogue, meanwhile, staggered sideways down the hall under the force of Arvin's blow. Both men dropped their burden at once; Glisena fell to the floor with a heavy thud.

There was no time to check if she was hurt. Arvin's blow had stunned the rogue instead of rendering him unconscious, and the second man—a beefy-looking fellow with a wind-reddened face and greasy hair—managed, despite his bonds, to twist up the loaded crossbow that hung from his belt. Arvin heard the trigger click and leaped aside from the doorway. The bolt snagged his cloak. The first rogue recovered and rushed down the hall, thrusting with his ice dagger. Arvin parried, and the point of the weapon scratched his left forearm. A shock of cold swept through his arm from his elbow to the tip of his abbreviated little finger. His hand went numb, and he dropped his dagger.

Greasy Hair was out of commission inside the room; the monkey's fist had wound its strands around his legs as well, and he'd fallen to the floor. But the first rogue had recovered enough to press home his attack. He feinted with his ice dagger, driving Arvin away from the weapon he'd just dropped. Arvin backed down the short hallway until the wall was at his back then put a deliberately worried look on his face.

The rogue lunged.

"Redditio!" Arvin cried, and his magical dagger flew up from the floor toward his ungloved hand. He caught it as the rogue completed his lunge; the ice dagger scored a line across Arvin's side as he twisted, tearing his shirt. Gasping from the sudden cold—it felt as though an ice-cold hand had clenched his guts—Arvin completed his twist and slammed his own weapon home. It sank to the hilt in the rogue's back.

The rogue went down. He fell to the floor, gurgling like a man whose lungs were filled with fever-fluid. Then he coughed a spray of blood. He wouldn't live long.

Arvin stood on the rogue's wrist and plucked the ice dagger out of his hand then glanced through the doorway at the second man. The fellow had strained against his magical bindings until the cords cut deep grooves into the flesh of his arms and legs, but the ensorcelled twine was holding.

Transferring both daggers to his gloved hand, Arvin touched his side. Crumbles of frozen blood came away from the wound, causing it to bleed slightly. Like the cut on his arm, it was no more than a scratch. "Nine lives," he whispered.

Inside the room, on the table, was a mug of ale. Arvin was tempted to take a hefty swallow but decided against it. He didn't want the rogues thinking his bravery needed a crutch. He glared down at the trussed man.

"It wasn't my idea," the fellow whined. He jerked his head at the rogue who lay dying in the hall. "Lewinn was the one who wanted to cut you out of the deal. He said we could keep the diamonds for ourselves. I said, 'No, Lewinn, we should deal fairly with the mind mage,' but he wouldn't listen. He—"

"Shut up," Arvin said.

Greasy Hair did.

The wounded rogue exhaled one last, gurgling breath then was still. Arvin grabbed his ankles and dragged him inside the room. He eased the door shut—so far, the other occupants of the inn hadn't reacted to the sounds of the fight, and he wanted to keep it that way—then knelt beside Glisena. Her eyes were closed, but her chest rose and fell evenly. Arvin lightly patted her cheek and called her name, but she didn't wake up.

"What have you done to her?" Arvin asked.

"She's drugged," Greasy Hair answered. His voice matched the mental voice Arvin had listened in on earlier, when the skinny rogue had forced him into the cooper's workshop.

Arvin frowned down at Glisena. "How did—"

"It was Lewinn's idea," Greasy Hair interrupted. "He posed as the innkeeper and brought her the ale, and—"

"How did you know she was here?" Arvin asked, glad he'd resisted the urge to drink.

"Lewinn spotted her, looking out the window. That's how we knew you had her." Greasy Hair paused. A too-innocent expression appeared on his face. "Listen, mind mage, the diamonds are in my pocket. Untie me, and I'll give them to you. The diamonds for the girl, just like we agreed, and our dealings will be over. All right?"

Arvin ignored him. He stood, thinking. Doubtless it had happened just the way Greasy Hair described. But how had Glisena wound up in Karrell's room?

It was possible—though it bordered on the miraculous—that Zelia had found a way to spirit Glisena out of the palace in the time it had taken Arvin to walk back to the inn. Could she have found a way past the wards and plucked Glisena out from under the very eyes of nine powerful clerics—ten, counting Marasa—and a watchful baron?

Possible, but hardly likely.

Unless Karrell had been the one to get Glisena out.

Karrell looked human enough; maybe she'd fooled the wards. And she had access to the palace. She might have been able to charm the clerics, to steal Glisena away and bring her here, to the room at the inn.

Whatever was going on, Arvin needed to get Glisena out of here.

Scooping the mug of ale off the table, he grabbed the rogue's greasy hair and wrenched his head back. "Drink it," he growled.

Greasy Hair struggled to wrench his head aside. "The diamonds aren't really in my pocket," he gasped. "But I can get them for you. Let me—"

Arvin poured the ale down his throat.

The man sputtered then swallowed. His eyes glazed then rolled—and he went limp.

Arvin pricked the fellow's arm with his dagger: no response. Greasy Hair wasn't feigning unconsciousness. Arvin spoke the command word that re-knotted the monkey's fist and shoved it back in his pocket. Then he reached inside his shirt for the brooch the baron had given him. He pinned it to the front of the thin rogue's shirt, where it was sure to be spotted. That would give Naneth something to puzzle over, if she came to claim Glisena and found one of the "baron's men" dead on the floor, next to an unconscious rogue.

Arvin removed the ice dagger's sheath from the dead rogue's belt, slid the weapon into it, and tucked it into his boot. Then he bent down and carefully picked up Glisena.

She was lighter than he'd expected—and cooler; her body no longer radiated heat. The drug the rogues had tricked her into drinking must have dampened her fever. It also seemed to have quieted the demon. Glisena's bulging stomach pressed up against Arvin's; he could no longer feel the demon kicking.

Arvin crept down the stairs, Glisena in his arms. He eased open the door at the bottom and peered out into the street. The street was deserted, except for a lone figure far down the block, walking toward the inn. Something about the person made Arvin uneasy; a second glance told him he'd been right to trust his instincts. The person moved with a swaying motion that instantly told Arvin her race: yuan-ti.

Zelia.

And she was moving toward the inn. Had she spotted him?

Arvin closed the door and hurried in the only other direction available: through the inn's common room, which had closed for the night. With Glisena in his arms, he wound his way between the tables, toward the inn's front door. Once again he looked cautiously outside. This time the street was empty.

Arvin hurried up the street. As he ran, slipping on patches of slush, he activated the lapis lazuli and visualized the one person he'd not yet contacted with it today who might be able to help: Marasa. Her face came into focus in his mind at once: drawn, worried-looking, and pale. Her left hand was raised, evoking Helm; her lips moved in prayer. Her eyes widened as a mental image of Arvin formed in her mind's eye.

Marasa, he thought, hailing her. *I found Glisena. She's unconscious; I'm carrying her back to the palace from the Fairwinds Inn. Send help. Hurry!*

Marasa's eyes widened in surprise. She glanced down then up at Arvin. *That's not possible,* she thought. *Glisena's here. I've been by her side all....* Suddenly, her expression grew wary. One last thought—only half-directed at Arvin, but it came through anyway—drifted through her mind: *Is this a trick?* Then the sending was broken.

Arvin slowed and stared down at the woman in his arms. Glisena was still at the palace? If this wasn't Glisena, who *was* it? He glanced around, spotted a sheltered doorway up the street, and stepped into it. With one hand, he undid the fastenings of his cloak, letting it fall to the ground. He spread it out with his foot then lowered the unconscious woman onto it. Then, closing his eyes so he could concentrate, he ran his fingertips across her face.

It took several moments of intense concentration for him to feel what was truly there. The face felt broader than Glisena's, and flatter. And the hair, when he ran it through his fingers, was wavy, not straight. And the ears. . . .

Yes. There it was. The woman's left earlobe was pierced, the piercing filled with an earring of carved stone.

"Karrell," Arvin said in a stunned whisper.

She'd done an amazing job of transforming her appearance. She hadn't polymorphed herself—that would have fooled Arvin's fingers, as well as his eyes. She must have used some sort of illusion. He touched her hair a second time and felt what he'd expected: a gritty powder. Back in Hlondeth, one of the assassins who had commissioned a magical rope from Arvin had used a similar magical powder. By sprinkling a pinch of it on his head, he could change his appearance to that of anyone he liked. He'd actually gloated about how he'd used the powder to assume the appearance of a woman's husband then stabbed the woman in front of her own daughter. The husband had been charged with the crime—and executed in the pits with his daughter watching and cursing his name.

Arvin was glad he wasn't working for the Guild anymore.

He stared down at Karrell, shaking his head. Whatever game she'd been playing had been a dangerous one. The rogues had interrupted it, Tymora be praised.

Arvin idly scratched his forehead. The scab was starting to itch again.

His hand froze in mid-scratch as he realized it wasn't the wound. That tickling sensation was Naneth scrying on him.

And if she could see him, she could see Karrell. Who still looked like Glisena.

Arvin cursed his ill luck. Why had Naneth chosen this precise moment to scry on him? If she recognized the spot where he was crouching, she might appear at any moment.

He glanced wildly around. Just a short distance up the street, in the intersection, was one of the statues of Helm's gauntlet. Maybe, if he was quick enough. . . .

Arvin scooped Karrell up and ran toward the gauntlet. Naneth's scrying ended when he was partway there. He scrambled up onto the dais and slapped his bare hand against the gauntlet. "Come on," he gasped, looking around for one of the clerics who was supposed to materialize when the gauntlet's protection was invoked. "Come *on*."

He heard a faint pop behind him: air being displaced as a person teleported. He turned, expecting to see one of the Eyes.

It was Naneth, standing perhaps a hundred paces away, beside the doorway Arvin had just bolted from.

Then Zelia appeared from around a corner, holding a piece of parchment in one hand.

With a sinking heart, Arvin recognized it as the drawing Karrell had made of him. The one he'd crumpled up, thrown into the fireplace, and forgotten.

Zelia had found it.

"Arvin," she said as she walked with slithering steps toward Arvin. "We meet again. You look unusually healthy . . . for a dead man." Laughter hissed softly from her lips.

No, not laughter. That hissing meant she was manifesting a power: a psionic attack. And Arvin had no energy left in his *muladhara* to counter it.

He tensed, but the mental agony he was bracing against didn't manifest. Then he realized that the gauntlet was protecting him. Zelia couldn't attack him. Not here.

He shifted Karrell in his arms so that her limp hand also touched the gauntlet. They were protected, for the moment, against spells. But if Naneth used a spell that wasn't directly hostile—if she got close enough to touch Karrell and teleport away with her, for example—they'd be in trouble.

"There you are," Zelia said to Naneth, gesturing at Arvin and Karrell. "The girl. As promised."

Naneth thanked her with a silent nod then walked briskly toward them.

A second faint pop sounded, right next to Arvin. Relief swept through him as he saw the newcomer's red cloak and brightly polished breastplate, emblazoned with the eye of Helm.

"The baron's daughter!" Arvin gasped, shifting Karrell so the cleric could see her face. "She's in danger."

Out of the corner of his eye, he saw Naneth break into a run. For a large woman, she moved surprisingly fast. "Detain that man!" she screamed. "He's an agent of Chondath. He's kidnapping the baron's daughter."

The cleric frowned then raised his gauntlet, turning the eye on its palm toward Arvin.

Arvin answered the question before the cleric even asked it. "I serve Lord Foesmasher," he said. As he spoke, a tingle swept through him: the gauntlet's truth-enforcing magic. He jerked his head at Naneth. "That woman's a sorcerer—an enemy of Foesmasher."

Naneth's hands were up, her fingers weaving a spell.

"Teleport us to the palace," Arvin shouted. "Now!"

The cleric had been summoning his weapon—a mace-shaped glow that had half-materialized in his fist. The glow vanished, and he clamped a hand on Arvin's wrist.

As he did, Naneth completed her spell. In the area next to the dais, up suddenly became down. Arvin fell into the air, legs flailing. Karrell tumbled from his arms. The cleric was still holding onto Arvin's wrist and was praying—a prayer Arvin recognized, though he'd heard it only once before, when the yuan-ti ambassador had been teleported away by the clerics in Mimph.

"Wait!" Arvin shouted. With his free hand, he twisted violently, trying to catch Karrell. He caught hold of her ankle as he had a dizzying glimpse of Naneth on the dais below, casting another spell while Zelia hissed furiously, manifesting a power.

Tendrils of thought wiggled their way into his mind like tiny serpents. Hissing, they slithered through his mind, tearing with their fangs at his thoughts. He felt his mind begin to fray, and with each strand that parted, his body became weaker. One leg went limp, his left arm suddenly stopped responding to his thoughts, his head lolled back on a weakened neck—and the fingers of his right hand, the one that was gripping Karrell's ankle, grew limp as severed strings. He tried to keep hold of her, but felt his fingers slipping, slipping....

Naneth gloated up at him, reaching for Karrell with her pudgy fingers, while Zelia hissed with laughter.

"No," Arvin gasped. With his last bit of strength, he forced his thumb and one finger to close around Karrell's ankle—just as Zelia hit him with a massive thrust of psionic energy that smashed into his mind like a fist. Reeling, still falling upward, he caught a glimpse of her savoring his defeat with her forked tongue.

And the street vanished as the cleric teleported Arvin away.

❂ ❂ ❂ ❂ ❂

Arvin groaned and rolled over. He ached in several places, there were sharp pains in his side and along his left arm, and his mind felt as though it were full of holes—the aftermath of Zelia's psionic attack.

The memory jolted him fully awake.

Karrell! Had she—

He looked wildly around. He was in the same chapel in which he had spoken to Foesmasher two nights ago—inside the palace. Relief rushed through him as he spotted Karrell farther along the bench he was lying on, just beyond his feet. The effects of the magical powder had worn off; she looked like herself again. She'd been teleported back with him. She was safe.

He touched the crystal at his neck. "Nine lives," he whispered. He glanced around, but saw they were alone in the room. Oddly, the cleric who had teleported them here had just left them. Or perhaps it was not so odd, given the events that were unfolding elsewhere in the palace. Arvin wondered if Glisena had given birth yet.

Karrell's chin was on her chest, her body slumped with exhaustion. She seemed to be sleeping, albeit restlessly. Her fingers twitched, as if plucking at something. Then she groaned in her sleep.

Fear swept through Arvin then, chilling him like an icy wind. Was Karrell having a nightmare—one drawn from the dark pit of Zelia's memories? Fingers trembling, he nudged her awake.

Karrell's eyes flew open. "Arvin! You have recovered. The cleric assured me you would, but I was worried, even so. He told me that I had been drugged, that Naneth had attacked you and—"

Arvin pulled her closer to him and anxiously ran his fingers over her temples, her hair, searching for traces of ectoplasm. He found none, but that meant nothing. If she had been seeded, it had been done some time ago.

"What are you doing?" Karrell asked.

"Did you meet with Zelia?"

Karrell pulled away, a wary expression on her face. "I said nothing that would give you away. My ring prevented her from learning about you."

"That doesn't matter—not now," Arvin said. He laughed bitterly. "Zelia knows I'm alive. She showed up at the inn, just as I was carrying you out. She saw me." He winced and rubbed his aching head. "She nearly killed me."

Karrell glanced away. She was silent for several moments. "I am sorry," she said at last.

"'Sorry' isn't going to help me now," Arvin said. He shook his head. "What in the Abyss were you *thinking?*"

Karrell met his eye. "That Zelia might know where Sibyl is hiding. And I was right. She—"

"Damn it, Karrell," Arvin exploded. "Zelia might have seeded you."

"Yes," Karrell said gravely. "I know. But it was a calculated risk. You found a way to root out a mind seed once before; I was confident in your ability to do it again, if need be." Then her voice lowered. "I just wish you had an equal confidence in me."

Arvin sighed and ran his hands through his hair. "Were you dreaming just now?"

"Yes." She frowned. "Why?"

"Was the dream...." He searched for the right word. He had found Zelia's memories foreign, disturbing—but perhaps Karrell wouldn't. She was a yuan-ti, after all, and female. "Did it seem to be a memory from someone else's life?"

"Ah. You are still worried about the mind seed. No, it was not Zelia's dream. It was one I have been having for many months. A troubling dream, in which I am bound tightly and cannot escape."

"Your own dream, then," Arvin said, feeling slightly relieved.

"No, not mine. Not mine alone."

"What do you mean?" Arvin asked sharply.

Karrell tilted her head and stared at the window. Pale winter sunlight shone through the stained glass, causing the blue-and-gold eye of Helm to glow. "I have talked to other yuan-ti. Many of us have been having troubling dreams. Dreams of someone who is embracing us who will not let go, or of being bound by ropes, or even—most strange, for a yuan-ti—of being a mouse, held tight by a serpent. No one knows what they mean. Not even Zelia."

Arvin nodded, completely at a loss. Whatever the dreams meant, they had little to do with their immediate problem. "If you start having strange thoughts while you're awake, tell me," he said. "Or strange dreams—stranger than the ones you've just described, I mean."

"I will," Karrell said with a grave nod. Then she said, "Tell me what happened. How did I come to be drugged?"

Arvin told her about the two rogues who hoped to sell "Glisena" to Chondath, about finding her unconscious in the room at the inn, and about trying to carry "Glisena" back to the palace, only to be confronted by Naneth. He also told her about their narrow escape, thanks to the cleric.

She listened, nodding.

Arvin paused. "So what were you doing, disguised as Glisena?"

"It was Zelia's idea," Karrell said.

Arvin waited, arms folded across his chest. He could tell, already, that he wasn't going to like the explanation. "Start from the beginning. Tell me all about your meeting. Don't leave out any details."

"I met with Zelia at the ambassador's residence," Karrell said. "I told her I was an agent of Yranil Suzur, *ssthaar* of the Jennestas—a ruler who, like Dediana

Extaminos, is wary of Sibyl's rise to power. Zelia agreed to speak with me."

"She agreed to meet with a complete stranger?"

Karrell's eyes lighted mischievously. "I think she found me . . . charming."

Arvin's eyebrows rose. "You charmed Zelia? I'm impressed."

"We spoke about Sibyl—about how dangerous she is. And yes, Zelia *does* know where Sibyl is hiding," Karrell continued. "As you guessed, she in Hlondeth. Sibyl has denned in an ancient temple beneath the city—a temple that was erected at the peak of the Serpentes Empire to honor the beast lord Varae, an aspect of Sseth. The temple was abandoned and forgotten long before Hlondeth was even built, but nobles of House Extaminos rediscovered it two years after Lord Shevron's death. They briefly worshiped there, and it was abandoned again. Sibyl, together with her followers, has turned it into a fully fledged temple once more."

"How did Zelia discover this?" Arvin asked.

Karrell gave a graceful shrug. "One of House Extaminos's spies learned it."

Arvin wondered if it had been another of Zelia's mind seeds. "Zelia might have been lying to you."

"She might have," Karrell agreed. "But to what end? She would have been foolish to throw away the opportunity I offered—an alliance with a group that is also working against Sibyl."

"Zelia breaks alliances as quickly as she makes them," Arvin countered. "Still, go on. You haven't explained why you were impersonating Glisena."

"To lure Naneth to me," Karrell said. "Zelia gave me the powder, and suggested I play the part of Glisena. She said she would contact Naneth and promise to deliver 'Glisena' to her—and ensure that Naneth teleported me to the Extaminos palace in Hlondeth. There, House Extaminos's spellcasters would subdue Naneth. And I would use a second pinch of the powder to change my appearance to match Naneth's. Then I would infiltrate the temple where Sibyl lairs, and—"

"Did Zelia give you a second pinch of powder?" Arvin asked.

"No."

"You *trusted* her? After what she did to me?"

Karrell winced. "I had to take the chance. The lives of thousands of people—"

"What about this person?" Arvin asked, thumping a hand against his chest. It felt hollow. "You were going to leave without even saying good-bye."

"There was no time," Karrell said, her dark eyes flashing. "And I would have returned. Once I had secured the Circled Serpent and carried it to a place of safety, I would have come back to you."

"If you'd lived," Arvin said bitterly. "And if you didn't, I'd never have known what had happened to you."

She lifted a hand to his face. "You would have contacted me," she said. Her fingers lightly touched the scab on his forehead. "With your stone. I would have told you, then, where I was."

Arvin turned away from her touch.

"Do you want the truth?" she asked.

Arvin glanced reluctantly back at her.

"I feared that you would try to talk me out of it," she said. She sighed. "And that you would succeed. I could not run that risk. Too much is at stake."

Arvin nodded. He stared at Helm's gauntlet for several long moments then turned to Karrell. "Zelia played you for a fool," he told her. "When she told you that you would be the one to infiltrate Sibyl's lair, she was lying."

Karrell tossed her head. "Of course you would say that."

"I'm not just *saying* that," Arvin told her. "I know that. I spied on Zelia, earlier tonight. Probably just after you met with her. When she was talking to Naneth."

"And?" Karrell prompted.

"Zelia planted a mind seed in her."

Karrell absorbed this news without reacting. "I thought Zelia might do that," she said evenly. "And I knew it would anger you, if you found out. What I do not understand is why you feel any sympathy for the midwife. After what she did to the baron's daughter—"

"I *don't* feel sympathy for her," Arvin said. "Naneth deserves what's coming to her." He shuddered, remembering the terrible headaches, the nightmarish dreams, the impulses that were not his own—impulses that had, just before the mind seed was due to blossom, driven him to kill an innocent man. "The point is that Zelia was using you to further her own ends."

"Zelia no more used me than I used her," Karrell countered. "I sought her out. I asked her to help me get close to Sibyl, and that is what she did." She frowned. "Or rather, what she tried to do. Our plan would have worked, if the rogues had not interfered."

"You're lucky they did," Arvin said. "Zelia never would have let you impersonate Naneth."

Karrell's eyes narrowed. "Why are you so certain of that?"

"Zelia planted a mind seed in me—remember?" He tapped his temple. "I know how her mind works. Zelia doesn't delegate—she does the job herself. Or rather, her mind seeds do. She probably would have let Naneth teleport you to the House Extaminos compound—but that's as far as your part in it would go. She'd let Naneth report to Sibyl that 'Glisena' had been delivered—thus ensuring that Naneth remained in Sibyl's good graces—then would have found a way, somehow, to stall the midwife for seven days, until the mind seed blossomed. You, meanwhile, would become superfluous—and would be disposed of."

"It is a convincing argument," Karrell said. "Except

for one point. Why would Zelia kill me? Why throw away a valuable ally?"

"She wouldn't have thrown you away," Arvin said grimly. "She'd have seeded you."

"Ah." Karrell remained silent for several moments. She stared out through the chapel's stained-glass window. Outside, a light snow had begun to fall. "Thank you for risking your life to save me," she said at last. "If I had listened to your warnings. . . ." A tear slid down her cheek. She brushed it angrily away. "It is just that so many lives are at stake. So much is resting on my shoulders. If Sibyl finds the second half of the Circled Serpent and uses it to unlock the door, the Night Serpent will escape."

"And the world will come to an end," Arvin whispered—believing it, this time. He held out his arms questioningly. Karrell nodded, and he embraced her. They kissed.

Several moments later she broke off the kiss and squared her shoulders. "At least Zelia has given me a starting point," she said. "The location of Sibyl's den. That is where the stolen half of the Circled Serpent must be." She met Arvin's eye. "I will go there," she said. "Alone, if need be. Unless. . . ."

Arvin hesitated. Recovering ancient artifacts wasn't what he'd signed on for, and the people Karrell hoped to save were strangers from a distant land. Whether they lived or died meant nothing to him personally. But the fact that they would die to further Sibyl's plans did.

"I'll do it," he said, taking her hand. "I'll come with you to Hlondeth, and help you find the Circled Serpent. But before we go anywhere, I need to meditate and restore my energies." He heard Karrell's stomach growl and gave her a brief smile. "And it sounds as though you need to eat." He laid a hand gently on her stomach. "Or as though someone does."

Karrell lifted his hand to her lips and kissed it then

rose to her feet. "I will find a servant," she said. "Someone who can bring us food."

Arvin nodded and watched her leave. Then he stripped off his shirt and pants, preparing himself for his meditations. He lowered himself to the floor and assumed the *bhujanga asana*. The stone tiles were cold against his bare legs and palms; the sensation helped him ignore his aches and pains, helped him focus.

Toward the end of his meditations, he heard hurried footsteps in the corridor outside the chapel. He rose to his feet as a soldier strode into the room. The soldier was one of those who had been standing vigil outside Glisena's chamber earlier—a man with short black hair and eyes as gray as steel. His eyes were wide and worried.

"The baron demands your presence," he announced. "At once."

Arvin looked around. "Where is Karrell? Have you seen her? She—"

"There is no time," the soldier said, gesturing impatiently. "High Watcher Davinu needs you."

Arvin nodded as he pulled on his shirt and pants. He told himself not to worry—Karrell was probably eating in the kitchen or somewhere else in the palace. She wouldn't abandon him a second time. Not after he'd promised to help her. He'd find her later, after the clerics had dealt with the demon.

As he followed the soldier from the room, he wondered what it would be like to listen in on a demon's thoughts as it was being born.

He shuddered. He was certain the experience wasn't going to be a pleasant one.

CHAPTER 15

As Arvin strode along behind the soldier, he glanced this way and that, looking for Karrell. He didn't think she'd desert him a second time, especially after he'd at last convinced her how dangerous Zelia was, but a lingering worry still nagged at him.

They passed the practice hall where servants were busy oiling and cleaning the equipment, and several rooms in which still more servants cleaned fireplaces, swept the floors, and dusted furniture. Arvin was amazed to see life at the palace apparently carrying on as if nothing untoward was happening. Only the clerics, it seemed, knew of the life-and-death struggle Glisena was facing.

They passed the council chamber where Arvin had first spoken to Foesmasher, following his arrival in Ormpetarr. Arvin glanced inside and saw two women polishing the many shields that hung on the wall. One of them caught his eye at once: a middle-aged woman with graying hair. It took Arvin a moment to remember where he had seen her before, but when he did, he halted abruptly.

The woman had been at Naneth's house, the night Foesmasher had burst into it, searching for the midwife—she'd been the one the soldiers had taken away for questioning. It seemed just a little coincidental that she should turn out to be one of the palace servants.

"I need to speak to someone," Arvin told the soldier. "It won't take long—no more than a moment."

The soldier grabbed Arvin's elbow. "There's no time. Lord Foesmasher—"

"Will want to hear what I'm about to find out," Arvin finished for him. "That servant," he said, nodding into the room, "is somehow involved in what's happened to Glisena. I intend to find out what she knows."

The soldier stared at him a moment, indecision in his eyes. Then his hand fell away. "Just be quick," he said.

"I will."

Arvin entered the council chamber and walked to the far end of the room, pretending to be admiring the model ships that stood on the table. As he passed the two servants, he manifested the power that would let him listen in on their thoughts. Silver sparkles erupted from his forehead, vanishing even as the woman with the graying hair turned around. Her eyes had a distant expression, as if she were listening to some half-heard sound. When they focused on Arvin, she nodded and bobbed a curtsey.

The other servant—a girl in her teens, glanced over her shoulder then continued with her work. Her thoughts were superficial: musings about one of the stable hands—how handsome he was—and a slight irritation that the baron's guest had trod on her clean floor. Arvin focused instead on the thoughts of the older woman, the one he suspected of being Naneth's spy. She was worried about something, but not clearly articulating her fears.

Arvin would help her along.

He gestured for her to approach. She did, holding a rag that smelled of beeswax. So far, her thoughts were a mix of annoyance at having been interrupted and puzzlement about what Arvin could possibly want. She didn't remember him.

He leaned toward her and spoke in a low voice. "I know who you serve," he said.

The woman frowned. Of course he did, she thought. She served the baron. What did this man *really* want with her?

Arvin was impressed. If the servant was a spy, she was a good one. "I know why you were at Naneth's home, the other night," he continued. "About your . . . arrangement with her."

That made her eyes widen. And her thoughts begin to flow. Who was this man, and how did he know about Naneth? Would he tell her husband? She prayed to Helm that he wouldn't. Ewainn was so proud—he would crumble if he knew the fault had been his, all along. She'd thought he'd find out, when she'd been hauled before the Eyes for questioning four nights ago, but all they'd wanted to know, it turned out, was where the midwife was. And just as well, that Naneth had disappeared. Now she wouldn't have to pay the midwife—coin Ewainn would notice was missing, sooner or later. If he'd pressed her, she might have had to explain to Ewainn that he wasn't the one who quickened a child in her—that the midwife had used magic to do it.

Arvin struggled to keep his expression neutral. This woman was pregnant? He'd assumed, when he'd overheard her protest to the baron's soldiers that she was just one of Naneth's customers, that she had gone to the midwife's home to arrange for Naneth to deliver a daughter's child. With her graying hair, he'd taken her to be a pending grandmother.

"I don't know what you're talking about, my lord," she choked out at last.

"Yes, you do," Arvin said, more gently, this time. He glanced pointedly down at her stomach; it had a slight but unmistakable bulge. "When did Naneth cast the spell?"

Her hands twisted the rag. "A tenday and a hand ago."

Arvin glanced once more at her stomach. She was three months along, at least. "What date?" he asked.

"The fifth."

Arvin nodded. The same night the demon had been bound into Glisena's womb. The night Glisena, thinking her pregnancy merely hastened along, had fled the palace.

Arvin stared at the servant, thinking furiously. Should he tell her that the child in her womb was really that of Glisena and Dmetrio? Seven days from now, Naneth would be as good as dead. No one except Arvin would ever know the baby wasn't the serving woman's.

Until the first time it turned into a serpent.

How would the woman's husband react to that, Arvin wondered.

In the doorway, the soldier cleared his throat impatiently. "'At *once*,' the baron said. Not a tenday from now."

Arvin touched the servant's hand. "Your name?" he asked gently.

Why does he want to know? she thought in a panicky voice. But she answered obediently, as her years of servitude dictated. "Belinna."

"We'll talk again, Belinna. Later. In private. There's something about your child that you need to know. In the meantime, your secret is safe with me." Ending his manifestation, he strode back to the soldier.

As he once more followed the soldier down the hall, he wondered whether he should tell Glisena he'd located her child. It would certainly bolster her for the ordeal she was about to face, but it would result in anguish for Belinna when Glisena reclaimed her child. Belinna had already come to regard the infant inside her as her own, to love it. That much Arvin had seen in her eyes and heard in her thoughts.

But would she love it still when it turned out to be half serpent?

They reached Glisena's chamber, and the soldier rapped on the door. Magical energy sparkled around the lock. It was opened a moment later by a haggard-looking Foesmasher. He ushered Arvin into the room then closed the door.

Glisena no longer lay on her bed; now she was seated on a birthing chair. Davinu and the other clerics still stood in a circle around her, praying with voices that were nearly hoarse; Arvin wondered how long they could continue without sleep. The shields still floated in a circle, surrounding them, but they were moving more slowly. Every now and then one would bob toward the ground like the head of a horse that had run too far and too long then rise again.

Marasa sat on a stool next to the birthing chair, holding Glisena's hand. A knife lay on a low, cloth-draped table beside her. To cut the cord once the demon was born, Arvin supposed. The room smelled of blood; rags under the birthing chair were stained a bright red.

The baron began to pace back and forth behind them, thumping a fist against his thigh. Each time his daughter groaned, his jaw clenched. "Can't you do something for her pain?" he growled at Marasa.

"I already have," the cleric said in an exhausted voice.

As Glisena bore down, panting, Marasa's face grew pale. Her free hand pressed against her own stomach, and she shuddered. Arvin, watching, realized that she must have cast a spell that allowed her to draw Glisena's hurts into her own body. There was a psionic power that did something similar—it operated on the same principles as the fate link that Tanju had taught Arvin, except that the damage and pain could only be channeled to the psion, himself. Arvin had declined it as something he didn't really want to learn. At the time, he couldn't think of anyone he cared enough about to want to inflict that kind of pain on himself.

Marasa exhaled through clenched teeth then gestured at one of the clerics. He stepped out of the circle and held his left hand out, palm toward her. Magical energy crackled faintly in the air as he cast a spell. Marasa shook her head, like a dog shaking off water. Her shoulders straightened, and her face resumed its natural color.

The baron continued pacing.

Davinu turned as Arvin approached. "The demon is a breach birth," he said. "We will need to cut it free. But before we begin, I need to know what it's thinking. Use your mind magic."

Glisena groaned, and Marasa shuddered. Another cleric stepped forward and healed her. As Glisena panted, blood trickled down onto the rags beneath the birthing chair. She looked up at Arvin, her face glistening with sweat. There was terror in her eyes— she was afraid of dying—but also something more: a question.

Arvin squatted beside her. The words came unbidden to his lips. "I found the person you asked me about," he said quietly. "She—or he—is safe."

The lines of strain on Glisena's face eased, just a little. "She," she panted, a mother's certainty burning in her eyes. "Take ... care of ... her."

"No need," Arvin whispered fiercely. "You'll make it through this."

Glisena shook her head. "Promise. That you'll ... take care ..." she gasped.

Arvin touched her shoulder. "I promise."

The clerics gently lifted Glisena onto the bed, reforming their circle there. Marasa pulled her stool up next to the bed. Davinu opened Glisena's night robe, exposing her stomach. The lines Naneth had drawn on it were almost gone; only the faintest traces of white remained. Davinu picked up the knife. It was silver, the blade inlaid with gold in the shape of a staring eye: Helm's symbol. Davinu held the knife out, and one of the clerics poured water over it from a silver chalice that also bore a stylized eye. Then he held it ready, waiting.

Arvin manifested his power. Sparkles of silver erupted from his third eye and drifted down onto Glisena. The thoughts of those in the room crowded in on him: Glisena's relief that Arvin had located her child, Marasa's fierce love for Glisena and grim determination to bear her pain, Davinu steeling himself for the surgery he was about to perform, and the other clerics' fervent prayers, all overlaid with a tight clench of fear. Davinu had given them careful instructions about what was to happen; the moment the blood cord was severed, he would banish the demon. Arvin expected to hear Foesmasher's thoughts as well—his anguish at seeing his "little dove" in such pain was clear for all to see—but something was shielding his thoughts. Was it a magical item, like Karrell's ring? Briefly, Arvin wondered where Karrell was—he hoped far from this part of the palace—then turned his mind back to the task at hand. Blotting out the overlapping babble of mental voices, he sent his consciousness deeper, and found the voice he'd dreaded hearing.

So tight, so confined ... but I will be free soon. If only I had my swords, I would slash my way out.

Arvin shuddered. "It's wishing it had its sword," he reported. "No, swords," he corrected. "Plural."

Distantly, he heard the clerics murmuring to each other.

"A balor, then?" one asked.

"Too large," another answered. "And the horns—they would have torn—"

Ah. That's better. I can turn.

"It's turning," Arvin said.

Glisena screamed as her stomach bulged. Something flickered between her legs then drew inside her again; it looked like the tip of a tail.

Foesmasher whirled, one hand on his sword hilt, his face twisted with anguish. Marasa clapped a hand on Glisena's stomach, drawing the pain into herself. "Do it," she gritted up at Davinu. "Now. Before it—" Her face paled as another spasm of pain rushed into her.

Davinu touched Glisena's forehead with a fingertip. "Hold," he commanded.

Glisena's body stiffened. Her chest, however, still rose and fell. And her stomach heaved.

Davinu lowered the point of the knife to her belly then took a deep breath. He began to cut.

Foesmasher stood rigid, eyes locked on Glisena, barely breathing. One fist was white-knuckled on his sword hilt; the other was pressed against his mouth.

The other clerics crowded around the bed, hands extended toward Glisena, chanting. "Guardian of the innocent, lord of the unsleeping eye, watch and protect this girl in her time of need...."

Blood sprayed onto Davinu's breastplate as he cut. The knife parted muscle, and something that glistened, and a layer of darker flesh that smelled of seared meat. Then came a rush of sulfurous-smelling liquid, and something could be seen writhing within. Arvin caught a glimpse of flailing arms and a long, serpentine tail.

Marasa groaned and swayed, nearly falling from her stool. One of the clerics steadied her.

I am wounded! It burns!

"You've cut the demon," Arvin said. "You've injured it."

Him again! Where is he? He will pay for this!

Arvin felt a chill run through him. He swallowed nervously. "It thinks ... that I'm the one who hurt—"

Davinu passed the knife to one of the clerics and grabbed the edges of the gaping hole he'd just cut in Glisena's bloody flesh. "Now," he shouted. "Pull it free."

One of the clerics plunged his hand into the wound and seized hold of the demon. He pulled, his free hand braced against Glisena's pelvis, and the demon suddenly came free. It was tiny, the size of a newborn child—but instead of legs, it had a thrashing tail fully twice the length of its body. It had six arms, a full head of sulfur-yellow hair and an upper body like that of a mature woman, with full, round breasts.

"A marilith?" the cleric holding it gasped. He had grabbed it by one of its arms and fought to maintain his grip on the blood-slicked flesh. The demon twisted violently, its tail lashing and flicking blood. A twisted pink cord spiraled down from its naval into Glisena's stomach.

Davinu seized the cord and motioned for the other cleric to cut it with the knife.

The demon twisted, knocking the knife out of the cleric's hand. As the cleric scrambled after the knife, the demon wrapped its tail around Davinu's neck. "You annoy me," it said in a voice deeper and more malevolent than any mortal man's. Then it constricted.

Davinu clawed at the tail that was choking him. "Cut ... cut...."

Behind him, the shields that had been circling through the air clunked to the floor.

Foesmasher drew his sword and lunged forward, slashing at the cord, but missed. His blade whistled through the air, narrowly missing the cleric who was holding the demon.

The demon slithered out of the cleric's grip, then thrust all six of its hands out at once, as if fending off foes. Tendrils of shadowy darkness sprang into being around it and coiled themselves around its body. Foesmasher shoved the cleric aside and thrust at the demon, but the tendrils coiled around the weapon, halting it. The darkness slithered up the blade and licked at Foesmasher's bare hand, and the baron dropped his sword. Foesmasher backed away, his fingers moving creakily as he tried to force his hands to obey him.

These mortals want to play with swords? the demon mused, tightening its grip on Davinu's neck.

Davinu's face purpled.

Then swords they shall have.

"Swords!" Arvin shouted. "The demon's going to use magic to—"

A loud whirring noise filled the air as thousands of tiny blades sprang into existence, forming a curtain of steel around the bed and enclosing Glisena, Marasa, Arvin, and Davinu inside it. The remaining clerics screamed as the blades slashed into them. The whirling weapons clattered off their breastplates but sliced into exposed arms, legs, faces, and throats; five of the clerics fell, mortally wounded. The remaining three staggered back, screaming, bloody but still on their feet. Foesmasher, well behind them, was still struggling to pick up his sword; the demon's magic seemed to have sapped the strength from his arms.

Outside the chamber, fists pounded on the magic-locked door. Arvin could hear the muffled shouting of the soldiers.

The demon, its tail still wrapped around Davinu's throat, glanced around the room. *Which one,* it mused, *was I supposed to kill?* It gave a mental sigh. *All of them, I suppose.*

Davinu leaned back—dangerously close to the whirling blades—pulling the birthing cord taught. "Cord..." he choked. "C-c-c...."

"You cannot banish me," the demon gloated in a voice like thick, bubbling blood. *Not while I am bound by—*

"*Shivis,*" Arvin shouted, summoning his dagger into his glove and leaping forward. The demon tried to twist aside but failed. With a clean stroke, Arvin severed the birthing cord.

Davinu staggered, the demon still wrapped around his throat. Blades clattered against the armor that shielded his back; one sliced through an unprotected spot near his shoulder, leaving a deep slash. He recoiled from the whirling curtain of steel and struggled to speak the words of the prayer that would banish the demon—Arvin could hear them echoing in Davinu's thoughts—but there was no air in his lungs.

"Marasa," Arvin shouted. "Banish the demon!"

Marasa, busy with Glisena, ignored him. She threw something to the floor—the afterbirth she had just pulled out of Glisena's wound—and pressed the two edges of the wound together, chanting a healing spell. She realized the danger—Arvin could hear it in her thoughts—but without a restorative spell, *now,* Glisena would bleed to death. Just a moment more, and Marasa would cast the banishing spell.

A moment they didn't have.

Davinu collapsed, unconscious. The demon released him and coiled its tail under itself, rising like a rearing snake, the lowermost pair of its six hands resting on its hips.

Outside the barrier of whirling blades, the three clerics who still stood were casting spells. One shouted commands at the demon while holding out a gauntleted hand; another had summoned a shimmering mace into his hand. The third chanted a prayer that caused a glowing sword to rush toward the demon, but the weapon broke apart before reaching its target, scattering into shimmers of light. Foesmasher, meanwhile, had finally picked up his sword and a shield and was trying to force his way through the barrier of blades. They thudded into the shield with a loud clatter, driving him back.

The demon eyed them scornfully. *Time to even the odds,* it thought. It cocked its head to the side. *Should it be dretches, or hezrou?*

Marasa continued to chant her prayer, running a finger along Glisena's wound. Slowly, the flesh knit itself back together.

"Marasa!" Arvin screamed. "The demon's going to summon—"

The demon stared at Arvin with slit eyes. "So it was you whose voice I heard."

An invisible force yanked Arvin's dagger from his hand.

Let's play.

The dagger reversed itself and drove, point-first, at Arvin's chest, forcing him to twist aside. He shouted the command word that should have caused it to fly back to his hand, but the demon's magic was stronger. The knife refused to obey. The demon, meanwhile, had begun the spell that would summon others of its kind; Arvin could hear the words of its summoning whispering through its mind. He glanced wildly at Marasa—she still hadn't finished healing Glisena—and the dagger thrust at him, slicing a nick out of his left ear.

No time.

The demon would finish its summoning before Marasa could banish it.

The dagger flew toward him again; he batted it away with his left hand. The blade sliced a line through the ensorcelled leather glove.

His glove.

Leaping toward the demon, he slapped his gloved hand down on its tail. *"Shivis!"* he cried.

The demon disappeared into the glove.

For several moments, no one spoke. A muffled pounding continued on the door—the soldiers outside, trying to break in—while the blades continued to whir through the air. Then, all at once, they clattered to the floor, together with Arvin's dagger. The three clerics hurried toward Davinu. Foesmasher stood gaping, his sword hanging limply from his fist.

Arvin held up his gloved hand, turning it slowly back and forth. "It worked."

Marasa uttered the final word of her prayer, sealing the wound shut. She started to turn toward Arvin but then suddenly tensed. She leaned over Glisena, pressing one hand to the girl's throat. Glisena's chest was no longer moving. Her eyes stared glassily at the ceiling. "No," she howled. "By Helm's mercy, *no!*"

A distant voice whispered into Arvin's mind. *The binding ends. I am free!*

The glove bulged. One of its seams split.

Ah. An exit.

The palm of the glove humped upward.

Terrified, Arvin yanked the glove from his hand and hurled it to the floor. "Marasa!" he shouted, allowing his manifestation to end. Too much was happening too fast. "The demon's breaking free!"

Foesmasher stared at his daughter. A pained look on his face, he caught Marasa's eye. "Is she . . .?"

Marasa hung her head. Foesmasher gave a grief-stricken sob.

The glove tore open with a loud ripping sound as the demon erupted from it. In the space of a heartbeat, the demon expanded to its full size. Even coiled on its tail, it loomed over Arvin; his head was barely level with its chest. The tail was as thick as a man's waist, and each of the demon's arms was twice the length of a human's. Each hand held a long sword that was utterly black, save for a glowing line of red that edged its wavy blade. Where the weapons had come from, Arvin had no idea. Tendrils of darkness still wreathed the demon: the magic it had used to sap the baron's strength earlier.

The demon stared at Arvin, chuckling. A forked tongue, black as the swords, flickered out of its mouth, savoring his fear.

Arvin backed slowly away. "Marasa," he croaked. "The demon—"

The cleric with the glowing mace rushed the demon, swinging his weapon, and shouted Helm's name.

Swifter than the eye could follow, the demon flicked one of its hands. Its sword sliced through the cleric's neck. The cleric fell to the floor in an expanding pool of blood, his head hanging by a thread of flesh. The other two clerics exchanged nervous glances. Behind them, the door finally burst open. One of the soldiers rushed into the room, three others crowding behind him. His eyes widened at the sight of the demon.

As if awakened from a nightmare, Marasa sprang into action. "By Helm's all-seeing might," she shouted, thrusting her palm out at the demon, "I order you to return to—"

The demon disappeared.

Arvin blinked. "Did you—"

The flat of a sword blade tapped him on the shoulder. He whirled.

The demon was behind him.

The four soldiers rushed it. With a whirlwind of motion, the demon cut them down.

Marasa spun on her heel, trying to bring her palm into line with the demon. "To return to the—"

This time the demon teleported behind her. Its tail lashed out, coiling around the cleric's torso like a whip. Then it squeezed.

"To—" Marasa grunted as the air was forced from her lungs.

The demon squeezed.

Roaring, Foesmasher slashed at the demon's tail with his sword. Once again, the tendrils of darkness blocked the weapon and slithered up it. This time, they sent Foesmasher staggering. He stumbled back on wobbly legs then fell.

Marasa struggled to draw air into her lungs, to finish her spell.

The demon squeezed tighter, hissing.

Arvin opened his suddenly dry mouth, closed it, opened it again, and—fighting down the fear that washed through him in chilling waves—at last found his voice. "Hey, demon!" he shouted. He reached down for the ice dagger that was still sheathed in his boot. He watched the tendrils of darkness that coiled around the demon as they shifted, seeking a pattern. "*I'm* the one you were supposed to kill."

He whipped his hand forward, throwing the dagger. Swift as thought, it flew toward the demon and caught it square in the chest. Cold exploded outward from the weapon, etching crackling lines of frost across the demon's bare skin.

The demon glanced down at the dagger that had buried itself to the hilt between its breasts. It laughed and plucked it out. "A pinprick," it rumbled. It snapped the blade in two and tossed the pieces aside. Then its eyes met Arvin's. "But even pinpricks annoy me."

Suddenly releasing Marasa, the demon slithered forward.

Marasa sagged, facedown, onto the floor.

Terrified, Arvin backed away from the approaching demon. Then he turned and ran. Leaping over the mangled remains of the soldiers, he sprinted out through the adjoining room and into the hall. Behind him, he heard the hiss of scales on stone. Soldiers ran toward him up the hall; he dodged around them, shouting at them to get out of the way. Metal clashed against metal and wet *thunks* sounded as the soldiers rushed up to attack the demon—and died. Arvin ran past the council chamber, past other rooms in which servants startled then screamed as they saw what was slithering after him, and past the practice hall.

As he ran, he manifested a sending. The image of Marasa formed in his mind's eye. She was being helped to her feet by someone Arvin couldn't see. She was shaky and unsteady—but alive. She startled as Arvin's face appeared in her mind.

I'm leading the demon to the chapel, Arvin sent, praying that the demon wasn't also capable of reading thoughts. *Get Foesmasher to teleport you there. I'll keep it busy until you can banish it.*

Arvin, she croaked. Even her mental voice sounded awful; absorbing Glisena's hurts had taken its toll. *I'll come as quickly as I can.*

"Little mouse," the demon taunted from behind Arvin. "I can smell your fear. What a tasty little morsel you will be."

A blade swished through the air just over Arvin's head. A second blade *thunked* into the doorframe next to him as he pelted into the chapel. He raced for the gauntlet at the far end of the room, his breathing ragged and heart pounding. Leaping onto the dais, he slapped both palms against the gauntlet. He skittered around behind it, both hands still on the polished silver, placing the statue between himself and the demon.

The demon halted at the edge of the dais. Lazily regarding him through slit eyes, it coiled its scaly tail under itself. "Little morsel," it hissed. "Come down from there."

"Make me," he said, staring defiantly into its eyes.

The demon bared its teeth, hissing. Its incisors were

long and curved, like a snake's. Arvin wondered if they held venom.

Footsteps sounded in the hallway: Marasa?

The demon's head started to turn.

One palm still pressed tight to the gauntlet, Arvin plunged his other hand into his pocket and found the monkey's fist. "Here," he said to the demon, hurling the knot of twine. "Catch."

Even as the monkey's fist unknotted, the demon raised its swords. Six blades flashed through the air, chopping the magical twine to pieces. The frayed remains fell at its feet. The demon cocked its head then frowned. "I grow weary of this."

"So do I," Arvin said in a loud voice, hoping to cover the sound of footsteps in the hall. Marasa would have a better chance if she was able to surprise the demon. She could banish it before it got a chance to teleport out of the spell's path.

"But I've got one more trick up my sleeve," Arvin bluffed. "One that's bound to—"

He faltered as he saw who was coming down the hall. Not Marasa, as he had desperately hoped, but Karrell.

"Arvin!" she called. "What is happening? Are you—"
She jerked to a halt just inside the room as she saw the demon. Her eyes widened.

The demon turned.

Karrell immediately began to cast a spell, but even as she raised her hands, the demon lashed out with one of its swords. Karrell twisted out of its path, but the blade caught her raised right hand. Blood sprayed and fingers flew to the floor. Karrell gasped and clutched her wounded hand.

The demon snaked its tail across the doorway, blocking it, and prodded Karrell with one of its swords. "Go ahead," it hissed with malicious delight. "Try to flee."

Arvin tried to manifest a distraction, but though a loud droning filled the air, the demon's eyes remained locked on Karrell. He leaned out from the dais and kicked the demon in the back. A shock of weakness flowed up his leg as his foot struck one of the black tendrils that coiled around the demon's body. Ignoring the numbness it caused, he shouted at the demon's back and kicked it a second time. "Hey, scale-face! Behind you!"

Almost absent-mindedly, the demon turned its head and slashed backhanded at him with one of its swords. Arvin flinched as the blade came to a jerking halt a palm's width from his head, halted by the magic of the gauntlet. A heartbeat later, a whirling circle of blades appeared, this time surrounding the gauntlet and trapping Arvin inside. Cursing, he shrank back from them, his sweaty palms still on the statue. A moment ago, the gauntlet had provided sanctuary. The demon had turned it into a prison.

The momentary distraction, however, gave Karrell the time she needed. The far end of the chapel was suddenly plunged into darkness, hiding her from sight.

The demon frowned then twisted, whipping its tail through the patch of darkness. Arvin heard Karrell gasp—and the tail yanked her back into the light. Caught within the demon's coils, Karrell fought to free herself, her wounded hand leaving smears of blood on the demon's scaly tail. The demon lapped at the blood with its long black tongue then smiled. "A yuan-ti?" it said. "*You* must be the one I'm supposed to kill." It tail squeezed—and Karrell exhaled in pain. Arvin heard a dull crack that sounded like a rib breaking.

Footsteps sounded in the hallway—more than one person, and running this time—and a woman's voice was shouting orders: Marasa?

Arvin looked wildly around the chapel. He was weaponless, and the monkey's fist—the last of his ensorcelled items—was lying on the floor in tatters. If he let go of the gauntlet, he'd be cut down before he took a single step. But Marasa was at last on her way. He and Karrell only needed to survive for a few moments more.

"Helm," he croaked. "Help us now. Do something."

The skies outside lightened. Dusk-red sunlight slanted in through the chapel's stained-glass windows, turning the blue eyes at their centers an eerie purple. The light beamed in, limning the image of Helm's eye on the chapel floor.

With a hiss, the demon thrust its sword at the nearest window, smashing a hole through the eye. Glass exploded outward. The skies outside darkened again as the sun continued its descent.

As a loose pane of glass fell from the broken window to shatter on the floor, Arvin realized there was a weapon he could use, after all. He reached out with his mind, sending a thread-thin line of glowing silver toward the broken window. With it, he seized one of the panes of glass and threw it at the demon's face. The demon batted it away with a sword, smashing it into bright blue shards, but Arvin hurled another pane of glass at it, and another, keeping up the distraction.

Four of the baron's soldiers—three men and a woman—charged into the chapel, swords in hand. The woman shouted a command, and Arvin's heart sank as he realized it hadn't been Marasa's voice he'd heard, after all. The soldiers leaped forward, engaging the demon.

The demon, however, needed only four swords to meet their attack. One of the men went down even before he'd managed to close with it, his throat slashed. With its fifth sword, the demon continued to knock away the panes of glass Arvin hurled at it. That left one more sword. This one it thrust at Karrell; it *thunked* into the wooden floor beside her head as she desperately twisted aside.

Karrell's face was purple now and her movements were jerky. The demon—still fighting the soldiers with three of its arms—yanked the sword free and flexed its tail, dragging Karrell across the floor.

The female soldier pressed the demon, shouting Helm's name. The demon thrust a sword through her stomach, spitting her, then flicked her limp body away. One of the two remaining soldiers turned to run; with a flash of steel, the demon lopped off his head. The other grimly continued to attack but met the same end.

Its opponents dead, the demon glanced down at Karrell, tongue flickering through its hissing smile.

Karrell's fear-filled eyes sought Arvin's. He could see that she realized she was about to die. Her lips tried to form a word, but there was no breath left in her body.

Arvin ended his manifestation; the pane of glass he'd been about to throw fell to the floor and shattered. Reaching deep inside himself, he manifested a different power—one whose secondary display filled the air with the scents of saffron and ginger. Then, for a heartbeat, he hesitated. He didn't want to make the same mistake he'd made with Tanglemane. If the demon died....

It was a gamble he had to take. Spells and steel hadn't defeated the demon; he doubted anything would. And if he didn't manifest his power, Karrell would die.

Guiding the energies with his mind, he coiled one loop around the demon, another around Karrell. Then he tied them together and yanked the knot tight.

"Demon!" he shouted. "I've just bound your fate to the yuan-ti woman. Kill her, and you'll die!"

It was a desperate lie. Karrell's death would mean little to the demon. She might cause it a slight wound, but no more.

Ignoring Arvin, the demon slashed at Karrell with its sword. This time, Karrell's reaction was slower; the sword sliced a line down her cheek as she wrenched her head aside. The demon grunted—then hissed and touched its own cheek with the back of a hand. The hand came away slick with green blood.

The demon turned to face Arvin and tried to speak, but no words came from its mouth. It seemed to be having trouble breathing. It frowned down at Karrell, who lay gasping on the floor, then uncoiled its tail from her. Then it stared, its eyes slit with malevolence, at Arvin. "Unbind me, sorcerer," it commanded.

Relief washed through Arvin. He glanced at Karrell.

Her lips formed silent words: "Thank you."

Arvin gave her a grim smile. Just a few moments more, and Marasa would surely appear and banish the demon. He stared back at it through the whirling blades that still surrounded the dais. "No," he told the demon. "You will remain bound."

The demon flicked a hand, and the blades disappeared. It cocked its head to the side and considered Arvin. "Mortal," it hissed. "Surely you can be persuaded." Its hand opened, revealing a glitter of gems. The demon tipped its hand, letting them spill from its palm onto the floor. "The yuan-ti means nothing to me; she may go. Unbind me from her, and these are yours."

Arvin smiled grimly. "A rogue tried to entice me with a similar offer a few days ago," he said. "He's dead now."

The demon clenched its fist—causing the swords to reappear—and pointed one of them at Arvin. "Unbind me!" it roared.

Arvin gripped the gauntlet with sweaty hands. "No."

"We seem to have reached an impasse," the demon hissed.

Outside the chapel, just beyond the spot where one of the soldier's bodies lay, Arvin saw a flash of silver: light, glinting off a polished breastplate. Marasa stepped into view in the doorway, her lips moving as she whispered a spell, her left hand—clad in a silver gauntlet whose palm was set with an enormous, glittering sapphire—extended toward the demon.

"Yes," Arvin answered. "It seems we have." He shrugged, a gesture that removed his hands for no more than a fraction of a heartbeat from the gauntlet. It had the desired effect; the demon lashed out with a sword, but before the blade connected, Arvin's hands were back on the gauntlet.

The demon glared at him, oblivious to Karrell, who had risen to her hands and knees and was crawling away, her wounded hand leaving a smear of blood on the floor, and to Marasa, who was casting her spell. Marasa swept her hand down toward the demon, the sapphire in her gauntlet glinting. "By Helm's all-seeing might, I order you, demon, back to the place from whence you came!" she shouted.

The demon rose from the floor, roaring, slashing wildly with its swords. A rent appeared in the air next to it; an angry boil that burst open, emitting a sulfurous stench. Dark shapes writhed inside the tear in the fabric of the planes, howling and thrashing. The demon tumbled toward them.

Karrell fell onto her side—had she slipped on her own blood? As she rose again, blood from her wounded hand streamed toward the hole in a thin red ribbon—a ribbon the demon grabbed in one clawed hand.

Arvin reeled, realizing he'd seen this once before: in the vision at Naneth's home.

Still roaring, the demon disappeared through the gap between the planes. Karrell was yanked after it, screaming.

The gap closed.

For a heartbeat, Arvin stood rooted to the spot, Karrell's scream echoing in his mind. Then he hurled himself across the chapel toward the spot where she'd disappeared. "Karrell!" he cried desperately. Tears streaming down his face, he clutched at empty air. He sagged to the ground and beat his fists against the floor. A fate link wasn't supposed to work that way; it transferred pain, wounds, even fatal injury from one individual to the next, but that was all.

What had gone wrong?

He felt a hand on his shoulder. He looked up and saw Marasa staring down at him. Her face was deeply lined and streaked with tears; her hair seemed even grayer than it had been before. "I'm sorry," she whispered. "I didn't realize. . . ."

Arvin looked up at her through tear-blurred eyes. "Karrell was still alive when she went into the Abyss. Is there any way she could still be—"

Marasa shook her head grimly. "No. She would never survive."

Arvin's shoulders slumped.

"She was pregnant," he whispered, "with my child." He shook his head and corrected himself. "With my *children*. They're all. . . ." His throat caught, preventing him from speaking further.

Marasa nodded but seemed too weary to offer any further comfort. Her hand fell away from his shoulder.

Outside, the skies darkened and a wet snow began to fall. A chill wind blew flakes of white in through the shattered window. A shard of blue—all that remained of Helm's eye—fell to the floor like a tear and broke, tinkling.

Arvin spotted Karrell's ring, lying on the floor in a pool of blood. Two severed fingers lay next to it. He picked the ring up and wiped it clean on his shirt, then stared for a long moment at the turquoise stone. Then he pressed the ring to his lips. "Forgive me," he whispered.

He slipped the ring onto the little finger of his left hand then clenched his hand shut, savoring the pain of his abbreviated little finger.

Karrell was dead.

So was Glisena.

Arvin had failed them both.

But Sibyl was still alive. And if she managed to get her hands on the second half of the Circled Serpent, many more would die.

He stared down at the ring on his finger. "I'll do it," he vowed. "Finish what you started. See to it that Sibyl never gets a chance to use the Circled Serpent."

In the darkening skies outside, thunder rumbled.

Arvin stood near the stern of the ship, watching the shoreline of Sespech fall away behind. Already the square buildings of Mimph were no more than tiny squares on the horizon, their lights slowly fading. The waters of the Vilhon Reach were as dark as the overcast evening sky above, a perfect counterpoint to his grim mood.

Seven days had passed since Karrell had disappeared into the Abyss. His eyes still teared whenever he thought of her. Her life had entwined with his only briefly, yet he still felt frayed by her loss. He thought back to what she'd told him on the day he'd discovered she was a yuan-ti. After they'd made love, she'd told him more about the beliefs of her religion. Every person's life was a maze, hedged with pain, disappointment, suffering, and self-doubt, she'd said. To find one's way through this jungle, one had to keep one's eyes on the "true path"—the course the gods had cleared for one through the thorny undergrowth.

Arvin had joked that he still hadn't found his true path—that he kept fumbling his way from one near-disaster to the next. Karrell had just smiled and told him he would find it, one day, by following his heart.

Arvin sighed. He *had* followed his heart—to Karrell—only to lose her.

On the day she disappeared—and every day after that—he'd tried to contact her with his lapis lazuli, but she'd never answered.

She was dead. And it was his fault.

He touched the chunk of crystal at his throat, wishing the gods had taken him instead. "Nine lives," he muttered.

He'd never thought of his continued survival as a curse before.

He watched as Mimph sank from sight, its lights seemingly extinguished by the cold waters of the Vilhon Reach. In distant Ormpetarr, a grieving Foesmasher would be mourning the loss of his daughter. Marasa had tried to summon Glisena's soul back to her dead body—that was what had taken Marasa so long to reach the chapel—but her attempt to resurrect the baron's daughter had been in vain. Glisena's death had been magical in nature, and irreversible—the contingency that allowed the binding to end and the demon to assume its full size.

At least Foesmasher still had his grandchild. He'd reacted amazingly well to the news that Belinna was carrying it. Instead of denouncing the "serpent," he'd begun to weep. "It's all I have left of her now," he'd moaned. Then, wiping away his tears, he'd summoned Belinna to his council chamber. Belinna, forewarned by Arvin that the child in her womb was not only half yuan-ti, but of royal blood, had responded hesitantly to the summons. That hesitancy had turned to amazement and joy when the baron announced she would be elevated to the position of royal nursemaid. That her child would, from the moment it was born, have everything it needed—as would she and her husband.

Despite his daughter's death, Foesmasher had also been generous to Arvin—very generous. With his coin pouch filled with gems and coins, Arvin would have no difficulty making a new life for himself anywhere he chose. But that could wait. For the moment, there were more pressing matters he had to attend to.

As for Naneth, there had been no sign of the midwife, despite the baron's soldiers having searched every corner of Ormpetarr. Arvin wondered where she was. Or rather, where the mind seed was that, even now, would be taking over her body. The seed would, no doubt, soon be on its way to infiltrate Sibyl's lair. There, Arvin was certain, it would face an unpleasant reception from Sibyl, who must by now have known that her plan to assassinate Dediana Extaminos had failed.

Nor had the baron's men been able to locate Zelia. Would she follow Dmetrio and the mind seed back to Hlondeth? If so, Arvin would have to tread carefully, starting the moment his ship docked there. Tymora willing, he would spot Zelia before she spotted him.

The ship rose and fell, its rigging creaked, and tielines fluttered against the taut canvas above. Arvin could no longer see Mimph; the gloom had swallowed it. "Farewell, Sespech," he said. "I doubt I'll see you again."

Then he turned to stare across the water at the dark line that was the north shore of the Vilhon Reach—at the faint green glow on the horizon that was Hlondeth. Somewhere beneath its streets, Sibyl was laired in an ancient temple, with her half of the Circled Serpent.

Somewhere in the city above, Dmetrio had his half.

Somehow, Arvin would have to find one or the other, before the two halves were joined.

R.A. SALVATORE'S
WAR OF THE SPIDER QUEEN

THE EPIC SAGA OF THE DARK ELVES CONTINUES.

EXTINCTION
Book IV
Lisa Smedman

For even a small group of drow, trust is the rarest commodity of all. When the expedition prepares for a return to the Abyss, what little trust there is crumbles under a rival goddess's hand.

ANNIHILATION
Book V
Philip Athans

Old alliances have been broken, and new bonds have been formed. While some finally embark for the Abyss itself, others stay behind to serve a new mistress—a goddess with plans of her own.

RESURRECTION
Book VI

The Spider Queen has been asleep for a long time, leaving the Underdark to suffer war and ruin. But if she finally returns, will things get better… or worse?

April 2005

The New York Times *best-seller now in paperback!*

CONDEMNATION
Book III
Richard Baker

The search for answers to Lolth's silence uncovers only more complex questions, allowing doubt and frustration to test the boundaries of already tenuous relationships. Sensing the holes in the armor of Menzoberranzan, a new, dangerous threat steps in to test the resolve of the Jewel of the Underdark, and finds it lacking.

Now in paperback!
DISSOLUTION, BOOK I
INSURRECTION, BOOK II

CHECK OUT THESE NEW TITLES FROM THE AUTHORS OF R.A. SALVATORE'S WAR OF THE SPIDER QUEEN SERIES!

VENOM'S TASTE
House of Serpents, Book I
Lisa Smedman

The New York Times Best-selling author of *Extinction*.
Serpents. Poison. Psionics. And the occasional evil death cult. Business as usual in the Vilhon Reach. Lisa Smedman breathes life into the treacherous yuan-ti race.

THE RAGE
The Year of Rogue Dragons, Book I
Richard Lee Byers

Every once in a while the dragons go mad. Without warning they darken the skies of Faerûn and kill and kill and kill. Richard Lee Byers, the new master of dragons, takes wing.

FORSAKEN HOUSE
The Last Mythal, Book I
Richard Baker

The New York Times Best-selling author of *Condemnation*.
The Retreat is at an end, and the elves of Faerûn find themselves at a turning point. In one direction lies peace and stagnation, in the other: war and destiny. *New York Times* best-selling author Richard Baker shows the elves their future.

THE RUBY GUARDIAN
Scions of Arrabar, Book II
Thomas M. Reid

Life and death both come at a price in the mercenary city-states of the Vilhon Reach. Vambran thought he knew the cost of both, but he still has a lot to learn. Thomas M. Reid makes humans the most dangerous monsters in Faerûn.

THE SAPPHIRE CRESCENT
Scions of Arrabar, Book I
Available Now

FATHER AND DAUGHTER COME FACE-TO-FACE IN THE STREETS OF WATERDEEP.

ELMINSTER'S DAUGHTER
The Elminster Series

Ed Greenwood

Like a silken shadow, the thief Narnra Shalace flits through the dank streets and dark corners of Waterdeep. Little does she know that she's about to come face-to-face with the most dangerous man in all Faerûn: her father. And amidst a vast conspiracy to overthrow all order in the Realms, she'll have to learn to trust again—and to love.

ELIMINSTER: THE MAKING OF A MAGE

ELMINSTER IN MYTH DRANNOR

THE TEMPTATION OF ELMINSTER

ELMINSTER IN HELL

Available Now!

Adventures in the Realms!

THE YELLOW SILK
The Rogues
Don Bassingthwaite

More than just the weather is cold and bitter in the wind-swept realm of Altumbel. When a stranger travels from the distant east to reclaim his family's greatest treasure, he finds just how cold and bitter a people can be.

DAWN OF NIGHT
The Erevis Cale Trilogy, Book II
Paul S. Kemp

He's left Sembia far behind. He's made new friends. He's made new enemies. And now Erevis Cale himself is changing into something, and he's not sure exactly what it is.

REALMS OF DRAGONS
The Year of Rogue Dragons
Edited by Philip Athans

All new stories by R.A. Salvatore, Richard Lee Byers, Ed Greenwood, Elaine Cunningham, and a host of **Forgotten Realms®** stars breathe new life into the great wyrms of Faerûn.

THERE ARE A HUNDRED GODS LOOKING
OVER FAERÛN, EACH WITH A THOUSAND
SERVANTS OR MORE. SERVANTS WE CALL...
THE PRIESTS

LADY OF POISON
Bruce R. Cordell

Evil has the Great Dale in its venomous grip. Monsters crawl from
the shadows, disease and poison ravage the townsfolk, and dark
cults gather in the night. Not all religions, after all, work for good.

MISTRESS OF NIGHT
Dave Gross

Fighting a goddess of secrets can be a dangerous game. Werewolves
stalk the moonlit night, goddesses clash in the heavens, and a lone
priestess will sacrifice everything to stop them.

QUEEN OF THE DEPTHS
Voronica Whitney-Robinson

Far below the waves, evil swims. The ocean goddess is a fickle
mistress who toys with man and ship alike. How can she be
trusted when the seas run red with blood?

May 2005

MAIDEN OF PAIN
Kameron M. Franklin

The book that **Forgotten Realms®** novel fans have been waiting
for—the result of an exhaustive international talent search. The
newest star in the skies of Faerûn tells a story of torture, sacrifice,
and betrayal.

July 2005

FROM *NEW YORK TIMES*

BEST-SELLING AUTHOR

R.A. SALVATORE

In taverns, around campfires, and in the loftiest council chambers of Faerûn, people whisper the tales of a lone dark elf who stumbled out of the merciless Underdark to the no less unforgiving wilderness of the World Above and carved a life for himself, then lived a legend...

THE LEGEND OF DRIZZT

For the first time in deluxe hardcover editions, all three volumes of the Dark Elf Trilogy take their rightful place at the beginning of one of the greatest fantasy epics of all time. Each title contains striking new cover art and portions of an all-new author interview, with the questions posed by none other than the readers themselves.

HOMELAND

Being born in Menzoberranzan means a hard life surrounded by evil.

EXILE

But the only thing worse is being driven from the city with hunters on your trail.

SOJOURN

Unless you can find your way out, never to return.

GO BEHIND ENEMY LINES WITH DRIZZT DO'URDEN IN THIS ALL NEW TRILOGY FROM BEST-SELLING AUTHOR R.A. SALVATORE.

THE HUNTER'S BLADES TRILOGY

The **New York Times** *best-seller now in paperback!*

THE LONE DROW
Book II

Alone and tired, cold and hungry, Drizzt Do'Urden has never been more dangerous. But neither have the rampaging orcs that have finally done the impossible—what for the dwarves of the North is the most horrifying nightmare ever—they've banded together.

New in hardcover!

THE TWO SWORDS
Book III

Drizzt has become the Hunter, but King Obould won't let himself become the Hunted and that means one of them will have to die. The Hunter's Blades trilogy draws to an explosive conclusion.

THE THOUSAND ORCS
Book I
Available Now!